OCT - - 2017

THE

RED
PYRAMID

THE

RED
PYRAMID

RICK RIORDAN

North Lake County
Public Library District
P.O. Box 820
Polson, MT 59860

DISNEP • HYPERION BOOKS
NEW YORK

First Edition

10 9 8 7

G475-5664-5 10264

Printed in the United States of America

Hieroglyph art by Michelle Gengaro-Kokmen

ISBN 978-1-4231-1338-6

Reinforced binding

Library of Congress Cataloging-in-Publication Data on file.

Visit www.hyperionbooksforchildren.com

*To all my librarian friends, champions of books,
true magicians in the House of Life. Without you,
this writer would be lost in the Duat.*

Contents

CONTENTS

WARNING

The following is a transcript of a digital recording. In certain places, the audio quality was poor, so some words and phrases represent the author's best guesses. Where possible, illustrations of important symbols mentioned in the recording have been added. Background noises such as scuffling, hitting, and cursing by the two speakers have not been transcribed. The author makes no claims for the authenticity of the recording. It seems impossible that the two young narrators are telling the truth, but you, the reader, must decide for yourself.

1. A Death at the Needle

WE ONLY HAVE A FEW HOURS, so listen carefully.

If you're hearing this story, you're already in danger. Sadie and I might be your only chance.

Go to the school. Find the locker. I won't tell you which school or which locker, because if you're the right person, you'll find it. The combination is 13/32/33. By the time you finish listening, you'll know what those numbers mean. Just remember the story we're about to tell you isn't complete yet. How it ends will depend on you.

The most important thing: when you open the package and find what's inside, *don't* keep it longer than a week. Sure, it'll be tempting. I mean, it will grant you almost unlimited power. But if you possess it too long, it will consume you. Learn its secrets quickly and pass it on. Hide it for the next person, the way Sadie and I did for you. Then be prepared for your life to get very interesting.

Okay, Sadie is telling me to stop stalling and get on with

1

the story. Fine. I guess it started in London, the night our dad blew up the British Museum.

My name is Carter Kane. I'm fourteen and my home is a suitcase.

You think I'm kidding? Since I was eight years old, my dad and I have traveled the world. I was born in L.A. but my dad's an archaeologist, so his work takes him all over. Mostly we go to Egypt, since that's his specialty. Go into a bookstore, find a book about Egypt, there's a pretty good chance it was written by Dr. Julius Kane. You want to know how Egyptians pulled the brains out of mummies, or built the pyramids, or cursed King Tut's tomb? My dad is your man. Of course, there are other reasons my dad moved around so much, but I didn't know his secret back then.

I didn't go to school. My dad homeschooled me, if you can call it "home" schooling when you don't have a home. He sort of taught me whatever he thought was important, so I learned a lot about Egypt and basketball stats and my dad's favorite musicians. I read a lot, too—pretty much anything I could get my hands on, from dad's history books to fantasy novels—because I spent a lot of time sitting around in hotels and airports and dig sites in foreign countries where I didn't know anybody. My dad was always telling me to put the book down and play some ball. You ever try to start a game of pick-up basketball in Aswan, Egypt? It's not easy.

Anyway, my dad trained me early to keep all my possessions in a single suitcase that fits in an airplane's overhead compartment. My dad packed the same way, except he was allowed an extra workbag for his archaeology tools. Rule number one: I was not allowed to look in his workbag. That's a rule I never broke until the day of the explosion.

It happened on Christmas Eve. We were in London for visitation day with my sister, Sadie.

See, Dad's only allowed two days a year with her—one in the winter, one in the summer—because our grandparents hate him. After our mom died, her parents (our grandparents) had this big court battle with Dad. After six lawyers, two fistfights, and a near fatal attack with a spatula (don't ask), they won the right to keep Sadie with them in England. She was only six, two years younger than me, and they couldn't keep us both—at least that was their excuse for not taking me. So Sadie was raised as a British schoolkid, and I traveled around with my dad. We only saw Sadie twice a year, which was fine with me.

[Shut up, Sadie. Yes—I'm getting to that part.]

So anyway, my dad and I had just flown into Heathrow after a couple of delays. It was a drizzly, cold afternoon. The whole taxi ride into the city, my dad seemed kind of nervous.

Now, my dad is a big guy. You wouldn't think anything could make him nervous. He has dark brown skin like mine, piercing brown eyes, a bald head, and a goatee, so he looks like a buff evil scientist. That afternoon he wore his cashmere winter coat and his best brown suit, the one he used for public lectures. Usually he exudes so much confidence that he dominates any room he walks into, but sometimes—like that afternoon—I saw another side to him that I didn't really understand. He kept looking over his shoulder like we were being hunted.

"Dad?" I said as we were getting off the A-40. "What's wrong?"

"No sign of them," he muttered. Then he must've realized he'd spoken aloud, because he looked at me kind of startled. "Nothing, Carter. Everything's fine."

Which bothered me because my dad's a terrible liar. I always knew when he was hiding something, but I also knew no amount of pestering would get the truth out of him. He was probably trying to protect me, though from what I didn't know. Sometimes I wondered if he had some dark secret in his past, some old enemy following him, maybe; but the idea seemed ridiculous. Dad was just an archaeologist.

The other thing that troubled me: Dad was clutching his workbag. Usually when he does that, it means we're in danger. Like the time gunmen stormed our hotel in Cairo. I heard shots coming from the lobby and ran downstairs to check on my dad. By the time I got there, he was just calmly zipping up his workbag while three unconscious gunmen hung by their feet from the chandelier, their robes falling over their heads so you could see their boxer shorts. Dad claimed not to have witnessed anything, and in the end the police blamed a freak chandelier malfunction.

Another time, we got caught in a riot in Paris. My dad found the nearest parked car, pushed me into the backseat, and told me to stay down. I pressed myself against the floorboards and kept my eyes shut tight. I could hear Dad in the driver's seat, rummaging in his bag, mumbling something to himself while the mob yelled and destroyed things outside. A few minutes later he told me it was safe to get up. Every other car on the block had been overturned and set on fire. Our car had been freshly washed and polished, and several twenty-euro notes had been tucked under the windshield wipers.

Anyway, I'd come to respect the bag. It was our good luck charm. But when my dad kept it close, it meant we were going to need good luck.

We drove through the city center, heading east toward my grandparents' flat. We passed the golden gates of Buckingham Palace, the big stone column in Trafalgar Square. London is a pretty cool place, but after you've traveled for so long, all cities start to blend together. Other kids I meet sometimes say, "Wow, you're so lucky you get to travel so much." But it's not like we spend our time sightseeing or have a lot of money to travel in style. We've stayed in some pretty rough places, and we hardly ever stay anywhere longer than a few days. Most of the time it feels like we're fugitives rather than tourists.

I mean, you wouldn't think my dad's work was dangerous. He does lectures on topics like "Can Egyptian Magic Really Kill You?" and "Favorite Punishments in the Egyptian Underworld" and other stuff most people wouldn't care about. But like I said, there's that other side to him. He's always very cautious, checking every hotel room before he lets me walk into it. He'll dart into a museum to see some artifacts, take a few notes, and rush out again like he's afraid to be caught on the security cameras.

One time when I was younger, we raced across the Charles de Gaulle airport to catch a last-minute flight, and Dad didn't relax until the plane was off the ground, I asked him point blank what he was running from, and he looked at me like I'd just pulled the pin out of a grenade. For a second I was scared he might actually tell me the truth. Then he said, "Carter, it's nothing." As if "nothing" were the most terrible thing in the world.

After that, I decided maybe it was better not to ask questions.

My grandparents, the Fausts, live in a housing development near Canary Wharf, right on the banks of the River Thames. The taxi let us off at the curb, and my dad asked the driver to wait.

We were halfway up the walk when Dad froze. He turned and looked behind us.

"What?" I asked.

Then I saw the man in the trench coat. He was across the street, leaning against a big dead tree. He was barrel shaped, with skin the color of roasted coffee. His coat and black pinstriped suit looked expensive. He had long braided hair and wore a black fedora pulled down low over his dark round glasses. He reminded me of a jazz musician, the kind my dad would always drag me to see in concert. Even though I couldn't see his eyes, I got the impression he was watching us. He might've been an old friend or colleague of Dad's. No matter where we went, Dad was always running into people he knew. But it did seem strange that the guy was waiting here, outside my grandparents'. And he didn't look happy.

"Carter," my dad said, "go on ahead."

"But—"

"Get your sister. I'll meet you back at the taxi."

He crossed the street toward the man in the trench coat, which left me with two choices: follow my dad and see what was going on, or do what I was told.

I decided on the slightly less dangerous path. I went to retrieve my sister.

Before I could even knock, Sadie opened the door.

"Late as usual," she said.

She was holding her cat, Muffin, who'd been a "going away" gift from Dad six years before. Muffin never seemed to get older or bigger. She had fuzzy yellow-and-black fur like a miniature leopard, alert yellow eyes, and pointy ears that were too tall for her head. A silver Egyptian pendant dangled from her collar. She didn't look anything like a muffin, but Sadie had been little when she named her, so I guess you have to cut her some slack.

Sadie hadn't changed much either since last summer.

[As I'm recording this, she's standing next to me, glaring, so I'd better be careful how I describe her.]

You would never guess she's my sister. First of all, she'd been living in England so long, she has a British accent. Second, she takes after our mom, who was white, so Sadie's skin is much lighter than mine. She has straight caramel-colored hair, not exactly blond but not brown, which she usually dyes with streaks of bright colors. That day it had red streaks down the left side. Her eyes are blue. I'm serious. *Blue* eyes, just like our mom's. She's only twelve, but she's exactly as tall as me, which is really annoying. She was chewing gum as usual, dressed for her day out with Dad in battered jeans, a leather jacket, and combat boots, like she was going to a concert and was hoping to stomp on some people. She had headphones dangling around her neck in case we bored her.

[Okay, she didn't hit me, so I guess I did an okay job of describing her.]

"Our plane was late," I told her.

She popped a bubble, rubbed Muffin's head, and tossed the cat inside. "Gran, going out!"

From somewhere in the house, Grandma Faust said something I couldn't make out, probably "Don't let them in!"

Sadie closed the door and regarded me as if I were a dead mouse her cat had just dragged in. "So, here you are again."

"Yep."

"Come on, then." She sighed. "Let's get on with it."

That's the way she was. No "Hi, how you been the last six months? So glad to see you!" or anything. But that was okay with me. When you only see each other twice a year, it's like you're distant cousins rather than siblings. We had absolutely nothing in common except our parents.

We trudged down the steps. I was thinking how she smelled like a combination of old people's house and bubble gum when she stopped so abruptly, I ran into her.

"Who's that?" she asked.

I'd almost forgotten about the dude in the trench coat. He and my dad were standing across the street next to the big tree, having what looked like a serious argument. Dad's back was turned so I couldn't see his face, but he gestured with his hands like he does when he's agitated. The other guy scowled and shook his head.

"Dunno," I said. "He was there when we pulled up."

"He looks familiar." Sadie frowned like she was trying to remember. "Come on."

"Dad wants us to wait in the cab," I said, even though I knew it was no use. Sadie was already on the move.

Instead of going straight across the street, she dashed up the sidewalk for half a block, ducking behind cars, then crossed to the opposite side and crouched under a low stone wall. She started sneaking toward our dad. I didn't have much choice but to follow her example, even though it made me feel kind of stupid.

"Six years in England," I muttered, "and she thinks she's James Bond."

Sadie swatted me without looking back and kept creeping forward.

A couple more steps and we were right behind the big dead tree. I could hear my dad on the other side, saying, "—have to, Amos. You know it's the right thing."

"No," said the other man, who must've been Amos. His voice was deep and even—very insistent. His accent was American. "If I don't stop you, Julius, *they* will. The Per Ankh is shadowing you."

Sadie turned to me and mouthed the words "Per *what*?"

I shook my head, just as mystified. "Let's get out of here," I whispered, because I figured we'd be spotted any minute and get in serious trouble. Sadie, of course, ignored me.

"They don't know my plan," my father was saying. "By the time they figure it out—"

"And the children?" Amos asked. The hairs stood up on the back of my neck. "What about them?"

"I've made arrangements to protect them," my dad said. "Besides, if I don't do this, we're all in danger. Now, back off."

"I can't, Julius."

"Then it's a duel you want?" Dad's tone turned deadly serious. "You never could beat me, Amos."

I hadn't seen my dad get violent since the Great Spatula Incident, and I wasn't anxious to see a repeat of *that*, but the two men seemed to be edging toward a fight.

Before I could react, Sadie popped up and shouted, "Dad!"

He looked surprised when she tackle-hugged him, but not nearly as surprised as the other guy, Amos. He backed up so quickly, he tripped over his own trench coat.

He'd taken off his glasses. I couldn't help thinking that Sadie was right. He did look familiar—like a very distant memory.

"I—I must be going," he said. He straightened his fedora and lumbered down the road.

Our dad watched him go. He kept one arm protectively around Sadie and one hand inside the workbag slung over his shoulder. Finally, when Amos disappeared around the corner, Dad relaxed. He took his hand out of the bag and smiled at Sadie. "Hello, sweetheart."

Sadie pushed away from him and crossed her arms. "Oh, now it's *sweetheart*, is it? You're late. Visitation Day's nearly over! And what was that about? Who's Amos, and what's the Per Ankh?"

Dad stiffened. He glanced at me like he was wondering how much we'd overheard.

"It's nothing," he said, trying to sound upbeat. "I have a wonderful evening planned. Who'd like a private tour of the British Museum?"

Sadie slumped in the back of the taxi between Dad and me.

"I can't believe it," she grumbled. "One evening together, and you want to do research."

Dad tried for a smile. "Sweetheart, it'll be fun. The curator of the Egyptian collection personally invited—"

"Right, big surprise." Sadie blew a strand of red-streaked hair out of her face. "Christmas Eve, and we're going to see some moldy old relics from Egypt. Do you ever think about *anything* else?"

Dad didn't get mad. He never gets mad at Sadie. He just stared out the window at the darkening sky and the rain.

"Yes," he said quietly. "I do."

Whenever Dad got quiet like that and stared off into nowhere, I knew he was thinking about our mom. The last few months, it had been happening a lot. I'd walk into our hotel room and find him with his cell phone in his hands, Mom's picture smiling up at him from the screen—her hair tucked under a headscarf, her blue eyes startlingly bright against the desert backdrop.

Or we'd be at some dig site. I'd see Dad staring at the horizon, and I'd know he was remembering how he'd met her—two young scientists in the Valley of the Kings, on a dig to discover a lost tomb. Dad was an Egyptologist. Mom was an anthropologist looking for ancient DNA. He'd told me the story a thousand times.

Our taxi snaked its way along the banks of the Thames. Just past Waterloo Bridge, my dad tensed.

"Driver," he said. "Stop here a moment."

The cabbie pulled over on the Victoria Embankment.

"What is it, Dad?" I asked.

He got out of the cab like he hadn't heard me. When Sadie and I joined him on the sidewalk, he was staring up at Cleopatra's Needle.

In case you've never seen it: the Needle is an obelisk, not a needle, and it doesn't have anything to do with Cleopatra. I guess the British just thought the name sounded cool when they brought it to London. It's about seventy feet tall, which would've been really impressive back in Ancient Egypt, but on the Thames, with all the tall buildings around, it looks small and sad. You could drive right by it and not even realize you'd just passed something that was a thousand years older than the city of London.

"God." Sadie walked around in a frustrated circle. "Do we have to stop for *every* monument?"

My dad stared at the top of the obelisk. "I had to see it again," he murmured. "Where it happened..."

A freezing wind blew off the river. I wanted to get back in the cab, but my dad was really starting to worry me. I'd never seen him so distracted.

"What, Dad?" I asked. "What happened here?"

"The last place I saw her."

Sadie stopped pacing. She scowled at me uncertainly, then back at Dad. "Hang on. Do you mean Mum?"

Dad brushed Sadie's hair behind her ear, and she was so surprised, she didn't even push him away.

I felt like the rain had frozen me solid. Mom's death had always been a forbidden subject. I knew she'd died in an accident in London. I knew my grandparents blamed my dad. But no one would ever tell us the details. I'd given up asking my dad, partly because it made him so sad, partly because he absolutely refused to tell me anything. "When you're older" was all he would say, which was the most frustrating response ever.

"You're telling us she died here," I said. "At Cleopatra's Needle? What happened?"

He lowered his head.

"Dad!" Sadie protested. "I go past this *every* day, and you mean to say—all this time—and I didn't even *know*?"

"Do you still have your cat?" Dad asked her, which seemed like a really stupid question.

"Of course I've still got the cat!" she said. "What does that have to do with anything?"

"And your amulet?"

Sadie's hand went to her neck. When we were little, right before Sadie went to live with our grandparents, Dad had given us both Egyptian amulets. Mine was an Eye of Horus, which was a popular protection symbol in Ancient Egypt.

In fact my dad says the modern pharmacist's symbol, ℞, is a simplified version of the Eye of Horus, because medicine is supposed to protect you.

Anyway, I always wore my amulet under my shirt, but I figured Sadie would've lost hers or thrown it away.

To my surprise, she nodded. "'Course I have it, Dad, but don't change the subject. Gran's always going on about how you caused Mum's death. That's not true, is it?"

We waited. For once, Sadie and I wanted exactly the same thing—the truth.

"The night your mother died," my father started, "here at the Needle—"

A sudden flash illuminated the embankment. I turned, half blind, and just for a moment I glimpsed two figures: a tall pale man with a forked beard and wearing cream-colored robes, and a coppery-skinned girl in dark blue robes and a headscarf—the kind of clothes I'd seen hundreds of times in Egypt. They were just standing there side by side, not twenty feet away, watching us. Then the light faded. The figures melted into a fuzzy afterimage. When my eyes readjusted to the darkness, they were gone.

"Um..." Sadie said nervously. "Did you just see that?"

"Get in the cab," my dad said, pushing us toward the curb. "We're out of time."

From that point on, Dad clammed up.

"This isn't the place to talk," he said, glancing behind us. He'd promised the cabbie an extra ten pounds if he got us to the museum in under five minutes, and the cabbie was doing his best.

"Dad," I tried, "those people at the river—"

"And the other bloke, Amos," Sadie said. "Are they Egyptian police or something?"

"Look, both of you," Dad said, "I'm going to need your help tonight. I know it's hard, but you have to be patient. I'll explain everything, I promise, after we get to the museum. I'm going to make everything right again."

"What do you mean?" Sadie insisted. "Make *what* right?"

Dad's expression was more than sad. It was almost guilty. With a chill, I thought about what Sadie had said: about our grandparents blaming him for Mom's death. That *couldn't* be what he was talking about, could it?

The cabbie swerved onto Great Russell Street and screeched to a halt in front of the museum's main gates.

"Just follow my lead," Dad told us. "When we meet the curator, act normal."

I was thinking that Sadie never acted *normal*, but I decided not to say anything.

We climbed out of the cab. I got our luggage while Dad paid the driver with a big wad of cash. Then he did something strange. He threw a handful of small objects into the backseat—they looked like stones, but it was too dark for me to be sure. "Keep driving," he told the cabbie. "Take us to Chelsea."

That made no sense since we were already out of the cab, but the driver sped off. I glanced at Dad, then back at the cab, and before it turned the corner and disappeared in the dark, I caught a weird glimpse of three passengers in the backseat: a man and two kids.

I blinked. There was no way the cab could've picked up another fare so fast. "Dad—"

"London cabs don't stay empty very long," he said matter-of-factly. "Come along, kids."

He marched off through the wrought iron gates. For a second, Sadie and I hesitated.

"Carter, *what* is going on?"

I shook my head. "I'm not sure I want to know."

"Well, stay out here in the cold if you want, but *I'm* not leaving without an explanation." She turned and marched after our dad.

Looking back on it, I should've run. I should've dragged Sadie out of there and gotten as far away as possible. Instead I followed her through the gates.

2. An Explosion for Christmas

I'D BEEN TO THE BRITISH MUSEUM BEFORE. In fact I've been in more museums than I like to admit—it makes me sound like a total geek.

[That's Sadie in the background, yelling that I *am* a total geek. Thanks, Sis.]

Anyway, the museum was closed and completely dark, but the curator and two security guards were waiting for us on the front steps.

"Dr. Kane!" The curator was a greasy little dude in a cheap suit. I'd seen mummies with more hair and better teeth. He shook my dad's hand like he was meeting a rock star. "Your last paper on Imhotep—brilliant! I don't know how you translated those spells!"

"Im-ho-who?" Sadie muttered to me.

"Imhotep," I said. "High priest, architect. Some say he was a magician. Designed the first step pyramid. You know."

"Don't know," Sadie said. "Don't care. But thanks."

Dad expressed his gratitude to the curator for hosting us on a holiday. Then he put his hand on my shoulder. "Dr. Martin, I'd like you to meet Carter and Sadie."

"Ah! Your son, obviously, and—" The curator looked hesitantly at Sadie. "And this young lady?"

"My daughter," Dad said.

Dr. Martin's stare went temporarily blank. Doesn't matter how open-minded or polite people think they are, there's always that moment of confusion that flashes across their faces when they realize Sadie is part of our family. I hate it, but over the years I've come to expect it.

The curator regained his smile. "Yes, yes, of course. Right this way, Dr. Kane. We're very honored!"

The security guards locked the doors behind us. They took our luggage, then one of them reached for Dad's workbag.

"Ah, no," Dad said with a tight smile. "I'll keep this one."

The guards stayed in the foyer as we followed the curator into the Great Court. It was ominous at night. Dim light from the glass-domed ceiling cast crosshatched shadows across the walls like a giant spiderweb. Our footsteps clicked on the white marble floor.

"So," Dad said, "the stone."

"Yes!" the curator said. "Though I can't imagine what new information you could glean from it. It's been studied to death—our most famous artifact, of course."

"Of course," Dad said. "But you may be surprised."

"What's he on about now?" Sadie whispered to me.

I didn't answer. I had a sneaking suspicion what stone they

were talking about, but I couldn't figure out why Dad would drag us out on Christmas Eve to see it.

I wondered what he'd been about to tell us at Cleopatra's Needle—something about our mother and the night she died. And why did he keep glancing around as if he expected those strange people we'd seen at the Needle to pop up again? We were locked in a museum surrounded by guards and high-tech security. Nobody could bother us in here—I hoped.

We turned left into the Egyptian wing. The walls were lined with massive statues of the pharaohs and gods, but my dad bypassed them all and went straight for the main attraction in the middle of the room.

"Beautiful," my father murmured. "And it's not a replica?"

"No, no," the curator promised. "We don't always keep the actual stone on display, but for you—this is quite real."

We were staring at a slab of dark gray rock about three feet tall and two feet wide. It sat on a pedestal, encased in a glass box. The flat surface of the stone was chiseled with three distinct bands of writing. The top part was Ancient Egyptian picture writing: hieroglyphics. The middle section...I had to rack my brain to remember what my dad called it: *Demotic*, a kind of writing from the period when the Greeks controlled Egypt and a lot of Greek words got mixed into Egyptian. The last lines were in Greek.

"The Rosetta Stone," I said.

"Isn't that a computer program?" Sadie asked.

I wanted to tell her how stupid she was, but the curator cut me off with a nervous laugh. "Young lady, the Rosetta Stone was the key to deciphering hieroglyphics! It was discovered by Napoleon's army in 1799 and—"

"Oh, right," Sadie said. "I remember now."

I knew she was just saying that to shut him up, but my dad wouldn't let it go.

"Sadie," he said, "until this stone was discovered, regular mortals...er, I mean, no one had been able to read hieroglyphics for centuries. The written language of Egypt had been completely forgotten. Then an Englishman named Thomas Young proved that the Rosetta Stone's three languages all conveyed the same message. A Frenchman named Champollion took up the work and cracked the code of hieroglyphics."

Sadie chewed her gum, unimpressed. "What's it say, then?"

Dad shrugged. "Nothing important. It's basically a thank-you letter from some priests to King Ptolemy V. When it was first carved, the stone was no big deal. But over the centuries...over the centuries it has become a powerful symbol. Perhaps the most important connection between Ancient Egypt and the modern world. I was a fool not to realize its potential sooner."

He'd lost me, and apparently the curator too.

"Dr. Kane?" he asked. "Are you quite all right?"

Dad breathed deeply. "My apologies, Dr. Martin. I was just...thinking aloud. If I could have the glass removed? And if you could bring me the papers I asked for from your archives."

Dr. Martin nodded. He pressed a code into a small remote control, and the front of the glass box clicked open.

"It will take a few minutes to retrieve the notes," Dr. Martin said. "For anyone else, I would hesitate to grant unguarded access to the stone, as you've requested. I trust you'll be careful."

He glanced at us kids like we were troublemakers.

"We'll be careful," Dad promised.

As soon as Dr. Martin's steps receded, Dad turned to us with a frantic look in his eyes. "Children, this is very important. You have to stay out of this room."

He slipped his workbag off his shoulder and unzipped it just enough to pull out a bike chain and padlock. "Follow Dr. Martin. You'll find his office at the end of the Great Court on the left. There's only one entrance. Once he's inside, wrap this around the door handles and lock it tight. We need to delay him."

"You want us to lock him in?" Sadie asked, suddenly interested. "Brilliant!"

"Dad," I said, "what's going on?"

"We don't have time for explanations," he said. "This will be our only chance. They're coming."

"Who's coming?" Sadie asked.

He took Sadie by the shoulders. "Sweetheart, I love you. And I'm sorry... I'm sorry for many things, but there's no time now. If this works, I promise I'll make everything better for all of us. Carter, you're my brave man. You have to trust me. Remember, lock up Dr. Martin. Then stay out of this room!"

Chaining the curator's door was easy. But as soon as we'd finished, we looked back the way we'd come and saw blue light streaming from the Egyptian gallery, as if our dad had installed a giant glowing aquarium.

Sadie locked eyes with me. "Honestly, do you have *any* idea what he's up to?"

"None," I said. "But he's been acting strange lately. Thinking a lot about Mom. He keeps her picture..."

I didn't want to say more. Fortunately Sadie nodded like she understood.

"What's in his workbag?" she asked.

"I don't know. He told me never to look."

Sadie raised an eyebrow. "And you never did? God, that is so like you, Carter. You're hopeless."

I wanted to defend myself, but just then a tremor shook the floor.

Startled, Sadie grabbed my arm. "He told us to stay put. I suppose you're going to follow that order too?"

Actually, that order was sounding pretty good to me, but Sadie sprinted down the hall, and after a moment's hesitation, I ran after her.

When we reached the entrance of the Egyptian gallery, we stopped dead in our tracks. Our dad stood in front of the Rosetta Stone with his back to us. A blue circle glowed on the floor around him, as if someone had switched on hidden neon tubes in the floor.

My dad had thrown off his overcoat. His workbag lay open at his feet, revealing a wooden box about two feet long, painted with Egyptian images.

"What's he holding?" Sadie whispered to me. "Is that a boomerang?"

Sure enough, when Dad raised his hand, he was brandishing

a curved white stick. It did look like a boomerang. But instead of throwing the stick, he touched it to the Rosetta Stone. Sadie caught her breath. Dad was *writing* on the stone. Wherever the boomerang made contact, glowing blue lines appeared on the granite. Hieroglyphs.

It made no sense. How could he write glowing words with a stick? But the image was bright and clear: ram's horns above a box and an X.

"*Open*," Sadie murmured. I stared at her, because it sounded like she had just translated the word, but that was impossible. I'd been hanging around Dad for years, and even I could read only a few hieroglyphs. They are seriously hard to learn.

Dad raised his arms. He chanted: "*Wo-seer, i-ei.*" And two more hieroglyphic symbols burned blue against the surface of the Rosetta Stone.

As stunned as I was, I recognized the first symbol. It was the name of the Egyptian god of the dead.

"Wo-seer," I whispered. I'd never heard it pronounced that way, but I knew what it meant. "Osiris."

"*Osiris, come,*" Sadie said, as if in a trance. Then her eyes widened. "No!" she shouted. "Dad, no!"

Our father turned in surprise. He started to say, "Children—" but it was too late. The ground rumbled. The blue light turned to searing white, and the Rosetta Stone exploded.

When I regained consciousness, the first thing I heard was laughter—horrible, gleeful laughter mixed with the blare of the museum's security alarms.

I felt like I'd just been run over by a tractor. I sat up, dazed, and spit a piece of Rosetta Stone out of my mouth. The gallery was in ruins. Waves of fire rippled in pools along the floor. Giant statues had toppled. Sarcophagi had been knocked off their pedestals. Pieces of the Rosetta Stone had exploded outward with such force that they'd embedded themselves in the columns, the walls, the other exhibits.

Sadie was passed out next to me, but she looked unharmed. I shook her shoulder, and she grunted. "Ugh."

In front of us, where the Rosetta Stone had been, stood a smoking, sheared-off pedestal. The floor was blackened in a starburst pattern, except for the glowing blue circle around our father.

He was facing our direction, but he didn't seem to be looking at us. A bloody cut ran across his scalp. He gripped the boomerang tightly.

I didn't understand what he was looking at. Then the horrible laughter echoed around the room again, and I realized it was coming from right in front of me.

Something stood between our father and us. At first, I could barely make it out—just a flicker of heat. But as I concentrated, it took on a vague form—the fiery outline of a man.

He was taller than Dad, and his laugh cut through me like a chainsaw.

"Well done," he said to my father. "Very well done, Julius."

"You were not summoned!" My father's voice trembled. He

held up the boomerang, but the fiery man flicked one finger, and the stick flew from Dad's hand, shattering against the wall.

"I am never summoned, Julius," the man purred. "But when you open a door, you must be prepared for guests to walk through."

"Back to the Duat!" my father roared. "I have the power of the Great King!"

"Oh, scary," the fiery man said with amusement. "And even if you knew how to use that power, which you do not, he was never my match. I am the strongest. Now you will share his fate."

I couldn't make sense of anything, but I knew that I had to help my dad. I tried to pick up the nearest chunk of stone, but I was so terrified my fingers felt frozen and numb. My hands were useless.

Dad shot me a silent look of warning: *Get out.* I realized he was intentionally keeping the fiery man's back to us, hoping Sadie and I would escape unnoticed.

Sadie was still groggy. I managed to drag her behind a column, into the shadows. When she started to protest, I clamped my hand over her mouth. That woke her up. She saw what was happening and stopped fighting.

Alarms blared. Fire circled around the doorways of the gallery. The guards had to be on their way, but I wasn't sure if that was a good thing for us.

Dad crouched to the floor, keeping his eyes on his enemy, and opened his painted wooden box. He brought out a small rod like a ruler. He muttered something under his breath and the rod elongated into a wooden staff as tall as he was.

Sadie made a squeaking sound. I couldn't believe my eyes either, but things only got weirder.

Dad threw his staff at the fiery man's feet, and it changed into an enormous serpent—ten feet long and as big around as I was—with coppery scales and glowing red eyes. It lunged at the fiery man, who effortlessly grabbed the serpent by its neck. The man's hand burst into white-hot flames, and the snake burned to ashes.

"An old trick, Julius," the fiery man chided.

My dad glanced at us, silently urging us again to run. Part of me refused to believe any of this was real. Maybe I was unconscious, having a nightmare. Next to me, Sadie picked up a chunk of stone.

"How many?" my dad asked quickly, trying to keep the fiery man's attention. "How many did I release?"

"Why, all five," the man said, as if explaining something to a child. "You should know we're a package deal, Julius. Soon I'll release even more, and they'll be very grateful. I shall be named king again."

"The Demon Days," my father said. "They'll stop you before it's too late."

The fiery man laughed. "You think the House can stop me? Those old fools can't even stop arguing among themselves. Now let the story be told anew. And this time you shall *never* rise!"

The fiery man waved his hand. The blue circle at Dad's feet went dark. Dad grabbed for his toolbox, but it skittered across the floor.

"Good-bye, Osiris," the fiery man said. With another flick of his hand, he conjured a glowing coffin around our dad. At first it was transparent, but as our father struggled and pounded on its sides, the coffin became more and more solid—a golden Egyptian sarcophagus inlaid with jewels. My dad caught my eyes one last time, and mouthed the word *Run!* before the coffin sank into the floor, as if the ground had turned to water.

"Dad!" I screamed.

Sadie threw her stone, but it sailed harmlessly through the fiery man's head.

He turned, and for one terrible moment, his face appeared in the flames. What I saw made no sense. It was as if someone had superimposed two different faces on top of each other— one almost human, with pale skin, cruel, angular features, and glowing red eyes, the other like an animal with dark fur and sharp fangs. Worse than a dog or a wolf or a lion—some animal I'd never seen before. Those red eyes stared at me, and I knew I was going to die.

Behind me, heavy footsteps echoed on the marble floor of the Great Court. Voices were barking orders. The security guards, maybe the police—but they'd never get here in time.

The fiery man lunged at us. A few inches from my face, something shoved him backward. The air sparked with electricity. The amulet around my neck grew uncomfortably hot.

The fiery man hissed, regarding me more carefully. "So... it's *you*."

The building shook again. At the opposite end of the room, part of the wall exploded in a brilliant flash of light. Two people stepped through the gap—the man and the girl we'd seen at the Needle, their robes swirling around them. Both of them held staffs.

The fiery man snarled. He looked at me one last time and said, "Soon, boy."

Then the entire room erupted in flames. A blast of heat sucked all the air of out my lungs and I crumpled to the floor.

The last thing I remember, the man with the forked beard and the girl in blue were standing over me. I heard the security guards running and shouting, getting closer. The girl crouched over me and drew a long curved knife from her belt.

"We must act quickly," she told the man.

"Not yet," he said with some reluctance. His thick accent sounded French. "We must be sure before we destroy them."

I closed my eyes and drifted into unconsciousness.

3. Imprisoned with My Cat

[Give me the bloody mic.]

Hullo. Sadie here. My brother's a rubbish storyteller. Sorry about that. But now you've got me, so all is well.

Let's see. The explosion. Rosetta Stone in a billion pieces. Fiery evil bloke. Dad boxed in a coffin. Creepy Frenchman and Arab girl with the knife. Us passing out. Right.

So when I woke up, the police were rushing about as you might expect. They separated me from my brother. I didn't really mind that part. He's a pain anyway. But they locked me in the curator's office for *ages*. And yes, they used *our* bicycle chain to do it. Cretins.

I was shattered, of course. I'd just been knocked out by a fiery whatever-it-was. I'd watched my dad get packed in a sarcophagus and shot through the floor. I tried to tell the police about all that, but did they care? No.

Worst of all: I had a lingering chill, as if someone was pushing ice-cold needles into the back of my neck. It had started when I looked at those blue glowing words Dad had drawn on the Rosetta Stone and I *knew* what they meant. A family disease, perhaps? Can knowledge of boring Egyptian stuff be hereditary? With my luck.

Long after my gum had gone stale, a policewoman finally retrieved me from the curator's office. She asked me no questions. She just trundled me into a police car and took me home. Even then, I wasn't allowed to explain to Gran and Gramps. The policewoman just tossed me into my room and I waited. And waited.

I don't like waiting.

I paced the floor. My room was nothing posh, just an attic space with a window and a bed and a desk. There wasn't much to do. Muffin sniffed my legs and her tail puffed up like a bottlebrush. I suppose she doesn't fancy the smell of museums. She hissed and disappeared under the bed.

"Thanks a lot," I muttered.

I opened the door, but the policewoman was standing guard.

"The inspector will be with you in a moment," she told me. "Please stay inside."

I could see downstairs—just a glimpse of Gramps pacing the room, wringing his hands, while Carter and a police inspector talked on the sofa. I couldn't make out what they were saying.

"Could I just use the loo?" I asked the nice officer.

"No." She closed the door in my face. As if I might rig an explosion in the toilet. Honestly.

I dug out my iPod and scrolled through my playlist. Nothing struck me. I threw it on my bed in disgust. When I'm too distracted for music, that is a very sad thing. I wondered why Carter got to talk to the police first. It wasn't fair.

I fiddled with the necklace Dad had given me. I'd never been sure what the symbol meant. Carter's was obviously an eye, but mine looked a bit like an angel, or perhaps a killer alien robot.

Why on earth had Dad asked if I still had it? *Of course* I still had it. It was the only gift he'd ever given me. Well, apart from Muffin, and with the cat's attitude, I'm not sure I would call her a proper gift.

Dad had practically abandoned me at age six, after all. The necklace was my one link to him. On good days I would stare at it and remember him fondly. On bad days (which were much more frequent) I would fling it across the room and stomp on it and curse him for not being around, which I found quite therapeutic. But in the end, I always put it back on.

At any rate, during the weirdness at the museum—and I'm not making this up—the necklace got *hotter*. I nearly took it off, but I couldn't help wondering if it truly was protecting me somehow.

I'll make things right, Dad had said, with that guilty look he often gives me.

Well, colossal fail, Dad.

What had he been thinking? I wanted to believe it had all been a bad dream: the glowing hieroglyphs, the snake staff, the coffin. Things like that simply don't happen. But I knew better. I couldn't dream anything as horrifying as that fiery man's face when he'd turned on us. "Soon, boy," he'd told Carter, as if he intended to track us down. Just the idea made my hands tremble. I also couldn't help wondering about our stop at Cleopatra's Needle, how Dad had insisted on seeing it, as if he were steeling his courage, as if what he did at the British Museum had something to do with my mum.

My eyes wandered across my room and fixed on my desk. *No*, I thought. *Not going to do it.*

But I walked over and opened the drawer. I shoved aside a few old mags, my stash of sweets, a stack of maths homework I'd forgotten to hand in, and a few pictures of me and my mates Liz and Emma trying on ridiculous hats in Camden Market. And there at the bottom of it all was the picture of Mum.

Gran and Gramps have loads of pictures. They keep a shrine to Ruby in the hall cupboard—Mum's childhood artwork, her O-level results, her graduation picture from university, her favorite jewelry. It's quite mental. I was determined not to be like them, living in the past. I barely remembered Mum, after all, and nothing could change the fact she was dead.

But I did keep the one picture. It was of Mum and me at our house in Los Angeles, just after I was born. She stood out on the balcony, the Pacific Ocean behind her, holding a wrinkled pudgy lump of baby that would some day grow up to be yours truly. Baby me was not much to look at, but Mum was gorgeous, even in shorts and a tattered T-shirt. Her eyes were deep blue. Her blond hair was clipped back. Her skin was perfect. Quite depressing compared to mine. People always say I look like her, but I couldn't even get the spot off my chin much less look so mature and beautiful.

[Stop smirking, Carter.]

The photo fascinated me because I hardly remembered our lives together at all. But the main reason I'd kept the photo was because of the symbol on Mum's T-shirt: one of those life symbols—an ankh.

My dead mother wearing the symbol for life. Nothing could've been sadder. But she smiled at the camera as if she knew a secret. As if my dad and she were sharing a private joke.

Something tugged at the back of my mind. That stocky man in the trench coat who'd been arguing with Dad across the street—he'd said something about the Per Ankh.

Had he meant *ankh* as in the symbol for life, and if so, what was a *per*? I supposed he didn't mean pear as in the fruit.

I had an eerie feeling that if I saw the words *Per Ankh* written in hieroglyphics, I would know what they meant.

I put down the picture of Mum. I picked up a pencil and turned over one of my old homework papers. I wondered what would happen if I tried to *draw* the words *Per Ankh*. Would the right design just occur to me?

As I touched pencil to paper, my bedroom door opened. "Miss Kane?"

I whirled and dropped the pencil.

A police inspector stood frowning in my doorway. "What are you doing?"

"Maths," I said.

My ceiling was quite low, so the inspector had to stoop to come in. He wore a lint-colored suit that matched his gray hair and his ashen face. "Now then, Sadie. I'm Chief Inspector Williams. Let's have a chat, shall we? Sit down."

I didn't sit, and neither did he, which must've annoyed him. It's hard to look in charge when you're hunched over like Quasimodo.

"Tell me everything, please," he said, "from the time your father came round to get you."

"I already told the police at the museum."

"Again, if you don't mind."

So I told him everything. Why not? His left eyebrow crept higher and higher as I told him the strange bits like the glowing letters and serpent staff.

"Well, Sadie," Inspector Williams said. "You've got quite an imagination."

"I'm not lying, Inspector. And I think your eyebrow is trying to escape."

He tried to look at his own eyebrows, then scowled. "Now, Sadie, I'm sure this is very hard on you. I understand you want to protect your father's reputation. But he's gone now—"

"You mean through the floor in a coffin," I insisted. "He's *not* dead."

Inspector Williams spread his hands. "Sadie, I'm very sorry. But we must find out why he did this act of . . . well . . ."

"Act of *what*?"

He cleared his throat uncomfortably. "Your father destroyed priceless artifacts and apparently killed himself in the process. We'd very much like to know why."

I stared at him. "Are you saying my father's a terrorist? Are you *mad*?"

"We've made calls to some of your father's associates. I understand his behavior had become erratic since your mother's death. He'd become withdrawn and obsessive in his studies, spending more and more time in Egypt—"

"He's a bloody Egyptologist! You should be looking for him, not asking stupid questions!"

"Sadie," he said, and I could hear in his voice that he was resisting the urge to strangle me. Strangely, I get this a lot from adults. "There are extremist groups in Egypt that object to Egyptian artifacts being kept in other countries' museums. These people might have approached your father. Perhaps in his state, your father became an easy target for them. If you've heard him mention any names—"

I stormed past him to the window. I was so angry I could hardly think. I refused to believe Dad was dead. No, no, no. And a terrorist? Please. Why did adults have to be so thick? They always say "tell the truth," and when you do, they don't believe you. What's the point?

I stared down at the dark street. Suddenly that cold tingly

feeling got worse than ever. I focused on the dead tree where I'd met Dad earlier. Standing there now, in the dim light of a streetlamp, looking up at me, was the pudgy bloke in the black trench coat and the round glasses and the fedora—the man Dad had called Amos.

I suppose I should've felt threatened by an odd man staring up at me in the dark of night. But his expression was full of concern. And he looked *so* familiar. It was driving me mad that I couldn't remember why.

Behind me, the inspector cleared his throat. "Sadie, no one blames you for the attack on the museum. We understand you were dragged into this against your will."

I turned from the window. "Against my will? I chained the curator in his office."

The inspector's eyebrow started to creep up again. "Be that as it may, surely you didn't understand what your father meant to do. Possibly your brother was involved?"

I snorted. "Carter? Please."

"So you are determined to protect him as well. You consider him a proper brother, do you?"

I couldn't believe it. I wanted to smack his face. "What's that supposed to mean? Because he doesn't *look* like me?"

The inspector blinked. "I only meant—"

"I *know* what you meant. Of course he's my brother!"

Inspector Williams held up his hands apologetically, but I was still seething. As much as Carter annoyed me, I hated it when people assumed we weren't related, or looked at my father askance when he said the three of us were a family— like we'd done something wrong. Stupid Dr. Martin at the museum. Inspector Williams. It happened every time Dad and Carter and I were together. *Every* bloody time.

"I'm sorry, Sadie," the inspector said. "I only want to make sure we separate the innocent from the guilty. It will go much easier for everyone if you cooperate. Any information. Anything your father said. People he might've mentioned."

"Amos," I blurted out, just to see his reaction. "He met a man named Amos."

Inspector Williams sighed. "Sadie, he couldn't have done. Surely you know that. We spoke with Amos not one hour ago, on the phone from his home in New York."

"He isn't in New York!" I insisted. "He's right—"

I glanced out the window and Amos was gone. Bloody typical.

"That's not possible," I said.

"Exactly," the inspector said.

"But he was here!" I exclaimed. "Who *is* he? One of Dad's colleagues? How did you know to call him?"

"Really, Sadie. This acting must stop."

"Acting?"

The inspector studied me for a moment, then set his jaw as if he'd made a decision. "We've already had the truth from Carter. I didn't want to upset you, but he told us everything. He understands there's no point protecting your father now. You might as well help us, and there will be no charges against you."

"You shouldn't lie to children!" I yelled, hoping my voice carried all the way downstairs. "Carter would never say a word against Dad, and neither will I!"

The inspector didn't even have the decency to look embarrassed.

He crossed his arms. "I'm sorry you feel that way, Sadie. I'm afraid it's time we went downstairs...to discuss consequences with your grandparents."

4. Kidnapped by a Not-So-Stranger

I JUST LOVE FAMILY MEETINGS. Very cozy, with the Christmas garlands round the fireplace and a nice pot of tea and a detective from Scotland Yard ready to arrest you.

Carter slumped on the sofa, cradling Dad's workbag. I wondered why the police had let him keep it. It should have been evidence or something, but the inspector didn't seem to notice it at all.

Carter looked awful—I mean even worse than usual. Honestly, the boy had never been in a proper school, and he dressed like a junior professor, with his khaki trousers and a button-down shirt and loafers. He's not bad looking, I suppose. He's reasonably tall and fit and his hair isn't hopeless. He's got Dad's eyes, and my mates Liz and Emma have even told me from his picture that he's *hot*, which I must take with a grain of salt because (a) he's my brother, and (b) my mates are a bit crazed. When it came to clothes, Carter wouldn't have known *hot* if it bit him on the bum.

[Oh, don't look at me like that, Carter. You know it's *true*.]

At any rate, I shouldn't have been too hard on him. He was taking Dad's disappearance even worse than I was.

Gran and Gramps sat on either side of him, looking quite nervous. The pot of tea and a plate of biscuits sat on the table, but no one was having any. Chief Inspector Williams ordered me into the only free chair. Then he paced in front of the fireplace importantly. Two more police stood by the front door—the woman from earlier and a big bloke who kept eyeing the biscuits.

"Mr. and Mrs. Faust," Inspector Williams said, "I'm afraid we have two uncooperative children."

Gran fidgeted with the trim of her dress. It's hard to believe she's related to Mum. Gran is frail and colorless, like a stick person really, while Mum in the photos always looked so happy and full of life. "They're just children," she managed. "Surely you can't blame them."

"*Pah!*" Gramps said. "This is ridiculous, Inspector. They aren't responsible!"

Gramps is a former rugby player. He has beefy arms, a belly much too big for his shirt, and eyes sunk deep in his face, as if someone had punched them (well, actually Dad *had* punched them years ago, but that's another story). Gramps is quite scary looking. Usually people got out of his way, but Inspector Williams didn't seem impressed.

"Mr. Faust," he said, "what do you imagine the morning headlines will read? 'British Museum attacked. Rosetta Stone destroyed.' Your son-in-law—"

"*Former* son-in-law," Gramps corrected.

"—was most likely vaporized in the explosion, or he ran off, in which case—"

"He didn't run off!" I shouted.

"We need to know where he is," the inspector continued. "And the only witnesses, your grandchildren, refuse to tell me the truth."

"We *did* tell you the truth," Carter said. "Dad isn't dead. He sank through the floor."

Inspector Williams glanced at Gramps, as if to say, *There, you see?* Then he turned to Carter. "Young man, your father has committed a criminal act. He's left you behind to deal with the consquences—"

"That's not true!" I snapped, my voice trembling with rage. I couldn't believe Dad would intentionally leave us at the mercy of police, of course. But the idea of him abandoning me—well, as I might have mentioned, that's a bit of a sore point.

"Dear, please," Gran told me, "the inspector is only doing his job."

"Badly!" I said.

"Let's all have some tea," Gran suggested.

"No!" Carter and I yelled at once, which made me feel bad for Gran, as she practically wilted into the sofa.

"We *can* charge you," the inspector warned, turning on me. "We can and we will—"

He froze. Then he blinked several times, as if he'd forgotten what he was doing.

Gramps frowned. "Er, Inspector?"

"Yes…" Chief Inspector Williams murmured dreamily. He reached in his pocket and took out a little blue booklet—an American passport. He threw it in Carter's lap.

"You're being deported," the inspector announced. "You're to leave the country within twenty-four hours. If we need to question you further, you'll be contacted through the FBI."

Carter's mouth fell open. He looked at me, and I knew I wasn't imagining how odd this was. The inspector had completely changed direction. He'd been about to arrest us. I was sure of it. And then out of the blue, he was deporting Carter? Even the other police officers looked confused.

"Sir?" the policewoman asked. "Are you sure—"

"Quiet, Linley. The two of you may go."

The cops hesitated until Williams made a shooing motion with his hand. Then they left, closing the door behind them.

"Hold on," Carter said. "My father's disappeared, and you want me to leave the country?"

"Your father is either dead or a fugitive, son," the inspector said. "Deportation is the kindest option. It's already been arranged."

"With whom?" Gramps demanded. "Who authorized this?"

"With…" The inspector got that funny blank look again. "With the proper authorities. Believe me, it's better than prison."

Carter looked too devastated to speak, but before I could feel sorry for him, Inspector Williams turned to me. "You, too, miss."

He might as well have hit me with a sledgehammer.

"You're deporting *me?*" I asked. "I live here!"

"You're an American citizen. And under the circumstances, it's best for you to return home."

I just stared at him. I couldn't remember any home except this flat. My mates at school, my room, *everything* I knew was here. "Where am I supposed to go?"

"Inspector," Gran said, her voice trembling. "This isn't fair. I can't believe—"

"I'll give you some time to say good-bye," the inspector interrupted. Then he frowned as if baffled by his own actions. "I—I must be going."

This made no sense, and the inspector seemed to realize it, but he walked to the front door anyway. When he opened it, I almost jumped out of my chair, because the man in black, Amos, was standing there. He'd lost his trench coat and hat somewhere, but was still wearing the same pinstripe suit and round glasses. His braided hair glittered with gold beads.

I thought the inspector would say something, or express surprise, but he didn't even acknowledge Amos. He walked right past him and into the night.

Amos came inside and closed the door. Gran and Gramps stood up.

"You," Gramps growled. "I should've known. If I was younger, I would beat you to a pulp."

"Hello, Mr. and Mrs. Faust," Amos said. He looked at Carter and me as if we were problems to be solved. "It's time we had a talk."

———

Amos made himself right at home. He flopped onto the sofa and poured himself tea. He munched on a biscuit, which was quite dangerous, because Gran's biscuits are horrid.

I thought Gramps's head would explode. His face went bright red. He came up behind Amos and raised his hand as if he were about to smack him, but Amos kept munching his biscuit.

"Please, sit down," he told us.

And we all sat. It was the strangest thing—as if we'd been waiting for his order. Even Gramps dropped his hand and moved round the sofa. He sat next to Amos with a disgusted sigh.

Amos sipped his tea and regarded me with some displeasure. That wasn't fair, I thought. I didn't look *that* bad, considering what we'd been through. Then he looked at Carter and grunted.

"Terrible timing," he muttered. "But there's no other way. They'll have to come with me."

"Excuse me?" I said. "I'm not going anywhere with some strange man with biscuit on his face!"

He did in fact have biscuit crumbs on his face, but he apparently didn't care, as he didn't bother to check.

"I'm no stranger, Sadie," he said. "Don't you remember?"

It was creepy hearing him talk to me in such a familiar way. I felt I *should* know him. I looked at Carter, but he seemed just as mystified as I was.

"No, Amos," Gran said, trembling. "You can't take Sadie. We had an agreement."

"Julius broke that agreement tonight," Amos said. "You

know you can't care for Sadie anymore—not after what's happened. Their only chance is to come with me."

"Why should we go anywhere with you?" Carter asked. "You almost got in a fight with Dad!"

Amos looked at the workbag in Carter's lap. "I see you kept your father's bag. That's good. You'll need it. As for getting into fights, Julius and I did that quite a lot. If you didn't notice, Carter, I was trying to *stop* him from doing something rash. If he'd listened to me, we wouldn't be in this situation."

I had no idea what he was on about, but Gramps apparently understood.

"You and your superstitions!" he said. "I told you we want none of it."

Amos pointed to the back patio. Through the glass doors, you could see the lights shining on the Thames. It was quite a nice view at night, when you couldn't notice how run-down some of the buildings were.

"Superstition, is it?" Amos asked. "And yet you found a place to live on the *east* bank of the river."

Gramps turned even redder. "That was Ruby's idea. Thought it would protect us. But she was wrong about many things, wasn't she? She trusted Julius and you, for one!"

Amos looked unfazed. He smelled interesting—like old-timey spices, copal and amber, like the incense shops in Covent Garden.

He finished his tea and looked straight at Gran. "Mrs. Faust, you know what's begun. The police are the least of your worries."

Gran swallowed. "You...*you* changed that inspector's mind. You made him deport Sadie."

"It was that or see the children arrested," Amos said.

"Hang on," I said. "You *changed* Inspector Williams's mind? How?"

Amos shrugged. "It's not permanent. In fact we should get to New York in the next hour or so before Inspector Williams begins to wonder why he let you go."

Carter laughed incredulously. "You can't get to New York from London in an hour. Not even the fastest plane—"

"No," Amos agreed. "Not a plane." He turned back to Gran as if everything had been settled. "Mrs. Faust, Carter and Sadie have only one safe option. You know that. They'll come to the mansion in Brooklyn. I can protect them there."

"You've got a mansion," Carter said. "In Brooklyn."

Amos gave him an amused smile. "The family mansion. You'll be safe there."

"But our dad—"

"Is beyond your help for now," Amos said sadly. "I'm sorry, Carter. I'll explain later, but Julius would want you to be safe. For that, we must move quickly. I'm afraid I'm all you've got."

That was a bit harsh, I thought. Carter glanced at Gran and Gramps. Then he nodded glumly. He knew that they didn't want him around. He'd always reminded them of our dad. And yes, it was a stupid reason not to take in your grandson, but there you are.

"Well, Carter can do what he wants," I said. "But *I live here*. And I'm not going off with some stranger, am I?"

I looked at Gran for support, but she was staring at the lace doilies on the table as if they were suddenly quite interesting.

"Gramps, surely..."

But he wouldn't meet my eyes either. He turned to Amos. "You can get them out of the country?"

"Hang on!" I protested.

Amos stood and wiped the crumbs off his jacket. He walked to the patio doors and stared out at the river. "The police will be back soon. Tell them anything you like. They won't find us."

"You're going to *kidnap* us?" I asked, stunned. I looked at Carter. "Do you believe this?"

Carter shouldered the workbag. Then he stood like he was ready to go. Possibly he just wanted to be out of Gran and Gramps's flat. "How do you plan to get to New York in an hour?" he asked Amos. "You said, not a plane."

"No," Amos agreed. He put his finger to the window and traced something in the condensation—another bloody hieroglyph.

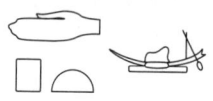

"A boat," I said—then realized I'd translated aloud, which I wasn't supposed to be able to do.

Amos peered at me over the top of his round glasses. "How did you—"

"I mean that last bit looks like a boat," I blurted out. "But that can't be what you mean. That's ridiculous."

"Look!" Carter cried.

I pressed in next to him at the patio doors. Down at the

quayside, a boat was docked. But not a regular boat, mind you. It was an Egyptian reed boat, with two torches burning in the front, and a big rudder in the back. A figure in a black trench coat and hat—possibly Amos's—stood at the tiller.

I'll admit, for once, I was at a loss for words.

"We're going in that," Carter said. "To Brooklyn."

"We'd better get started," Amos said.

I whirled back to my grandmother. "Gran, please!"

She brushed a tear from her cheek. "It's for the best, my dear. You should take Muffin."

"Ah, yes," Amos said. "We can't forget the cat."

He turned towards the stairs. As if on cue, Muffin raced down in a leopard-spotted streak and leaped into my arms. She *never* does that.

"Who are you?" I asked Amos. It was clear I was running out of options, but I at least wanted answers. "We can't just go off with some stranger."

"I'm not a stranger." Amos smiled at me. "I'm family."

And suddenly I remembered his face smiling down at me, saying, "Happy birthday, Sadie." A memory so distant, I'd almost forgotten.

"Uncle Amos?" I asked hazily.

"That's right, Sadie," he said. "I'm Julius's brother. Now come along. We have a long way to go."

5. We Meet the Monkey

IT'S CARTER AGAIN. SORRY. We had to turn off the tape for a while because we were being followed by—well, we'll get to that later.

Sadie was telling you how we left London, right?

So anyway, we followed Amos down to the weird boat docked at the quayside. I cradled Dad's workbag under my arm. I still couldn't believe he was gone. I felt guilty leaving London without him, but I believed Amos about one thing: right now Dad was beyond our help. I didn't trust Amos, but I figured if I wanted to find out what had happened to Dad, I was going to have to go along with him. He was the only one who seemed to know anything.

Amos stepped aboard the reed boat. Sadie jumped right on, but I hesitated. I'd seen boats like this on the Nile before, and they never seemed very sturdy.

It was basically woven together from coils of plant fiber— like a giant floating rug. I figured the torches at the front couldn't be a good idea, because if we didn't sink, we'd burn. At the back, the tiller was manned by a little guy wearing Amos's black trench coat and hat. The hat was shoved down on his head so I couldn't see his face. His hands and feet were lost in the folds of the coat.

"How does this thing move?" I asked Amos. "You've got no sail."

"Trust me." Amos offered me a hand.

The night was cold, but when I stepped on board I suddenly felt warmer, as if the torchlight were casting a protective glow over us. In the middle of the boat was a hut made from woven mats. From Sadie's arms, Muffin sniffed at it and growled.

"Take a seat inside," Amos suggested. "The trip might be a little rough."

"I'll stand, thanks." Sadie nodded at the little guy in back. "Who's your driver?"

Amos acted as if he hadn't heard the question. "Hang on, everyone!" He nodded to the steersman, and the boat lurched forward.

The feeling was hard to describe. You know that tingle in the pit of your stomach when you're on a roller coaster and it goes into free fall? It was kind of like that, except we weren't falling, and the feeling didn't go away. The boat moved with astounding speed. The lights of the city blurred, then were swallowed in a thick fog. Strange sounds echoed in the dark: slithering and hissing, distant screams, voices whispering in languages I didn't understand.

The tingling turned to nausea. The sounds got louder, until I was about to scream myself. Then suddenly the boat slowed.

The noises stopped, and the fog dissipated. City lights came back, brighter than before.

Above us loomed a bridge, much taller than any bridge in London. My stomach did a slow roll. To the left, I saw a familiar skyline—the Chrysler Building, the Empire State Building.

"Impossible," I said. "That's New York."

Sadie looked as green as I felt. She was still cradling Muffin, whose eyes were closed. The cat seemed to be purring. "It can't be," Sadie said. "We only traveled a few minutes."

And yet here we were, sailing up the East River, right under the Williamsburg Bridge. We glided to a stop next to a small dock on the Brooklyn side of the river. In front of us was an industrial yard filled with piles of scrap metal and old construction equipment. In the center of it all, right at the water's edge, rose a huge factory warehouse heavily painted with graffiti, the windows boarded up.

"That is not a mansion," Sadie said. Her powers of perception are really amazing.

"Look again." Amos pointed to the top of the building.

"How . . . how did you . . ." My voice failed me. I wasn't sure why I hadn't seen it before, but now it was obvious: a five-story mansion perched on the roof of the warehouse, like another layer of a cake. "You couldn't build a mansion up there!"

"Long story," Amos said. "But we needed a private location."

"And is this the east shore?" Sadie asked. "You said something about that in London—my grandparents living on the east shore."

Amos smiled. "Yes. Very good, Sadie. In ancient times, the east bank of the Nile was always the side of the living, the side

51

where the sun rises. The dead were buried west of the river. It was considered bad luck, even dangerous, to live there. The tradition is still strong among . . . our people."

"Our people?" I asked, but Sadie muscled in with another question.

"So you can't live in Manhattan?" she asked.

Amos's brow furrowed as he looked across at the Empire State Building. "Manhattan has other problems. Other gods. It's best we stay separate."

"Other *what*?" Sadie demanded.

"Nothing." Amos walked past us to the steersman. He plucked off the man's hat and coat—and there was no one underneath. The steersman simply wasn't there. Amos put on his fedora, folded his coat over his arm, then waved toward a metal staircase that wound all the way up the side of the warehouse to the mansion on the roof.

"All ashore," he said. "And welcome to the Twenty-first Nome."

"Gnome?" I asked, as we followed him up the stairs. "Like those little runty guys?"

"Heavens, no," Amos said. "I hate gnomes. They smell horrible."

"But you said—"

"*Nome*, n-o-m-e. As in a district, a region. The term is from ancient times, when Egypt was divided into forty-two provinces. Today, the system is a little different. We've gone global. The world is divided into three hundred and sixty nomes. Egypt, of course, is the First. Greater New York is the Twenty-first."

Sadie glanced at me and twirled her finger around her temple.

"No, Sadie," Amos said without looking back. "I'm not crazy. There's much you need to learn."

We reached the top of the stairs. Looking up at the mansion, it was hard to understand what I was seeing. The house was at least fifty feet tall, built of enormous limestone blocks and steel-framed windows. There were hieroglyphs engraved around the windows, and the walls were lit up so the place looked like a cross between a modern museum and an ancient temple. But the weirdest thing was that if I glanced away, the whole building seemed to disappear. I tried it several times just to be sure. If I looked for the mansion from the corner of my eye, it wasn't there. I had to force my eyes to refocus on it, and even that took a lot of willpower.

Amos stopped before the entrance, which was the size of a garage door—a dark heavy square of timber with no visible handle or lock. "Carter, after you."

"Um, how do I—"

"How do you think?"

Great, another mystery. I was about to suggest we ram Amos's head against it and see if that worked. Then I looked at the door again, and I had the strangest feeling. I stretched out my arm. Slowly, without touching the door, I raised my hand and the door followed my movement—sliding upward until it disappeared into the ceiling.

Sadie looked stunned. "How..."

"I don't know," I admitted, a little embarrassed. "Motion sensor, maybe?"

"Interesting." Amos sounded a little troubled. "Not the way I would've done it, but very good. Remarkably good."

"Thanks, I think."

Sadie tried to go inside first, but as soon as she stepped on the threshold, Muffin wailed and almost clawed her way out of Sadie's arms.

Sadie stumbled backward. "What was that about, cat?"

"Oh, of course," Amos said. "My apologies." He put his hand on the cat's head and said, very formally, "You may enter."

"The cat needs permission?" I asked.

"Special circumstances," Amos said, which wasn't much of an explanation, but he walked inside without saying another word. We followed, and this time Muffin stayed quiet.

"Oh my god..." Sadie's jaw dropped. She craned her neck to look at the ceiling, and I thought the gum might fall out of her mouth.

"Yes," Amos said. "This is the Great Room."

I could see why he called it that. The cedar-beamed ceiling was four stories high, held up by carved stone pillars engraved with hieroglyphs. A weird assortment of musical instruments and Ancient Egyptian weapons decorated the walls. Three levels of balconies ringed the room, with rows of doors all looking out on the main area. The fireplace was big enough to park a car in, with a plasma-screen TV above the mantel and massive leather sofas on either side. On the floor was a snakeskin rug, except it was forty feet long and fifteen feet wide—bigger than any snake. Outside, through glass walls, I could see the terrace that wrapped around the house. It had a swimming pool, a dining area, and a blazing fire pit. And at the far end of the Great Room was a set of double doors marked with the Eye of Horus, and chained with half a dozen padlocks. I wondered what could possibly be behind them.

But the real showstopper was the statue in the center of the Great Room. It was thirty feet tall, made of black marble. I could tell it was of an Egyptian god because the figure had a human body and an animal's head—like a stork or a crane, with a long neck and a really long beak.

The god was dressed ancient-style in a kilt, sash, and neck collar. He held a scribe's stylus in one hand, and an open scroll in the other, as if he had just written the hieroglyphs inscribed there: an ankh—the Egyptian looped cross—with a rectangle traced around its top.

"That's it!" Sadie exclaimed. "Per Ankh."

I stared at her in disbelief. "All right, how can you read that?"

"I don't know," she said. "But it's obvious, isn't it? The top one is shaped like the floor plan of a house."

"How did you get that? It's just a box." The thing was, she

was right. I recognized the symbol, and it *was* supposed to be a simplified picture of a house with a doorway, but that wouldn't be obvious to most people, especially people named Sadie. Yet she looked absolutely positive.

"It's a house," she insisted. "And the bottom picture is the ankh, the symbol for life. Per Ankh—the House of Life."

"Very good, Sadie." Amos looked impressed. "And this is a statue of the only god still allowed in the House of Life—at least, normally. Do you recognize him, Carter?"

Just then it clicked: the bird was an ibis, an Egyptian river bird. "Thoth," I said. "The god of knowledge. He invented writing."

"Indeed," Amos said.

"Why the animal heads?" Sadie asked. "All those Egyptian gods have animal heads. They look so silly."

"They don't normally appear that way," Amos said. "Not in real life."

"Real life?" I asked. "Come on. You sound like you've met them in person."

Amos's expression didn't reassure me. He looked as if he were remembering something unpleasant. "The gods could appear in many forms—usually fully human or fully animal, but occasionally as a hybrid form like this. They are primal forces, you understand, a sort of bridge between humanity and nature. They are depicted with animal heads to show that they exist in two different worlds at once. Do you understand?"

"Not even a little," Sadie said.

"*Mmm.*" Amos didn't sound surprised. "Yes, we have much training to do. At any rate, the god before you, Thoth, founded the House of Life, for which this mansion is the regional headquarters. Or at least . . . it used to be. I'm the only member left in the Twenty-first Nome. Or I *was*, until you two came along."

"Hang on." I had so many questions I could hardly think where to start. "What *is* the House of Life? Why is Thoth the only god allowed here, and why are you—"

"Carter, I understand how you feel." Amos smiled sympathetically. "But these things are better discussed in daylight. You need to get some sleep, and I don't want you to have nightmares."

"You think I can sleep?"

"*Mrow.*" Muffin stretched in Sadie's arms and let loose a huge yawn.

Amos clapped his hands. "Khufu!"

I thought he'd sneezed, because Khufu is a weird name, but then a little dude about three feet tall with gold fur and a purple shirt came clambering down the stairs. It took me a second to realize it was a baboon wearing an L.A. Lakers jersey.

The baboon did a flip and landed in front of us. He showed off his fangs and made a sound that was half roar, half belch. His breath smelled like nacho-flavored Doritos.

All I could think to say was, "The Lakers are my home team!"

The baboon slapped his head with both hands and belched again.

"Oh, Khufu likes you," Amos said. "You'll get along famously."

"Right." Sadie looked dazed. "You've got a monkey butler. Why not?"

Muffin purred in Sadie's arms as if the baboon didn't bother her at all.

"*Agh!*" Khufu grunted at me.

Amos chuckled. "He wants to go one-on-one with you, Carter. To, ah, see your game."

I shifted from foot to foot. "Um, yeah. Sure. Maybe tomorrow. But how can you understand—"

"Carter, I'm afraid you'll have a lot to get used to," Amos said. "But if you're going to survive and save your father, you have to get some rest."

"Sorry," Sadie said, "did you say 'survive and save our father'? Could you expand on that?"

"Tomorrow," Amos said. "We'll begin your orientation in the morning. Khufu, show them to their rooms, please."

"*Agh-uhh!*" the baboon grunted. He turned and waddled up the stairs. Unfortunately, the Lakers jersey didn't completely cover his multicolored rear.

We were about to follow when Amos said, "Carter, the workbag, please. It's best if I lock it in the library."

I hesitated. I'd almost forgotten the bag on my shoulder, but it was all I had left of my father. I didn't even have our luggage because it was still locked up at the British Museum. Honestly, I'd been surprised that the police hadn't taken the workbag too, but none of them seemed to notice it.

"You'll get it back," Amos promised. "When the time is right."

He asked nicely enough, but something in his eyes told me that I really didn't have a choice.

I handed over the bag. Amos took it gingerly, as if it were full of explosives.

"See you in the morning." He turned and strode toward the chained-up doors. They unlatched themselves and opened just enough for Amos to slip through without showing us anything on the other side. Then the chains locked again behind him.

I looked at Sadie, unsure what to do. Staying by ourselves in the Great Room with the creepy statue of Thoth didn't seem like much fun, so we followed Khufu up the stairs.

Sadie and I got adjoining rooms on the third floor, and I've got to admit, they were way cooler than any place I'd ever stayed before.

I had my own kitchenette, fully stocked with my favorite snacks: ginger ale—[No, Sadie. It's not an old person's soda! Be quiet!]—Twix, and Skittles. It seemed impossible. How did Amos know what I liked? The TV, computer, and stereo system were totally high-tech. The bathroom was stocked with my regular brand of toothpaste, deodorant, everything. The king-size bed was awesome, too, though the pillow was a little strange. Instead of a cloth pillow, it was an ivory headrest like I'd seen in Egyptian tombs. It was decorated with lions and (of course) more hieroglyphs.

The room even had a deck that looked out on New York Harbor, with views of Manhattan and the Statue of Liberty in the distance, but the sliding glass doors were locked shut somehow. That was my first indication that something was wrong.

I turned to look for Khufu, but he was gone. The door to my room was shut. I tried to open it, but it was locked.

A muffled voice came from the next room. "Carter?"

"Sadie." I tried the door to her adjoining room, but it was locked too.

"We're prisoners," she said. "Do you think Amos...I mean, can we trust him?"

After all I'd seen today, I didn't trust *anything*, but I could hear the fear in Sadie's voice. It triggered an unfamiliar feeling in me, like I needed to reassure her. The idea seemed ridiculous. Sadie had always seemed so much braver than me—doing what she wanted, never caring about the consequences. I was the one who got scared. But right now, I felt like I needed to play a role I hadn't played in a long, long time: big brother.

"It'll be okay." I tried to sound confident. "Look, if Amos wanted to hurt us, he could've done it by now. Try to get some sleep."

"Carter?"

"Yeah?"

"It was magic, wasn't it? What happened to Dad at the museum. Amos's boat. This house. All of it's magic."

"I think so."

I could hear her sigh. "Good. At least I'm not going mad."

"Don't let the bedbugs bite," I called. And I realized I hadn't said that to Sadie since we had lived together in Los Angeles, when Mom was still alive.

"I miss Dad," she said. "I hardly ever saw him, I know, but...I miss him."

My eyes got a little teary, but I took a deep breath. I was *not* going to go all weak. Sadie needed me. Dad needed us.

"We'll find him," I told her. "Pleasant dreams."

I listened, but the only thing I heard was Muffin meowing and scampering around, exploring her new space. At least *she* didn't seem unhappy.

I got ready for bed and crawled in. The covers were comfortable and warm, but the pillow was just too weird. It gave me neck cramps, so I put it on the floor and went to sleep without it.

My first big mistake.

C
A
R
T
E
R

6. Breakfast with a Crocodile

HOW TO DESCRIBE IT? Not a nightmare. It was much more real and frightening.

As I slept, I felt myself go weightless. I drifted up, turned, and saw my own sleeping form below.

I'm dying, I thought. But that wasn't it, either. I wasn't a ghost. I had a new shimmering golden form with wings instead of arms. I was some kind of bird. [No, Sadie, not a chicken. Will you let me tell the story, please?]

I knew I wasn't dreaming, because I don't dream in color. I certainly don't dream in all five senses. The room smelled faintly of jasmine. I could hear the carbonation bubbles pinging in the can of ginger ale I'd opened on my nightstand. I could feel a cold wind ruffling through my feathers, and I realized the windows were open. I didn't want to leave, but a strong current pulled me out of the room like a leaf in a storm.

The lights of the mansion faded below me. The skyline of New York blurred and disappeared. I shot through the mist and darkness, strange voices whispering all around me. My stomach tingled as it had earlier that night on Amos's barge. Then the mist cleared, and I was in a different place.

I floated above a barren mountain. Far below, a grid of city lights stretched across the valley floor. Definitely not New York. It was nighttime, but I could tell I was in the desert. The wind was so dry, the skin on my face was like paper. And I know that doesn't make sense, but my face felt like my normal face, as if that part of me hadn't transformed into a bird. [Fine, Sadie. Call me the Carter-headed chicken. Happy?]

Below me on a ridge stood two figures. They didn't seem to notice me, and I realized I wasn't glowing anymore. In fact I was pretty much invisible, floating in the darkness. I couldn't make out the two figures clearly, except to recognize that they weren't human. Staring harder, I could see that one was short, squat, and hairless, with slimy skin that glistened in the starlight—like an amphibian standing on its hind legs. The other was tall and scarecrow skinny, with rooster claws instead of feet. I couldn't see his face very well, but it looked red and moist and...well, let's just say I was glad I couldn't see it better.

"Where is he?" the toadie-looking one croaked nervously.

"Hasn't taken a permanent host yet," the rooster-footed guy chided. "He can only appear for a short time."

"You're sure this is the place?"

"Yes, fool! He'll be here as soon—"

A fiery form appeared on the ridge. The two creatures fell to the ground, groveling in the dirt, and I prayed like crazy that I really was invisible.

"My lord!" the toad said.

Even in the dark, the newcomer was hard to see—just the silhouette of a man outlined in flames.

"What do they call this place?" the man asked. And as soon as he spoke, I knew for sure he was the guy who'd attacked my dad at the British Museum. All the fear I'd felt at the museum came rushing back, paralyzing me. I remembered trying to pick up that stupid rock to throw, but I hadn't been able to do even that. I'd completely failed my dad.

"My lord," Rooster Foot said. "The mountain is called Camelback. The city is called Phoenix."

The fiery man laughed—a booming sound like thunder. "Phoenix. How appropriate! And the desert so much like home. All it needs now is to be scoured of life. The desert should be a sterile place, don't you think?"

"Oh yes, my lord," the toadie agreed. "But what of the other four?"

"One is already entombed," the fiery man said. "The second is weak. She will be easily manipulated. That leaves only two. And they will be dealt with soon enough."

"Er...how?" the toadie asked.

The fiery man glowed brighter. "You are an inquisitive little tadpole, aren't you?" He pointed at the toad and the poor creature's skin began to steam.

"No!" the toadie begged. "No-o-o-o!"

I could hardly watch. I don't want to describe it. But if you've heard what happens when cruel kids pour salt on snails, you'll have a pretty good idea of what happened to the toadie. Soon there was nothing left.

Rooster Foot took a nervous step back. I couldn't blame him.

"We will build my temple here," the fiery man said, as if nothing had happened. "This mountain shall serve as my place of worship. When it is complete, I will summon the greatest storm ever known. I will cleanse everything. *Everything.*"

"Yes, my lord," Rooster Foot agreed quickly. "And, ah, if I may suggest, my lord, to increase your power..." The creature bowed and scraped and moved forward, as if he wanted to whisper in the fiery man's ear.

Just when I thought Rooster Foot was going to become fried chicken for sure, he said something to the fiery dude that I couldn't make out, and the fiery dude burned brighter.

"Excellent! If you can do this, you will be rewarded. If not..."

"I understand, my lord."

"Go then," the fiery man said. "Unleash our forces. Start with the longnecks. That should soften them up. Collect the younglings and bring them to me. I want them alive, before they have time to learn their powers. Do not fail me."

"No, lord."

"Phoenix," the fiery man mused. "I like that very much." He swept his hand across the horizon, as if he were imagining the city in flames. "Soon I will rise from your ashes. It will be a lovely birthday present."

I woke with my heart pounding, back in my own body. I felt hot, as if the fiery guy were starting to burn me. Then I realized that there was a cat on my chest.

Muffin stared at me, her eyes half closed. *"Mrow."*

"How did you get in?" I muttered.

I sat up, and for a second I wasn't sure where I was. Some hotel in another city? I almost called for my dad...and then I remembered.

Yesterday. The museum. The sarcophagus.

It all crashed down on me so hard I could barely breathe.

Stop, I told myself. *You don't have time for grief.* And this is going to sound weird, but the voice in my head almost sounded like a different person—older, stronger. Either that was a good sign, or I was going crazy.

Remember what you saw, the voice said. *He's after you. You have to be ready.*

I shivered. I wanted to believe I'd just had a bad dream, but I knew better. I'd been through too much in the last day to doubt what I'd seen. Somehow, I'd actually left my body while I slept. I'd *been* to Phoenix—thousands of miles away. The fiery dude was there. I hadn't understood much of what he'd said, but he'd talked about sending his forces to capture the younglings. Gee, wonder who that could be?

Muffin jumped off the bed and sniffed at the ivory headrest, looking up at me as if she were trying to tell me something.

"You can have it," I told her. "It's uncomfortable."

She butted her head against it and stared at me accusingly. *"Mrow."*

"Whatever, cat."

I got up and showered. When I tried to get dressed, I found that my old clothes had disappeared in the night. Everything in the closet was my size, but way different than what I was used to—baggy drawstring pants and loose shirts, all plain white linen, and robes for cold weather, kind of what the *fellahin*, the peasants in Egypt, wear. It wasn't exactly my style.

Sadie likes to tell me that I don't *have* a style. She complains that I dress like I'm an old man—button-down shirt, slacks, dress shoes. Okay, maybe. But here's the thing. My dad had always drilled into my head that I had to dress my best.

I remember the first time he explained it to me. I was ten. We were on our way to the airport in Athens, and it was like 112 degrees outside, and I was complaining that I wanted to wear shorts and a T-shirt. Why couldn't I be comfortable? We weren't going anywhere important that day—just traveling.

My dad put his hand on my shoulder. "Carter, you're getting older. You're an African American man. People will judge you more harshly, and so you must always look impeccable."

"That isn't fair!" I insisted.

"Fairness does not mean everyone gets the same," Dad said. "Fairness means everyone gets what they need. And the only way to get what you need is to make it happen *yourself*. Do you understand?"

I told him I didn't. But still I did what he asked—like caring about Egypt, and basketball, and music. Like traveling with only one suitcase. I dressed the way Dad wanted me to, because Dad was usually right. In fact I'd never known him to be wrong...until the night at the British Museum.

Anyway, I put on the linen clothes from the closet. The slipper shoes were comfortable, though I doubted they'd be much good to run in.

The door to Sadie's room was open, but she wasn't there.

Thankfully my bedroom door wasn't locked anymore. Muffin joined me and we walked downstairs, passing a lot of unoccupied bedrooms on the way. The mansion could've easily slept a hundred people, but instead it felt empty and sad.

Down in the Great Room, Khufu the baboon sat on the sofa with a basketball between his legs and a chunk of strange-looking meat in his hands. It was covered in pink feathers. ESPN was on the television, and Khufu was watching highlights from the games the night before.

"Hey," I said, though I felt a little weird talking to him. "Lakers win?"

Khufu looked at me and patted his basketball like he wanted a game. *"Agh, agh."*

He had a pink feather hanging from his chin, and the sight made my stomach do a slow roll.

"Um, yeah," I said. "We'll play later, okay?"

I could see Sadie and Amos out on the terrace, eating breakfast by the pool. It should've been freezing out there, but the fire pit was blazing, and neither Amos nor Sadie looked cold. I headed their way, then hesitated in front of the statue of Thoth. In the daylight, the bird-headed god didn't look quite so scary. Still, I could swear those beady eyes were watching me expectantly.

What had the fiery guy said last night? Something about catching us before we learned our powers. It sounded ridiculous, but for a moment I felt a surge of strength—like the night before when I'd opened the front door just by raising my hand. I felt like I could lift anything, even this thirty-foot-tall statue if I wanted to. In a kind of trance, I stepped forward.

Muffin meowed impatiently and butted my foot. The feeling dissolved.

"You're right," I told the cat. "Stupid idea."

Besides, I could smell breakfast now—French toast, bacon, hot chocolate—and I couldn't blame Muffin for being in a hurry. I followed her out to the terrace.

"Ah, Carter," Amos said. "Merry Christmas, my boy. Join us."

"About time," Sadie grumbled. "I've been up for ages."

But she held my eyes for a moment, like she was thinking the same thing I was: *Christmas.* We hadn't spent a Christmas morning together since Mom died. I wondered if Sadie remembered how we used to make god's-eye decorations out of yarn and Popsicle sticks.

Amos poured himself a cup of coffee. His clothes were similar to those he'd worn the day before, and I had to admit the guy had style. His tailored suit was made of blue wool, he wore a matching fedora, and his hair was freshly braided with dark blue lapis lazuli, one of the stones the Egyptians often used for jewelry. Even his glasses matched. The round lenses were tinted blue. A tenor sax rested on a stand near the fire pit, and I could totally picture him playing out here, serenading the East River.

As for Sadie, she was dressed in a white linen pajama outfit like me, but somehow she'd managed to keep her combat boots. She'd probably slept with them on. She looked pretty comical with the red-streaked hair and the outfit, but since I wasn't dressed any better, I could hardly make fun of her.

"Um . . . Amos?" I asked. "You didn't have any pet birds, did you? Khufu's eating something with pink feathers."

"*Mmm.*" Amos sipped his coffee. "Sorry if that disturbed you. Khufu's very picky. He only eats foods that end in *-o*. Doritos, burritos, flamingos."

I blinked. "Did you say—"

"Carter," Sadie warned. She looked a little queasy, like she'd already had this conversation. "Don't ask."

"Okay," I said. "Not asking."

"Please, Carter, help yourself." Amos waved toward a buffet table piled high with food. "Then we can get started with the explanations."

I didn't see any flamingo on the buffet table, which was fine by me, but there was just about everything else. I snagged some pancakes with butter and syrup, some bacon, and a glass of OJ.

Then I noticed movement in the corner of my eye. I glanced at the swimming pool. Something long and pale was gliding just under the surface of the water.

I almost dropped my plate. "Is that—"

"A crocodile," Amos confirmed. "For good luck. He's albino, but please don't mention that. He's sensitive."

"His name is Philip of Macedonia," Sadie informed me.

I wasn't sure how Sadie was taking this all so calmly, but I figured if she wasn't freaking out, I shouldn't either.

"That's a long name," I said.

"He's a long crocodile," Sadie said. "Oh, and he likes bacon."

To prove her point, she tossed a piece of bacon over her shoulder. Philip lunged out of the water and snapped up the treat. His hide was pure white and his eyes were pink. His mouth was so big, he could've snapped up an entire pig.

"He's quite harmless to my friends," Amos assured me. "In the old days, no temple would be complete without a lake full of crocodiles. They are powerful magic creatures."

"Right," I said. "So the baboon, the crocodile... any other pets I should know about?"

Amos thought for a moment. "Visible ones? No, I think that's it."

I took a seat as far from the pool as possible. Muffin circled my legs and purred. I hoped she had enough sense to stay away from magic crocodiles named Philip.

"So, Amos," I said between bites of pancake. "Explanations."

"Yes," he agreed. "Where to start..."

"Our dad," Sadie suggested. "What happened to him?"

Amos took a deep breath. "Julius was attempting to summon a god. Unfortunately, it worked."

It was kind of hard to take Amos seriously, talking about summoning gods while he spread butter on a bagel.

"Any god in particular?" I asked casually. "Or did he just order a generic god?"

Sadie kicked me under the table. She was scowling, as if she actually believed what Amos was saying.

Amos took a bite of bagel. "There are many Egyptian gods, Carter. But your dad was after one in particular."

He looked at me meaningfully.

"Osiris," I remembered. "When Dad was standing in front

of the Rosetta Stone, he said, 'Osiris, come.' But Osiris is a legend. He's make-believe."

"I wish that were true." Amos stared across the East River at the Manhattan skyline, gleaming in the morning sun. "The Ancient Egyptians were not fools, Carter. They built the pyramids. They created the first great nation state. Their civilization lasted thousands of years."

"Yeah," I said. "And now they're gone."

Amos shook his head. "A legacy that powerful does not disappear. Next to the Egyptians, the Greeks and Romans were babies. Our modern nations like Great Britain and America? Blinks of an eye. The very oldest root of civilization, at least of Western civilization, is Egypt. Look at the pyramid on the dollar bill. Look at the Washington Monument—the world's largest Egyptian obelisk. Egypt is still very much alive. And so, unfortunately, are her gods."

"Come on," I argued. "I mean...even if I believe there's a real thing called magic. Believing in ancient gods is totally different. You're joking, right?"

But as I said it, I thought about the fiery guy in the museum, the way his face had shifted between human and animal. And the statue of Thoth—how its eyes had followed me.

"Carter," Amos said, "the Egyptians would not have been stupid enough to believe in imaginary gods. The beings they described in their myths are very, very real. In the old days, the priests of Egypt would call upon these gods to channel their power and perform great feats. That is the origin of what we now call magic. Like many things, magic was first invented by the Egyptians. Each temple had a branch of magicians called the House of Life. Their magicians were famed throughout the ancient world."

"And you're an Egyptian magician."

Amos nodded. "So was your father. You saw it for yourself last night."

I hesitated. It was hard to deny my dad had done some weird stuff at the museum—some stuff that looked like magic.

"But he's an archaeologist," I said stubbornly.

"That's his cover story. You'll remember that he specialized in translating ancient spells, which are very difficult to understand unless you work magic yourself. Our family, the Kane family, has been part of the House of Life almost since the beginning. And your mother's family is almost as ancient."

"The Fausts?" I tried to imagine Grandma and Grandpa Faust doing magic, but unless watching rugby on TV and burning cookies was magical, I couldn't see it.

"They had not practiced magic for many generations," Amos admitted. "Not until your mother came along. But yes, a very ancient bloodline."

Sadie shook her head in disbelief. "So now Mum was magic, too. Are you joking?"

"No jokes," Amos promised. "The two of you... you combine the blood of two ancient families, both of which have a long, complicated history with the gods. You are the most powerful Kane children to be born in many centuries."

I tried to let that sink in. At the moment, I didn't feel powerful. I felt queasy. "You're telling me our parents secretly worshipped animal-headed gods?" I asked.

"Not worshipped," Amos corrected. "By the end of the

ancient times, Egyptians had learned that their gods were not to be worshipped. They are powerful beings, primeval forces, but they are not divine in the sense one might think of God. They are created entities, like mortals, only much more powerful. We can respect them, fear them, use their power, or even fight them to keep them under control—"

"*Fight* gods?" Sadie interrupted.

"Constantly," Amos assured her. "But we don't worship them. Thoth taught us that."

I looked at Sadie for help. The old guy had to be crazy. But Sadie was looking like she believed every word.

"So..." I said. "Why did Dad break the Rosetta Stone?"

"Oh, I'm sure he didn't mean to break it," Amos said. "That would've horrified him. In fact, I imagine my brethren in London have repaired the damage by now. The curators will soon check their vaults and discover that the Rosetta Stone miraculously survived the explosion."

"But it was blown into a million pieces!" I said. "How could they repair it?"

Amos picked up a saucer and threw it onto the stone floor. The saucer shattered instantly.

"That was *to destroy*," Amos said. "I could've done it by magic—*ha-di*—but it's simpler just to smash it. And now..." Amos held out his hand. "Join. *Hi-nehm.*"

A blue hieroglyphic symbol burned in the air above his palm.

The pieces of the saucer flew into his hand and reassembled like a puzzle, even the smallest bits of dust gluing themselves into place. Amos put the perfect saucer back on the table.

"Some trick," I managed. I tried to sound calm about it, but I was thinking of all the odd things that had happened to my dad and me over the years, like those gunmen in the Cairo hotel who'd ended up hanging by their feet from a chandelier. Was it possible my dad had made that happen with some kind of spell?

Amos poured milk in the saucer, and put it on the floor. Muffin came padding over. "At any rate, your father would never intentionally damage a relic. He simply didn't realize how much power the Rosetta Stone contained. You see, as Egypt faded, its magic collected and concentrated into its remaining relics. Most of these, of course, are still in Egypt. But you can find some in almost every major museum. A magician can use these artifacts as focal points to work more powerful spells."

"I don't get it," I said.

Amos spread his hands. "I'm sorry, Carter. It takes years of study to understand magic, and I'm trying to explain it to you in a single morning. The important thing is, for the past six years your father has been looking for a way to summon Osiris, and last night he thought he had found the right artifact to do it."

"Wait, why did he want Osiris?"

Sadie gave me a troubled look. "Carter, Osiris was the lord of the dead. Dad was talking about making things right. He was talking about Mum."

Suddenly the morning seemed colder. The fire pit sputtered in the wind coming off the river.

"He wanted to bring Mom back from the dead?" I said. "But that's crazy!"

Amos hesitated. "It would've been dangerous. Inadvisable. Foolish. But not crazy. Your father is a powerful magician. If, in fact, that is what he was after, he might have accomplished it, using the power of Osiris."

I stared at Sadie. "You're actually buying this?"

"You saw the magic at the museum. The fiery bloke. Dad summoned something from the stone."

"Yeah," I said, thinking of my dream. "But that wasn't Osiris, was it?"

"No," Amos said. "Your father got more than he bargained for. He did release the spirit of Osiris. In fact, I think he successfully joined with the god—"

"Joined with?"

Amos held up his hand. "Another long conversation. For now, let's just say he drew the power of Osiris into himself. But he never got the chance to use it because, according to what Sadie has told me, it appears that Julius released *five* gods from the Rosetta Stone. Five gods who were all trapped together."

I glanced at Sadie. "You told him everything?"

"He's going to help us, Carter."

I wasn't quite ready to trust this guy, even if he was our uncle, but I decided I didn't have much choice.

"Okay, yeah," I said. "The fiery guy said something like 'You released all five.' What did he mean?"

Amos sipped his coffee. The faraway look on his face reminded me of my dad. "I don't want to scare you."

"Too late."

"The gods of Egypt are very dangerous. For the last two thousand years or so, we magicians have spent much of our time binding and banishing them whenever they appear. In fact, our most important law, issued by Chief Lector Iskandar in Roman times, forbids unleashing the gods or using their power. Your father broke that law once before."

Sadie's face paled. "Does this have something to do with Mum's death? Cleopatra's Needle in London?"

"It has *everything* to do with that, Sadie. Your parents... well, they thought they were doing something good. They took a terrible risk, and it cost your mother her life. Your father took the blame. He was exiled, I suppose you would say. Banished. He was forced to move around constantly because the House monitored his activities. They feared he would continue his ...research. As indeed he did."

I thought about the times Dad would look over his shoulder as he copied some ancient inscriptions, or wake me up at three or four in the morning and insist it was time to change hotels, or warn me not to look in his workbag or copy certain pictures from old temple walls—as if our lives depended on it.

"Is that why you never came round?" Sadie asked Amos. "Because Dad was banished?"

"The House forbade me to see him. I loved Julius. It hurt me to stay away from my brother, and from you children. But I could not see you—until last night, when I simply had no choice but to try to help. Julius has been obsessed with finding Osiris for years. He was consumed with grief because of what happened to your mother. When I learned that Julius was about to break the law again, to try to set things right, I had to stop him. A second offense would've meant a death sentence. Unfortunately, I failed. I should've known he was too stubborn."

I looked down at my plate. My food had gotten cold. Muffin leaped onto the table and rubbed against my hand. When I didn't object, she started eating my bacon.

"Last night at the museum," I said, "the girl with the knife, the man with the forked beard—they were magicians too? From the House of Life?"

"Yes," Amos said. "Keeping an eye on your father. You are fortunate they let you go."

"The girl wanted to kill us," I remembered. "But the guy with the beard said, *not yet.*"

"They don't kill unless it is absolutely necessary," Amos said. "They will wait to see if you are a threat."

"Why would we be a threat?" Sadie demanded. "We're children! The summoning wasn't our idea."

Amos pushed away his plate. "There is a reason you two were raised separately."

"Because the Fausts took Dad to court," I said matter-of-factly. "And Dad lost."

"It was much more than that," Amos said. "The House insisted you two be separated. Your father wanted to keep you both, even though he knew how dangerous it was."

Sadie looked like she'd been smacked between the eyes. "He did?"

"Of course. But the House intervened and made sure your grandparents got custody of you, Sadie. If you and Carter were raised together, you could become very powerful. Perhaps you have already sensed changes over the past day."

I thought about the surges of strength I'd been feeling, and the way Sadie suddenly seemed to know how to read Ancient Egyptian. Then I thought of something even further back.

"Your sixth birthday," I told Sadie.

"The cake," she said immediately, the memory passing between us like an electric spark.

At Sadie's sixth birthday party, the last one we'd shared as a family, Sadie and I had a huge argument. I don't remember what it was about. I think I wanted to blow out the candles for her. We started yelling. She grabbed my shirt. I pushed her. I remember Dad rushing toward us, trying to intervene, but before he could, Sadie's birthday cake exploded. Icing splattered the walls, our parents, the faces of Sadie's little six-year-old friends. Dad and Mom separated us. They sent me to my room. Later, they said we must've hit the cake by accident as we were fighting, but I knew we hadn't. Something much weirder had made it explode, as if it had responded to our anger. I remembered Sadie crying with a chunk of cake on her forehead, an upside-down candle stuck to the ceiling with its wick still burning, and an adult visitor, one of my parents' friends, his glasses speckled with white frosting.

I turned to Amos. "That was you. You were at Sadie's party."

"Vanilla icing," he recalled. "Very tasty. But it was clear even then that you two would be difficult to raise in the same household."

"And so..." I faltered. "What happens to us now?"

I didn't want to admit it, but I couldn't stand the thought of being separated from Sadie again. She wasn't much, but she was all I had.

"You must be trained properly," Amos said, "whether the House approves or not."

"Why wouldn't they approve?" I asked.

"I will explain everything, don't worry. But we must start your lessons if we are to stand any chance of finding your father and putting things right. Otherwise the entire world is in danger. If we only knew where—"

"Phoenix," I blurted out.

Amos stared at me. "What?"

"Last night I had...well, not a dream, exactly..." I felt stupid, but I told him what had happened while I slept.

Judging from Amos's expression, the news was even worse than I thought.

"You're *sure* he said 'birthday present'?" he asked.

"Yeah, but what does that mean?"

"And a permanent host," Amos said. "He didn't have one yet?"

"Well, that's what the rooster-footed guy said—"

"That was a demon," Amos said. "A minion of chaos. And if demons are coming through to the mortal world, we don't have much time. This is bad, very bad."

"If you live in Phoenix," I said.

"Carter, our enemy won't stop in Phoenix. If he's grown so powerful so fast... What did he say about the storm, exactly?"

"He said: 'I will summon the greatest storm ever known.'"

Amos scowled. "The last time he said that, he created the Sahara. A storm that large could destroy North America, generating enough chaos energy to give him an almost invincible form."

"What are you talking about? Who *is* this guy?"

Amos waved away the question. "More important right now: why didn't you sleep with the headrest?"

I shrugged. "It was uncomfortable." I looked at Sadie for support. "You didn't use it, did you?"

Sadie rolled her eyes. "Well, of course I did. It was *obviously* there for a reason."

Sometimes I really hate my sister. [Ow! That's my foot!]

"Carter," Amos said, "sleep is dangerous. It's a doorway into the Duat."

"Lovely," Sadie grumbled. "Another strange word."

"Ah... yes, sorry," Amos said. "The Duat is the world of spirits and magic. It exists beneath the waking world like a vast ocean, with many layers and regions. We submerged just under its surface last night to reach New York, because travel through the Duat is much faster. Carter, your consciousness also passed through its shallowest currents as you slept, which is how you witnessed what happened in Phoenix. Fortunately, you survived that experience. But the deeper you go into the Duat, the more horrible things you encounter, and the more difficult it is to return. There are entire realms filled with demons, palaces where the gods exist in their pure forms, so powerful their mere presence would burn a human to ashes. There are prisons that hold beings of unspeakable evil, and some chasms so deep and chaotic that not even the gods dare explore them. Now that your powers are stirring, you must not sleep without protection, or you leave yourself open to attacks from the Duat or ... unintended journeys through it. The headrest is enchanted, to keep your consciousness anchored to your body."

"You mean I actually *did* ..." My mouth tasted like metal. "Could he have killed me?"

Amos's expression was grave. "The fact that your soul can travel like that means you are progressing faster than I thought. Faster than should be possible. If the Red Lord had noticed you—"

"The Red Lord?" Sadie said. "That's the fiery bloke?"

Amos rose. "I must find out more. We can't simply wait for him to find you. And if he releases the storm on his birthday, at the height of his powers—"

"You mean you're going to Phoenix?" I could barely get the words out. "Amos, that fiery man defeated Dad like his magic was a joke! Now he's got demons, and he's getting stronger, and—you'll be killed!"

Amos gave me a dry smile, like he'd already weighed the dangers and didn't need a reminder. His expression reminded me painfully of Dad's. "Don't count your uncle out so quickly, Carter. I've got some magic of my own. Besides, I must see what is happening for myself if we're to have any chance at saving your father and stopping the Red Lord. I'll be quick and careful. Just stay here. Muffin will guard you."

I blinked. "The cat will guard us? You can't just leave us here! What about our training?"

"When I return," Amos promised. "Don't worry, the mansion is protected. Just do not leave. Do not be tricked into opening the door for anyone. And whatever happens, *do not* go into the library. I absolutely forbid it. I will be back by sunset."

Before we could protest, Amos walked calmly to the edge of the terrace and jumped.

"No!" Sadie screamed. We ran to the railing and looked over. Below was a hundred-foot drop into the East River. There was no sign of Amos. He'd simply vanished.

Philip of Macedonia splashed in his pool. Muffin jumped onto the railing and insisted we pet her.

We were alone in a strange mansion with a baboon, a crocodile, and a weird cat. And apparently, the entire world was in danger.

I looked at Sadie. "What do we do now?"

She crossed her arms. "Well, that's obvious, isn't it? We explore the library."

7. I Drop a Little Man on His Head

HONESTLY, CARTER IS SO THICK sometimes I can't believe we're related.

I mean when someone says *I forbid it,* that's a good sign it's worth doing. I made for the library straightaway.

"Hold on!" Carter cried. "You can't just—"

"Brother dear," I said, "did your soul leave your body again while Amos was talking, or did you actually *hear* him? Egyptian gods *real.* Red Lord *bad.* Red Lord's birthday: very soon, very bad. House of Life: fussy old magicians who hate our family because Dad was a bit of a rebel, whom by the way you could take a lesson from. Which leaves us—*just us*—with Dad missing, an evil god about to destroy the world, and an uncle who just jumped off the building—and I *can't* actually blame him." I took a breath. [Yes, Carter, I do have to breathe occasionally.] "Am I missing anything? Oh, yes, I also have a brother who is supposedly quite powerful from an ancient bloodline, blah, blah, et cetera, but is too afraid to visit a library. Now, coming or not?"

Carter blinked as if I'd just hit him, which I suppose I had in a way.

"I just..." He faltered. "I just think we should be careful."

I realized the poor boy was quite scared, which I couldn't hold against him, but it did startle me. Carter was my *big* brother, after all—older, more sophisticated, the one who traveled the world with Dad. Big brothers are the ones who are supposed to pull their punches. Little sisters—well, we should be able to hit as hard as we like, shouldn't we? But I realized that possibly, just possibly, I'd been a bit harsh with him.

"Look," I said. "We need to help Dad, yes? There's got to be some powerful stuff in that library, otherwise Amos wouldn't keep it locked up. You do want to help Dad?"

Carter shifted uncomfortably. "Yeah...of course."

Well, that was one problem sorted, so we headed for the library. But as soon as Khufu saw what we were up to, he scrambled off the sofa with his basketball and jumped in front of the library doors. Who knew baboons were so speedy? He barked at us, and I have to say baboons have *enormous* fangs. And they're not any prettier when they've been chewing up exotic pink birds.

Carter tried to reason with him. "Khufu, we're not going to steal anything. We just want—"

"*Agh!*" Khufu dribbled his basketball angrily.

"Carter," I said, "you're not helping. Look here, Khufu. I

have...ta-da!" I held up a little yellow box of cereal I'd taken from the buffet table. "Cheerios! Ends with an *-o*. Yumsies!"

"Aghhh!" Khufu grunted, more excited now than angry.

"Want it?" I coaxed. "Just take it to the couch and pretend you didn't see us, yes?"

I threw the cereal towards the couch, and the baboon lunged after it. He grabbed the box in midair and was so excited, he ran straight up the wall and sat on the fireplace mantel, where he began gingerly picking out Cheerios and eating them one at a time.

Carter looked at me with grudging admiration. "How did you—"

"Some of us think ahead. Now, let's open these doors."

That was not so easily done. They were made of thick wood laced with giant steel chains and padlocked. *Complete* overkill.

Carter stepped forward. He tried to raise the doors by lifting his hand, which had been quite impressive the night before, only now accomplished nothing.

He shook the chains the old-fashioned way, then yanked on the padlocks.

"No good," he said.

Ice needles tingled on the back of my neck. It was almost as if someone—or something—was whispering an idea in my head. "What was that word Amos used at breakfast with the saucer?"

"For 'join'?" Carter said. "*Hi-nehm* or something."

"No, the other one, for 'destroy'."

"Uh, *ha-di.* But you'd need to know magic and the hieroglyphics, wouldn't you? And even then—"

I raised my hand toward the door. I pointed with two fingers and my thumb—an odd gesture I'd never made before, like a make-believe gun except with the thumb parallel to the ground.

"*Ha-di!*"

Bright gold hieroglyphs burned against the largest padlock.

And the doors exploded. Carter hit the floor as chains shattered and splinters flew all over the Great Room. When the dust cleared, Carter got up, covered in wood shavings. I seemed to be fine. Muffin circled my feet, mewing contentedly, as if this were all very normal.

Carter stared at me. "How exactly—"

"Don't know," I admitted. "But the library's open."

"Think you overdid it a little? We're going to be in so much trouble—"

"We'll just figure out a way to zap the door back, won't we?"

"No more zapping, please," Carter said. "That explosion could've killed us."

"Oh, do you think if you tried that spell on a person—"

"No!" He stepped back nervously.

I felt gratified that I could make him squirm, but I tried not to smile. "Let's just explore the library, shall we?"

The truth was, I couldn't have *ha-di*-ed anyone. As soon as I stepped forward, I felt so faint that I almost collapsed.

Carter caught me as I stumbled. "You okay?"

"Fine," I managed, though I didn't feel fine. "I'm tired"—my stomach rumbled—"and famished."

"You just ate a huge breakfast."

It was true, but I felt as if I hadn't had food in weeks.

"Never mind," I told him. "I'll manage."

Carter studied me skeptically. "Those hieroglyphs you created were golden. Dad and Amos both used blue. Why?"

"Maybe everyone has his own color," I suggested. "Maybe you'll get hot pink."

"Very funny."

"Come on, pink wizard," I said. "Inside we go."

The library was so amazing, I almost forgot my dizziness. It was bigger than I'd imagined, a round chamber sunk deep into solid rock, like a giant well. This didn't make sense, as the mansion was sitting on top of a warehouse, but then again nothing else about the place was exactly normal.

From the platform where we stood, a staircase descended three stories to the bottom floor. The walls, floor, and domed ceiling were all decorated with multicolored pictures of people, gods, and monsters. I'd seen such illustrations in Dad's books (yes, all right, sometimes when I was in the Piccadilly bookshop I'd wander into the Egypt section and sneak a look at Dad's books, just to feel some connection to him, not because I wanted to read them) but the pictures in the books had always been faded and smudged. These in the library looked newly painted, making the entire room a work of art.

"It's beautiful," I said.

A blue starry sky glittered on the ceiling, but it wasn't a solid field of blue. Rather, the sky was painted in a strange swirling pattern. I realized it was shaped like a woman. She lay curled on her side—her body, arms, and legs dark blue and dotted with stars. Below, the library floor was done in a similar way, the green-and-brown earth shaped into a man's body, dotted with forests and hills and cities. A river snaked across his chest.

The library had no books. Not even bookshelves. Instead, the walls were honeycombed with round cubbyholes, each one holding a sort of plastic cylinder.

At each of the four compass points, a ceramic statue stood on a pedestal. The statues were half-size humans wearing kilts and sandals, with glossy black wedge-shaped haircuts and black eyeliner around their eyes.

[Carter says the eyeliner stuff is called kohl, as if it matters.]

At any rate, one statue held a stylus and scroll. Another held a box. Another held a short, hooked staff. The last was empty-handed.

"Sadie." Carter pointed to the center of the room. Sitting on a long stone table was Dad's workbag.

Carter started down the stairs, but I grabbed his arm. "Hang on. What about traps?"

He frowned. "Traps?"

"Didn't Egyptian tombs have traps?"

"Well...sometimes. But this isn't a tomb. Besides, more often they had curses, like the burning curse, the donkey curse—"

"Oh, lovely. That sounds so much better."

He trotted down the steps, which made me feel quite

ridiculous, as I'm usually the one to forge ahead. But I supposed if someone had to get cursed with a burning skin rash or attacked by a magical donkey, it was better Carter than me.

We made it to the middle of the room with no excitement. Carter opened the bag. Still no traps or curses. He brought out the strange box Dad had used in the British Museum.

It was made of wood, and about the right size to hold a loaf of French bread. The lid was decorated much like the library, with gods and monsters and sideways-walking people.

"How did the Egyptians move like that?" I wondered. "All sideways with their arms and legs out. It seems quite silly."

Carter gave me one of his *God, you're stupid* looks. "They didn't walk like that in real life, Sadie."

"Well, why are they painted like that, then?"

"They thought paintings were like magic. If you painted yourself, you had to show all your arms and legs. Otherwise, in the afterlife you might be reborn without all your pieces."

"Then why the sideways faces? They never look straight at you. Doesn't that mean they'll lose the other side of their face?"

Carter hesitated. "I think they were afraid the picture would be *too* human if it was looking right at you. It might try to *become* you."

"So is there anything they *weren't* afraid of?"

"Little sisters," Carter said. "If they talked too much, the Egyptians threw them to the crocodiles."

He had me for a second. I wasn't used to him displaying a sense of humor. Then I punched him. "Just open the bloody box."

The first thing he pulled out was a lump of white gunk.

"Wax," Carter pronounced.

"Fascinating." I picked up a wooden stylus and a palette with small indentations in its surface for ink, then a few glass jars of the ink itself—black, red, and gold. "And a prehistoric painting set."

Carter pulled out several lengths of brown twine, a small ebony cat statue, and a thick roll of paper. No, not paper. Papyrus. I remembered Dad explaining how the Egyptians made it from a river plant because they never invented paper. The stuff was so thick and rough, it made me wonder if the poor Egyptians had had to use toilet papyrus. If so, no wonder they walked sideways.

Finally I pulled out a wax figurine.

"*Ew*," I said.

He was a tiny man, crudely fashioned, as if the maker had been in a hurry. His arms were crossed over his chest, his mouth was open, and his legs were cut off at the knees. A lock of human hair was wrapped round his waist.

Muffin jumped on the table and sniffed the little man. She seemed to think him quite interesting.

"There's nothing here," Carter said.

"What do you want?" I asked. "We've got wax, some toilet papyrus, an ugly statue—"

"Something to explain what happened to Dad. How do we get him back? Who was that fiery man he summoned?"

I held up the wax man. "You heard him, warty little troll. Tell us what you know."

I was just messing about. But the wax man became soft and warm like flesh. He said, "I answer the call."

I screamed and dropped him on his tiny head. Well, can you blame me?

"*Ow!*" he said.

Muffin came over to have a sniff, and the little man started cursing in another language, possibly Ancient Egyptian. When that didn't work, he screeched in English: "Go away! I'm not a mouse!"

I scooped up Muffin and put her on the floor.

Carter's face had gone as soft and waxy as the little man's. "What *are* you?" he asked.

"I'm a *shabti*, of course!" The figurine rubbed his dented head. He still looked quite lumpish, only now he was a living lump. "Master calls me Doughboy, though I find the name insulting. You may call me Supreme-Force-Who-Crushes-His-Enemies!"

"All right, Doughboy," I said.

He scowled at me, I think, though it was hard to tell with his mashed-up face.

"*You* weren't supposed to trigger me! Only the master does that."

"The master, meaning Dad," I guessed. "*Er*, Julius Kane?"

"That's him," Doughboy grumbled. "Are we done yet? Have I fulfilled my service?"

Carter stared at me blankly, but I thought I was beginning to understand.

"So, Doughboy," I told the lump. "You were triggered when I picked you up and gave you a direct order: *Tell us what you know.* Is that correct?"

Doughboy crossed his stubby arms. "You're just toying with me now. *Of course* that's correct. Only the master is supposed to be able to trigger me, by the way. I don't know how you did it, but he'll blast you to pieces when he finds out."

Carter cleared his throat. "Doughboy, the master is our dad, and he's missing. He's been magically sent away somehow and we need your help—"

"Master is gone?" Doughboy smiled so widely, I thought his wax face would split open. "Free at last! See you, suckers!"

He lunged for the end of the table but forgot he had no feet. He landed on his face, then began crawling toward the edge, dragging himself with his hands. "Free! Free!"

He fell off the table and onto the floor with a thud, but that didn't seem to discourage him. "Free! Free!"

He made it another centimeter or two before I picked him up and threw him in Dad's magic box. Doughboy tried to get out, but the box was just tall enough that he couldn't reach the rim. I wondered if it had been designed that way.

"Trapped!" he wailed. "Trapped!"

"Oh, shut up," I told him. "*I'm* the mistress now. And you'll answer my questions."

Carter raised his eyebrow. "How come *you* get to be in charge?"

"Because I was smart enough to activate him."

"You were just joking around!"

I ignored my brother, which is one of my many talents. "Now, Doughboy, first off, what's a *shabti*?"

"Will you let me out of the box if I tell you?"

"You *have* to tell me," I pointed out. "And no, I won't."

He sighed. "*Shabti* means *answerer*, as even the stupidest slave could tell you."

Carter snapped his fingers. "I remember now! The Egyptians made models out of wax or clay—servants to do every kind of job they could imagine in the afterlife. They were supposed to come to life when their master called, so the deceased person could, like, kick back and relax and let the *shabti* do all his work for eternity."

"First," Doughboy snipped, "that is typical of humans! Lazing around while we do all the work. Second, afterlife work is only *one* function of *shabti*. We are also used by magicians for a great number of things in *this* life, because magicians would be total incompetents without us. Third, if you know so much, why are you asking me?"

"Why did Dad cut off your legs," I wondered, "and leave you with a mouth?"

"I—" Doughboy clapped his little hands over his mouth. "Oh, very funny. Threaten the wax statue. Big bully! He cut my legs off so I wouldn't run away or come to life in perfect form and try to kill him, naturally. Magicians are very mean. They maim statues to control them. They are afraid of us!"

"Would you come to life and try to kill him, had he made you perfectly?"

"Probably," Doughboy admitted. "Are we done?"

"Not by half," I said. "What happened to our dad?"

Doughboy shrugged. "How should I know? But I see his wand and staff aren't in the box."

"No," Carter said. "The staff—the thing that turned into

a snake—it got incinerated. And the wand . . . is that the boomerang thing?"

"The *boomerang thing?*" Doughboy said. "Gods of Eternal Egypt, you're dense. Of course that's his wand."

"It got shattered," I said.

"Tell me how," Doughboy demanded.

Carter told him the story. I wasn't sure that was the best idea, but I supposed a ten-centimeter-tall statue couldn't do us *that* much harm.

"This is wonderful!" Doughboy cried.

"Why?" I asked. "Is Dad still alive?"

"No!" Doughboy said. "He's almost certainly dead. The five gods of the Demon Days released? Wonderful! And anyone who duels with the Red Lord—"

"Wait," I said. "I order you to tell me what happened."

"Ha!" Doughboy said. "I only have to tell you what I *know.* Making educated guesses is a completely different task. I declare my service fulfilled!"

With that, he turned back to lifeless wax.

"Wait!" I picked him up again and shook him. "Tell me your educated guesses!"

Nothing happened.

"Maybe he's got a timer," Carter said. "Like only once a day. Or maybe you broke him."

"Carter, make a *helpful* suggestion! What do we do now?"

He looked at the four ceramic statues on their pedestals. "Maybe—"

"Other *shabti?*"

"Worth a shot."

If the statues were *answerers*, they weren't very good at it. We tried holding them while giving them orders, though they were quite heavy. We tried pointing at them and shouting. We tried asking nicely. They gave us no answers at all.

I grew so frustrated I wanted to *ha-di* them into a million pieces, but I was still so hungry and tired, I had the feeling that spell would not be good for my health.

Finally we decided to check the cubbyholes round the walls. The plastic cylinders were the kind you might find at a drive-through bank—the kind that shoot up and down the pneumatic tubes. Inside each case was a papyrus scroll. Some looked new. Some looked thousands of years old. Each canister was labeled in hieroglyphs and (fortunately) in English.

"*The Book of the Heavenly Cow*," Carter read on one. "What kind of name is that? What've you got, *The Heavenly Badger*?"

"No," I said. "*The Book of Slaying Apophis*."

Muffin meowed in the corner. When I looked over, her tail was puffed up.

"What's wrong with her?" I asked.

"Apophis was a giant snake monster," Carter muttered. "He was bad news."

Muffin turned and raced up the stairs, back into the Great Room. Cats. No accounting for them.

Carter opened another scroll. "Sadie, look at this."

He'd found a papyrus that was quite long, and most of the text on it seemed to be lines of hieroglyphs.

"Can you read any of this?" Carter asked.

I frowned at the writing, and the odd thing was, I *couldn't* read it—except for one line at the top. "Only that bit where the title should be. It says... *Blood of the Great House.* What does that mean?"

"Great house," Carter mused. "What do the words sound like in Egyptian?"

"Per-roh. Oh, it's *pharaoh,* isn't it? But I thought a pharaoh was a king?"

"It is," Carter said. "The word literally means 'great house,' like the king's mansion. Sort of like referring to the president as 'the White House.' So here it probably means more like *Blood of the Pharaohs,* all of them, the whole lineage of all the dynasties, not just one guy."

"So why do I care about the pharaohs' blood, and why can't I read any of the rest?"

Carter stared at the lines. Suddenly his eyes widened. "They're names. Look, they're all written inside cartouches."

"Excuse me?" I asked, because *cartouche* sounded like a rather rude word, and I pride myself on knowing those.

"The circles," Carter explained. "They symbolize magic ropes. They're supposed to protect the holder of the name from evil magic." He eyed me. "And possibly also from other magicians reading their names."

"Oh, you're mental," I said. But I looked at the lines, and saw what he meant. All the other words were protected by cartouches, and I couldn't make sense of them.

97

"Sadie," Carter said, his voice urgent. He pointed to a cartouche at the very end of the list—the last entry in what looked to be a catalogue of thousands.

Inside the circle were two simple symbols, a basket and a wave.

"KN," Carter announced. "I know this one. It's our name, KANE."

"Missing a few letters, isn't it?"

Carter shook his head. "Egyptians usually didn't write vowels. Only consonants. You have to figure out the vowel sounds from context."

"They really *were* nutters. So that could be KON or IKON or KNEE or AKNE."

"It could be," Carter agreed. "But it's our name, Kane. I asked Dad to write it for me in hieroglyphs once, and that's how he did it. But why are we in this list? And what is 'blood of the pharaohs'?"

That icy tingle started on the back of my neck. I remembered what Amos had said, about both sides of our family being very ancient. Carter's eyes met mine, and judging from his expression, he was having the same thought.

"There's no way," I protested.

"Must be some kind of joke," he agreed. "Nobody keeps family records that far back."

I swallowed, my throat suddenly very dry. So many odd things had happened to us in the last day, but it was only when I saw our name in that book that I finally began to believe all this mad Egyptian stuff was real. Gods, magicians, monsters... and our family was tied into it.

Ever since breakfast, when it occurred to me that Dad had been trying to bring Mum back from the dead, a horrible emotion had been trying to take hold of me. And it wasn't dread. Yes, the whole idea was creepy, *much* creepier than the shrine my grandparents kept in the hall cupboard to my dead mother. And yes, I told you I try not to live in the past and nothing could change the fact that my mum was gone. But I'm a liar. The truth was, I'd had one dream ever since I was six: to see my mum again. To actually get to know her, talk to her, go shopping, do *anything*. Just be with her once so I could have a better memory to hold on to. The feeling I was trying to shake was *hope*. I knew I was setting myself up for colossal hurt. But if it really *were* possible to bring her back, then I would've blown up any number of Rosetta Stones to make it happen.

"Let's keep looking," I said.

After a few more minutes, I found a picture of some of animal-headed gods, five in a row, with a starry woman figure arching over them protectively like an umbrella. Dad had released five gods. *Hmm.*

"Carter," I called. "What's this, then?"

He came to have a look and his eyes lit up.

"That's it!" he announced. "These five... and up here, their mother, Nut."

I laughed. "A goddess named Nut? Is her last name Case?"

"Very funny," Carter said. "She was the goddess of the sky."

He pointed to the painted ceiling—the lady with the blue star-spangled skin, same as in the scroll.

"So what about her?" I asked.

Carter knit his eyebrows. "Something about the Demon Days. It had to do with the birth of these five gods, but it's been a long time since Dad told me the story. This whole scroll is written in hieratic, I think. That's like hieroglyph cursive. Can you read it?"

I shook my head. Apparently, my particular brand of insanity only applied to regular hieroglyphs.

"I wish I could find the story in English," Carter said.

Just then there was a cracking noise behind us. The empty-handed clay statue hopped off his pedestal and marched towards us. Carter and I scrambled to get out of his way, but he walked straight past us, grabbed a cylinder from its cubbyhole and brought it to Carter.

"It's a retrieval *shabti*," I said. "A clay librarian!"

Carter swallowed nervously and took the cylinder. "*Um* . . . thanks."

The statue marched back to his pedestal, jumped on, and hardened again into regular clay.

"I wonder . . ." I faced the *shabti*. "Sandwich and chips, please!"

Sadly, none of the statues jumped down to serve me. Perhaps food wasn't allowed in the library.

Carter uncapped the cylinder and unrolled the papyrus. He sighed with relief. "This version is in English."

As he scanned the text, his frown got deeper.

"You don't look happy," I noticed.

"Because I remember the story now. The five gods . . . if Dad really released them, it isn't good news."

"Hang on," I said. "Start from the beginning."

Carter took a shaky breath. "Okay. So the sky goddess, Nut, was married to the earth god, Geb."

"That would be this chap on the floor?" I tapped my foot on the big green man with the river and hills and forests all over his body.

"Right," Carter said. "Anyway, Geb and Nut wanted to have kids, but the king of the gods, Ra—he was the sun god—heard this bad prophecy that a child of Nut—"

"Child of Nut," I snickered. "Sorry, go on."

"—a child of Geb and Nut would one day replace Ra as king. So when Ra learned that Nut was pregnant, Ra freaked out. He forbade Nut to give birth to her children on any day or night of the year."

I crossed my arms. "So what, she had to stay pregnant forever? That's awfully mean."

Carter shook his head. "Nut figured out a way. She set up a game of dice with the moon god, Khons. Every time Khons lost, he had to give Nut some of his moonlight. He lost so many times, Nut won enough moonlight to create five *new* days and tag them on to the end of the year."

"Oh, please," I said. "First, how can you gamble moonlight? And if you did, how could you make extra days out of it?"

"It's a story!" Carter protested. "Anyway, the Egyptian calendar had three hundred and sixty days in the year, just like the three hundred and sixty degrees in a circle. Nut created five days and added them to the end of the year—days that were not part of the regular year."

"The Demon Days," I guessed. "So the myth explains why

a year has three hundred and sixty-five days. And I suppose she had her children—"

"During those five days," Carter agreed. "One kid per day."

"Again, how do you have five children in a row, each on a different day?"

"They're gods," Carter said. "They can do stuff like that."

"Makes as much sense as the name Nut. But please, go on."

"So when Ra found out, he was furious, but it was too late. The children were already born. Their names were Osiris—"

"The one Dad was after."

"Then Horus, Set, Isis, and, um..." Carter consulted his scroll. "Nephthys. I always forget that one."

"And the fiery man in the museum said, *you have released all five.*"

"Exactly. What if they were imprisoned together and Dad didn't realize it? They were born together, so maybe they had to be summoned back into the world together. The thing is, one of these guys, Set, was a really bad dude. Like, the villain of Egyptian mythology. The god of evil and chaos and desert storms."

I shivered. "Did he perhaps have something to do with fire?"

Carter pointed to one of the figures in the picture. The god had an animal head, but I couldn't quite make out which sort of animal: Dog? Anteater? Evil bunny rabbit? Whichever it was, his hair and his clothes were bright red.

"The Red Lord," I said.

"Sadie, there's more," Carter said. "Those five days—the Demon Days—were bad luck in Ancient Egypt. You had to be careful, wear good luck charms, and not do anything important or dangerous on those days. And in the British Museum, Dad told Set: *They'll stop you before the Demon Days are over.*"

"Surely you don't think he meant *us*," I said. "*We're* supposed to stop this Set character?"

Carter nodded. "And if the last five days of *our* calendar year still count as the Egyptian Demon Days—they'd start on December 27, the day after tomorrow."

The *shabti* seemed to be staring at me expectantly, but I had not the slightest idea what to do. Demon Days and evil bunny gods—if I heard *one* more impossible thing, my head would explode.

And the worst of it? The little insistent voice in the back of my head saying: *It's not impossible. To save Dad, we must defeat Set.*

As if that had been on my to-do list for Christmas hols. See Dad—check. Develop strange powers—check. Defeat an evil god of chaos—check. The whole idea was mad!

Suddenly there was a loud crash, as if something had broken in the Great Room. Khufu began barking in alarm.

Carter and I locked eyes. Then we ran for the stairs.

8. Muffin Plays with Knives

OUR BABOON WAS GOING completely sky goddess—which is to say, *nuts*.

He swung from column to column, bouncing along the balconies, overturning pots and statues. Then he ran back to the terrace windows, stared outside for a moment, and proceeded to go berserk again.

Muffin was also at the window. She crouched on all fours with her tail twitching as if she were stalking a bird.

"Perhaps it's just a passing flamingo," I suggested hopefully, but I'm not sure Carter could hear me over the screaming baboon.

We ran to the glass doors. At first I didn't see any problem. Then water exploded from the pool, and my heart nearly jumped out of my chest. Two enormous creatures, most definitely not flamingos, were thrashing about with our crocodile, Philip of Macedonia.

I couldn't make out what they were, only that they were fighting Philip two against one. They disappeared under the boiling water, and Khufu ran screaming through the Great Room again, bonking himself on the head with his empty Cheerios box, which I must say was not particularly helpful.

"Longnecks," Carter said incredulously. "Sadie, did you *see* those things?"

I couldn't find an answer. Then one of the creatures was thrown out of the pool. It slammed into the doors right in front of us, and I jumped back in alarm. On the other side of the glass was the most terrifying animal I'd ever seen. Its body was like a leopard's—lean and sinewy, with golden spotted fur—but its neck was completely wrong. It was green and scaly and at least as long as the rest of its body. It had a cat's head, but no normal cat's. When it turned its glowing red eyes towards us, it howled, showing a forked tongue and fangs dripping with green venom.

I realized my legs were shaking and I was making a very undignified whimpering sound.

The cat-serpent jumped back into the pool to join its companion in beating up Philip, who spun and snapped but seemed unable to hurt his attackers.

"We have to help Philip!" I cried. "He'll be killed!"

I reached for the door handle, but Muffin growled at me.

Carter said, "Sadie, no! You heard Amos. We can't open the doors for any reason. The house is protected by magic. Philip will have to beat them on his own."

"But what if he can't? Philip!"

The old crocodile turned. For a second his pink reptilian eye focused on me as if he could sense my concern. Then the cat-snakes bit at his underbelly and Philip rose up so that only the tip of his tail still touched the water. His body began to glow. A low hum filled the air, like an airplane engine starting up. When Philip came down, he slammed into the terrace with all his might.

The entire house shook. Cracks appeared in the concrete terrace outside, and the swimming pool split right down the middle as the far end crumbled into empty space.

"No!" I cried.

But the edge of the terrace ripped free, plunging Philip and the monsters straight into the East River.

My whole body began to tremble. "He sacrificed himself. He killed the monsters."

"Sadie . . ." Carter's voice was faint. "What if he didn't? What if they come back?"

"Don't say that!"

"I—I recognized them, Sadie. Those creatures. Come on."

"Where?" I demanded, but he ran straight back to the library.

Carter marched up to the *shabti* who'd helped us before. "Bring me the . . . *gah*, what's it called?"

"What?" I asked.

"Something Dad showed me. It's a big stone plate or something. Had a picture of the first pharaoh, the guy who united Upper and Lower Egypt into one kingdom. His name . . ." His eyes lit up. "Narmer! Bring me the Narmer Plate!"

Nothing happened.

"No," Carter decided. "Not a plate. It was...one of those things that holds paint. A palette. Bring me the Narmer Palette!"

The empty-handed *shabti* didn't move, but across the room, the statue with the little hook came to life. He jumped off his pedestal and disappeared in a cloud of dust. A heartbeat later, he reappeared on the table. At his feet was a wedge of flat gray stone, shaped like a shield and about as long as my forearm.

"No!" Carter protested. "I meant a *picture* of it! Oh great, I think this is the *real* artifact. The *shabti* must've stolen it from the Cairo Museum. We've got to return—"

"Hang on," I said. "We might as well have a look."

The surface of the stone was carved with the picture of a man smashing another man in the face with what looked like a spoon.

"That's Narmer with the spoon," I guessed. "Angry because the other bloke stole his breakfast cereal?"

Carter shook his head. "He's conquering his enemies and uniting Egypt. See his hat? That's the crown of Lower Egypt, before the two countries united."

"The bit that looks like a bowling pin?"

"You're impossible," Carter grumbled.

"He looks like Dad, doesn't he?"

"Sadie, be serious!"

"I *am* serious. Look at his profile."

Carter decided to ignore me. He examined the stone like he was afraid to touch it. "I need to see the back but I don't want to turn it over. We might damage—"

I grabbed the stone and flipped it over.

"Sadie! You could've broken it!"

"That's what mend spells are for, yes?"

We examined the back of the stone, and I had to admit I was impressed by Carter's memory. Two cat-snake monsters stood in the center of the palette, their necks entwined. On either side, Egyptian men with ropes were trying to capture the creatures.

"They're called serpopards," Carter said. "Serpent leopards."

"Fascinating," I said. "But what *are* serpopards?"

"No one knows exactly. Dad thought they were creatures of chaos—very bad news, and they've been around forever. This stone is one of the oldest artifacts from Egypt. Those pictures were carved five thousand years ago."

"So why are five-thousand-year-old monsters attacking our house?"

"Last night, in Phoenix, the fiery man ordered his servants to capture us. He said to send the longnecks first."

I had a metallic taste in my mouth, and I wished I hadn't

chewed my last piece of gum. "Well...good thing they're at the bottom of the East River."

Just then Khufu rushed into the library, screaming and slapping his head.

"Suppose I shouldn't have said that," I muttered.

Carter told the *shabti* to return the Narmer Palette, and both statue and stone disappeared. Then we followed the baboon upstairs.

The serpopards were back, their fur wet and slimy from the river, and they weren't happy. They prowled the broken ledge of the terrace, their snake necks whipping round as they sniffed the doors, looking for a way in. They spit poison that steamed and bubbled on the glass. Their forked tongues darted in and out.

"*Agh, agh!*" Khufu picked up Muffin, who was sitting on the sofa, and offered me the cat.

"I really don't think that will help," I told him.

"AGH!" Khufu insisted.

Neither *Muffin* nor *cat* ended in -o, so I guessed Khufu was not trying to offer me a snack, but I didn't know what he was on about. I took the cat just to shut him up.

"*Mrow?*" Muffin looked up at me.

"It'll be all right," I promised, trying not to sound scared out of my mind. "The house is protected by magic."

"Sadie," Carter said. "They've found something."

The serpopards had converged at the left-hand door and were intently sniffing the handle.

"Isn't it locked?" I asked.

Both monsters smashed their ugly faces against the glass. The door shuddered. Blue hieroglyphs glowed along the door-frame, but their light was faint.

"I don't like this," Carter murmured.

I prayed that the monsters would give up. Or that perhaps Philip of Macedonia would climb back to the terrace (do crocodiles climb?) and renew the fight.

Instead, the monsters smashed their heads against the glass again. This time a web of cracks appeared. The blue hiero-glyphs flickered and died.

"AGH!" Khufu screamed. He waved his hand vaguely at the cat.

"Maybe if I try the *ha-di* spell," I said.

Carter shook his head. "You almost fainted after you blew up those doors. I don't want you passing out, or worse."

Carter once again surprised me. He tugged a strange sword from one of Amos's wall displays. The blade had an odd crescent-moon curve and looked horribly impractical.

"You can't be serious," I said.

"Unless—unless you've got a better idea," he stammered, his face beading with perspiration. "It's me, you, and the ba-boon against *those* things."

I'm sure Carter was trying to be brave in his own extremely unbrave way, but he was shaking worse than I was. If anyone was going to pass out, I feared it would be him, and I didn't fancy him doing that while holding a sharp object.

Then the serpopards struck a third time, and the door shat-tered. We backed up to the foot of Thoth's statue as the crea-tures stalked into the great room. Khufu threw his basketball, which bounced harmlessly off the first monster's head. Then he launched himself at the serpopard.

"Khufu, don't!" Carter yelled.

But the baboon sank his fangs into the monster's neck. The serpopard lashed around, trying to bite him. Khufu leaped off, but the monster was quick. It used its head like a bat and smacked poor Khufu in midair, sending him straight through the shattered door, over the broken terrace, and into the void.

I wanted to sob, but there wasn't time. The serpopards came toward us. We couldn't outrun them. Carter raised his sword. I pointed my hand at the first monster and tried to speak the *ha-di* spell, but my voice stuck in my throat.

"*Mrow!*" Muffin said, more insistently. Why was the cat still nestled in my arm and not running away in terror?

Then I remembered something Amos had said: *Muffin will protect you.* Was that what Khufu had been trying to remind me? It seemed impossible, but I stammered, "M-muffin, I order you to protect us."

I tossed her on the floor. Just for a moment, the silver pendant on her collar seemed to gleam. Then the cat arched her back leisurely, sat down, and began licking a front paw. Well, really, what was I expecting—heroics?

The two red-eyed monsters bared their fangs. They raised their heads and prepared to strike—and an explosion of dry air blasted through the room. It was so powerful, it knocked Carter and me to the floor. The serpopards stumbled and backed away.

I staggered to my feet and realized that the center of the blast had been *Muffin.* My cat was no longer there. In her place was a woman—small and lithe like a gymnast. Her jet-black hair was tied in a ponytail. She wore a skintight leopard-skin jumpsuit and Muffin's pendant around her neck.

She turned and grinned at me, and her eyes were still Muffin's—yellow with black feline pupils. "About time," she chided.

The serpopards got over their shock and charged the cat woman. Their heads struck with lightning speed. They should've ripped her in two, but the cat lady leaped straight up, flipping three times, and landed above them, perched on the mantel.

She flexed her wrists, and two enormous knives shot from her sleeves into her hands. "A-a-ah, fun!"

The monsters charged. She launched herself between them, dancing and dodging with incredible grace, letting them lash at her futilely while she threaded their necks together. When she stepped away, the serpopards were hopelessly intertwined. The more they struggled, the tighter the knots became. They trampled back and forth, knocking over furniture and roaring in frustration.

"Poor things," the cat woman purred. "Let me help."

Her knives flashed, and the two monsters' heads thudded to the floor at her feet. Their bodies collapsed and dissolved into enormous piles of sand.

"So much for my playthings," the woman said sadly. "From sand they come, and to sand they return."

She turned towards us, and the knives shot back into her sleeves. "Carter, Sadie, we should leave. Worse will be coming."

Carter made a choking sound. "*Worse?* Who—how—what—"

"All in good time." The woman stretched her arms above her head with great satisfaction. "So good to be in human form again! Now, Sadie, can you open us a door through the Duat, please?"

I blinked. "Um...no. I mean—I don't know how."

The woman narrowed her eyes, clearly disappointed. "Shame. We'll need more power, then. An obelisk."

"But that's in London," I protested. "We can't—"

"There's a nearer one in Central Park. I try to avoid Manhattan, but this is an emergency. We'll just pop over and open a portal."

"A portal to where?" I demanded. "Who are you, and why are you my cat?"

The woman smiled. "For now, we just want a portal out of danger. As for my name, it's *not* Muffin, thank you very much. It's—"

"Bast," Carter interrupted. "Your pendant—it's the symbol of Bast, goddess of cats. I thought it was just decoration but ...that's you, isn't it?"

"Very good, Carter," Bast said. "Now come, while we can still make it out of here alive."

9. We Run from Four Guys in Skirts

So, yeah. Our cat was a goddess.

What else is new?

She didn't give us much time to talk about it. She ordered me to the library to grab my dad's magic kit, and when I came back she was arguing with Sadie about Khufu and Philip.

"We have to search for them!" Sadie insisted.

"They'll be fine," said Bast. "However, *we* will not be, unless we leave now."

I raised my hand. "*Um*, excuse me, Miss Goddess Lady? Amos told us the house was—"

"Safe?" Bast snorted. "Carter, the defenses were too easily breached. Someone *sabotaged* them."

"What do you mean? Who—"

"Only a magician of the House could've done it."

"Another magician?" I asked. "Why would another magician want to sabotage Amos's house?"

"Oh, Carter," Bast sighed. "So young, so innocent.

114

Magicians are devious creatures. Could be a million reasons why one would backstab another, but we don't have time to discuss it. Now, come on!"

She grabbed our arms and led us out the front door. She'd sheathed her knives, but she still had some wicked sharp claws for fingernails that hurt as they dug into my skin. As soon as we stepped outside, the cold wind stung my eyes. We climbed down a long flight of metal stairs into the industrial yard that surrounded the factory.

Dad's workbag was heavy on my shoulder. The curved sword I'd strapped across my back felt cold against my thin linen clothes. I'd started to sweat during the serpopard attack, and now my perspiration felt like it was turning to ice.

I looked around for more monsters, but the yard seemed abandoned. Old construction equipment lay in rusting heaps—a bulldozer, a crane with a wrecking ball, a couple of cement mixers. Piles of sheet metal and stacks of crates made a maze of obstacles between the house and the street a few hundred yards away.

We were about halfway across the yard when an old gray tomcat stepped in our path. One of his ears was torn. His left eye was swollen shut. Judging from his scars, he'd spent most of his life fighting.

Bast crouched and stared at the cat. He looked up at her calmly.

"Thank you," Bast said.

The old tomcat trotted off toward the river.

"What was that about?" Sadie asked.

"One of my subjects, offering help. He'll spread the news

about our predicament. Soon every cat in New York will be on alert."

"He was so battered," Sadie said. "If he's your subject, couldn't you heal him?"

"And take away his marks of honor? A cat's battle scars are part of his identity. I couldn't—" Suddenly Bast tensed. She dragged us behind a stack of crates.

"What is it?" I whispered.

She flexed her wrists and her knives slid into her hands. She peeped over the top of the crates, every muscle in her body trembling. I tried to see what she was looking at, but there was nothing except the old wrecking-ball crane.

Bast's mouth twitched with excitement. Her eyes were fixed on the huge metal ball. I'd seen kittens look like that when they stalked catnip toy mice, or pieces of string, or rubber balls. . . . Balls? No. Bast was an ancient goddess. Surely she wouldn't—

"This could be it." She shifted her weight. "Stay very *very* still."

"There's no one there," Sadie hissed.

I started to say, "*Um* . . . "

Bast lunged over the crates. She flew thirty feet through the air, knives flashing, and landed on the wrecking ball with such force that she broke the chain. The cat goddess and the huge metal sphere smashed into the dirt and went rolling across the yard.

"*Rowww!*" Bast wailed. The wrecking ball rolled straight over her, but she didn't appear hurt. She leaped off and pounced again. Her knives sliced through the metal like wet clay. Within seconds, the wrecking ball was reduced to a mound of scraps.

Bast sheathed her blades. "Safe now!"

Sadie and I looked at each other.

"You saved us from a metal ball," Sadie said.

"You never know," Bast said. "It could've been hostile."

Just then a deep *boom!* shook the ground. I looked back at the mansion. Tendrils of blue fire curled from the top windows.

"Come on," Bast said. "Our time is up!"

I thought maybe she'd whisk us off by magic, or at least hail a taxi. Instead, Bast borrowed a silver Lexus convertible.

"Oh, yes," she purred. "I like this one! Come along, children."

"But this isn't yours," I pointed out.

"My dear, I'm a cat. Everything I *see* is mine." She touched the ignition and the keyhole sparked. The engine began to purr. [No, Sadie. Not like a cat, like an engine.]

"Bast," I said, "you can't just—"

Sadie elbowed me. "We'll work out how to return it later, Carter. Right now we've got an emergency."

She pointed back toward the mansion. Blue flames and smoke now billowed from every window. But that wasn't the scary part—coming down the stairs were four men carrying a large box, like an oversize coffin with long handles sticking out at both ends. The box was covered with a black shroud and looked big enough for at least two bodies. The four men wore only kilts and sandals. Their coppery skin glinted in the sun as if made of metal.

"Oh, that's bad," Bast said. "In the car, please."

I decided not to ask questions. Sadie beat me to the shotgun seat so I climbed in back. The four metallic guys with the box were racing across the yard, coming straight for us at an unbelievable speed. Before I even had my seat belt on, Bast hit the gas.

We tore through the streets of Brooklyn, weaving insanely through traffic, riding over sidewalks, narrowly missing pedestrians.

Bast drove with reflexes that were...well, catlike. Any human trying to drive so fast would've had a dozen wrecks, but she got us safely onto the Williamsburg Bridge.

I thought for sure we must've lost our pursuers, but when I looked back, the four copper men with the black box were weaving in and out of traffic. They appeared to be jogging at a normal pace, but they passed cars that were doing fifty. Their bodies blurred like choppy images in an old movie, as if they were out of sync with the regular stream of time.

"What *are* they?" I asked. "*Shabti?*"

"No, carriers." Bast glanced in the rearview mirror. "Summoned straight from the Duat. They'll stop at nothing to find their victims, throw them in the sedan—"

"The what?" Sadie interrupted.

"The large box," Bast said. "It's a kind of carriage. The carriers capture you, beat you senseless, throw you in, and carry you back to their master. They never lose their prey, and they never give up."

"But what do they want us for?"

"Trust me," Bast growled, "you don't want to know."

I thought about the fiery man last night in Phoenix—how he'd fried one of his servants into a grease spot. I was pretty sure I didn't want to meet him face-to-face again.

"Bast," I said, "if you're a goddess, can't you just snap your fingers and disintegrate those guys? Or wave your hand and teleport us away?"

"Wouldn't that be nice? But my power in this host is limited."

"You mean Muffin?" Sadie asked. "But you're not a cat anymore."

"She's still my host, Sadie, my anchor on this side of the Duat—and a very imperfect one. Your call for help allowed me to assume human shape, but that alone takes a great deal of power. Besides, even when I'm in a *powerful* host, Set's magic is stronger than mine."

"Could you please say something I actually understand?" I pleaded.

"Carter, we don't have time for a full discussion on gods and hosts and the limits of magic! We have to get you to safety."

Bast floored the accelerator and shot up the middle of the bridge. The four carriers with the sedan raced after us, blurring the air as they moved, but no cars swerved to avoid them. No one panicked or even looked at them.

"How can people not see them?" I said. "Don't they notice four copper men in skirts running up the bridge with a weird black box?"

Bast shrugged. "Cats can hear many sounds you can't.

Some animals see things in the ultraviolet spectrum that are invisible to humans. Magic is similar. Did you notice the mansion when you first arrived?"

"Well ... no."

"And you are born to magic," Bast said. "Imagine how hard it would be for a regular mortal."

"Born to magic?" I remembered what Amos had said about our family being in the House of Life for a long time. "If magic, like, runs in the family, why haven't I ever been able to do it before?"

Bast smiled in the mirror. "Your sister understands."

Sadie's ears turned red. "No, I don't! I still can't believe you're a *goddess*. All these years, you've been eating crunchy treats, sleeping on my head—"

"I made a deal with your father," Bast said. "He let me remain in the world as long as I assumed a minor form, a normal housecat, so I could protect and watch over you. It was the least I could do after—" She stopped abruptly.

A horrible thought occurred to me. My stomach fluttered, and it had nothing to do with how fast we were going. "After our mom's death?" I guessed.

Bast stared straight ahead out the windshield.

"That's it, isn't it?" I said. "Dad and Mom did some kind of magic ritual at Cleopatra's Needle. Something went wrong. Our mom died and ... and they released you?"

"That's not important right now," Bast said. "The point is I agreed to look after Sadie. And I will."

She was hiding something. I was sure of it, but her tone made it clear that the subject was closed.

"If you gods are so powerful and helpful," I said, "why does the House of Life forbid magicians from summoning you?"

Bast swerved into the fast lane. "Magicians are paranoid. Your best hope is to stay with me. We'll get as far away as possible from New York. Then we'll get help and challenge Set."

"What help?" Sadie asked.

Bast raised an eyebrow. "Why, we'll summon more gods, of course."

10. Bast Goes Green

[Sadie, stop it! Yeah, I'm getting to that part.] Sorry, she keeps trying to distract me by setting fire to my—never mind. Where was I?

We barreled off the Williamsburg Bridge into Manhattan and headed north on Clinton Street.

"They're still following," Sadie warned.

Sure enough, the carriers were only a block behind us, weaving around cars and trampling over sidewalk displays of tourist junk.

"We'll buy some time." Bast growled deep in her throat—a sound so low and powerful it made my teeth buzz. She yanked the wheel and swerved right onto East Houston.

I looked back. Just as the carriers turned the corner, a horde of cats materialized all around them. Some jumped from windows. Some ran from the sidewalks and alleys. Some crawled from the storm drains. All of them converged on the carriers in a wave of fur and claws—climbing up their copper legs, scratching their backs, clinging to their faces, and weighing down the sedan box. The carriers stumbled, dropping the box. They began blindly swatting at the cats. Two cars swerved to avoid the animals and collided, blocking the entire street, and the carriers went down under the mass of angry felines. We turned onto the FDR Drive, and the scene disappeared from view.

"Nice," I admitted.

"It won't hold them long," Bast said. "Now—Central Park!"

Bast ditched the Lexus at the Metropolitan Museum of Art.

"We'll run from here," she said. "It's just behind the museum."

When she said run, she meant it. Sadie and I had to sprint to keep up, and Bast wasn't even breaking a sweat. She didn't stop for little things like hot dog stands or parked cars. Anything under ten feet tall she leaped over with ease, leaving us to scramble around the obstacles as best we could.

We ran into the park on the East Drive. As soon as we turned north, the obelisk loomed above us. A little over seventy feet tall, it looked like an exact copy of the needle in London. It was tucked away on a grassy hill, so it actually felt isolated, which is hard to achieve in the center of New York. There was no one around except a couple of joggers farther down the path. I could hear the traffic behind us on Fifth Avenue, but even that seemed far away.

We stopped at the obelisk's base. Bast sniffed the air as if smelling for trouble. Once I was standing still, I realized just how cold I was. The sun was directly overhead, but the wind ripped right through my borrowed linen clothes.

"I wish I'd grabbed something warmer," I muttered. "A wool coat would be nice."

"No, it wouldn't," Bast said, scanning the horizon. "You're dressed for magic."

Sadie shivered. "We have to freeze to be magical?"

"Magicians avoid animal products," Bast said absently. "Fur, leather, wool, any of that. The residual life aura can interfere with spells."

"My boots seem all right," Sadie noted.

"Leather," Bast said with distaste. "You may have a higher tolerance, so a bit of leather won't bother your magic. I don't know. But linen clothing is always best, or cotton—plant material. At any rate, Sadie, I think we're clear for the moment. There's a window of auspicious time starting right now, at eleven thirty, but it won't last long. Get started."

Sadie blinked. "Me? Why me? You're the goddess!"

"I'm not good at portals," Bast said. "Cats are protectors. Just control your emotions. Panic or fear will kill a spell. We *have* to get out of here before Set summons the other gods to his cause."

I frowned. "You mean Set's got, like, other evil gods on speed dial?"

Bast glanced nervously toward the trees. "Evil and good may not be the best way to think of it, Carter. As a magician, you must think about chaos and order. *Those* are the two forces that control the universe. Set is all about chaos."

"But what about the other gods Dad released?" I persisted. "Aren't they good guys? Isis, Osiris, Horus, Nephthys—where are they?"

Bast fixed her eyes on me. "That's a good question, Carter."

A Siamese cat broke through the bushes and ran up to Bast. They looked at each other for a moment. Then the Siamese dashed away.

"The carriers are close," Bast announced. "And something else...something much stronger, closing in from the east. I think the carriers' master has grown impatient."

My heart did a flip. "*Set* is coming?"

"No," Bast said. "Perhaps a minion. Or an ally. My cats are having trouble describing what they're seeing, and I *don't* want to find out. Sadie, now is the time. Just concentrate on opening a gateway to the Duat. I'll keep off the attackers. Combat magic is my specialty."

"Like what you did in the mansion?" I asked.

Bast showed her pointed teeth. "No, that was just combat."

The woods rustled, and the carriers emerged. Their sedan chair's shroud had been shredded by cat claws. The carriers themselves were scratched and dented. One walked with a limp, his leg bent backward at the knee. Another had a car fender wrapped around his neck.

The four metal men carefully set down their sedan chair. They looked at us and drew golden metal clubs from their belts.

"Sadie, get to work," Bast ordered. "Carter, you're welcome to help me."

The cat goddess unsheathed her knives. Her body began

to glow with a green hue. An aura surrounded her, growing larger, like a bubble of energy, and lifting her off the ground. The aura took shape until Bast was encased in a holographic projection about four times her normal size. It was an image of the goddess in her ancient form—a twenty-foot-tall woman with the head of a cat. Floating in midair in the center of the hologram, Bast stepped forward. The giant cat goddess moved with her. It didn't seem possible that a see-through image could have substance, but its foot shook the ground. Bast raised her hand. The glowing green warrior did the same, unsheathing claws as long and sharp as rapiers. Bast swiped the sidewalk in front of her and shredded the pavement to concrete ribbons. She turned and smiled at me. The giant cat's head did likewise, baring horrible fangs that could've bitten me in half.

"*This,*" Bast said, "is combat magic."

At first I was too stunned to do anything but watch as Bast launched her green war machine into the middle of the carriers.

She slashed one carrier to pieces with a single swipe, then stepped on another and flattened him into a metal pancake. The other two carriers attacked her holographic legs, but their metal clubs bounced harmlessly off the ghostly light with showers of sparks.

Meanwhile Sadie stood in front of the obelisk with her arms raised, shouting: "Open, you stupid piece of rock!"

Finally I drew my sword. My hands were shaking. I didn't want to charge into battle, but I felt like I should help. And if I *had* to fight, I figured having a twenty-foot-tall glowing cat warrior on my side was the way to do it. "Sadie, I—I'm going to help Bast. Keep trying!"

"I *am*!"

I ran forward just as Bast sliced the other two carriers apart like loaves of bread. With relief, I thought: *Well, that's it.*

Then all four carriers began to re-form. The flat one peeled himself off the pavement. The sliced ones' pieces clicked together like magnets, and the carriers stood up good as new.

"Carter, help me hack them apart!" Bast called. "They need to be in smaller pieces!"

I tried to stay out of Bast's way as she sliced and stomped. Then as soon as she disabled a carrier, I went to work chopping its remains into smaller pieces. They seemed more like Play-Doh than metal, because my blade mashed them up pretty easily.

Another few minutes and I was surrounded by piles of coppery rubble. Bast made a glowing fist and smashed the sedan into kindling.

"That wasn't so hard," I said. "What were we running for?"

Inside her glowing shell, Bast's face was coated with sweat. It hadn't occurred to me that a goddess could get tired, but her magic avatar must've taken a lot of effort.

"We're not safe yet," she warned. "Sadie, how's it coming?"

"It's not," Sadie complained. "Isn't there another way?"

Before Bast could answer, the bushes rustled with a new sound—like rain, except more *slithery*.

A chill ran up my back. "What...what is that?"

"No," Bast murmured. "It can't be. Not her."

Then the bushes exploded. A thousand brown creepy-crawlies poured from the woods in a carpet of grossness—all pincers and stinging tails.

I wanted to yell, "Scorpions!" But my voice wouldn't work. My legs started trembling. I *hate* scorpions. They're everywhere in Egypt. Many times I'd found them in my hotel bed or shower. Once I'd even found one in my sock.

"Sadie!" Bast called urgently.

"Nothing!" Sadie moaned.

The scorpions kept coming—thousands upon thousands. Out of the woods a woman appeared, walking fearlessly through the middle of the arachnids. She wore brown robes with gold jewelry glinting around her neck and arms. Her long black hair was cut Ancient Egyptian–style with a strange crown on top. Then I realized it wasn't a crown—she had a live, supersize scorpion nesting on her head. Millions of the little nasties swirled around her like she was the center of their storm.

"Serqet," Bast growled.

"The scorpion goddess," I guessed. Maybe that should've terrified me, but I was already pretty much at my maximum. "Can you take her?"

Bast's expression didn't reassure me.

"Carter, Sadie," she said, "this is going to get ugly. Get to the museum. Find the temple. It may protect you."

"What temple?" I asked.

"And what about you?" Sadie added.

"I'll be fine. I'll catch up." But when Bast looked at me, I could tell she wasn't sure. She was just buying us time.

"Go!" she ordered. She turned her giant green cat warrior to face the mass of scorpions.

Embarrassing truth? In the face of those scorpions, I didn't even pretend to be brave. I grabbed Sadie's arm and we ran.

S
A
D
I
E

11. We Meet the Human Flamethrower

Right, I'm taking the microphone. There is *no chance* Carter would tell this part properly, as it's about Zia. [Shut up, Carter. You know it's true.]

Oh, who is Zia? Sorry, getting ahead of myself.

We raced to the entrance of the museum, and I had no idea why, except that a giant glowing cat woman had told us to. Now, you must realize I was already devastated by everything that had happened. First, I'd lost my father. Second, my loving grandparents had kicked me out of the flat. Then I'd discovered I was apparently "blood of the pharaohs," born to a magical family, and all sorts of rubbish that sounded quite impressive but only brought me loads of trouble. And as soon as I'd found a new home—a mansion with proper breakfast and friendly pets and quite a nice room for me, by the way— Uncle Amos disappeared, my lovely new crocodile and baboon friends were tossed in a river, and the mansion was set on fire.

And if *that* wasn't enough, my faithful cat Muffin had decided to engage in a hopeless battle with a swarm of scorpions.

Do you call it a "swarm" for scorpions? A herd? A gaggle? Oh, never mind.

The point is I couldn't believe I'd been asked to open a magic doorway when clearly I had no such skill, and now my brother was dragging me away. I felt like an utter failure. [And no comments from you, Carter. As I recall, *you* weren't much help at the time, either.]

"We can't just leave Bast!" I shouted. "Look!"

Carter kept running, dragging me along, but I could see quite clearly what was happening back at the obelisk. A mass of scorpions had crawled up Bast's glowing green legs and were wriggling into the hologram like it was gelatin. Bast smashed hundreds of them with her feet and fists, but there were simply too many. Soon they were up to her waist, and her ghostly shell began to flicker. Meanwhile, the brown-robed goddess advanced slowly, and I had a feeling she would be worse than any number of scorpions.

Carter pulled me through a row of bushes and I lost sight of Bast. We burst onto Fifth Avenue, which seemed ridiculously normal after the magic battle. We ran down the sidewalk, shoved through a knot of pedestrians, and climbed the steps of the Met.

A banner above the entrance announced some sort of special Christmas event, which I suppose is why the museum was open on a holiday, but I didn't bother reading the details. We pushed straight inside.

What did it look like? Well, it was a museum: huge entry hall, lots of columns and so on. I can't claim I spent much time admiring the decor. I do remember it had queues for the ticket windows, because we ran right past them. There were also security guards, because they yelled at us as we dashed into the exhibits. By luck, we ended up in the Egyptian area, in front of a reconstructed tomb sort of place with narrow corridors. Carter probably could've told you what the structure was supposed to be, but honestly I didn't care.

"Come on," I said.

We slipped inside the exhibit, which proved quite enough to lose the security guards, or perhaps they had better things to do than pursue naughty children.

When we popped out again, we sneaked around until we were sure we weren't being followed. The Egypt wing wasn't crowded—just a few clumps of old people and a foreign tour group with a guide explaining a sarcophagus in French. "Et voici la momie!"

Strangely, no one seemed to notice the enormous sword on Carter's back, which surely must've been a security issue (and much more interesting than the exhibits). A few old people did give us odd looks, but I suspect that was because we were dressed in linen pajamas, drenched in sweat, and covered in grass and leaves. My hair was probably a nightmare as well.

I found an empty room and pulled Carter aside. The glass cases were full of *shabti*. A few days earlier I wouldn't have given them a second thought. Now, I kept glancing at the statues, sure they'd come to life any minute and try to bash me on the head.

"What now?" I asked Carter. "Did you see any temple?"

"No." He knit his eyebrows as if trying hard to remember. "I think there's a rebuilt temple down that hall...or is that in the Brooklyn Museum? Maybe the one in Munich? Sorry, I've been to so many museums with Dad that they all get mixed together."

I sighed in exasperation. "Poor boy, forced to travel the world, skip school, and spend time with Dad while I get a whole two days a year with him!"

"Hey!" Carter turned on me with surprising force. "You get a *home*! You get friends and a normal life and don't wake up each morning wondering what country you're in! You don't—"

The glass case next to us shattered, spraying glass at our feet.

Carter looked at me, bewildered. "Did we just—"

"Like my exploding birthday cake," I grumbled, trying not to let on how startled I was. "You need to control your temper."

"*Me?*"

Alarms began to blare. Red lights pulsed through the corridor. A garbled voice came on the loudspeaker and said something about proceeding calmly to the exits. The French tour group ran past us, screaming in panic, followed by a crowd of remarkably fast old people with walkers and canes.

"Let's finish arguing later, shall we?" I told Carter. "Come on!"

We ran down another corridor, and the sirens died as suddenly as they'd started. The blood-red lights kept pulsing in eerie silence. Then I heard it: the slithering, clacking sounds of scorpions.

"What about Bast?" My voice choked up. "Is she—"

"Don't think about it," Carter said, though, judging from his face, that's *exactly* what he was thinking about. "Keep moving!"

Soon we were hopelessly lost. As far as I could tell, the Egyptian part of the museum was designed to be as confusing as possible, with dead ends and halls that doubled back on themselves. We passed hieroglyphic scrolls, gold jewelry, sarcophagi, statues of pharaohs, and huge chunks of limestone. Why would someone display a rock? Aren't there enough of those in the world?

We saw no one, but the slithering sounds grew louder no matter which way we ran. Finally I rounded a corner and smacked straight into someone.

I yelped and scrambled backwards, only to stumble into Carter. We both fell on our bums in a most unflattering way. It's a miracle Carter didn't impale himself on his own sword.

At first I didn't recognize the girl standing in front of us, which seems strange, looking back on it. Perhaps she was using some sort of magic aura, or perhaps I just didn't want to believe it was *her*.

She looked a bit taller than me. Probably older, too, but not by much. Her black hair was trimmed along her jawline and longer in the front so that it swept over her eyes. She had caramel-colored skin and pretty, vaguely Arab features. Her eyes—lined in black kohl, Egyptian style—were a strange amber color that was either quite beautiful or a bit scary; I couldn't decide which. She had a backpack on her shoulder, and wore sandals and loose-fitting linen clothes like ours. She looked as if she were on her way to a martial arts class. God, now that I think of it, we probably looked the same way. How embarrassing.

I slowly began to realize I'd seen her before. She was the girl with the knife from the British Museum. Before I could say anything, Carter sprang to his feet. He moved in front of me and brandished his sword as if trying to *protect* me. Can you believe the nerve?

"Get—get back!" he stammered.

The girl reached into her sleeve and produced a curved white piece of ivory—an Egyptian wand.

She flicked it to one side, and Carter's sword flew out of his hands and clattered to the floor.

"Don't embarrass yourself," the girl said sternly. "Where is Amos?"

Carter looked too stunned to speak. The girl turned towards me. Her golden eyes were both beautiful *and* scary, I decided, and I didn't like her a bit.

"Well?" she demanded.

I didn't see why I needed to tell her a bloody thing, but an uncomfortable pressure started building in my chest, like a burp trying to get free. I heard myself say, "Amos is gone. He left this morning."

"And the cat demon?"

"That's *my* cat," I said. "And she's a goddess, not a demon. She saved us from the scorpions!"

Carter unfroze. He snatched up his sword and pointed it at the girl again. Full credit for persistence, I suppose.

"Who are you?" he demanded. "What do you want?"

"My name is Zia Rashid." She tilted her head as if listening.

Right on cue, the entire building rumbled. Dust sprinkled from the ceiling, and the slithering sounds of scorpions doubled in volume behind us.

"And right now," Zia continued, sounding a bit disappointed, "I must save your miserable lives. Let's go."

I suppose we could've refused, but our choices seemed to be Zia or the scorpions, so we ran after her.

She passed a case full of statues and casually tapped the glass with her wand. Tiny granite pharaohs and limestone gods stirred at her command. They hopped off their pedestals and crashed through the glass. Some wielded weapons. Others simply cracked their stone knuckles. They let us pass, but stared down the corridor behind us as if waiting for the enemy.

"Hurry," Zia told us. "These will only—"

"Buy us time," I guessed. "Yes, we've heard that before."

"You talk too much," Zia said without stopping.

I was about to make a withering retort. Honestly, I would've put her in her place quite properly. But just then we emerged into an enormous room and my voice abandoned me.

"Whoa," Carter said.

I couldn't help agreeing with him. The place was extremely *whoa*.

The room was the size of a football stadium. One wall was made completely of glass and looked out on the park. In the middle of the room, on a raised platform, an ancient building had been reconstructed. There was a freestanding stone gateway about eight meters tall, and behind that an open courtyard and square structure made of uneven sandstone blocks carved all over on the outside with images of gods and pharaohs and hieroglyphs. Flanking the building's entrance were two columns bathed in eerie light.

"An Egyptian temple," I guessed.

"The Temple of Dendur," Zia said. "Actually it was built by the Romans—"

"When they occupied Egypt," Carter said, like this was delightful information. "Augustus commissioned it."

"Yes," Zia said.

"Fascinating," I murmured. "Would you two like to be left alone with a history textbook?"

Zia scowled at me. "At any rate, the temple was dedicated to Isis, so it will have enough power to open a gate."

"To summon more gods?" I asked.

Zia's eyes flashed angrily. "Accuse me of that again, and I will cut out your tongue. I meant a gateway to get you out of here."

I felt completely lost, but I was getting used to that. We followed Zia up the steps and through the temple's stone gateway.

The courtyard was empty, abandoned by the fleeing museum visitors, which made it feel quite creepy. Giant carvings of gods stared down at me. Hieroglyphic inscriptions were everywhere, and I was afraid that if I concentrated too hard, I might be able to read them.

Zia stopped at the front steps of the temple. She held up her wand and wrote in the air. A familiar hieroglyph burned between the columns.

Open—the same symbol Dad had used at the Rosetta Stone. I waited for something to blow up, but the hieroglyph simply faded.

Zia opened her backpack. "We'll make our stand here until the gate can be opened."

"Why not just open it now?" Carter asked.

"Portals can only appear at auspicious moments," Zia said. "Sunrise, sunset, midnight, eclipses, astrological alignments, the exact time of a god's birth—"

"Oh, come on," I said. "How can you possibly know all that?"

"It takes years to memorize the complete calendar," Zia said. "But the next auspicious moment is easy: high noon. Ten and a half minutes from now."

She didn't check a watch. I wondered how she knew the time so precisely, but I decided it wasn't the most important question.

"Why should we trust you?" I asked. "As I recall, at the British Museum, you wanted to gut us with a knife."

"That would've been simpler." Zia sighed. "Unfortunately, my superiors think you might be *innocents*. So for now, I can't kill you. But I also can't allow you to fall into the hands of the Red Lord. And so . . . you can trust me."

"Well, I'm convinced," I said. "I feel all warm and fuzzy inside."

Zia reached in her bag and took out four little statues—animal-headed men, each about five centimeters tall. She handed them to me. "Put the Sons of Horus around us at the cardinal points."

"Excuse me?"

"North, south, east, west." She spoke slowly, as if I were an idiot.

"I know compass directions! But—"

"That's north." Zia pointed out the wall of glass. "Figure out the rest."

I did what she asked, though I didn't see how the little men would help. Meanwhile, Zia gave Carter a piece of chalk and told him to draw a circle around us, connecting the statues.

"Magic protection," Carter said. "Like what Dad did at the British Museum."

"Yes," I grumbled. "And we saw how well *that* worked."

Carter ignored me. What else is new? He was so eager to please Zia that he jumped right to the task of drawing his sidewalk art.

Then Zia took something else from her bag—a plain wooden rod like the one our dad had used in London. She spoke a word under her breath, and the rod expanded into a two-meter-long black staff topped with a carved lion's head. She twirled it around single-handedly like a baton—just showing off, I was sure—while holding the wand in her other hand.

Carter finished the chalk circle as the first scorpions appeared at the gallery's entrance.

"How much longer on that gate?" I asked, hoping I didn't sound as terrified as I felt.

"Stay inside the circle no matter what," Zia said. "When the gate opens, jump through. And keep behind me!"

She touched her wand to the chalk circle, spoke another word, and the circle began to glow dark red.

Hundreds of scorpions swarmed towards the temple, turning the floor into a living mass of claws and stingers. Then the woman in brown, Serqet, entered the gallery. She smiled at us coldly.

"Zia," I said, "that's a goddess. She defeated *Bast*. What chance do *you* have?"

Zia held up her staff and the carved lion's head burst into flames—a small red fireball so bright, it lit the entire room. "I am a scribe in the House of Life, Sadie Kane. I am trained to fight gods."

12. A Jump Through the Hourglass

WELL, THAT WAS ALL VERY IMPRESSIVE, I suppose. You should've seen Carter's face—he looked like an excited puppy. [Oh, stop shoving me. You did!]

But I felt much less sure of Miss Zia "I'm-So-Magical" Rashid when the army of scorpions scuttled towards us. I wouldn't have thought it possible so many scorpions existed in the world, much less in Manhattan. The glowing circle round us seemed like insignificant protection against the millions of arachnids crawling over one another, many layers deep, and the woman in brown, who was even more horrible.

From a distance she looked all right, but as she got closer I saw that Serqet's pale skin glistened like an insect shell. Her eyes were beady black. Her long, dark hair was unnaturally thick, as if made from a million bristling bug antennae. And when she opened her mouth, sideways mandibles snapped and retracted outside her regular human teeth.

The goddess stopped about twenty meters away, studying us. Her hateful black eyes fixed on Zia. "Give me the younglings."

Her voice was harsh and raspy, as if she hadn't spoken in centuries.

Zia crossed her staff and wand. "I am mistress of the elements, Scribe of the First Nome. Leave or be destroyed."

Serqet clicked her mandibles in a gruesome foamy grin. Some of her scorpions advanced, but when the first one touched the glowing lines of our protective circle, it sizzled and turned to ashes. Mark my words, *nothing* smells worse than burned scorpion.

The rest of the horrible things retreated, swirling round the goddess and crawling up her legs. With a shudder, I realized they were wriggling into her robes. After a few seconds, all the scorpions had disappeared into the brown folds of her clothes.

The air seemed to darken behind Serqet, as if she were casting an enormous shadow. Then the darkness rose up and took the form of a massive scorpion tail, arcing over Serqet's head. It lashed down at us at blazing speed, but Zia raised her wand and the sting glanced off the ivory tip with a hissing sound. Steam rolled off Zia's wand, smelling of sulfur.

Zia pointed her staff towards the goddess, engulfing her body in fire. Serqet screamed and staggered backwards, but the fire died almost instantly. It left Serqet's robes seared and smoking, but the goddess looked more enraged than hurt.

"Your days are past, magician. The House is weak. Lord Set will lay waste to this land."

Zia threw her wand like a boomerang. It smashed into the shadowy scorpion tail and exploded in a blinding flash of light. Serqet lurched back and averted her eyes, and as she did, Zia reached into her sleeve and brought out something small—something closed inside her fist.

The wand was a diversion, I thought. *A magician's sleight of hand.*

Then Zia did something reckless: she leaped out of the magic circle—the very thing she'd warned us not to do.

"Zia!" Carter called. "The gate!"

I glanced behind me, and my heart almost stopped. The space between the two columns at the temple's entrance was now a vertical tunnel of sand, as if I were looking into the funnel of an enormous sideways hourglass. I could feel it tugging at me, pulling me towards it with magical gravity.

"I'm not going in *there*," I insisted, but another flash of light brought my attention back to Zia.

She and the goddess were involved in a dangerous dance. Zia twirled and spun with her fiery staff, and everywhere she passed, she left a trail of flames burning in the air. I had to admit it: Zia was almost as graceful and impressive as Bast.

I had the oddest desire to help. I wanted—very badly, in fact—to step outside the circle and engage in combat. It was a completely mad urge, of course. What could I possibly have done? But still I felt I shouldn't—or *couldn't*—jump through the gate without helping Zia.

"Sadie!" Carter grabbed me and pulled me back. Without my even realizing it, my foot had almost stepped across the line of chalk. "What are you thinking?"

I didn't have an answer, but I stared at Zia and mumbled in a sort of trance, "She's going to use ribbons. They won't work."

"What?" Carter demanded. "Come on, we've got to go through the gate!"

Just then Zia opened her fist and small red tendrils of cloth fluttered into the air. *Ribbons.* How had I known? They zipped about like living things—like eels in water—and began to grow larger.

Serqet was still concentrating on the fire, trying to keep Zia from caging her. At first she didn't seem to notice the ribbons, which grew until they were several meters long. I counted five, six, seven of them in all. They zipped around, orbiting Serqet, ripping through her shadow scorpion as if it were a harmless illusion. Finally they wrapped around Serqet's body, pinning her arms and legs. She screamed as if the ribbons burned her. She dropped to her knees, and the shadow scorpion disintegrated into an inky haze.

Zia spun to a stop. She pointed her staff at the goddess's face. The ribbons began to glow, and the goddess hissed in pain, cursing in a language I didn't know.

"I bind you with the Seven Ribbons of Hathor," Zia said. "Release your host or your essence will burn forever."

"Your *death* will last forever!" Serqet snarled. "You have made an enemy of Set!"

Zia twisted her staff, and Serqet fell sideways, writhing and smoking.

"I will...not..." the goddess hissed. But then her black eyes turned milky white, and she lay still.

"The gate!" Carter warned. "Zia, come on! I think it's closing!"

He was right. The tunnel of sand seemed to be moving a bit more slowly. The tug of its magic did not feel as strong.

Zia approached the fallen goddess. She touched Serqet's forehead, and black smoke billowed from the goddess's mouth. Serqet transformed and shrank until we were looking at a completely different woman wrapped in red ribbons. She had pale skin and black hair, but otherwise she didn't look anything like Serqet. She looked, well, *human*.

"Who is that?" I asked.

"The host," Zia said. "Some poor mortal who—"

She looked up with a start. The black haze was no longer dissipating. It was getting thicker and darker again, swirling into a more solid form.

"Impossible," Zia said. "The ribbons are too powerful. Serqet *can't* re-form unless—"

"Well, she *is* re-forming," Carter yelled, "and our exit is closing! Let's go!"

I couldn't believe he was willing to jump into a churning wall of sand, but as I watched the black cloud take the shape of a two-story-tall scorpion—a very *angry* scorpion—I made my decision.

"Coming!" I yelled.

"Zia!" Carter yelled. "Now!"

"Perhaps you're right," the magician decided. She turned, and together we ran and plunged straight into the swirling vortex.

13. I Face the Killer Turkey

My turn.

First of all, Sadie's "puppy dog" comment was totally out of line. I was *not* starry-eyed about Zia. It's just that I don't meet a lot of people who can throw fireballs and battle gods. [Stop making faces at me, Sadie. You look like Khufu.]

Anyway, we plunged into the sand tunnel.

Everything went dark. My stomach tingled with that top-of-the-roller-coaster weightlessness as I hurtled forward. Hot winds whipped around me, and my skin burned.

Then I tumbled out onto a cold tile floor, and Sadie and Zia crashed on top of me.

"*Ow!*" I grumbled.

The first thing I noticed was the fine layer of sand covering my body like powdered sugar. Then my eyes adjusted to the harsh light. We were in a big building like a shopping mall, with crowds bustling around us.

No...not a mall. It was a two-level airport concourse, with

shops, lots of windows, and polished steel columns. Outside, it was dark, so I knew we must be in a different time zone. Announcements echoed over the intercom in a language that sounded like Arabic.

Sadie spit sand out of her mouth. "Yuck!"

"Come on," Zia said. "We can't stay here."

I struggled to my feet. People were streaming past—some in Western clothes, some in robes and headscarves. A family arguing in German rushed by and almost ran over me with their suitcases.

Then I turned and saw something I recognized. In the middle of the concourse stood a life-size replica of an Ancient Egyptian boat made from glowing display cases—a sales counter for perfume and jewelry.

"This is the Cairo airport," I said.

"Yes," Zia said. "Now, let's go!"

"Why the rush? Can Serqet...can she follow us through that sand gate?"

Zia shook her head. "An artifact overheats whenever it creates a gate. It requires a twelve-hour cooldown before it can be used again. But we still have to worry about airport security. Unless you'd like to meet the Egyptian police, you'll come with me *now*."

She grabbed our arms and steered us through the crowd. We must've looked like beggars in our old-fashioned clothes, covered head-to-toe in sand. People gave us a wide berth, but nobody tried to stop us.

"Why are we here?" Sadie demanded.

"To see the ruins of Heliopolis," Zia said.

"Inside an *airport?*" Sadie asked.

I remembered something Dad had told me years ago, and my scalp tingled.

"Sadie, the ruins are *under* us." I looked at Zia. "That's right, isn't it?"

She nodded. "The ancient city was pillaged centuries ago. Some of its monuments were carted away, like Cleopatra's two needles. Most of its temples were broken down to make new buildings. What was left disappeared under Cairo's suburbs. The largest section is under this airport."

"And how does that help us?" Sadie asked.

Zia kicked open a maintenance door. On the other side was a broom closet. Zia muttered a command—"*Sahad*"—and the image of the closet shimmered and disappeared, revealing a set of stone steps leading down.

"Because not *all* Heliopolis is in ruins," Zia said. "Follow closely. And *touch nothing.*"

The stairs must've led down about seven million miles, because we descended *forever*. The passage had been made for miniature people, too. We had to crouch and crawl most of the way, and even so, I bonked my head on the ceiling a dozen times. The only light was from a ball of fire in Zia's palm, which made shadows dance across the walls.

I'd been in places like this before—tunnels inside pyramids, tombs my dad had excavated—but I've never liked them. Millions of tons of rock above me seemed to crush the air out of my lungs.

Finally we reached the bottom. The tunnel opened up, and

Zia stopped abruptly. After my eyes adjusted, I saw why. We were standing at the edge of a chasm.

A single wooden plank spanned the void. On the opposite ledge, two jackal-headed granite warriors flanked a doorway, their spears crossed over the entrance.

Sadie sighed. "Please, no more psychotic statues."

"Do not joke," Zia warned. "This is an entrance to the First Nome, the oldest branch of the House of Life, headquarters for all magicians. My job was to bring you here safely, but I cannot help you cross. Each magician must unbar the path for herself, and the challenge is different for each supplicant."

She looked at Sadie expectantly, which annoyed me. First Bast, now Zia—both of them treated Sadie like she should have some kind of superpowers. I mean, okay, so she'd been able to blast the library doors apart, but why didn't anyone look at *me* to do cool tricks?

Plus, I was still annoyed with Sadie for the comments she'd made at the museum in New York—how I had it so good traveling the world with Dad. She had no idea how often I wanted to complain about the constant traveling, how many days I wished I didn't have to get on a plane and could just be like a normal kid going to school and making friends. But I couldn't complain. *You always have to look impeccable,* Dad had told me. And he didn't just mean my clothes. He meant my attitude. With Mom gone, I was all he had. Dad needed me to be strong. Most days, I didn't mind. I loved my dad. But it was also hard.

Sadie didn't understand that. *She* had it easy. And now

she seemed to be getting all the attention, as if *she* were the special one. It wasn't fair.

Then I heard Dad's voice in my head: "Fairness means everyone gets what they need. And the only way to get what you need is to make it happen yourself."

I don't know what got into me, but I drew my sword and marched across the plank. It was like my legs were working by themselves, not waiting for my brain. Part of me thought: *This is a really bad idea.* But part of me answered: *No, we do not fear this.* And the voice didn't sound like mine.

"Carter!" Sadie cried.

I kept walking. I tried not to look down at the yawning void under my feet, but the sheer size of the chasm made me dizzy. I felt like one of those gyroscope toys, spinning and wobbling as I crossed the narrow plank.

As I got closer to the opposite side, the doorway between the two statues began to glow, like a curtain of red light.

I took a deep breath. Maybe the red light was a portal, like the gate of sand. If I just charged through fast enough...

Then the first dagger shot out of the tunnel.

My sword was in motion before I realized it. The dagger should've impaled me in the chest, but somehow I deflected it with my blade and sent it sailing into the abyss. Two more daggers shot out of the tunnel. I'd never had the best reflexes, but now they sped up. I ducked one dagger and hooked the other with the curved blade of my sword, turned the dagger and flung it back into the tunnel. *How the heck did I do that?*

I advanced to the end of the plank and slashed through

the red light, which flickered and died. I waited for the statues to come alive, but nothing happened. The only sound was a dagger clattering against the rocks in the chasm far below.

The doorway began to glow again. The red light coalesced into a strange form: a five-foot-tall bird with a man's head. I raised my sword, but Zia yelled, "Carter, no!"

The bird creature folded his wings. His eyes, lined with kohl, narrowed as they studied me. A black ornamental wig glistened on his head, and his face was etched with wrinkles. One of those fake braided pharaoh beards was stuck on his chin like a backward ponytail. He didn't look hostile, except for the red flickering light all around him, and the fact that from the neck down he was the world's largest killer turkey.

Then a chilling thought occurred to me: This was a bird with a human head, the same form I'd imagined taking when I slept in Amos's house, when my soul left my body and flew to Phoenix. I had no idea what that meant, but it scared me.

The bird creature scratched at the stone floor. Then, unexpectedly, he smiled.

"*Pari, niswa nafeer,*" he told me, or at least that's what it sounded like.

Zia gasped. She and Sadie were standing behind me now, their faces pale. Apparently they'd managed to cross the chasm without my noticing.

Finally Zia seemed to collect herself. She bowed to the bird creature. Sadie followed her example.

The creature winked at me, as if we'd just shared a joke. Then he vanished. The red light faded. The statues retracted their arms, uncrossing their spears from the entrance.

"That's it?" I asked. "What did the turkey say?"

Zia looked at me with something like fear. "That was *not* a turkey, Carter. That was a *ba*."

I'd heard my dad use that word before, but I couldn't place it. "Another monster?"

"A human soul," Zia said. "In this case, a spirit of the dead. A magician from ancient times, come back to serve as a guardian. They watch the entrances of the House."

She studied my face as if I'd just developed some terrible rash.

"What?" I demanded. "Why are you looking at me that way?"

"Nothing," she said. "We must hurry."

She squeezed by me on the ledge and disappeared into the tunnel.

Sadie was staring at me too.

"All right," I said. "What did the bird guy say? You understood it?"

She nodded uneasily. "He mistook you for someone else. He must have bad eyesight."

"Because?"

"Because he said, 'Go forth, good king.'"

I was in a daze after that. We passed through the tunnel and entered a vast underground city of halls and chambers, but I only remember bits and pieces of it.

The ceilings soared to twenty or thirty feet, so it didn't feel like we were underground. Every chamber was lined with massive stone columns like the ones I'd seen in Egyptian ruins, but these were in perfect condition, brightly painted to resemble palm trees, with carved green fronds at the top, so I felt like I was walking through a petrified forest. Fires burned in copper braziers. They didn't seem to make any smoke, but the air smelled good, like a marketplace for spices—cinnamon, clove, nutmeg, and others I couldn't identify. The city smelled like Zia. I realized that this was her home.

We saw a few other people—mostly older men and women. Some wore linen robes, some modern clothes. One guy in a business suit walked past with a black leopard on a leash, as if that were completely normal. Another guy barked orders to a small army of brooms, mops, and buckets that were scuttling around, cleaning up the city.

"Like that cartoon," Sadie said. "Where Mickey Mouse tries to do magic and the brooms keep splitting and toting water."

"'The Sorcerer's Apprentice,'" Zia said. "You do know that was based on an Egyptian story, don't you?"

Sadie just stared back. I knew how she felt. It was too much to process.

We walked through a hall of jackal-headed statues, and I could swear their eyes watched us as we passed. A few minutes later, Zia led us through an open-air market—if you can call anything "open-air" underground—with dozens of stalls selling weird items like boomerang wands, animated clay dolls, parrots, cobras, papyrus scrolls, and hundreds of different glittering amulets.

Next we crossed a path of stones over a dark river teeming with fish. I thought they were perch until I saw their vicious teeth.

"Are those piranhas?" I asked.

"Tiger fish from the Nile," Zia said. "Like piranhas, except these can weigh up to sixteen pounds."

I watched my step more closely after that.

We turned a corner and passed an ornate building carved out of black rock. Seated pharaohs were chiseled into the walls, and the doorway was shaped like a coiled serpent.

"What's in there?" Sadie asked.

We peeked inside and saw rows of children—maybe two dozen in all, about six to ten years old or so—sitting cross-legged on cushions. They were hunched over brass bowls, peering intently into some sort of liquid and speaking under their breath. At first I thought it was a classroom, but there was no sign of a teacher, and the chamber was lit only by a few candles. Judging by the number of empty seats, the room was meant to hold twice as many kids.

"Our initiates," Zia said, "learning to scry. The First Nome must keep in contact with our brethren all over the world. We use our youngest as . . . operators, I suppose you would say."

"So you've got bases like this all over the world?"

"Most are much smaller, but yes."

I remembered what Amos had told us about the nomes. "Egypt is the First Nome. New York is the Twenty-first. What's the last one, the Three-hundred-and-sixtieth?"

"That would be Antarctica," Zia said. "A punishment assignment. Nothing there but a couple of cold magicians and some magic penguins."

"Magic penguins?"

"Don't ask."

Sadie pointed to the children inside. "How does it work? They see images in the water?"

"It's oil," Zia said. "But yes."

"So few," Sadie said. "Are these the only initiates in the whole city?"

"In the whole *world*," Zia corrected. "There were more before—" She stopped herself.

"Before what?" I asked.

"Nothing," Zia said darkly. "Initiates do our scrying because young minds are most receptive. Magicians begin training no later than the age of ten … with a few dangerous exceptions."

"You mean us," I said.

She glanced at me apprehensively, and I knew she was still thinking about what the bird spirit had called me: a *good king*. It seemed so unreal, like our family name in that *Blood of the Pharaohs* scroll. How could I be related to some ancient kings? And even if I was, *I* certainly wasn't a king. I had no kingdom. I didn't even have my single suitcase anymore.

"They'll be waiting for you," Zia said. "Come along."

We walked so far, my feet began to ache.

Finally we arrived at a crossroads. On the right was a massive set of bronze doors with fires blazing on either side; on the left, a twenty-foot-tall sphinx carved into the wall. A doorway nestled between its paws, but it was bricked in and covered in cobwebs.

"That looks like the Sphinx at Giza," I said.

"That's because we are directly under the *real* Sphinx," Zia said. "That tunnel leads straight up to it. Or it used to, before it was sealed."

"But..." I did some quick calculations in my head. "The Sphinx is, like, twenty miles from the Cairo Airport."

"Roughly."

"No way we've walked that far."

Zia actually smiled, and I couldn't help noticing how pretty her eyes were. "Distance changes in magic places, Carter. Surely you've learned that by now."

Sadie cleared her throat. "So why is the tunnel closed, then?"

"The Sphinx was too popular with archaeologists," Zia said. "They kept digging around. Finally, in the 1980s, they discovered the first part of the tunnel under the Sphinx."

"Dad told me about that!" I said. "But he said the tunnel was a dead end."

"It was when we got through with it. We couldn't let the archaeologists know how much they're missing. Egypt's leading archaeologist recently speculated that they've only discovered thirty percent of the ancient ruins in Egypt. In truth, they've only discovered one tenth, and not even the *interesting* tenth."

"What about King Tut's tomb?" I protested.

"That boy king?" Zia rolled her eyes. "*Boring.* You should see some of the *good* tombs."

I felt a little hurt. Dad had named me after Howard Carter, the guy who discovered King Tut's tomb, so I'd always felt a personal attachment to it. If that wasn't a "good" tomb, I wondered what was.

Zia turned to face the bronze doors.

"This is the Hall of Ages." She placed her palm against the seal, which bore the symbol of the House of Life.

The hieroglyphs began to glow, and the doors swung open.

Zia turned to us, her expression deadly serious. "You are about to meet the Chief Lector. Behave yourselves, unless you wish to be turned into insects."

14. A French Guy Almost Kills Us

THE LAST COUPLE OF DAYS I'd seen a lot of crazy things, but the Hall of Ages took the prize.

Double rows of stone pillars held up a ceiling so high, you could've parked a blimp under it with no trouble. A shimmering blue carpet that looked like water ran down the center of the hall, which was so long, I couldn't see the end even though it was brightly lit. Balls of fire floated around like helium basketballs, changing color whenever they bumped into one another. Millions of tiny hieroglyphic symbols also drifted through the air, randomly combining into words and then breaking apart.

I grabbed a pair of glowing red legs.

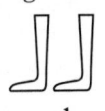

They walked across my palm before jumping off and dissolving.

But the weirdest things were the *displays*.

I don't know what else to call them. Between the columns on either side of us, images shifted, coming into focus and then blurring out again like holograms in a sandstorm.

"Come on," Zia told us. "And don't spend too much time looking."

It was impossible not to. The first twenty feet or so, the magical scenes cast a golden light across the hall. A blazing sun rose above an ocean. A mountain emerged from the water, and I had the feeling I was watching the beginning of the world. Giants strode across the Nile Valley: a man with black skin and the head of a jackal, a lioness with bloody fangs, a beautiful woman with wings of light.

Sadie stepped off the rug. In a trance, she reached toward the images.

"Stay on the carpet!" Zia grabbed Sadie's hand and pulled her back toward the center of the hall. "You are seeing the Age of the Gods. No mortal should dwell on these images."

"But..." Sadie blinked. "They're only pictures, aren't they?"

"Memories," Zia said, "so powerful they could destroy your mind."

"Oh," Sadie said in a small voice.

We kept walking. The images changed to silver. I saw armies clashing—Egyptians in kilts and sandals and leather armor, fighting with spears. A tall, dark-skinned man in red-and-white armor placed a double crown on his head: Narmer, the king who united Upper and Lower Egypt. Sadie was right: he did look a bit like Dad.

"This is the Old Kingdom," I guessed. "The first great age of Egypt."

Zia nodded. As we walked down the hall, we saw workers building the first step pyramid out of stone. Another few steps, and the biggest pyramid of all rose from the desert at Giza. Its outer layer of smooth white casing stones gleamed in the sun. Ten thousand workers gathered at its base and knelt before the pharaoh, who raised his hands to the sun, dedicating his own tomb.

"Khufu," I said.

"The baboon?" Sadie asked, suddenly interested.

"No, the pharaoh who built the Great Pyramid," I said. "It was the tallest structure in the world for almost four thousand years."

Another few steps, and the images turned from silver to coppery.

"The Middle Kingdom," Zia announced. "A bloody, chaotic time. And yet this is when the House of Life came to maturity."

The scenes shifted more rapidly. We watched armies fighting, temples being built, ships sailing on the Nile, and magicians throwing fire. Every step covered hundreds of years, and yet the hall still went on forever. For the first time I understood just how ancient Egypt was.

We crossed another threshold, and the light turned bronze.

"The New Kingdom," I guessed. "The last time Egypt was ruled by Egyptians."

Zia said nothing, but I watched scenes passing that my dad had described to me: Hatshepsut, the greatest female pharaoh, putting on a fake beard and ruling Egypt as a man; Ramesses the Great leading his chariots into battle.

I saw magicians dueling in a palace. A man in tattered robes, with a shaggy black beard and wild eyes, threw down his staff, which turned into a serpent and devoured a dozen other snakes.

I got a lump in my throat. "Is that—"

"Musa," Zia said. "Or Moshe, as his own people knew him. You call him Moses. The only foreigner ever to defeat the House in a magic duel."

I stared at her. "You're kidding, right?"

"We would not kid about such a thing."

The scene shifted again. I saw a man standing over a table of battle figurines: wooden toy ships, soldiers, and chariots. The man was dressed like a pharaoh, but his face looked oddly familiar. He looked up and seemed to smile right at me. With a chill, I realized he had the same face as the *ba*, the bird-faced spirit who'd challenged me on the bridge.

"Who is that?" I asked.

"Nectanebo II," Zia said. "The last native Egyptian king, and the last sorcerer pharaoh. He could move entire armies, create or destroy navies by moving pieces on his board, but in the end, it was not enough."

We stepped over another line and the images shimmered blue. "These are the Ptolemaic times," Zia said. "Alexander the Great conquered the known world, including Egypt. He set up his general Ptolemy as the new pharaoh, and founded a line of Greek kings to rule over Egypt."

The Ptolemaic section of the hall was shorter, and seemed sad compared to all the others. The temples were smaller. The kings and queens looked desperate, or lazy, or simply apathetic.

There were no great battles...except toward the end. I saw Romans march into the city of Alexandria. I saw a woman with dark hair and a white dress drop a snake into her blouse.

"Cleopatra," Zia said, "the seventh queen of that name. She tried to stand against the might of Rome, and she lost. When she took her life, the last line of pharaohs ended. Egypt, the great nation, faded. Our language was forgotten. The ancient rites were suppressed. The House of Life survived, but we were forced into hiding."

We passed into an area of red light, and history began to look familiar. I saw Arab armies riding into Egypt, then the Turks. Napoleon marched his army under the shadow of the pyramids. The British came and built the Suez Canal. Slowly Cairo grew into a modern city. And the old ruins faded farther and farther under the sands of the desert.

"Each year," Zia said, "the Hall of Ages grows longer to encompass our history. Up until the present."

I was so dazed I didn't even realize we'd reached the end of the hall until Sadie grabbed my arm.

In front of us stood a dais and on it an empty throne, a gilded wooden chair with a flail and a shepherd's crook carved in the back—the ancient symbols of the pharaoh.

On the step below the throne sat the oldest man I'd ever seen. His skin was like lunch-bag paper—brown, thin, and crinkled. White linen robes hung loosely off his small frame. A leopard skin was draped around his shoulders, and his hand shakily held a big wooden staff, which I was sure he was going to drop any minute. But weirdest of all, the glowing hieroglyphs in the air seemed to be coming *from him*. Multicolored symbols popped up all around him and floated away as if he were some sort of magic bubble machine.

At first I wasn't sure he was even alive. His milky eyes stared into space. Then he focused on me, and electricity coursed through my body.

He wasn't just looking at me. He was scanning me—reading my entire being.

Hide, something inside me said.

I didn't know where the voice came from, but my stomach clenched. My whole body tensed as if I were bracing for a hit, and the electrical feeling subsided.

The old man raised an eyebrow as if I'd surprised him. He glanced behind him and said something in a language I didn't recognize.

A second man stepped out of the shadows. I wanted to yelp. He was the guy who'd been with Zia in the British Museum—the one with the cream-colored robes and the forked beard.

The bearded man glared at Sadie and me.

"I am Desjardins," he said with a French accent. "My master, Chief Lector Iskandar, welcomes you to the House of Life."

I couldn't think what to say to that, so of course I asked a stupid question. "He's really old. Why isn't he sitting on the throne?"

Desjardins' nostrils flared, but the old dude, Iskandar, just chuckled, and said something else in that other language.

Desjardins translated stiffly: "The master says thank you for noticing; he is in fact *really* old. But the throne is for the pharaoh. It has been vacant since the fall of Egypt to Rome. It is...*comment dit-on?* Symbolic. The Chief Lector's role is to serve and protect the pharaoh. Therefore he sits at the foot of the throne."

I looked at Iskandar a little nervously. I wondered how many years he'd been sitting on that step. "If you...if he can understand English...what language is he speaking?"

Desjardins sniffed. "The Chief Lector understands many things. But he prefers to speak Alexandrian Greek, his birth tongue."

Sadie cleared her throat. "Sorry, his *birth* tongue? Wasn't Alexander the Great way back in the blue section, thousands of years ago? You make it sound like Lord Salamander is—"

"Lord *Iskandar*," Desjardins hissed. "Show respect!"

Something clicked in my mind: back in Brooklyn, Amos had talked about the magicians' law against summoning gods—a law made in Roman times by the Chief Lector... Iskandar. Surely it had to be a different guy. Maybe we were talking to Iskandar the XXVII or something.

The old man looked me in the eyes. He smiled, as if he knew exactly what I was thinking. He said something else in Greek, and Desjardins translated.

"The master says not to worry. You will not be held responsible for the past crimes of your family. At least, not until we have investigated you further."

"Gee...thanks," I said.

"Do not mock our generosity, boy," Desjardins warned. "Your father broke our most important law twice: once at Cleopatra's Needle, when he tried to summon the gods and your mother died assisting him. Then again at the British

Museum, when your father was foolish enough to use the Rosetta Stone itself. Now your uncle too is missing—"

"You know what's happened to Amos?" Sadie blurted out.

Desjardins scowled. "Not yet," he admitted.

"You have to find him!" Sadie cried. "Don't you have some sort of GPS magic or—"

"We are searching," Desjardins said. "But you cannot worry about Amos. You must stay here. You must be...trained."

I got the impression he was going to say a different word, something not as nice as *trained*.

Iskandar spoke directly to me. His tone sounded kindly.

"The master warns that the Demon Days begin tomorrow at sunset," Desjardins translated. "You must be kept safe."

"But we have to find our dad!" I said. "Dangerous gods are on the loose out there. We saw Serqet. And Set!"

At these names, Iskandar's expression tightened. He turned and gave Desjardins what sounded like an order. Desjardins protested. Iskandar repeated his statement.

Desjardins clearly didn't like it, but he bowed to his master. Then he turned toward me. "The Chief Lector wishes to hear your story."

So I told him, with Sadie jumping in whenever I stopped to take a breath. The funny thing was, we both left out certain things without planning to. We didn't mention Sadie's magic abilities, or the encounter with the *ba* who'd called me a king. It was like I literally *couldn't* mention those things. Whenever I tried, the voice inside my head whispered, *Not that part. Be silent.*

When I was done, I glanced at Zia. She said nothing, but she was studying me with a troubled expression.

Iskandar traced a circle on the step with the butt of his staff. More hieroglyphs popped into the air and floated away.

After several seconds, Desjardins seemed to grow impatient. He stepped forward and glared at us. "You are lying. That could not have been Set. He would need a powerful host to remain in this world. *Very* powerful."

"Look, you," Sadie said. "I don't know what all this rubbish is about hosts, but I saw Set with my own eyes. You were there at the British Museum—you must have done, too. And if Carter saw him in Phoenix, Arizona, then..." She looked at me doubtfully. "Then he's probably not crazy."

"Thanks, Sis," I mumbled, but Sadie was just getting started.

"And as for Serqet, she's real too! Our friend, my cat, Bast, died protecting us!"

"So," Desjardins said coldly, "you admit to consorting with gods. That makes our investigation much easier. Bast is not your *friend*. The gods caused the downfall of Egypt. It is forbidden to call on their powers. Magicians are sworn to keep the gods from interfering in the mortal world. We must use all our power to fight them."

"Bast said you were paranoid," Sadie added.

The magician clenched his fists, and the air tingled with the weird smell of ozone, like during a thunderstorm. The hairs on my neck stood straight up. Before anything bad could happen, Zia stepped in front of us.

"Lord Desjardins," she pleaded, "there *was* something

strange. When I ensnared the scorpion goddess, she re-formed almost instantly. I could not return her to the Duat, even with the Seven Ribbons. I could only break her hold on the host for a moment. Perhaps the rumors of other escapes—"

"What other escapes?" I asked.

She glanced at me reluctantly. "Other gods, *many* of them, released since last night from artifacts all over the world. Like a chain reaction—"

"Zia!" Desjardins snapped. "That information is not for sharing."

"Look," I said, "lord, sir, whatever—Bast warned us this would happen. She said Set would release more gods."

"Master," Zia pleaded, "if Ma'at is weakening, if Set is increasing chaos, perhaps that is why I could not banish Serqet."

"Ridiculous," Desjardins said. "You are skilled, Zia, but perhaps you were not skilled enough for this encounter. And as for these two, the contamination must be contained."

Zia's face reddened. She turned her attention to Iskandar. "Master, please. Give me a chance with them."

"You forget your place," Desjardins snapped. "These two are guilty and must be destroyed."

My throat started closing up. I looked at Sadie. If we had to make a run for it down that long hall, I didn't like our chances....

The old man finally looked up. He smiled at Zia with true affection. For a second I wondered if she were his great-great-great-granddaughter or something. He spoke in Greek, and Zia bowed deeply.

Desjardins looked ready to explode. He swept his robes away from his feet and marched behind the throne.

"The Chief Lector will allow Zia to test you," he growled. "Meanwhile, I will seek out the truth—or the lies—in your story. You will be punished for the lies."

I turned to Iskandar and copied Zia's bow. Sadie did the same.

"Thank you, master," I said.

The old man studied me for a long time. Again I felt as if he were trying to burn into my soul—not in an angry way. More out of concern. Then he mumbled something, and I understood two words: *Nectanebo* and *ba*.

He opened his hand and a flood of glowing hieroglyphs poured out, swarming around the dais. There was a blinding flash of light, and when I could see again, the dais was empty. The two men were gone.

Zia turned toward us, her expression grim. "I will show you to your quarters. In the morning, your testing begins. We will see what magic you know, and how you know it."

I wasn't sure what she meant by that, but I exchanged an uneasy look with Sadie.

"Sounds fun," Sadie ventured. "And if we fail this test?"

Zia regarded her coldly. "This is not the sort of test you fail, Sadie Kane. You pass or you die."

15. A Godly Birthday Party

THEY TOOK CARTER TO A DIFFERENT dormitory, so I don't know how he slept. But *I* couldn't get a wink.

It would've been hard enough with Zia's comments about passing our tests or dying, but the girls' dormitory just wasn't as posh as Amos's mansion. The stone walls sweated moisture. Creepy pictures of Egyptian monsters danced across the ceiling in the torchlight. I got a floating cot to sleep in, and the other girls in training—*initiates*, Zia had called them—were much younger than me, so when the old dorm matron told them to go to sleep straightaway, they actually *obeyed*. The matron waved her hand and the torches went out. She shut the door behind her, and I could hear the sound of locks clicking.

Lovely. Imprisoned in a nursery school dungeon.

I stared into the dark until I heard the other girls snoring. A single thought kept bothering me: an urge I just couldn't shake. Finally I crept out of bed and tugged on my boots.

I felt my way to the door. I tugged at the handle. Locked, as I suspected. I was tempted to kick it till I remembered what Zia had done in the Cairo Airport broom closet.

I pressed my palm against the door and whispered, *"Sahad."* Locks clicked. The door swung open. Handy trick.

Outside, the corridors were dark and empty. Apparently, there wasn't much nightlife in the First Nome. I sneaked through the city back the way we'd come and saw nothing but an occasional cobra slithering across the floor. After the last couple of days, that didn't even faze me. I thought about trying to find Carter, but I wasn't sure where they'd taken him, and honestly, I wanted to do this on my own.

After our last argument in New York, I wasn't sure how I felt about my brother. The idea that he could be jealous of *my* life while he got to travel the world with Dad—please! And he had the nerve to call my life *normal*? All right, I had a few mates at school like Liz and Emma, but my life was hardly easy. If Carter made a social faux pas or met people he didn't like, he could just move on! I had to stay put. I couldn't answer simple questions like "Where are your parents?" or "What does your family do?" or even "Where are you from?" without exposing just how odd my situation was. I was always the *different* girl. The mixed-race girl, the American who wasn't American, the girl whose mother had died, the girl with the absent father, the girl who made trouble in class, the girl who couldn't concentrate on her lessons. After a while one learns that blending in simply doesn't work. If people are going to single me out, I might as well give them something to stare at. Red stripes in my hair? Why not! Combat boots with the school uniform? Absolutely.

Headmaster says, "I'll have to call your parents, young lady." I say, "Good luck." Carter didn't know anything about my life.

But enough of that. The point was, I decided to do this particular bit of exploring alone, and after a few wrong turns, I found my way back to the Hall of Ages.

What was I up to, you may ask? I certainly didn't want to meet Monsieur Evil again or creepy old Lord Salamander.

But I *did* want to see those images—*memories*, Zia had called them.

I pushed open the bronze doors. Inside, the hall seemed deserted. No balls of fire floated around the ceiling. No glowing hieroglyphs. But images still shimmered between the columns, washing the hall with strange, multicolored light.

I took a few nervous steps.

I wanted another look at the Age of the Gods. On our first trip through the hall, something about those images had shaken me. I knew Carter thought I'd gone into a dangerous trance, and Zia had warned that the scenes would melt my brain; but I had a feeling she was just trying to scare me off. I felt a connection to those images, like there was an answer within—a vital piece of information I needed.

I stepped off the carpet and approached the curtain of golden light. I saw sand dunes shifting in the wind, storm clouds brewing, crocodiles sliding down the Nile. I saw a vast hall full of revelers. I touched the image.

And I was in the palace of the gods.

Huge beings swirled around me, changing shape from human to animal to pure energy. On a throne in the center of the room sat a muscular African man in rich black robes. He had a handsome face and warm brown eyes. His hands looked strong enough to crush rocks.

The other gods celebrated round him. Music played—a sound so powerful that the air burned. At the man's side stood a beautiful woman in white, her belly swollen as if she were a few months pregnant. Her form flickered; at times she seemed to have multicolored wings. Then she turned in my direction and I gasped. She had my mother's face.

She didn't seem to notice me. In fact, none of the gods did, until a voice behind me said, "Are you a ghost?"

I turned and saw a good-looking boy of about sixteen, dressed in black robes. His complexion was pale, but he had lovely brown eyes like the man on the throne. His black hair was long and tousled—rather wild, but it worked for me. He tilted his head, and it finally occurred to me that he'd asked me a question.

I tried to think of something to say. Excuse me? Hello? Marry me? Anything would've done. But all I could manage was a shake of the head.

"Not a ghost, eh?" he mused. "A *ba* then?" He gestured towards the throne. "Watch, but do not interfere."

Somehow I wasn't interested in watching the throne so much, but the boy in black dissolved into a shadow and disappeared, leaving me no further distraction.

"Isis," said the man on the throne.

The pregnant woman turned towards him and beamed. "My lord Osiris. Happy birthday."

"Thank you, my love. And soon we shall mark the birth

of our son—Horus, the great one! His new incarnation shall be his greatest yet. He shall bring peace and prosperity to the world."

Isis took her husband's hand. Music kept playing around them, gods celebrating, the very air swirling in a dance of creation.

Suddenly the palace doors blew open. A hot wind made the torches sputter.

A man strode into the hall. He was tall and strong, almost a twin to Osiris, but with dark red skin, blood-colored robes, and a pointed beard. He looked human, except when he smiled. Then his teeth turned to fangs. His face flickered—sometimes human, sometimes strangely wolflike. I had to stifle a scream, because I'd seen that wolfish face before.

The dancing stopped. The music died.

Osiris rose from his throne. "Set," he said in a dangerous tone. "Why have you come?"

Set laughed, and the tension in the room broke. Despite his cruel eyes, he had a wonderful laugh—nothing like the screeching he'd done at the British Museum. It was carefree and friendly, as if he couldn't possibly mean any harm.

"I come to celebrate my brother's birthday, of course!" he exclaimed. "And I bring entertainment!"

He gestured behind him. Four huge men with the heads of wolves marched into the room, carrying a jewel-encrusted golden coffin.

My heart began to race. It was the same box Set had used to imprison my dad at the British Museum.

No! I wanted to scream. *Don't trust him!*

But the assembled gods oohed and aahed, admiring the box, which was painted with gold and red hieroglyphs, trimmed with jade and opals. The wolf-men set down the box, and I saw it had no lid. The interior was lined with black linen.

"This sleeping casket," Set announced, "was made by my finest craftsmen, using the most expensive materials. Its value is beyond measure. The god who lies within, even for a night, will see his powers increase tenfold! His wisdom will never falter. His strength will never fail. It is a gift"—he smiled slyly at Osiris—"for the *one and only* god who fits within perfectly!"

I wouldn't have queued up first, but the gods surged forward. They pushed each other out of the way to get at the golden coffin. Some climbed in but were too short. Others were much too big. Even when they tried to change their shapes, the gods had no luck, as if the magic of the box were thwarting them. No one fit exactly. Gods grumbled and complained as others, anxious to try, pushed them to the floor.

Set turned to Osiris with a good-natured laugh. "Well, brother, we have no winner yet. Will you try? Only the best of the gods can succeed."

Osiris's eyes gleamed. Apparently he wasn't the god of brains, because he seemed completely taken in by the box's beauty. All the other gods looked at him expectantly, and I could see what he was thinking: if he fit in the box, what a brilliant birthday present. Even Set, his wicked brother, would have to admit that he was the rightful king of the gods.

Only Isis seemed troubled. She laid her hand on her husband's shoulder. "My lord, do not. Set does not bring presents."

"I am offended!" Set sounded genuinely hurt. "Can I not celebrate my brother's birthday? Are we so estranged that I cannot even apologize to the king?"

Osiris smiled at Isis. "My dear, it is only a game. Fear nothing."

He rose from his throne. The gods applauded as he approached the box.

"All hail Osiris!" Set cried.

The king of the gods lowered himself into the box, and when he glanced in my direction, just for a moment, he had my father's face.

No! I thought again. *Don't do it!*

But Osiris lay down. The coffin fit him exactly.

A cheer went up from the gods, but before Osiris could rise, Set clapped his hands. A golden lid materialized above the box and slammed down on top of it.

Osiris shouted in rage, but his cries were muffled.

Golden latches fastened around the lid. The other gods surged forward to intervene—even the boy in black I'd seen earlier reappeared—but Set was faster. He stamped his foot so hard, the stone floor trembled. The gods toppled over each other like dominoes. The wolf-men drew their spears, and the gods scrambled away in terror.

Set said a magic word, and a boiling cauldron appeared out of thin air. It poured its contents over the coffin—molten lead, coating the box, sealing it shut, probably heating the interior to a thousand degrees.

"Villain!" Isis wailed. She advanced on Set and began to speak a spell, but Set held up his hand. Isis rose from the floor, clawing at her mouth, her lips pressed as if an invisible force were suffocating her.

"Not today, lovely Isis," Set purred. "Today, I am king. And your child shall never be born!"

Suddenly, another goddess—a slender woman in a blue dress—charged out of the crowd. "Husband, no!"

She tackled Set, who momentarily lost his concentration. Isis fell to the floor, gasping. The other goddess yelled, "Flee!"

Isis turned and ran.

Set rose. I thought he would hit the goddess in blue, but he only snarled. "Foolish wife! Whose side are you on?"

He stamped his foot again, and the golden coffin sank into the floor.

Set raced after Isis. At the edge of the palace, Isis turned into a small bird of prey and soared into the air. Set sprouted demon's wings and launched himself in pursuit.

Then suddenly *I* was the bird. I was Isis, flying desperately over the Nile. I could sense Set behind me—closing. Closing.

You must escape, the voice of Isis said in my mind. *Avenge Osiris. Crown Horus king!*

Just when I thought my heart would burst, I felt a hand on my shoulder. The images evaporated.

The old master, Iskandar, stood next to me, his face pinched with concern. Glowing hieroglyphs danced round him.

"Forgive the interruption," he said in perfect English. "But you were almost dead."

That's when my knees turned to water, and I lost consciousness.

———

When I awoke, I was curled at Iskandar's feet on the steps below the empty throne. We were alone in the hall, which was mostly dark except for the light from the hieroglyphs that always seemed to glow around him.

"Welcome back," he said. "You're lucky you survived."

I wasn't so sure. My head felt like it had been boiled in oil.

"I'm sorry," I said. "I didn't mean to—"

"Look at the images? And yet you did. Your *ba* left your body and entered the past. Hadn't you been warned?"

"Yes," I admitted. "But...I was drawn to the pictures."

"*Mmm.*" Iskandar stared into space, as if remembering something from long ago. "They *are* hard to resist."

"You speak perfect English," I noticed.

Iskandar smiled. "How do you know I'm speaking English? Perhaps you are speaking Greek."

I hoped he was kidding, but I couldn't tell. He seemed so frail and warm, and yet...it was like sitting next to a nuclear reactor. I had a feeling he was full of more danger than I wanted to know.

"You're not really *that* old, are you?" I asked. "I mean, old enough to remember Ptolemaic times?"

"I am *exactly* that old, my dear. I was born in the reign of Cleopatra VII."

"Oh, please."

"I assure you, it's true. It was my sorrow to behold the last days of Egypt, before that foolhardy queen lost our kingdom to the Romans. I was the last magician to be trained before the House went underground. Many of our most powerful secrets were lost, including the spells my master used to extend my life.

Magicians these days still live long—sometimes centuries—but I have been alive for two millennia."

"So you're immortal?"

His chuckle turned into a racking cough. He doubled over and cupped his hands over his mouth. I wanted to help, but I wasn't sure how. The glowing hieroglyphs flickered and dimmed around him.

Finally the coughing subsided.

He took a shaky breath. "Hardly immortal, my dear. In fact..." His voice trailed off. "But never mind that. What did you see in your vision?"

I probably should've kept quiet. I didn't want to be turned into a bug for breaking any rules, and the vision had terrified me—especially the moment when I'd changed into the bird of prey. But Iskandar's kindly expression made it hard to hold back. I ended up telling him everything. Well, almost everything. I left out the bit about the good-looking boy, and yes, I know it was silly, but I was *embarrassed*. I reckoned that part could've been my own crazed imagination at work, as Ancient Egyptian gods could *not* have been that gorgeous.

Iskandar sat for a moment, tapping his staff against the steps. "You saw a very old event, Sadie—Set taking the throne of Egypt by force. He hid Osiris's coffin, you know, and Isis searched the entire world to find it."

"So she got him back eventually?"

"Not exactly. Osiris was resurrected—but only in the Underworld. He became the king of the dead. When their son, Horus, grew up, Horus challenged Set for the throne of Egypt and won after many hard battles. That is why Horus was called the Avenger. As I said—an old story, but one that the gods have repeated many times in our history."

"Repeated?"

"The gods follow patterns. In some ways they are quite predictable: acting out the same squabbles, the same jealousies down through the ages. Only the settings change, and the hosts."

There was that word again: *hosts.* I thought about the poor woman in the New York museum who'd turned into the goddess Serqet.

"In my vision," I said, "Isis and Osiris were married. Horus was about to be born as their son. But in another story Carter told me, all three of them were siblings, children of the sky goddess."

"Yes," Iskandar agreed. "This can be confusing for those who do not know the nature of gods. They cannot walk the earth in their pure form—at least, not for more than a few moments. They must have hosts."

"Humans, you mean."

"Or powerful objects, such as statues, amulets, monuments, certain models of cars. But they *prefer* human form. You see gods have great power, but only humans have creativity, the power to change history rather than simply repeat it. Humans can...how do you moderns say it...think outside the cup."

"The box," I suggested.

"Yes. The combination of human creativity and godly power can be quite formidable. At any rate, when Osiris and Isis first walked the earth, their hosts were brother and sister. But mortal hosts are not permanent. They die, they wear out.

Later in history, Osiris and Isis took new forms—humans who were husband and wife. Horus, who in one lifetime was their brother, was born into a new life as their son."

"That's confusing," I said. "And a little gross."

Iskandar shrugged. "The gods do not think of relationships the way we humans do. Their hosts are merely like changes of clothes. This is why the ancient stories seem so mixed up. Sometimes the gods are described as married, or siblings, or parent and child, depending on their hosts. The pharaoh himself was called a living god, you know. Egyptologists believe this was just a lot of propaganda, but in fact it was often literally true. The greatest of the pharaohs became hosts for gods, usually Horus. He gave them power and wisdom, and let them build Egypt into a mighty empire."

"But that's good, isn't it? Why is it against the law to host a god?"

Iskandar's face darkened. "Gods have different agendas than humans do, Sadie. They can overpower their hosts, literally burn them out. That is why so many hosts die young. Tutankhamen, poor boy, died at nineteen. Cleopatra VII was even worse. She tried to host the spirit of Isis without knowing what she was doing, and it shattered her mind. In the old days, the House of Life taught the use of divine magic. Initiates could study the path of Horus, or Isis, or Sekhmet, or any number of gods, learning to channel their powers. We had many more initiates back then."

Iskandar looked round the empty hall, as if imagining it filled with magicians. "Some adepts could call upon the gods only from time to time. Others attempted to host their spirits…with varying degrees of success. The ultimate goal was to become the 'eye' of the god—a perfect union of the two souls, mortal and immortal. Very few achieved this, even among the pharaohs, who were born to the task. Many destroyed themselves trying." He turned up his palm, which had the most deeply etched lifeline I'd ever seen. "When Egypt finally fell to the Romans, it became clear to us—to *me*—that mankind, our rulers, even the strongest magicians, no longer had the strength of will to master a god's power. The only ones who could…" His voice faltered.

"What?"

"Nothing, my dear. I talk too much. An old man's weakness."

"It's the blood of the pharaohs, isn't it?"

He fixed me in his gaze. His eyes no longer looked milky. They burned with intensity. "You are a remarkable young girl. You remind me of your mother."

My mouth fell open. "You knew her?"

"Of course. She trained here, as did your father. Your mother…well, aside from being a brilliant scientist, she had the gift of divination. One of the most difficult forms of magic, and she was the first in centuries to possess it."

"Divination?"

"Seeing the future. Tricky business, never perfect, but she saw things that made her seek advice from…*unconventional* places, things that made even *this* old man question some long-held beliefs…"

He drifted off into Memoryland again, which was infuriating enough when my grandparents did it, but when it's an all-powerful magician who has valuable information, it's enough to drive one mad.

"Iskandar?"

He looked at me with mild surprise, as if he'd forgotten I was there. "I'm sorry, Sadie. I should come to the point: you have a hard path ahead of you, but I'm convinced now it's a path you must take, for all our sakes. Your brother will need your guidance."

I was tempted to laugh. "Carter, need my guidance? For what? What path do you mean?"

"All in good time. Things must take their course."

Typical adult answer. I tried to bite back my frustration. "And what if I need guidance?"

"Zia," he said, without hesitation. "She is my best pupil, and she is wise. When the time comes, she will know how to help you."

"Right," I said, a bit disappointed. "Zia."

"For now you should rest, my dear. And it seems I, too, can rest at last." He sounded sad but relieved. I didn't know what he was talking about, but he didn't give me the chance to ask.

"I am sorry our time together was so brief," he said. "Sleep well, Sadie Kane."

"But—"

Iskandar touched my forehead. And I fell into a deep, dreamless sleep.

16. How Zia Lost Her Eyebrows

S
A
D
I
E

I WOKE TO A BUCKET OF ICE WATER IN MY FACE.

"Sadie! Get up," Zia said.

"God!" I yelled. "Was that *necessary?*"

"No," Zia admitted.

I wanted to strangle her, except I was dripping wet, shivering, and still disoriented. How long had I slept? It felt like only a few minutes, but the dormitory was empty. All the other cots were made. The girls must've already gone to their morning lessons.

Zia tossed me a towel and some fresh linen clothes. "We'll meet Carter in the cleansing room."

"I just *got* a bath, thanks very much. What I need is a proper breakfast."

"The cleansing prepares you for magic." Zia slung her bag of tricks over her shoulder and unfolded the long black staff she'd used in New York. "If you survive, we'll see about food."

I was tired of being reminded that I might die, but I got dressed and followed her out.

After another endless series of tunnels, we came to a chamber with a roaring waterfall. There was no ceiling, just a shaft above us that seemed to go up forever. Water fell from the darkness into a fountain, splashing over a five-meter-tall statue of that bird-headed god. What was his name—Tooth? No, Thoth. The water cascaded over his head, collected in his palms, then spilled out into the pool.

Carter stood beside the fountain. He was dressed in linen with Dad's workbag over one shoulder and his sword strapped to his back. His hair was rumpled, as if he hadn't slept well. At least he hadn't been doused in ice water. Seeing him, I felt a strange sense of relief. I thought about Iskandar's words last night: *Your brother will need your guidance.*

"What?" Carter asked. "You're staring at me funny."

"Nothing," I said quickly. "How'd you sleep?"

"Badly. I'll . . . I'll tell you about it later."

Was it my imagination, or did he frown in Zia's direction? *Hmm,* possible romantic trouble between Miss Magic and my brother? I made a mental note to interrogate him next time we were alone.

Zia went to a nearby cabinet. She brought out two ceramic cups, dipped them into the fountain, then offered them to us. "Drink."

I glanced at Carter. "After you."

"It's only water," Zia assured me, "but purified by contact with Thoth. It will focus your mind."

I didn't see how a statue could purify water. Then I

remembered what Iskandar had said, how gods could inhabit anything.

I took a drink. Immediately I felt like I'd had a good strong cup of Gran's tea. My brain buzzed. My eyesight sharpened. I felt so hyperactive, I almost didn't miss my chewing gum—almost.

Carter sipped from his cup. "Wow."

"Now the tattoos," Zia announced.

"Brilliant!" I said.

"On your tongue," she added.

"Excuse me?"

Zia stuck out her tongue. Right in the middle was a blue hieroglyph.

"Nith ith Naat," she tried to say with her tongue out. Then she realized her mistake and stuck her tongue back in. "I mean, this is Ma'at, the symbol of order and harmony. It will help you speak magic clearly. One mistake with a spell—"

"Let me guess," I said. "We'll die."

From her cabinet of horrors, Zia produced a fine-tipped paintbrush and a bowl of blue dye. "It doesn't hurt. And it's not permanent."

"How does it taste?" Carter wondered.

Zia smiled. "Stick out your tongue."

To answer Carter's question, the tattoo tasted like burning car tires.

"*Ugh.*" I spit a blue gob of "order and harmony" into the fountain. "Never mind breakfast. Lost my appetite."

Zia pulled a leather satchel out of the cabinet. "Carter will be allowed to keep your father's magic implements, plus a new staff and wand. Generally speaking, the wand is for defense, the staff is for offense, although, Carter, you may prefer to use your *khopesh*."

"*Khopesh?*"

"The curved sword," Zia said. "A favored weapon of the pharaoh's guard. It can be used in combat magic. As for Sadie, you will need a full kit."

"How come *he* gets Dad's kit?" I complained.

"He is the eldest," she said, as if that explained everything. Typical.

Zia tossed me the leather satchel. Inside was an ivory wand, a rod that I supposed turned into a staff, some paper, an ink set, a bit of twine, and a lovely chunk of wax. I was less than thrilled.

"What about a little wax man?" I asked. "I want a Doughboy."

"If you mean a figurine, you must make one yourself. You will be taught how, if you have the skill. We will determine your specialty later."

"Specialty?" Carter asked. "You mean like Nectanebo specialized in statues?"

Zia nodded. "Nectanebo was extremely skilled in statuary magic. He could make *shabti* so lifelike, they could pass for human. No one has ever been greater at statuary...except perhaps Iskandar. But there are many other disciplines: Healer. Amulet maker. Animal charmer. Elementalist. Combat magician. Necromancer."

"Diviner?" I asked.

Zia looked at me curiously. "Yes, although that is quite rare. Why do you—"

I cleared my throat. "So how do we know our specialty?"

"It will become clear soon enough," Zia promised, "but a good magician knows a bit of everything, which is why we start with a basic test. Let us go to the library."

The First Nome's library was like Amos's, but a hundred times bigger, with circular rooms lined with honeycomb shelves that seemed to go on forever, like the world's largest beehive. Clay *shabti* statues kept popping in and out, retrieving scroll canisters and disappearing, but we saw no other people.

Zia brought us to a wooden table and spread out a long, blank papyrus scroll. She picked up a stylus and dipped it in ink.

"The Egyptian word *shesh* means scribe or writer, but it can also mean magician. This is because magic, at its most basic, turns words into reality. You will create a scroll. Using your own magic, you will send power into the words on paper. When spoken, the words will unleash the magic."

She handed the stylus to Carter.

"I don't get it," he protested.

"A simple word," she suggested. "It can be anything."

"In English?"

Zia curled her lip. "If you must. Any language will work, but hieroglyphics are best. They are the language of creation, of magic, of Ma'at. You must be careful, however."

Before she could explain, Carter drew a simple hieroglyph of a bird.

The picture wriggled, peeled itself off the papyrus, and flew away. It splattered Carter's head with some hieroglyphic droppings on its way out. I couldn't help laughing at Carter's expression.

"A beginner's mistake," Zia said, scowling at me to be quiet. "If you use a symbol that stands for something alive, it is wise to write it only partially—leave off a wing, or the legs. Otherwise the magic you channel could make it come alive."

"And poop on its creator." Carter sighed, wiping off his hair with a bit of scrap papyrus. "That's why our father's wax statue, Doughboy, has no legs, right?"

"The same principle," Zia agreed. "Now, try again."

Carter stared at Zia's staff, which was covered in hieroglyphics. He picked the most obvious one and copied it on the papyrus—the symbol for fire.

Uh-oh, I thought. But the word did not come alive, which would've been rather exciting. It simply dissolved.

"Keep trying," Zia urged.

"Why am I so tired?" Carter wondered.

He definitely looked exhausted. His face was beaded with sweat.

"You're channeling magic from within," Zia said. "For me, fire is easy. But it may not be the most natural type of magic for you. Try something else. Summon...summon a sword."

Zia showed him how to form the hieroglyph, and Carter wrote it on the papyrus. Nothing happened.

"Speak it," Zia said.

"Sword," Carter said. The word glowed and vanished, and a butter knife lay on the papyrus.

I laughed. "Terrifying!"

Carter looked like he was about to pass out, but he managed

a grin. He picked up the knife and threatened to poke me with it.

"Very good for a first time," Zia said. "Remember, you are not creating the knife yourself. You are summoning it from Ma'at—the creative power of the universe. Hieroglyphs are the code we use. That's why they are called Divine Words. The more powerful the magician, the easier it becomes to control the language."

I caught my breath. "Those hieroglyphs floating in the Hall of Ages. They seemed to gather around Iskandar. Was he summoning them?"

"Not exactly," Zia said. "His presence is so strong, he makes the language of the universe visible simply by being in the room. No matter what our specialty, each magician's greatest hope is to become a speaker of the Divine Words—to know the language of creation so well that we can fashion reality simply by speaking, not even using a scroll."

"Like saying *shatter*," I ventured. "And having a door explode."

Zia scowled. "Yes, but such a thing would take years of practice."

"Really? Well—"

Out of the corner of my eye, I saw Carter shaking his head, silently warning me to shut up.

"*Um . . .*" I stammered. "Some day, I'll learn to do that."

Zia raised an eyebrow. "First, master the scroll."

I was getting tired of her attitude, so I picked up the stylus and wrote *Fire* in English.

Zia leaned forward and frowned. "You shouldn't—"

Before she could finish, a column of flame erupted in her face. I screamed, sure I'd done something horrible, but when the fire died Zia was still there, looking astonished, her eyebrows singed and her bangs smoldering.

"Oh, god," I said. "Sorry, sorry. Do I die now?"

For three heartbeats, Zia stared at me.

"Now," she announced. "I think you are ready to duel."

We used another magic gateway, which Zia summoned right on the library wall. We stepped into a circle of swirling sand and popped out the other side, covered in dust and grit, in the front of some ruins. The harsh sunlight almost blinded me.

"I hate portals," Carter muttered, brushing the sand out of his hair.

Then he looked around and his eyes widened. "This is Luxor! That's, like, hundreds of miles south of Cairo."

I sighed. "And that amazes you after teleporting from New York?"

He was too busy checking out our surroundings to answer.

I suppose the ruins were all right, though once you've seen one pile of crumbly Egyptian stuff, you've seen them all, I say. We stood on a wide avenue flanked by human-headed beasties, most of which were broken. The road went on behind us as far as I could see, but in front of us it ended at a temple much bigger than the one in the New York museum.

The walls were at least six stories high. Big stone pharaohs stood guard on either side of the entrance, and a single obelisk stood on the left-hand side. It looked as if one used to stand on the right as well, but it was now gone.

"Luxor is a modern name," Zia said. "This was once the city of Thebes. This temple was one of the most important in Egypt. It is the best place for us to practice."

"Because it's already destroyed?" I asked.

Zia gave me one of her famous scowls. "No, Sadie—because it is still full of magic. And it was sacred to your family."

"Our family?" Carter asked.

Zia didn't explain, as usual. She just gestured for us to follow.

"I don't like those ugly sphinxes," I mumbled as we walked down the path.

"Those ugly sphinxes are creatures of law and order," Zia said, "protectors of Egypt. They are on *our* side."

"If you say so."

Carter nudged me as we passed the obelisk. "You know the missing one is in Paris."

I rolled my eyes. "Thank you, Mr. Wikipedia. I thought they were in New York and London."

"That's a different pair," Carter said, like I was supposed to care. "The other *Luxor* obelisk is in Paris."

"Wish I was in Paris," I said. "Lot better than this place."

We walked into a dusty courtyard surrounded by crumbling pillars and statues with various missing body parts. Still, I could tell the place had once been quite impressive.

"Where are the people?" I asked. "Middle of the day, winter holidays. Shouldn't there be loads of tourists?"

Zia made a distasteful expression. "Usually, yes. I have encouraged them to stay away for a few hours."

"How?"

"Common minds are easy to manipulate." She looked pointedly at me, and I remembered how she'd forced me to talk in the New York museum. Oh, yes, she was just *begging* for more scorched eyebrows.

"Now, to the duel." She summoned her staff and drew two circles in the sand about ten meters apart. She directed me to stand in one of them and Carter in the other.

"I've got to duel *him*?" I asked.

I found the idea preposterous. The only thing Carter had shown aptitude for was summoning butter knives and pooping birds. Well, all right, and that bit on the chasm bridge deflecting the daggers, but still—what if I hurt him? As annoying as Carter might be, I didn't want to accidentally summon that glyph I'd made in Amos's house and explode him to bits.

Perhaps Carter was thinking the same thing, because he'd started to sweat. "What if we do something wrong?" he asked.

"I will oversee the duel," Zia promised. "We will start slowly. The first magician to knock the other out of his or her circle wins."

"But we haven't been trained!" I protested.

"One learns by doing," Zia said. "This is not school, Sadie. You cannot learn magic by sitting at a desk and taking notes. You can only learn magic by doing magic."

"But—"

"Summon whatever power you can," Zia said. "Use whatever you have available. Begin!"

I looked at Carter doubtfully. *Use whatever I have?* I opened the leather satchel and looked inside. A lump of wax? Probably not. I drew the wand and rod. Immediately, the rod expanded until I was holding a two-meter-long white staff.

Carter drew his sword, though I couldn't imagine what he'd do with it. Rather hard to hit me from ten meters away.

I wanted this over, so I raised my staff like I'd seen Zia do. I thought the word *Fire*.

A small flame sputtered to life on the end of the staff. I willed it to get bigger. The fire momentarily brightened, but then my eyesight went fuzzy. The flame died. I fell to my knees, feeling as if I'd run a marathon.

"You okay?" Carter called.

"No," I complained.

"If she knocks herself out, do I win?" he asked.

"Shut up!" I said.

"Sadie, you must be careful," Zia called. "You drew from your own reserves, not from the staff. You can quickly deplete your magic."

I got shakily to my feet. "Explain?"

"A magician begins a duel full of magic, the way you might be full after a good meal—"

"Which I never got," I reminded her.

"Each time you do magic," Zia continued, "you expend energy. You can draw energy from *yourself*, but you must know your limits. Otherwise you could exhaust yourself, or worse."

I swallowed and looked at my smoldering staff. "How much worse?"

"You could literally burn up."

I hesitated, thinking how to ask my next question without saying too much. "But I've done magic before. Sometimes it doesn't exhaust me. Why?"

From around her neck, Zia unclasped an amulet. She threw it into the air, and with a flash it turned into a giant vulture. The massive black bird soared over the ruins. As soon as it was out of sight, Zia extended her hand and the amulet appeared in her palm.

"Magic can be drawn from many sources," she said. "It can be stored in scrolls, wands, or staffs. Amulets are especially powerful. Magic can also be drawn straight from Ma'at, using the Divine Words, but this is difficult. Or"—she locked eyes with me—"it can be summoned from the gods."

"Why are you looking at me?" I demanded. "I didn't summon any gods. They just seem to *find* me!"

She put on her necklace but said nothing.

"Hold on," Carter said. "You claimed this place was sacred to our family."

"It was," Zia agreed.

"But wasn't this . . ." Carter frowned. "Didn't the pharaohs have a yearly festival here or something?"

"Indeed," she said. "The pharaoh would walk down the processional path all the way from Karnak to Luxor. He would enter the temple and become one with the gods. Sometimes, this was purely ceremonial. Sometimes, with the great pharaohs like Ramesses, here—" Zia pointed to one of the huge crumbling statues.

"They actually hosted the gods," I interrupted, remembering what Iskandar had said.

Zia narrowed her eyes. "And yet you claim to know nothing of your family's past."

"Wait a second," Carter protested. "You're saying we're related to—"

"The gods choose their hosts carefully," Zia said. "They always prefer the blood of the pharaohs. When a magician has the blood of *two* royal families…"

I exchanged looks with Carter. Something Bast said came back to me: "Your family was born to magic." And Amos had told us that both sides of our family had a complicated history with the gods, and that Carter and I were the most powerful children to be born in centuries. A bad feeling settled over me, like an itchy blanket prickling against my skin.

"Our parents were from different royal lines," I said. "Dad …he must've been descended from Narmer, the first pharaoh. I told you he looked like that picture!"

"That's not possible," Carter said. "That was five thousand years ago." But I could see his mind was racing. "Then the Fausts…" He turned to Zia. "Ramesses the Great built this courtyard. You're telling me our mom's family is descended from him?"

Zia sighed. "Don't tell me your parents kept this from you. Why do you think you are so dangerous to us?"

"You think we're hosting gods," I said, absolutely stunned. "That's what you're worried about—just because of something our great-times-a-thousand grandparents did? That's completely daft."

"Then prove it!" Zia said. "Duel, and show me how weak your magic is!"

She turned her back on us, as if we were completely unimportant.

Something inside me snapped. I'd had the worst two days ever. I'd lost my father, my home, and my cat, been attacked by monsters and had ice water dumped on my head. Now this *witch* was turning her back on me. She didn't want to train us. She wanted to see how dangerous we were.

Well, fine.

"Um, Sadie?" Carter called. He must've seen from my expression that I was beyond reason.

I focused on my staff. *Maybe not fire. Cats have always liked me. Maybe . . .*

I threw my staff straight at Zia. It hit the ground at her heels and immediately transformed into a snarling she-lion. Zia whirled in surprise, but then everything went wrong.

The lion turned and charged at Carter, as if she knew I was supposed to be dueling him.

I had a split second to think: *What have I done?*

Then the cat lunged . . . and Carter's form flickered. He rose off the ground, surrounded by a golden holographic shell like the one Bast had used, except that his giant image was a warrior with the head of a falcon. Carter swung his sword, and the falcon warrior did likewise, slicing the lion with a shimmering blade of energy. The cat dissolved in midair, and my staff clattered to the ground, cut neatly in half.

Carter's avatar shimmered, then disappeared. He dropped to the ground and grinned. "Fun."

He didn't even look tired. Once I got over my relief that

I hadn't killed him, I realized I didn't feel tired either. If anything, I had *more* energy.

I turned defiantly to Zia. "Well? Better, right?"

Her face was ashen. "The falcon. He—he summoned—"

Before she could finish, footsteps pounded on the stones. A young initiate raced into the courtyard, looking panicked. Tears streaked his dusty face. He said something to Zia in hurried Arabic. When Zia got his message, she sat down hard in the sand. She covered her face and began to tremble.

Carter and I left our dueling circles and ran to her.

"Zia?" Carter said. "What's wrong?"

She took a deep breath, trying to gather her composure. When she looked up, her eyes were red. She said something to the adept, who nodded and ran back the way he'd come.

"News from the First Nome," she said shakily. "Iskandar..." Her voice broke.

I felt as if a giant fist had punched me in the stomach. I thought about Iskandar's strange words last night: *It seems I, too, can rest at last.* "He's dead, isn't he? That's what he meant."

Zia stared at me. "What do you mean: 'That's what he meant'?"

"I..." I was about to say that I'd spoken with Iskandar the night before. Then I realized this might not be a good thing to mention. "Nothing. How did it happen?"

"In his sleep," Zia said. "He—he had been ailing for years, of course. But still..."

"It's okay," Carter said. "I know he was important to you."

She wiped at her tears, then rose unsteadily. "You don't

understand. Desjardins is next in line. As soon as he is named Chief Lector, he will order you executed."

"But we haven't done anything!" I said.

Zia's eyes flashed with anger. "You still don't realize how dangerous you are? You are hosting gods."

"Ridiculous," I insisted, but an uneasy feeling was building inside me. If it were true…no, it couldn't be! Besides, how could anyone, even a poxy old nutter like Desjardins, seriously execute children for something they weren't even aware of?

"He will order me to bring you in," Zia warned, "and I will have to obey."

"You can't!" Carter cried. "You *saw* what happened in the museum. We're not the problem. Set is. And if Desjardins isn't taking that seriously…well, maybe he's part of the problem too."

Zia gripped her staff. I was sure she was going to fry us with a fireball, but she hesitated.

"Zia." I decided to take a risk. "Iskandar talked with me last night. He caught me sneaking around the Hall of Ages."

She looked at me in shock. I reckoned I had only seconds before that shock turned to anger.

"He said you were his best pupil," I recalled. "He said you were wise. He also said Carter and I have a difficult path ahead of us, and you would know how to help us when the time came."

Her staff smoldered. Her eyes reminded me of glass about to shatter.

"Desjardins will kill us," I persisted. "Do you think that's what Iskandar had in mind?"

I counted to five, six, seven. Just when I was sure she was going to blast us, she lowered her staff. "Use the obelisk."

"What?" I asked.

"The obelisk at the entrance, fool! You have five minutes, perhaps less, before Desjardins sends orders for your execution. Flee, and destroy Set. The Demon Days begin at sundown. All portals will stop working. You need to get as close as possible to Set before that happens."

"Hold on," I said. "I meant you should come with us and help us! We can't even use an obelisk, much less destroy Set!"

"I cannot betray the House," she said. "You have four minutes now. If you can't operate the obelisk, you'll die."

That was enough incentive for me. I started to drag Carter off, but Zia called: "Sadie?"

When I looked back, Zia's eyes were full of bitterness.

"Desjardins will order me to hunt you down," she warned. "Do you understand?"

Unfortunately, I did. The next time we met, we would be enemies.

I grabbed Carter's hand and ran.

C
A
R
T
E
R

17. A Bad Trip to Paris

OKAY, BEFORE I GET TO THE demon fruit bats, I should back up.

The night before we fled Luxor, I didn't get much sleep—first because of an out-of-body experience, then a run-in with Zia. [Stop smirking, Sadie. It wasn't a *good* run-in.]

After lights out, I tried to sleep. Honest. I even used the stupid magic headrest they gave me instead of a pillow, but it didn't help. As soon as I managed to shut my eyes, my *ba* decided to take a little trip.

Just like before, I felt myself floating above my body, taking on a winged form. Then the current of the Duat swept me away at blurring speed. When my vision cleared, I found myself in a dark cavern. Uncle Amos was sneaking through it, finding his way with a faint blue light that flickered on the top of his staff. I wanted to call to him, but my voice didn't work. I'm not sure how he could miss me, floating a few feet away in glowing chicken form, but apparently I was invisible to him.

He stepped forward and the ground at his feet suddenly blazed to life with a red hieroglyph. Amos cried out, but his mouth froze half open. Coils of light wrapped around his legs like vines. Soon red tendrils completely entwined him, and Amos stood petrified, his unblinking eyes staring straight ahead.

I tried to fly to him, but I was stuck in place, floating helplessly, so I could only observe.

Laughter echoed through the cavern. A horde of *things* emerged from the darkness—toad creatures, animal-headed demons, and even stranger monsters half hidden in the gloom. They'd been lying in ambush, I realized—waiting for Amos. In front of them appeared a fiery silhouette—Set, but his form was much clearer now, and this time it wasn't human. His body was emaciated, slimy, and black, and his head was that of a feral beast.

"*Bon soir*, Amos," Set said. "How nice of you to come. We're going to have so much fun!"

I sat bolt upright in bed, back in my own body, with my heart pounding.

Amos had been captured. I knew it for certain. And even worse...Set had known somehow that Amos was coming. I thought back to something Bast had said, about how the serpopards had broken in to the mansion. She'd said the defenses had been sabotaged, and only a magician of the House could've done it. A horrible suspicion started building inside me.

I stared into the dark for a long time, listening to the little kid next to me mumbling spells in his sleep. When I couldn't stand it any longer, I opened the door with a push of my mind, the way I'd done at Amos's mansion, and I sneaked out.

I was wandering through the empty marketplace, thinking about Dad and Amos, replaying the events over and over, trying to figure out what I could've done differently to save them, when I spotted Zia.

She was hurrying across the courtyard as if she were being chased, but what really caught my attention was the shimmering black cloud around her, as if someone had wrapped her in a glittery shadow. She came to a section of blank wall and waved her hand. Suddenly a doorway appeared. Zia glanced nervously behind her and ducked inside.

Of course I followed.

I moved quietly up to the doorway. I could hear Zia's voice inside, but I couldn't make out what she was saying. Then the doorway began to solidify, turning back into a wall, and I made a split-second decision. I jumped through.

Inside, Zia was alone with her back to me. She was kneeling at a stone altar, chanting something under her breath. The walls were decorated with Ancient Egyptian drawings and modern photographs.

The glittery shadow no longer surrounded Zia, but something even stranger was happening. I'd been planning to tell Zia about my nightmare, but that went completely out of my thoughts when I saw what she was doing. She cupped her palms, the way you might hold a bird, and a glowing blue sphere appeared, about the size of a golf ball. Still chanting, she raised her hands. The sphere flew up, straight through the ceiling, and vanished.

Some instinct told me this was *not* something I was sup-posed to see.

I thought about backing out of the room. Only problem: the door was gone. No other exits. It was only a matter of time before—*Uh-oh.*

Maybe I'd made a noise. Maybe her magical senses had kicked in. But faster than I could react, Zia pulled her wand and turned on me, flames flickering down the edge of the boomerang.

"Hi," I said nervously.

Her expression turned from anger to surprise, then back to anger. "Carter, what are you doing here?"

"Just walking around. I saw you in the courtyard, so—"

"What do you mean you *saw* me?"

"Well...you were running, and you had this black shim-mery stuff around you, and—"

"You *saw* that? Impossible."

"Why? What was it?"

She dropped her wand and the fire died. "I don't appreciate being followed, Carter."

"Sorry. I thought you might be in trouble."

She started to say something, but apparently changed her mind. "In trouble...that's true enough."

She sat down heavily and sighed. In the candlelight, her amber eyes looked dark and sad.

She stared at the photos behind the altar, and I realized she was in some of them. There she was as a little girl, stand-ing barefoot outside a mud-brick house, squinting resentfully at the camera as if she didn't want her picture taken. Next to that, a wider shot showed a whole village on the Nile—the kind of place my dad took me to sometimes, where nothing had changed much in the last two thousand years. A crowd of villagers grinned and waved at the camera as if they were celebrating, and above them little Zia rode on the shoulders of a man who must've been her father. Another photo was a family shot: Zia holding hands with her mother and father. They could've been any *fellahin* family anywhere in Egypt, but her dad had especially kindly, twinkling eyes—I thought he must have a good sense of humor. Her mom's face was unveiled, and she laughed as if her husband had just cracked a joke.

"Your folks look cool," I said. "Is that home?"

Zia seemed like she wanted to get angry, but she kept her emotions under control. Or maybe she just didn't have the energy. "It *was* my home. The village no longer exists."

I waited, not sure I dared to ask. We locked eyes, and I could tell she was deciding how much to tell me.

"My father was a farmer," she said, "but he also worked for archaeologists. In his spare time he'd scour the desert for artifacts and new sites where they might want to dig."

I nodded. What Zia described was pretty common. Egyptians have been making extra money that way for centuries.

"One night when I was eight, my father found a statue," she said. "Small but very rare: a statue of a monster, carved from red stone. It had been buried in a pit with a lot of other statues that were all smashed. But somehow this one survived. He brought it home. He didn't know... He didn't realize magicians imprison monsters and spirits inside such statues, and break them to destroy their essence. My father brought the unbroken statue into our village, and…and accidentally unleashed…"

Her voice faltered. She stared at the picture of her father smiling and holding her hand.

"Zia, I'm sorry."

She knit her eyebrows. "Iskandar found me. He and the other magicians destroyed the monster…but not in time. They found me curled in a fire pit under some reeds where my mother had hidden me. I was the only survivor."

I tried to imagine how Zia would've looked when Iskandar found her—a little girl who'd lost everything, alone in the ruins of her village. It was hard to picture her that way.

"So this room is a shrine to your family," I guessed. "You come here to remember them."

Zia looked at me blankly. "That's the problem, Carter. I *can't* remember. Iskandar tells me about my past. He gave me these pictures, explained what happened. But…I have no memory at all."

I was about to say, "You were only eight." Then I realized I'd been the same age when my mom died, when Sadie and I were split up. I remembered all of that so clearly. I could still see our house in Los Angeles and the way the stars looked at night from our back porch overlooking the ocean. My dad would tell us wild stories about the constellations. Then every night before bed, Sadie and I would cuddle up with Mom on the sofa, fighting for her attention, and she'd tell us not to believe a word of Dad's stories. She'd explain the science behind the stars, talk about physics and chemistry as if we were her college students. Looking back on it, I wondered if she'd been trying to warn us: Don't believe in those gods and myths. They're too dangerous.

I remembered our last trip to London as a family, how nervous Mom and Dad seemed on the plane. I remembered our dad coming back to our grandparents' flat after Mom had died, and telling us there had been an accident. Even before he explained, I knew it was bad, because I'd never seen my dad cry before.

The little details that *did* fade drove me crazy—like the smell of Mom's perfume, or the way her voice sounded. The older I got, the harder I held on to those things. I couldn't imagine not remembering anything. How could Zia stand it?

"Maybe..." I struggled to find the right words. "Maybe you just—"

She held up her hand. "Carter, believe me. I've tried to remember. It's no use. Iskandar is the only family I've ever had."

"What about friends?"

Zia stared at me as if I'd used a foreign term. I realized I hadn't seen anyone close to our age in the First Nome. Everyone was either much younger or much older.

"I don't have time for friends," she said. "Besides, when initiates turn thirteen, they're assigned to other nomes around the world. I am the only one who stayed here. I like being alone. It's fine."

The hairs stood up on the back of my neck. I'd said almost the same thing, many times, when people asked me what it was like being homeschooled by my dad. Didn't I miss having friends? Didn't I want a normal life? "I like being alone. It's fine."

I tried to picture Zia going to a regular public high school, learning a locker combination, hanging out in the cafeteria. I couldn't picture it. I imagined she would be as lost as I would.

"Tell you what," I said. "After the testing, after the Demon Days, when things settle down—"

"Things won't settle down."

"—I'm going to take you to the mall."

She blinked. "The mall? For what reason?"

"To hang out," I said. "We'll get some hamburgers. See a movie."

Zia hesitated. "Is this what you'd call a 'date'?"

My expression must've been priceless, because Zia actually cracked a smile. "You look like a cow hit with a shovel."

"I didn't mean...I just meant..."

She laughed, and suddenly it was easier to imagine her as a regular high school kid.

"I will look forward to this *mall*, Carter," she said. "You are either a very interesting person...or a very dangerous one."

"Let's go with interesting."

She waved her hand, and the door reappeared. "Go now. And be careful. The next time you sneak up on me, you might not be so fortunate."

At the doorway, I turned. "Zia, what was that black shimmery stuff?"

Her smile faded. "An invisibility spell. Only very powerful magicians are able to see through it. *You* should not have."

She stared at me for answers, but I didn't have any.

"Maybe it was...wearing off or something," I managed. "And, can I ask, the blue sphere?"

She frowned. "The what?"

"The thing you released that went into the ceiling."

She looked mystified. "I . . . I don't know what you mean. Perhaps the candlelight was playing tricks on your eyes."

Awkward silence. Either she was lying to me, or I was going crazy, or . . . I didn't know what. I realized I hadn't told her about my vision of Amos and Set, but I felt that I'd already pushed her as far as I could for one night.

"Okay," I said. "Good night."

I made my way back to the dorm, but I didn't get to sleep again for a long time.

Fast-forward to Luxor. Maybe now you understand why I didn't want to leave Zia behind, and why I didn't believe Zia would actually hurt us.

On the other hand, I knew she wasn't lying about Desjardins. That guy wouldn't think twice about turning us into escargots. And the fact that Set had spoken French in my dream—"*Bon soir*, Amos." Was that just a coincidence . . . or was something a *lot* worse going on?

Anyway, when Sadie tugged on my arm, I followed.

We ran out of the temple and headed for the obelisk. But naturally, it wasn't that simple. We're the Kane family. Nothing is *ever* that simple.

Just as we reached the obelisk, I heard the *slish*-ing sound of a magic portal. About a hundred yards down the path, a bald magician in white robes stepped out of a whirling sand vortex.

"Hurry," I told Sadie. I grabbed the staff-rod from my bag

and threw it to her. "Since I cut yours in half. I'll stick with the sword."

"But I don't know what I'm doing!" she protested, searching the obelisk's base as if she hoped to find a secret switch.

The magician regained his balance and spit the sand out of his mouth. Then he spotted us. "Stop!"

"Yeah," I muttered. "That's gonna happen."

"Paris." Sadie turned to me. "You said the other obelisk is in Paris, right?"

"Right. *Um*, not to rush you, but..."

The magician raised his staff and started chanting.

I fumbled for the hilt of my sword. My legs felt like they were turning to butter. I wondered if I could pull off that hawk warrior thing again. That had been cool, but it had also been just a duel. And the test at the chasm bridge, when I'd deflected those daggers—that hadn't seemed like *me*. Every time I'd drawn this sword so far, I'd had help: Zia had been there, or Bast. I'd never felt completely alone. This time, it was just me. I was crazy to think I could hold off a full-fledged magician. I was no warrior. Everything I knew about swords came from reading books—the history of Alexander the Great, *The Three Musketeers*—as if that could help! With Sadie occupied at the obelisk, I was on my own.

No you're not, said a voice inside me.

Great, I thought. *I'm on my own* and *going crazy*.

At the far end of the avenue, the magician called out: "Serve the House of Life!"

But I got the feeling he wasn't talking to me.

The air between us began to shimmer. Waves of heat flowed from the double lines of sphinxes, making them look as if they were moving. Then I realized they *were* moving. Each one cracked down the middle, and ghostly apparitions appeared from the stone like locusts breaking out of their shells. Not all of them were in good shape. The spirit creatures from broken statues had missing heads or feet. Some limped along on only three legs. But at least a dozen attack sphinxes were in perfect condition, and they all came toward us—each one the size of a Doberman, made of milky white smoke and hot vapor. So much for the sphinxes being on *our* side.

"Soon!" I warned Sadie.

"Paris!" she called, and raised her staff and wand. "I want to go there *now*. Two tickets. First-class would be nice!"

The sphinxes advanced. The nearest one launched itself toward me, and with sheer luck I managed to slice it in half. The monster evaporated into smoke, but it let out a blast of heat so intense I thought my face was going to melt right off.

Two more sphinx ghosts loped toward me. A dozen more were only a few steps behind. I could feel my pulse pounding in my neck.

Suddenly the ground shook. The sky darkened, and Sadie yelled, "Yes!"

The obelisk glowed with purple light, humming with power. Sadie touched the stone and yelped. She was sucked inside and disappeared.

"Sadie!" I yelled.

In my moment of distraction, two of the sphinxes slammed

into me, knocking me to the ground. My sword skittered away. My rib cage went *crack!* and my chest erupted in pain. The heat coming off the creatures was unbearable—it was like being crushed under a hot oven.

I stretched out my fingers toward the obelisk. Just a few inches too far. I could hear the other sphinxes coming, the magician chanting, "Hold him! Hold him!"

With my last bit of strength, I lurched toward the obelisk, every nerve in my body screaming with pain. My fingertips touched the base, and the world went black.

Suddenly I was lying on cold, wet stone. I was in the middle of a huge public plaza. Rain was pouring down, and the chilly air told me I was no longer in Egypt. Sadie was somewhere close by, yelling in alarm.

The bad news: I'd brought the two sphinxes with me. One jumped off me and bounded after Sadie. The other was still on my chest, glaring down at me, its back steaming in the rain, its smoky white eyes inches from my face.

I tried to remember the Egyptian word for *fire*. Maybe if I could set the monster ablaze...but my mind was too full of panic. I heard an explosion off to my right, in the direction Sadie had run. I hoped she'd gotten away, but I couldn't be sure.

The sphinx opened its mouth and formed smoky fangs that had no business on an Ancient Egyptian king. It was about to chomp my face when a dark form loomed up behind it and shouted, "*Mange des muffins!*"

Slice!

The sphinx dissolved into smoke.

I tried to rise but couldn't. Sadie stumbled over. "Carter! Oh god, are you okay?"

I blinked at the other person—the one who had saved me: a tall, thin figure in a black, hooded raincoat. What had she yelled: *Eat muffins?* What kind of battle cry was that?

She threw off her coat, and a woman in a leopard-skin acrobatic suit grinned down at me, showing off her fangs and her lamplike yellow eyes.

"Miss me?" asked Bast.

18. When Fruit Bats Go Bad

We huddled under the eaves of a big white government building and watched the rain pour down on the Place de la Concorde. It was a miserable day to be in Paris. The winter skies were heavy and low, and the cold, wet air soaked right into my bones. There were no tourists, no foot traffic. Everyone with any sense was inside by a fire enjoying a hot drink.

To our right, the River Seine wound sluggishly through the city. Across the enormous plaza, the gardens of the Tuileries were shrouded in a soupy haze.

The Egyptian obelisk rose up lonely and dark in the middle of the square. We waited for more enemies to pop out of it, but none came. I remembered what Zia had said about artifacts needing a twelve-hour cooldown before they could be used again. I hoped she was right.

"Hold still," Bast told me.

I winced as she pressed her hand against my chest. She whispered something in Egyptian, and the pain slowly subsided.

213

"Broken rib," she announced. "Better now, but you should rest for at least a few minutes."

"What about the magicians?"

"I wouldn't worry about them just yet. The House will assume you teleported somewhere else."

"Why?"

"Paris is the Fourteenth Nome—Desjardins' headquarters. You would be insane trying to hide in his home territory."

"Great." I sighed.

"And your amulets *do* shield you," Bast added. "I could find Sadie anywhere because of my promise to protect her. But the amulets will keep you veiled from the eyes of Set and from other magicians."

I thought about the dark room in the First Nome with all the children looking into bowls of oil. Were they looking for us right now? The thought was creepy.

I tried to sit up and winced again.

"Stay still," Bast ordered. "Really, Carter, you should learn to fall like a cat."

"I'll work on that," I promised. "How are you even alive? Is it that 'nine lives' thing?"

"Oh, that's just a silly legend. I'm *immortal.*"

"But the scorpions!" Sadie scrunched in closer, shivering and drawing Bast's raincoat around her shoulders. "We saw them overwhelm you!"

Bast made a purring sound. "Dear Sadie, you do care! I must say I've worked for *many* children of the pharaohs, but you two—" She looked genuinely touched. "Well, I'm sorry if I worried you. It's true the scorpions reduced my power to almost nothing. I held them off as long as I could. Then I had just enough energy to revert to Muffin's form and slip into the Duat."

"I thought you weren't good at portals," I said.

"Well, first off, Carter, there are many ways in and out of the Duat. It has many different regions and layers—the Abyss, the River of Night, the Land of the Dead, the Land of Demons—"

"Sounds lovely," Sadie muttered.

"Anyway, portals are like doors. They pass through the Duat to connect one part of the mortal world to another. And yes, I'm not good at those. But I *am* a creature of the Duat. If I'm on my own, slipping into the nearest layer for a quick escape is relatively easy."

"And if they'd killed you?" I asked. "I mean, killed Muffin?"

"That would've banished me deep into the Duat. It would've been rather like putting my feet in concrete and dropping me into the middle of the sea. It would've taken years, perhaps centuries, before I would've been strong enough to return to the mortal world. Fortunately, that didn't happen. I came back straightaway, but by the time I got to the museum, the magicians had already captured you."

"We weren't exactly *captured*," I said.

"Really, Carter? How long were you in the First Nome before they decided to kill you?"

"Um, about twenty-four hours."

Bast whistled. "They've gotten friendlier! They used to blast godlings to dust in the first few minutes."

"We're *not*—wait, what did you call us?"

Sadie answered, sounding as if in a trance: "'Godlings.' That's what we are, aren't we? That's why Zia was so frightened of us, why Desjardins wants to kill us."

Bast patted Sadie's knee. "You always were bright, dear."

"Hold on," I said. "You mean hosts for *gods*? That's not possible. I think I'd know if..."

Then I thought about the voice in my head, warning me to hide when I met Iskandar. I thought about all the things I was suddenly able to do—like fight with a sword and summon a magical shell of armor. Those were not things I'd covered in home school.

"Carter," Sadie said. "When the Rosetta Stone shattered, it let out five gods, right? Dad joined with Osiris. Amos told us that. Set...I don't know. He got away somehow. But you and I—"

"The amulets protected us." I clutched the Eye of Horus around my neck. "Dad said they would."

"*If* we had stayed out of the room, as Dad told us to," Sadie recalled. "But we were there, watching. We wanted to help him. We practically *asked* for power, Carter."

Bast nodded. "That makes all the difference. An invitation."

"And since then..." Sadie looked at me tentatively, almost daring me to make fun of her. "I've had this feeling. Like a voice inside me...."

By now the cold rain had soaked right through my clothes. If Sadie hadn't said something, maybe I could've denied what was happening a little longer. But I thought about what Amos had said about our family having a long history with the gods. I thought about what Zia had told us about our lineage: "The gods choose their hosts carefully. They always prefer the blood of the pharaohs."

"Okay," I admitted. "I've been hearing a voice too. So either we're both going crazy—"

"The amulet." Sadie pulled it from her shirt collar and held it for Bast to see. "It's the symbol of a goddess, isn't it?"

I hadn't seen her amulet in a long time. It was different from mine. It reminded me of an ankh, or maybe some kind of fancy tie.

"That is a *tyet*," Bast said. "A magic knot. And yes, it is often called—"

"The Knot of Isis," Sadie said. I didn't see how she could know that, but she looked absolutely certain. "In the Hall of Ages, I saw an image of Isis, and then I *was* Isis, trying to get away from Set, and—oh, god. That's it, isn't it? I'm her."

She grabbed her shirt like she physically wanted to pull the goddess away from her. All I could do was stare. My sister, with her ratty red-highlighted hair and her linen pajamas and her combat boots—how could she possibly worry about being possessed by a *goddess*? What goddess would want her, except maybe the goddess of chewing gum?

But then . . . I'd been hearing a voice inside me too. A voice that was definitely not mine. I looked at my amulet, the Eye of Horus. I thought about the myths I knew—how Horus, the son of Osiris, had to avenge his father by defeating Set. And at Luxor I'd summoned an avatar with the head of a falcon.

I was afraid to try it, but I thought: *Horus?*

Well, it's about time, the other voice said. *Hello, Carter.*

"Oh, no," I said, panic rising in my chest. "No, no, no. Somebody get a can opener. I've got a god stuck in my head."

Bast's eyes lit up. "You communicated with Horus directly? That's excellent progress!"

"Progress?" I banged my palms against my head. "Get him out!"

Calm down, Horus said.

"Don't tell me to calm down!"

Bast frowned. "I didn't."

"Talking to him!" I pointed at my forehead.

"This is awful," Sadie wailed. "How do I get rid of her?"

Bast sniffed. "First off, Sadie, you don't have *all* of her. Gods are very powerful. We can exist in many places at once. But yes, part of Isis's spirit now resides inside you. Just as Carter now carries the spirit of Horus. And frankly, you both should feel honored."

"Right, very honored," I said. "Always wanted to be possessed!"

Bast rolled her eyes. "Please, Carter, it's *not* possession. Besides, you and Horus want the same thing—to defeat Set, just as Horus did millennia ago, when Set first killed Osiris. If you don't, your father is doomed, and Set will become king of the earth."

I glanced at Sadie, but she was no help. She ripped the amulet off her neck and threw it down. "Isis got in through the amulet, didn't she? Well, I'll just—"

"I really wouldn't do that," Bast warned.

But Sadie pulled out her wand and smashed the amulet. Blue sparks shot up from the ivory boomerang. Sadie yelped and dropped her wand, which was now smoking. Her hand was covered in black scorch marks. The amulet was fine. *"Ow!"* she said.

Bast sighed. She put her hand on Sadie's, and the burn marks faded. "I *did* tell you. Isis channeled her power through the amulet, yes, but she's not there now. She's in *you*. And even so, magical amulets are practically indestructible."

"So what are we supposed to do?" Sadie said.

"Well, for starters," Bast said, "Carter must use the power of Horus to defeat Set."

"Oh, is that all?" I said. "All by myself?"

"No, no. Sadie can help."

"Oh, super."

"I'll guide you as much as possible," Bast promised, "but in the end, the two of you must fight. Only Horus and Isis can defeat Set and avenge the death of Osiris. That's the way it was before. That's the way it must be now."

"Then we get our dad back?" I asked.

Bast's smile wavered. "If all goes well."

She wasn't telling us everything. No surprise. But my brain was too fuzzy to figure out what I was missing.

I looked down at my hands. They didn't seem any different—no stronger, no godlier. "If I've got the powers of a god, then why am I so..."

"Lame?" Sadie offered.

"Shut up," I said. "Why can't I use my powers better?"

"Takes practice," Bast said. "Unless you wish to give over

control to Horus. Then he would use your form, and you would not have to worry."

I could, a voice said inside me. *Let me fight Set. You can trust me.*

Yeah, right, I told him. *How can I be sure you wouldn't get me killed and just move on to some other host? How can I be sure you're not influencing my thoughts right now?*

I would not do that, the voice said. *I chose you because of your potential, Carter, and because we have the same goal. Upon my honor, if you let me control—*

"No," I said.

I realized I'd spoke aloud; Sadie and Bast were both looking at me.

"I mean I'm not giving up control," I said. "This is *our* fight. Our dad's locked in a coffin. Our uncle's been captured."

"Captured?" Sadie asked. I realized with a shock that I hadn't told her about my last little *ba* trip. There just hadn't been time.

When I gave her the details, she looked stricken. "God, no."

"Yeah," I agreed. "And Set spoke in French—'Bon soir.' Sadie, what you said about Set getting away—maybe he didn't. If he was looking for a powerful host—"

"Desjardins," Sadie finished.

Bast growled deep in her throat. "Desjardins was in London the night your father broke the Rosetta Stone, wasn't he? Desjardins has always been full of anger, full of ambition. In many ways, he would be the perfect host for Set. If Set managed to possess Desjardins' body, that would mean the

Red Lord now controls the man who is Chief Lector of the House.... By Ra's throne, Carter, I hope you're wrong. The two of you will have to learn to use the power of the gods quickly. Whatever Set is planning, he'll do it on his birthday, when he's strongest. That's the third Demon Day—three days from now."

"But I've already used Isis's powers, haven't I?" Sadie asked. "I've summoned hieroglyphs. I activated the obelisk at Luxor. Was that her or me?"

"Both, dear," Bast said. "You and Carter have great abilities on your own, but the power of the gods has hastened your development, and given you an extra reservoir to draw on. What would've taken you years to learn, you've accomplished in days. The more you channel the power of the gods, the more powerful you will become."

"And the more dangerous it gets," I guessed. "The magicians told us hosting the gods can burn you out, kill you, drive you crazy."

Bast fixed her eyes on me. Just for a second they were the eyes of a predator—ancient, powerful, dangerous. "Not everyone can host a god, Carter. That's true. But *you* two are *both* blood of the pharaohs. You combine *two* ancient bloodlines. That's very rare, very powerful. And besides, if you think you can survive *without* the power of the gods, think again. Don't repeat your mother's—" She stopped herself.

"What?" Sadie demanded. "What about our mother?"

"I shouldn't have said that."

"Tell us, cat!" Sadie said.

I was afraid Bast might unsheathe her knives. Instead she

leaned against the wall and stared out at the rain. "When your parents released me from Cleopatra's Needle...there was much more energy than they expected. Your father spoke the actual summoning spell, and the blast would've killed him instantly, but your mother threw up a shield. In that split second, I offered her my help. I offered to merge our spirits and help protect them. But she would not accept my help. She chose to tap her own reservoir...."

"Her own magic," Sadie murmured.

Bast nodded sadly. "When a magician commits herself to a spell, there is no turning back. If she overreaches her power ...well, your mother used her last bit of energy protecting your father. To save him, she sacrificed herself. She literally—"

"Burned up," I said. "That's what Zia warned us about."

The rain kept pouring down. I realized I was shivering.

Sadie wiped a tear from her cheek. She picked up her amulet and glared at it resentfully. "We've got to save Dad. If he's really got the spirit of Osiris..."

She didn't finish, but I knew what she was thinking. I thought about Mom when I was little, her arm around my shoulders as we stood on the back deck of our house in L.A. She'd pointed out the stars to me: Polaris, Orion's Belt, Sirius. Then she'd smile at me, and I'd feel like I was more important than any constellation in the sky. My mom had sacrificed herself to save Dad's life. She'd used so much magic, she literally burned up. How could I ever be that brave? Yet I had to try to save Dad. Otherwise I'd feel like Mom's sacrifice had been for nothing. And maybe if we could rescue Dad, he could set things right, even bring back our mom.

Is that possible? I asked Horus, but his voice was silent.

"All right," I decided. "So how do we stop Set?"

Bast thought for a moment, then smiled. I got the feeling that whatever she was about to suggest, I wasn't going to like it. "There *might* be a way without completely giving yourself over to the gods. There's a book by Thoth—one of the rare spell books written by the god of wisdom himself. The one I'm thinking of details a way to overcome Set. It is the prized possession of a certain magician. All we need to do is sneak into his fortress, steal it, and leave before sunset, while we can still create a portal to the United States."

"Perfect," Sadie said.

"Hold up," I said. "Which magician? And where's the fortress?"

Bast stared at me as if I were a bit slow. "Why, I think we already discussed him. Desjardins. His house is right here in Paris."

Once I saw Desjardins' house, I hated him even more. It was a huge mansion on the other side of the Tuileries, on the rue des Pyramides.

"Pyramids Road?" Sadie said. "Obvious, much?"

"Maybe he couldn't find a place on Stupid Evil Magician Street," I suggested.

The house was spectacular. The spikes atop its wrought iron fence were gilded. Even in the winter rain, the front garden was bursting with flowers. Five stories of white marble walls and black-shuttered windows loomed before us, the whole thing topped off by a roof garden. I'd seen royal palaces smaller than this place.

I pointed to the front door, which was painted bright red. "Isn't red a bad color in Egypt? The color of Set?"

Bast scratched her chin. "Now that you mention it, yes. It's the color of chaos and destruction."

"I thought black was the evil color," Sadie said.

"No, dear. As usual, modern folk have it backward. Black is the color of good soil, like the soil of the Nile. You can grow food in black soil. Food is good. Therefore black is good. Red is the color of desert sand. Nothing grows in the desert. Therefore red is evil." She frowned. "It *is* strange that Desjardins has a red door."

"Well, I'm excited," Sadie grumbled. "Let's go knock."

"There will be guards," Bast said. "And traps. And alarms. You can bet the house is heavily charmed to keep out gods."

"Magicians can do that?" I asked. I imagined a big can of pesticide labeled *God-Away*.

"Alas, yes," Bast said. "I will not be able to cross the threshold uninvited. You, however—"

"I thought we're gods too," Sadie said.

"That's the beauty of it," Bast said. "As hosts, you are still quite human. I have taken full possession of Muffin, so I am pretty much *me*—a goddess. But you are still—well, yourselves. Clear?"

"No," I said.

"I suggest you turn into birds," Bast said. "You can fly to the roof garden and make your way in. Plus, I like birds."

"First problem," I said, "we don't know how to turn into birds."

"Easily fixed! And a good test at channeling godly power.

Both Isis and Horus have bird forms. Simply imagine yourselves as birds, and birds you shall become."

"Just like that," Sadie said. "You won't pounce on us?"

Bast looked offended. "Perish the thought!"

I wished she hadn't used the word *perish*.

"Okay," I said. "Here goes."

I thought: *You in there, Horus?*

What? he said testily.

Bird form, please.

Oh, I see. You don't trust me. But now you need my help.

Man, come on. Just do the falcon thing.

Would you settle for an emu?

I decided talking wasn't going to help, so I closed my eyes
and imagined I was a falcon. Right away, my skin began to
burn. I had trouble breathing. I opened my eyes and gasped.

I was really, really short—eye-level with Bast's shins. I was
covered in feathers, and my feet had turned into wicked claws,
kind of like my *ba* form, but this was real flesh and blood.
My clothes and bag were gone, as if they'd melted into my
feathers. My eyesight had completely changed, too. I could
see a hundred and eighty degrees around, and the detail was
incredible. Every leaf on every tree popped out. I spotted a
cockroach a hundred yards away, scurrying into a sewer drain.
I could see every pore on Bast's face, now looming above me
and grinning.

"Better late than never," she said. "Took you almost ten
minutes."

Huh? The change had seemed instantaneous. Then I
looked next to me and saw a beautiful gray bird of prey, a

little bit smaller than me, with black-tipped wings and golden eyes. I'm not sure how, but I knew it was a kite—like the *bird* kite, not the kind with a string.

The kite let out a chirping sound—"*Ha, ha, ha.*" Sadie was laughing at me.

I opened my own beak, but no sound came out.

"Oh, you two look delicious," Bast said, licking her lips. "No, no—er, I mean wonderful. Now, off you go!"

I spread my majestic wings. I had really done it! I was a noble falcon, lord of the sky. I launched myself off the sidewalk and flew straight into the fence.

"*Ha—ha—ha,*" Sadie chirped behind me.

Bast crouched down and began making weird chittering noises. *Uh-oh.* She was imitating birds. I'd seen enough cats do this when they were stalking. Suddenly my own obituary flashed in my head: *Carter Kane, 14, died tragically in Paris when he was eaten by his sister's cat, Muffin.*

I spread my wings, kicked off with my feet, and with three strong flaps, I was soaring through the rain. Sadie was right behind me. Together we spiraled up into the air.

I have to admit: it felt amazing. Ever since I was a little kid, I'd had dreams in which I was flying, and I always hated waking up. Now it wasn't a dream or even a *ba* trip. It was one hundred percent real. I sailed on the cold air currents above the rooftops of Paris. I could see the river, the Louvre Museum, the gardens and palaces. And a mouse—yum.

Hang on, Carter, I thought. *Not hunting mice.* I zeroed in on Desjardins' mansion, tucked in my wings, and shot downward.

I saw the rooftop garden, the double glass doors leading

inside, and the voice inside me said: *Don't stop. It's an illusion. You've got to punch through their magic barriers.*

It was a crazy thought. I was plummeting so fast I would smack against the glass and become a feathery pancake, but I didn't slow down.

I rammed straight into the doors—and sailed through them as if they didn't exist. I spread my wings and landed on a table. Sadie sailed in right behind me.

We were alone in the middle of a library. So far, so good.

I closed my eyes and thought about returning to my normal form. When I opened my eyes again, I was regular old Carter, sitting on a table in my regular clothes, my workbag back on my shoulder.

Sadie was still a kite.

"You can turn back now," I told her.

She tilted her head and regarded me quizzically. She let out a frustrated croak.

I cracked a smile. "You can't, can you? You're stuck?"

She pecked my hand with her extremely sharp beak.

"*Ow!*" I complained. "It's not my fault. Keep trying."

She closed her eyes and ruffled her feathers until she looked like she was going to explode, but she stayed a kite.

"Don't worry," I said, trying to keep a straight face. "Bast will help once we get out of here."

"*Ha—ha—ha.*"

"Just keep watch. I'm going to look around."

The room was huge—more like a traditional library than a magician's lair. The furniture was dark mahogany. Every wall was covered with floor-to-ceiling bookcases. Books overflowed onto the floor. Some were stacked on tables or stuffed into smaller shelves. A big easy chair by the window looked like the kind of place Sherlock Holmes would sit smoking a pipe.

Every step I took, the floorboards creaked, which made me wince. I couldn't hear anyone else in the house, but I didn't want to take any chances.

Aside from the glass doors to the rooftop, the only other exit was a solid wooden door that locked from the inside. I turned the deadbolt. Then I wedged a chair up under the handle. I doubted that would keep magicians out for very long, but it might buy me a few seconds if things went bad.

I searched the bookshelves for what seemed like ages. All different types of books were jammed together—nothing alphabetized, nothing numbered. Most of the titles weren't in English. None were in hieroglyphics. I was hoping for something with big gold lettering that said *The Book of Thoth*, but no such luck.

"What would a *Book of Thoth* even look like?" I wondered.

Sadie turned her head and glared at me. I was pretty sure she was telling me to hurry up.

I wished there were *shabti* to fetch things, like the ones in Amos's library, but I didn't see any. Or maybe...

I slung Dad's bag off my shoulder. I set his magic box on the table and slid open the top. The little wax figure was still there, right where I'd left him. I picked him up and said, "Doughboy, help me find *The Book of Thoth* in this library."

His waxy eyes opened immediately. "And why should I help you?"

"Because you have no choice."

"I hate that argument! Fine—hold me up. I can't see the shelves."

I walked him around the room, showing him the books. I felt pretty stupid giving the wax doll a tour, but probably not as stupid as Sadie felt. She was still in bird form, scuttling back and forth on the table and snapping her beak in frustration as she tried to change back.

"Hold it!" Doughboy announced. "This one is ancient—right here."

I pulled down a thin volume bound in linen. It was so tiny, I would've missed it, but sure enough, the front cover was inscribed in hieroglyphics. I brought it over to the table and carefully opened it. It was more like a map than a book, unfolding into four parts until I was looking at a wide, long papyrus scroll with writing so old I could barely make out the characters.

I glanced at Sadie. "I bet you could read this to me if you weren't a bird."

She tried to peck me again, but I moved my hand.

"Doughboy," I said. "What is this scroll?"

"A spell lost in time!" he pronounced. "Ancient words of tremendous power!"

"Well?" I demanded. "Does it tell how to defeat Set?"

"Better! The title reads: *The Book of Summoning Fruit Bats*!"

I stared at him. "Are you serious?"

"Would I joke about such a thing?"

"Who would want to summon fruit bats?"

"Ha—ha—ha," Sadie croaked.

I pushed the scroll away and we went back to searching.

After about ten minutes, Doughboy squealed with delight. "Oh, look! I remember this painting."

It was a small oil portrait in a gilded frame, hanging on the end of a bookshelf. It must've been important, because it was bordered by little silk curtains. A light shone upon the portrait dude's face so he seemed about to tell a ghost story.

"Isn't that the guy who plays Wolverine?" I asked, because he had some serious jowl hair going on.

"You disgust me!" Doughboy said. "That is Jean-François Champollion."

It took me a second, but I remembered the name. "The guy who deciphered hieroglyphics from the Rosetta Stone."

"Of course. Desjardins' great uncle."

I looked at Champollion's picture again, and I could see the resemblance. They had the same fierce black eyes. "Great uncle? But wouldn't that make Desjardins—"

"About two hundred years old," Doughboy confirmed. "Still a youngster. You know that when Champollion first deciphered hieroglyphics, he fell into a coma for five days? He became the first man outside the House of Life to ever unleash their magic, and it almost killed him. Naturally, that got the attention of the First Nome. Champollion died before he could join the House of Life, but the Chief Lector accepted his descendants for training. Desjardins is very proud of his family . . . but a little sensitive too, because he's such a newcomer."

"That's why he didn't get along with our family," I guessed. "We're like . . . ancient."

Doughboy cackled. "And your father breaking the Rosetta Stone? Desjardins would've viewed that as an insult to his family honor! Oh, you should've seen the arguments Master Julius and Desjardins had in this room."

"You've been here before?"

"Many times! I've been everywhere. I'm all-knowing."

I tried to imagine Dad and Desjardins having an argument in here. It wasn't hard. If Desjardins hated our family, and if gods tended to find hosts who shared their goals, then it made total sense that Set would try to merge with him. Both wanted power, both were resentful and angry, both wanted to smash Sadie and me to a pulp. And if Set was now secretly controlling the Chief Lector...A drop of sweat trickled down the side of my face. I wanted to get out of this mansion.

Suddenly there was a banging sound below us, like someone closing a door downstairs.

"Show me where *The Book of Thoth* is," I ordered Doughboy. "Quick!"

As we moved down the shelves, Doughboy grew so warm in my hands, I was afraid he would melt. He kept a running commentary on the books.

"Ah, *Mastery of the Five Elements*!"

"Is that the one we want?" I asked.

"No, but a good one. How to tame the five essential elements of the universe—earth, air, water, fire, and cheese!"

"Cheese?"

He scratched his wax head. "I'm pretty sure that's the fifth, yes. But moving right along!"

We turned to the next shelf. "No," he announced. "No. Boring. Boring. Oh, Clive Cussler! No. No."

I was about to give up hope when he said, "There."

I froze. "Where—here?"

"The blue book with the gold trim," he said. "The one that's—"

I pulled it out, and the entire room began to shake.

"—trapped," Doughboy continued.

Sadie squawked urgently. I turned and saw her take flight. Something small and black swooped down from the ceiling. Sadie clashed with it in midair, and the black thing disappeared down her throat.

Before I could even register how gross that was, alarms blared downstairs. More black forms dropped from the ceiling and seemed to multiply in the air, swirling into a funnel cloud of fur and wings.

"There's your answer," Doughboy told me. "*Desjardins* would want to summon fruit bats. You mess with the wrong books, you trigger a plague of fruit bats. That's the trap!"

The things were on me like I was a ripe mango—diving at my face, clawing at my arms. I clutched the book and ran to the table, but I could hardly see. "Sadie, get out of here!" I yelled.

"SAW!" she cried, which I hoped meant yes.

I found Dad's workbag and shoved the book and Doughboy inside. The library door rattled. Voices yelled in French.

Horus, bird time! I thought desperately. *And no emu, please!*

I ran for the glass doors. At the last second, I found myself flying—once again a falcon, bursting into the cold rain. I knew with the senses of a predator that I was being followed by approximately four thousand angry fruit bats.

But falcons are wicked fast. Once outside, I raced north,

hoping to draw the bats away from Sadie and Bast. I outdistanced the bats easily but let them keep close enough that they wouldn't give up. Then, with a burst of speed, I turned in a tight circle and shot back toward Sadie and Bast in a hundred-mile-an-hour dive.

Bast looked up in surprise as I plummeted to the sidewalk, tumbling over myself as I turned back into a human. Sadie caught my arm, and only then did I realize she was back to normal as well.

"That was awful!" she announced.

"Exit strategy, quick!" I pointed at the sky, where an angry black cloud of fruit bats was getting closer and closer.

"The Louvre." Bast grabbed our hands. "It's got the closest portal."

Three blocks away. We'd never make it.

Then the red door of Desjardins' house blasted open, but we didn't wait to see what came out of it. We ran for our lives down the rue des Pyramides.

S
A
D
I
E

19. A Picnic in the Sky

[Right, Carter. Give me the mic.]

So I'd been to the Louvre once before on holiday, but I hadn't been chased by vicious fruit bats. I would've been terrified, except I was too busy being angry with Carter. I couldn't believe the way he'd treated my bird problem. Honestly, I thought I would be a kite *forever*, suffocating inside a little feathery prison. And he had the nerve to make fun!

I promised myself I'd get revenge, but for the time being we had enough worries staying alive.

We raced along in the cold rain. It was all I could do to avoid slipping on the slick pavements. I glanced back and saw two figures chasing us—men with shaved heads and goatees and black raincoats. They might've passed for normal mortals except they each carried a glowing staff. Not a good sign.

The bats were literally at our heels. One nipped my leg. Another buzzed my hair. I had to force myself to keep running.

My stomach still felt queasy from eating one of the little pests when I was a kite—and no, that had *not* been my idea. Totally a defensive instinct!

"Sadie," Bast called as we ran. "You'll have only seconds to open the portal."

"Where is it?" I yelled.

We dashed across the rue de Rivoli into a wide plaza surrounded by the wings of the Louvre. Bast made straight for the glass pyramid at the entrance, glowing in the dusk.

"You can't be serious," I said. "That isn't a *real* pyramid."

"Of course it's real," Bast said. "The *shape* gives a pyramid its power. It is a ramp to the heavens."

The bats were all around us now—biting our arms, flying around our feet. As their numbers increased, it got harder to see or move.

Carter reached for his sword, then apparently remembered it wasn't there anymore. He'd lost it at Luxor. He swore and rummaged around in his workbag.

"Don't slow down!" Bast warned.

Carter pulled out his wand. In total frustration, he threw it at a bat. I thought this a pointless gesture, but the wand glowed white-hot and thumped the bat solidly on the head, knocking it out of the air. The wand ricocheted through the swarm, thumping six, seven, eight of the little monsters before returning to Carter's hand.

"Not bad," I said. "Keep it up!"

We arrived at the base of the pyramid. The plaza was thankfully empty. The last thing I wanted was my embarrassing death by fruit bats posted on YouTube.

"One minute until sundown," Bast warned. "Our last chance for summoning is *now*."

She unsheathed her knives and started slicing bats out of the air, trying to keep them away from me. Carter's wand flew wildly, knocking fruit bats every which way. I faced the pyramid and tried to think of a portal, the way I'd done at Luxor, but it was almost impossible to concentrate.

Where do you wish to go? Isis said in my mind.

God, I don't care! America!

I realized I was crying. I hated to, but shock and fear were starting to overwhelm me. Where did I want to go? Home, of course! Back to my flat in London—back to my own room, my grandparents, my mates at school and my *old life*. But I couldn't. I had to think about my father and our mission. We had to get to Set.

America, I thought. *Now!*

My burst of emotion must've had some effect. The pyramid trembled. Its glass walls shimmered and the top of the structure began to glow.

A swirling sand vortex appeared, all right. Only one problem: it was hovering above the very top of the pyramid.

"Climb!" Bast said. Easy for her—she was a cat.

"The side is too steep!" Carter objected.

He'd done a good job with the bats. Dazed heaps littered the pavement, but more still flew round us, biting every bit of exposed skin, and the magicians were closing in.

"I'll toss you," Bast said.

"Excuse me?" Carter protested, but she picked him up by his collar and pants and tossed him up the side of the pyramid.

He skittered to the top in a very undignified manner and slipped straight through the portal.

"Now you, Sadie," Bast said. "Come on!"

Before I could move, a man's voice yelled, "Stop!"

Stupidly, I froze. The voice was so powerful, it was hard not to.

The two magicians were approaching. The taller one spoke in perfect English: "Surrender, Miss Kane, and return our master's property."

"Sadie, don't listen," Bast warned. "Come here."

"The cat goddess deceives you," the magician said. "She abandoned her post. She endangered us all. She will lead you to ruin."

I could tell he meant it. He was absolutely convinced of what he said.

I turned to Bast. Her expression had changed. She looked wounded, even grief-stricken.

"What does he mean?" I said. "What did you do wrong?"

"We have to leave," she warned. "Or they will kill us."

I looked at the portal. Carter was already through. That decided it. I wasn't going to be separated from him. As annoying as he was, Carter was the only person I had left. (How is that for depressing?)

"Toss me," I said.

Bast grabbed me. "See you in America." Then she chucked me up the side of the pyramid.

I heard the magician roar, "Surrender!" And an explosion rattled the glass next to my head. Then I plunged into the hot vortex of sand.

I woke in a small room with industrial carpeting, gray walls, and metal-framed windows. I felt as if I were inside a high-tech refrigerator. I sat up groggily and discovered I was coated in cold, wet sand.

"*Ugh*," I said. "Where are we?"

Carter and Bast stood by the window. Apparently they'd been conscious for a while, because they'd both brushed themselves off.

"You've got to see this view," Carter said.

I got shakily to my feet and nearly fell down again when I saw how high we were.

An entire city spread out below us—I mean *far* below, well over a hundred meters. I could almost believe we were still in Paris, because a river curved off to our left, and the land was mostly flat. There were white government buildings clustered around networks of parks and circular roads, all spread out under a winter sky. But the light was wrong. It was still afternoon here, so we must've traveled west. And as my eyes made their way to the other end of a long rectangular green space, I found myself staring at a mansion that looked oddly familiar.

"Is that...the White House?"

Carter nodded. "You got us to America, all right. Washington, D.C."

"But we're sky high!"

Bast chuckled. "You didn't specify any particular American city, did you?"

"Well...no."

"So you got the default portal for the U.S.—the largest single source of Egyptian power in North America."

I stared at her uncomprehendingly.

"The biggest obelisk ever constructed," she said. "The Washington Monument."

I had another moment of vertigo and moved away from the window. Carter grabbed my shoulder and helped me sit down.

"You should rest," he said. "You passed out for . . . how long, Bast?"

"Two hours and thirty-two minutes," she said. "I'm sorry, Sadie. Opening more than one portal a day *is* extremely taxing, even with Isis helping."

Carter frowned. "But we need her to do it again, right? It's not sunset here yet. We can still use portals. Let's open one and get to Arizona. That's where Set is."

Bast pursed her lips. "Sadie can't summon another portal. It would overextend her powers. I don't have the talent. And you, Carter . . . well, your abilities lie elsewhere. No offense."

"Oh, no," he grumbled. "I'm sure you'll call me next time you need to boomerang some fruit bats."

"Besides," Bast said, "when a portal is used, it needs time to cool down. No one will be able to use the Washington Monument—"

"For another twelve hours." Carter cursed. "I forgot about that."

Bast nodded. "And by then, the Demon Days will have begun."

"So we need another way to Arizona," Carter said.

I suppose he didn't mean to make me feel guilty, but I did. I hadn't thought things through, and now we were stuck in Washington.

I glanced at Bast out the corner of my eye. I wanted to ask her what the men at the Louvre had meant about her leading us to ruin, but I was afraid to. I wanted to believe she was on our side. Perhaps if I gave her a chance, she'd volunteer the information.

"At least those magicians can't follow us," I prompted.

Bast hesitated. "Not through the portal, no. But there are other magicians in America. And worse...Set's minions."

My heart climbed into my throat. The House of Life was scary enough, but when I remembered Set, and what his minions had done to Amos's house...

"What about Thoth's spellbook?" I said. "Did we at least find a way to fight Set?"

Carter pointed to the corner of the room. Spread out on Bast's raincoat was Dad's magic toolbox and the blue book we'd stolen from Desjardins.

"Maybe you can make sense of it," Carter said. "Bast and I couldn't read it. Even Doughboy was stumped."

I picked up the book, which was actually a scroll folded into sections. The papyrus was so brittle, I was afraid to touch it. Hieroglyphs and illustrations crowded the page, but I couldn't make sense of them. My ability to read the language seemed to be switched off.

Isis? I asked. *A little help?*

Her voice was silent. Maybe I'd worn her out. Or maybe

she was cross with me for not letting her take over my body, the way Horus had asked Carter to do. Selfish of me, I know.

I closed the book in frustration. "All that work for nothing."

"Now, now," Bast said. "It's not so bad."

"Right," I said. "We're stuck in Washington, D.C. We have two days to make it to Arizona and stop a god we don't know how to stop. And if we can't, we'll never see our dad or Amos again, and the world might end."

"That's the spirit!" Bast said brightly. "Now, let's have a picnic."

She snapped her fingers. The air shimmered, and a pile of Friskies cans and two jugs of milk appeared on the carpet.

"*Um*," Carter said, "can you conjure any people food?"

Bast blinked. "Well, no accounting for taste."

The air shimmered again. A plate of grilled cheese sandwiches and crisps appeared, along with a six-pack of Coke.

"Yum," I said.

Carter muttered something under his breath. I suppose grilled cheese wasn't his favorite, but he picked up a sandwich.

"We should leave soon," he said between bites. "I mean . . . tourists and all."

Bast shook her head. "The Washington Monument closes at six o'clock. The tourists are gone now. We might as well stay the night. If we must travel during the Demon Days, best to do it in daylight hours."

We all must've been exhausted, because we didn't talk again until we'd finished our food. I ate three sandwiches and drank two Cokes. Bast made the whole place smell like fish

Friskies, then started licking her hand as if preparing for a cat bath.

"Could you not do that?" I asked. "It's disturbing."

"Oh." She smiled. "Sorry."

I closed my eyes and leaned against the wall. It felt good to rest, but I realized the room wasn't actually quiet. The entire building seemed to be humming ever so slightly, sending a tremble through my skull that made my teeth buzz. I opened my eyes and sat up. I could still feel it.

"What is that?" I asked. "The wind?"

"Magic energy," Bast said. "I told you, this is a powerful monument."

"But it's modern. Like the Louvre pyramid. Why is it magic?"

"The Ancient Egyptians were excellent builders, Sadie. They picked shapes—obelisks, pyramids—that were charged with symbolic magic. An obelisk represents a sunbeam frozen in stone—a life-giving ray from the original king of the gods, Ra. It doesn't matter *when* the structure was built: it is still Egyptian. That's why any obelisk can be used for opening gates to the Duat, or releasing great beings of power—"

"Or trapping them," I said. "The way you were trapped in Cleopatra's Needle."

Her expression darkened. "I wasn't actually trapped *in* the obelisk. My prison was a magically created abyss deep in the Duat, and the obelisk was the door your parents used to release me. But, yes. All symbols of Egypt are concentrated nodes of magic power. So an obelisk can definitely be used to imprison gods."

An idea was nagging at the back of my mind, but I couldn't quite pin it down. Something about my mother, and Cleopatra's Needle, and my father's last promise in the British Museum: *I'll put things right.*

Then I thought back to the Louvre, and the comment the magician had made. Bast looked so cross at the moment I was almost afraid to ask, but it was the only way I'd get an answer. "The magician said you abandoned your post. What did he mean?"

Carter frowned. "When was this?"

I told him what had happened after Bast chucked him through the portal.

Bast stacked her empty Friskies cans. She didn't look eager to reply.

"When I was imprisoned," she said at last, "I—I wasn't alone. I was locked inside with a . . . creature of chaos."

"Is that bad?" I asked.

Judging from Bast's expression, the answer was yes. "Magicians often do this—lock a god up together with a monster so we have no time to try escaping our prison. For eons, I fought this monster. When your parents released me—"

"The monster got out?"

Bast hesitated a little too long for my taste.

"No. My enemy couldn't have escaped." She took a deep breath. "Your mother's final act of magic sealed that gate. The enemy was still inside. But that's what the magician meant. As far as he was concerned, my 'post' was battling that monster forever."

It had the ring of truth, as if she were sharing a painful

memory, but it didn't explain the other bit the magician had said: *She endangered us all.* I was getting up the nerve to ask exactly what the monster had been, when Bast stood up.

"I should go scout," she said abruptly. "I'll be back."

We listened to her footsteps echo down the stairwell.

"She's hiding something," Carter said.

"Work that out yourself, did you?" I asked.

He looked away, and immediately I felt bad.

"I'm sorry," I said. "It's just...what are we going to do?"

"Rescue Dad. What else can we do?" He picked up his wand and turned it in his fingers. "Do you think he really meant to...you know, bring Mom back?"

I wanted to say yes. More than anything, I wanted to believe that was possible. But I found myself shaking my head. Something about it didn't seem right. "Iskandar told me something about Mum," I said. "She was a diviner. She could see the future. He said she made him rethink some old ideas."

It was my first chance to tell Carter about my conversation with the old magician, so I gave him the details.

Carter knit his eyebrows. "You think that has something to do with why Mom died—she saw something in the future?"

"I don't know." I tried to think back to when I was six, but my memory was frustratingly fuzzy. "When they took us to England the last time, did she and Dad seem like they were in a hurry—like they were doing something really important?"

"Definitely."

"Would you say freeing Bast was really important? I mean— I love her, of course—but *worth dying for* important?"

Carter hesitated. "Probably not."

"Well, there you are. I think Dad and Mum were up to something bigger, something they didn't complete. Possibly that's what Dad was after at the British Museum—completing the task, whatever it was. *Making things right.* And this whole business about our family going back a billion years to some god-hosting pharaohs—why didn't anyone *tell* us? Why didn't Dad?"

Carter didn't answer for a long time.

"Maybe Dad was protecting us," he said. "The House of Life doesn't trust our family, especially after what Dad and Mom did. Amos said we were raised apart for a reason, so we wouldn't, like, trigger each other's magic."

"Bloody awful reason to keep us apart," I muttered.

Carter looked at me strangely, and I realized what I'd said might have been construed as a compliment.

"I just mean they should've been honest," I rushed on. "Not that I *wanted* more time with my annoying brother, of course."

He nodded seriously. "Of course."

We sat listening to the magic hum of the obelisk. I tried to remember the last time Carter and I had simply spent time like this together, talking.

"Is your, *um*..." I tapped the side of my head. "Your *friend* being any help?"

"Not much," he admitted. "Yours?"

I shook my head. "Carter, are you scared?"

"A little." He dug his wand into the carpet. "No, a lot."

I looked at the blue book we'd stolen—pages full of wonderful secrets I couldn't read. "What if we can't do it?"

"I don't know," he said. "That book about mastering the element of cheese would've been more helpful."

"Or summoning fruit bats."

"Please, not the fruit bats."

We shared a weary smile, and it felt rather good. But it changed nothing. We were still in serious trouble with no clear plan.

"Why don't you sleep on it?" he suggested. "You used a lot of energy today. I'll keep watch until Bast gets back."

He actually sounded concerned for me. How cute.

I didn't want to sleep. I didn't want to miss anything. But I realized my eyelids *were* incredibly heavy.

"All right, then," I said. "Don't let the bedbugs bite."

I lay down to sleep, but my soul—my *ba*—had other ideas.

20. I Visit the Star-Spangled Goddess

I HADN'T REALIZED HOW UNSETTLING it would be. Carter had explained how his *ba* left his body while he slept, but having it happen to me was another thing altogether. It was much worse than my vision in the Hall of Ages.

There I was, floating in the air as a glowing birdlike spirit. And there was my body below me, fast asleep. Just trying to describe it gives me a headache.

My first thought as I gazed down on my sleeping form: *God, I look awful.* Bad enough looking in a mirror or seeing pictures of myself on my friends' Web pages. Seeing myself in person was simply *wrong*. My hair was a rat's nest, the linen pajamas were not in the least flattering, and the spot on my chin was *enormous*.

My second thought as I examined the strange shimmering form of my *ba*: *This won't do at all.* I didn't care if I was invisible to the mortal eye or not. After my bad experience as a kite, I simply refused to go about as a glowing Sadie-headed chicken. That's fine for Carter, but I have standards.

I could feel the currents of the Duat tugging at me, trying to pull my *ba* to wherever souls go when they have visions, but I wasn't ready. I concentrated hard, and imagined my normal appearance (well, all right, perhaps my appearance as I'd *like* it to be, a bit better than normal). And *voilà*, my *ba* morphed into a human form, still see-through and glowing, mind you, but more like a proper ghost.

Well, at least that's sorted, I thought. And I allowed the currents to sweep me away. The world melted to black.

At first, I was nowhere—just a dark void. Then a young man stepped out of the shadows.

"You again," he said.

I stammered. "*Uh . . .*"

Honestly, you know me well enough by now. That's *not* like me. But this was the boy I'd seen in my Hall of Ages vision—the very handsome boy with the black robes and tousled hair. His dark brown eyes had the most unnerving effect on me, and I was *very* glad I'd changed out of my glowing chicken outfit.

I tried again, and managed three entire words. "What are you..."

"Doing here?" he said, gallantly finishing my sentence. "Spirit travel and death are very similar."

"Not sure what that means," I said. "Should I be worried?"

He tilted his head as if considering the question. "Not this trip. She only wants to talk to you. Go ahead."

He waved his hand and a doorway opened in the darkness. I was pulled towards it.

"See you again?" I asked.

But the boy was gone.

I found myself standing in a luxury flat in the middle of the sky. It had no walls, no ceiling, and a see-through floor looking straight down at city lights from the height of an airplane. Clouds drifted below my feet. The air should've been freezing cold and too thin to breathe, but I felt warm and comfortable.

Black leather sofas made a U round a glass coffee table on a blood-red rug. A fire burned in a slate fireplace. Bookshelves and paintings hovered in the air where the walls should've been. A black granite bar stood in the corner, and in the shadows behind it, a woman was making tea.

"Hello, my child," she said.

She stepped into the light, and I gasped. She wore an Egyptian kilt from the waist down. From the waist up, she wore only a bikini top, and her skin...her skin was dark blue, covered with stars. I don't mean *painted* stars. She had the entire cosmos living on her skin: gleaming constellations, galaxies too bright to look at, glowing nebulae of pink and blue dust. Her features seemed to disappear into the stars that shifted across her face. Her hair was long and as black as midnight.

"You're the Nut," I said. Then I realized maybe that had come out wrong. "I mean...the sky goddess."

The goddess smiled. Her bright white teeth were like a new galaxy bursting into existence. "Nut is fine. And believe me, I've heard all the jokes about my name."

She poured a second cup from her teapot. "Let's sit and talk. Care for some *sahlab*?"

"Uh, it's not tea?"

"No, an Egyptian drink. You've heard of hot chocolate? This is rather like hot vanilla."

I would've preferred tea, as I hadn't had a proper cup in ages. But I supposed one didn't turn down a goddess. "*Um*... yeah. Thanks."

We sat together on the sofa. To my surprise, my glowing spirity hands had no trouble holding a teacup, and I could drink quite easily. The *sahlab* was sweet and tasty, with just a hint of cinnamon and coconut. It warmed me up nicely and filled the air with the smell of vanilla. For the first time in days I felt safe. Then I remembered I was only here in spirit.

Nut set down her cup. "I suppose you're wondering why I've brought you here."

"Where exactly is 'here'? And, ah, who's your doorman?"

I hoped she'd drop some information about the boy in black, but she only smiled. "I must keep my secrets, dear. I can't have the House of Life trying to find me. Let's just say I've built this home with a nice city view."

"Is that..." I gestured to her starry blue skin. "*Um*...are you inside a human host?"

"No, dear. The sky itself is my body. This is merely a manifestation."

"But I thought—"

"Gods need a physical host outside the Duat? It's somewhat easier for me, being a spirit of the air. I was one of the few gods who was never imprisoned, because the House of Life could never catch me. I'm used to being...*free-form*." Suddenly Nut and the entire apartment flickered. I felt like I would drop through the floor. Then the sofa became stable again.

"Please don't do that again," I begged.

"My apologies," Nut said. "The point is, each god is different. But all my brethren are free now, all finding places in this modern world of yours. They won't be imprisoned again."

"The magicians won't like that."

"No," Nut agreed. "That's the first reason you are here. A battle between the gods and the House of Life would serve only chaos. You must make the magicians understand this."

"They won't listen to me. They think I'm a godling."

"You *are* a godling, dear." She touched my hair gently, and I felt Isis stirring within me, struggling to speak using my voice.

"I'm Sadie Kane," I said. "I didn't ask for Isis to hitch a ride."

"The gods have known your family for generations, Sadie. In the olden days, we worked together for the benefit of Egypt."

"The magicians said that gods caused the fall of the empire."

"That is a long and pointless debate," Nut said, and I could hear an edge of anger in her voice. "All empires fall. But *the idea* of Egypt is eternal—the triumph of civilization, the forces of Ma'at overcoming the forces of chaos. That battle is fought generation after generation. Now it's your turn."

"I know, I know," I said. "We have to defeat Set."

"But is it that simple, Sadie? Set is my son, too. In the old days, he was Ra's strongest lieutenant. He protected the sun god's boat from the serpent Apophis. Now *there* was evil. Apophis was the embodiment of chaos. He hated Creation from the moment the first mountain appeared out of the sea. He hated the gods, mortals, and everything they built. And yet Set fought against him. Set was one of us."

"Then he turned evil?"

Nut shrugged. "Set has always been Set, for better or worse. But he is still part of our family. It is difficult to lose any member of your family . . . is it not?"

My throat tightened. "That's hardly fair."

"Don't speak to me of fairness," Nut said. "For five thousand years, I have been kept apart from my husband, Geb."

I vaguely remembered Carter saying something about this, but it seemed different listening to her now, hearing the pain in her voice.

"What happened?" I asked.

"Punishment for bearing my children," she said bitterly. "I disobeyed Ra's wishes, and so he ordered my own father, Shu—"

"Hang on," I said. "Shoe?"

"S-h-u," she said. "The god of the wind."

"Oh." I wished these gods had names that weren't common household objects. "Go on, please."

"Ra ordered my father, Shu, to keep us apart, forever. I am exiled to the sky, while my beloved Geb cannot leave the ground."

"What happens if you try?"

Nut closed her eyes and spread her hands. A hole opened where she was sitting, and she fell through the air. Instantly, the clouds below us flickered with lightning. Winds raged across the flat, throwing books off the shelves, ripping away paintings and flinging them into the void. My teacup leaped out of my hand. I grabbed the sofa to avoid getting blown away myself.

Below me, lightning struck Nut's form. The wind pushed her violently upward, shooting past me. Then the winds died. Nut settled back onto the couch. She waved her hand and the flat repaired itself. Everything returned to normal.

"*That* happens," she said sadly.

"Oh."

She gazed at the city lights far below. "It has given me appreciation for my children, even Set. He has done horrible things, yes. It is his nature. But he is still my son, and still one of the gods. He acts his part. Perhaps the way to defeat him is not the way you would imagine."

"Hints, please?"

"Seek out Thoth. He has found a new home in Memphis."

"Memphis... Egypt?"

Nut smiled. "Memphis, Tennessee. Although the old bird probably *thinks* it is Egypt. He so rarely takes his beak out of his books, I doubt he would know the difference. You will find him there. He can advise you. Be wary, though: Thoth often asks for favors. He is sometimes hard to predict."

"Getting used to that," I said. "How are we supposed to get there?"

"I am goddess of the sky. I can guarantee you safe travel as far as Memphis." She waved her hand, and a folder appeared in my lap. Inside were three plane tickets—Washington to Memphis, first-class.

I raised my eyebrow. "I suppose you get a lot of frequent flyer miles?"

"Something like that," Nut agreed. "But as you get closer to

Set, you will be beyond my help. And I cannot protect you on the ground. Which reminds me: You need to wake up soon. Set's minion is closing in on your hideout."

I sat up straight. "How soon?"

"Minutes."

"Send my spirit back, then!" I pinched my ghostly arm, which hurt just like it would on my normal arm, but nothing happened.

"Soon, Sadie," Nut promised. "But two more things you must know. I had five children during the Demon Days. If your father released all of them, you should consider: Where is the fifth?"

I racked my brain trying to remember the names of all of Nut's five children. Bit difficult without my brother, the Human Wikipedia, around to keep track of such trivia for me. There was Osiris, the king, and Isis, his queen; Set, the evil god, and Horus, the avenger. But the fifth child of Nut, the one Carter said he could never remember...Then I recalled my vision in the Hall of Ages—Osiris's birthday and the woman in blue who'd helped Isis escape Set. "You mean Nephthys, Set's wife?"

"Consider it," Nut said again. "And lastly...a favor."

She opened her hand and produced an envelope sealed with red wax. "If you see Geb...will you give him this?"

I'd been asked to pass notes before, but never between gods. Honestly, Nut's anguished expression was no different than those of my love-struck friends back at school. I wondered if she'd ever written on her notebook: GEB + NUT = TRUE LOVE or MRS. GEB.

"Least I can do," I promised. "Now, about sending me back..."

"Safe travels, Sadie," the goddess said. "And Isis, restrain yourself."

The spirit of Isis rumbled inside me, as if I'd eaten a bad curry.

"Wait," I said, "what do you mean restrain—"

Before I could finish, my vision went black.

I snapped awake, back in my own body at the Washington Monument. "Leave now!"

Carter and Bast jumped in surprise. They were already awake, packing their things.

"What's wrong?" Carter asked.

I told them about my vision while I frantically searched my pockets. Nothing. I checked my magician's bag. Tucked inside with my wand and rod were three plane tickets and a sealed envelope.

Bast examined the tickets. "Excellent! First class serves salmon."

"But what about Set's minion?" I asked.

Carter glanced out the window. His eyes widened. "Yeah, *um*...it's here."

21. Aunt Kitty to the Rescue

I'D SEEN PICTURES OF THE CREATURE BEFORE, but pictures didn't come close to capturing how horrible it was in real life.

"The Set animal," Bast said, confirming my fear.

Far below, the creature prowled the base of the monument, leaving tracks in the new-fallen snow. I had trouble judging its size, but it must've been at least as big as a horse, with legs just as long. It had an unnaturally lean, muscled body with shiny reddish gray fur. You could almost mistake it for a huge greyhound—except for the tail and the head. The tail was reptilian, forked at the end with triangular points, like squid tentacles. It lashed around as if it had a mind of its own.

The creature's head was the strangest part. Its oversize ears stuck straight up like rabbit ears, but they were shaped more like ice cream cones, curled inward and wider on the top than the bottom. They could rotate almost three hundred and sixty degrees, so they could hear anything. The creature's snout was long and curved like an anteater's—only anteaters don't have razor-sharp teeth.

"Its eyes are glowing," I said. "That can't be good."

"How can you see that far?" Sadie demanded.

She stood next to me, squinting at the tiny figure in the snow, and I realized she had a point. The animal was at least five hundred feet below us. How was I able to see its eyes?

"You still have the sight of the falcon," Bast guessed. "And you're right, Carter. The glowing eyes mean the creature has caught our scent."

I looked at her and almost jumped out of my skin. Her hair was sticking straight up all over her head, like she'd stuck her finger in a light socket.

"*Um*, Bast?" I asked.

"What?"

Sadie and I exchanged looks. She mouthed the word *scared*. Then I remembered how Muffin's tail would always poof up when something startled her.

"Nothing," I said, though if the Set animal was so dangerous that it gave our goddess light-socket hair, that had to be a very bad sign. "How do we get out of here?"

"You don't understand," Bast said. "The Set animal is the perfect hunter. If it has our scent, there is no stopping it."

"Why is it called the 'Set animal'?" Sadie asked nervously. "Doesn't it have a name?"

"If it did," Bast said, "you would not want to speak it. It is merely known as the Set animal—the Red Lord's symbolic creature. It shares his strength, cunning...and his evil nature."

"Lovely," Sadie said.

The animal sniffed at the monument and recoiled, snarling.

"It doesn't seem to like the obelisk," I noticed.

"No," Bast said. "Too much Ma'at energy. But that won't hold it back for long."

As if on cue, the Set animal leaped onto the side of the monument. It began climbing like a lion scaling a tree, digging its claws into the stone.

"That's messed up," I said. "Elevator or stairs?"

"Both are too slow," Bast said. "Back away from the window."

She unsheathed her knives and sliced through the glass. She punched out the window, setting off alarm bells. Freezing air blasted into the observation room.

"You'll need to fly," Bast yelled over the wind. "It's the only way."

"No!" Sadie's face went pale. "Not the kite again."

"Sadie, it's okay," I said.

She shook her head, terrified.

I grabbed her hand. "I'll stay with you. I'll make sure you turn back."

"The Set animal is halfway up," Bast warned. "We're running out of time."

Sadie glanced at Bast. "What about you? You can't fly."

"I'll jump," she said. "Cats always land on their feet."

"It's over a hundred meters!" Sadie cried.

"A hundred and seventy," Bast said. "I'll distract the Set animal, buy you some time."

"You'll be killed." Sadie's voice sounded close to breaking. "Please, I can't lose you too."

Bast looked a little surprised. Then she smiled and put her hand on Sadie's shoulder. "I'll be fine, dear. Meet me at Reagan National, terminal A. Be ready to run."

Before I could argue, Bast jumped out the window. My heart just about stopped. She plummeted straight toward the pavement. I was sure she'd die, but as she fell she spread her arms and legs and seemed to relax.

She hurtled straight past the Set animal, which let out a horrible scream like a wounded man on a battlefield, then turned and leaped after her.

Bast hit the ground with both feet and took off running. She must've been doing sixty miles an hour, easy. The Set animal wasn't as agile. It crashed so hard, the pavement cracked. It stumbled for a few steps but didn't appear hurt. Then it loped after Bast and was soon gaining on her.

"She won't make it," Sadie fretted.

"Never bet against a cat," I said. "We've got to do our part. Ready?"

She took a deep breath. "All right. Before I change my mind."

Instantly, a black-winged kite appeared in front of me, flapping its wings to keep its balance in the intense wind. I willed myself to become a falcon. It was even easier than before.

A moment later, we soared into the cold morning air over Washington, D.C.

Finding the airport was easy. Reagan National was so close, I could see the planes landing across the Potomac.

The hard part was remembering what I was doing. Every

time I saw a mouse or a squirrel, I instinctively veered toward it. A couple of times I caught myself about to dive, and I had to fight the urge. Once I looked over and realized I was a mile away from Sadie, who was off doing her own hunting. I had to force myself to fly next to her and get her attention.

It takes willpower to stay human, the voice of Horus warned. *The more time you spend as a bird of prey, the more you think like one.*

Now you tell me, I thought.

I could help, he urged. *Give me control.*

Not today, bird-head.

Finally, I steered Sadie toward the airport, and we started hunting for a place to change back to human form. We landed at the top of a parking garage.

I willed myself to turn human. Nothing happened.

Panic started building in my throat. I closed my eyes and pictured my dad's face. I thought about how much I missed him, how much I needed to find him.

When I opened my eyes, I was back to normal. Unfortunately, Sadie was still a kite. She flapped around me and cawed frantically. *"Ha—ha—ha!"* There was a wild look in her eyes, and this time I understood how scared she was. Bird form had been hard enough for her to break out of the first time. If the second time took even more energy, she could be in serious trouble.

"It's all right." I crouched down, careful to move slowly. "Sadie, don't force it. You have to relax."

"Ha!" She tucked in her wings. Her chest was heaving.

"Listen, it helped me to focus on Dad. Remember what's

important to you. Close your eyes and think about your human life."

She closed her eyes, but almost instantly cried out in frustration and flapped her wings.

"Stop," I said. "Don't fly away!"

She tilted her head and gurgled in a pleading way. I started talking to her the way I would to a scared animal. I wasn't really paying attention to the words. I was just trying to keep my tone calm. But after a minute I realized I was telling her about my travels with Dad, and the memories that had helped me get out of bird form. I told her about the time Dad and I got stuck in the Venice airport and I ate so many cannoli, I got sick. I told her about the time in Egypt when I found the scorpion in my sock, and Dad managed to kill it with a TV remote control. I told her how we'd gotten separated once in the London Underground and how scared I was until Dad finally found me. I told her some pretty embarrassing stories that I'd never shared with anyone, because who could I share them with? And it seemed to me that Sadie listened. At least she stopped flapping her wings. Her breathing slowed. She became very still, and her eyes didn't look so panicked.

"Okay, Sadie," I said at last. "I've got an idea. Here's what we're going to do."

I took Dad's magic box out of its leather bag. I wrapped the bag around my forearm and tied it with the straps as best I could. "Hop on."

Sadie flew up and perched at my wrist. Even with my make-shift armguard, her sharp talons dug into my skin.

"We'll get you out of this," I said. "Keep trying. Relax, and focus on your human life. You'll figure it out, Sadie. I know you will. I'll carry you until then."

"*Ha.*"

"Come on," I said. "Let's find Bast."

With my sister perched on my arm, I walked to the elevator. A businessman with a rolling suitcase was waiting by the doors. His eyes widened when he saw me. I must've looked pretty strange—a tall black kid in dirty, ragged Egyptian clothes, with a weird box tucked under one arm and a bird of prey perched on the other.

"How's it going?" I said.

"I'll take the stairs." He hurried off.

The elevator took me to the ground level. Sadie and I crossed to the departures curb. I looked around desperately, hoping to see Bast, but instead I caught the attention of a curbside policeman. The guy frowned and started lumbering in my direction.

"Stay calm," I told Sadie. Resisting the urge to run, I turned and walked through the revolving doors.

Here's the thing—I always get a little edgy around police. I remember when I was like seven or eight and still a cute little kid, it wasn't a problem; but as soon as I hit eleven, I started to get the Look, like *What's that kid doing here? Is he going to steal something?* I mean it's ridiculous, but it's a fact. I'm not saying it happens with *every* police officer, but when it doesn't happen—let's just say it's a pleasant surprise.

This was not one of the pleasant times. I knew the cop was going to follow me, and I knew I had to act calm and walk like I had a purpose...which is not easy with a kite on your arm.

Christmas vacation, so the airport was pretty full—mostly families standing in line at the ticket counters, kids arguing and parents labeling luggage. I wondered what that would be like: a normal family trip, no magic problems or monsters chasing you.

Stop it, I told myself. *You've got work to do.*

But I didn't know where to go. Would Bast be inside security? Outside? The crowds parted as I walked through the terminal. People stared at Sadie. I knew I couldn't wander around looking lost. It was only a matter of time before the cops—

"Young man."

I turned. It was the police officer from outside. Sadie squawked, and the cop backed up, resting his hand on his nightstick.

"You can't have pets in here," he told me.

"I have tickets...." I tried to reach my pockets. Then I remembered that Bast had our tickets.

The cop scowled. "You'd better come with me."

Suddenly a woman's voice called: "There you are, Carter!"

Bast was hurrying over, pushing her way through the crowd. I'd never been happier to see an Egyptian god in my life.

Somehow she'd managed to change clothes. She wore a rose-colored pantsuit, lots of gold jewelry, and a cashmere coat, so she looked like a wealthy businesswoman. Ignoring the cop, she sized up my appearance and wrinkled her nose. "Carter, I *told* you not to wear those horrible falconry clothes. Honestly, you look like you've been sleeping in the wild!"

She took out a handkerchief and made a big production of wiping my face, while the policeman stared.

"*Uh*, ma'am," he finally managed. "Is this your—"

"Nephew," Bast lied. "I'm so sorry, officer. We're heading to Memphis for a falconry competition. I hope he hasn't caused any problems. We're going to miss our flight!"

"*Um*, the falcon can't fly..."

Bast giggled. "Well, of course it can fly, officer. It's a bird!"

His face reddened. "I mean on a plane."

"Oh! We have the paperwork." To my amazement, she pulled out an envelope and handed it to the cop, along with our tickets.

"I see," the cop said. He looked our tickets over. "You bought...a first class ticket for your falcon."

"It's a black kite, actually," Bast said. "But yes, it's a very temperamental bird. A prizewinner, you know. Give it a coach seat and try to offer it pretzels, and I won't be held responsible for the consequences. No, we *always* fly first class, don't we, Carter?"

"*Um*, yeah...Aunt Kitty."

She flashed me a look that said: *I'll get you for that.* Then she went back to smiling at the cop, who handed back our tickets and Sadie's "paperwork."

"Well, if you'll excuse us, officer. That's a very handsome uniform, by the way. Do you work out?" Before he could respond, Bast grabbed my arm and hurried me toward the security checkpoint. "Don't look back," she said under her breath.

As soon as we turned the corner, Bast pulled me aside by the vending machines.

"The Set animal is close," she said. "We've got a few minutes at best. What's wrong with Sadie?"

"She can't..." I stammered. "I don't know exactly."

"Well, we'll have to figure it out on the plane."

"How did you change clothes?" I asked. "And the document for the bird..."

She waved her hand dismissively. "Oh, mortal minds are weak. That 'document' is an empty ticket sleeve. And my clothes haven't really changed. It's just a glamour."

I looked at her more closely, and I saw she was right. Her new clothes flickered like a mirage over her usual leopard-skin bodysuit. As soon as she pointed it out, the magic seemed flimsy and obvious.

"We'll try to make it to the gate before the Set animal," she said. "It will be easier if you stow your things in the Duat."

"What?"

"You don't really want to tote that box around under your arm, do you? Use the Duat as a storage bin."

"How?"

Bast rolled her eyes. "Honestly, what do they teach magicians these days?"

"We had about twenty seconds of training!"

"Just imagine a space in the air, like a shelf or a treasure chest—"

"A locker?" I asked. "I've never had a school locker."

"Fine. Give it a combination lock—anything you want. Imagine opening the locker with your combination. Then shove the box inside. When you need it again, just call it to mind, and it will appear."

I was skeptical, but I imagined a locker. I gave it a combination: 13/32/33—retired numbers for the Lakers, obviously:

Chamberlain, Johnson, Abdul-Jabbar. I held out my dad's magic box and let it go, sure it would smash to the floor. Instead, the box disappeared.

"Cool," I said. "Are you sure I can get it back?"

"No," Bast said. "Now, come on!"

22. Leroy Meets the Locker of Doom

C A R T E R

I'D NEVER GONE THROUGH SECURITY with a live bird of prey before. I thought it would cause a holdup, but instead the guards moved us into a special line. They checked our paperwork. Bast smiled a lot, flirted with the guards and told them they must be working out, and they waved us through. Bast's knives didn't set off the alarms, so maybe she'd stored them in the Duat. The guards didn't even try to put Sadie through the X-ray machine.

I was retrieving my shoes when I heard a scream from the other side of security.

Bast cursed in Egyptian. "We were too slow."

I looked back and saw the Set animal charging through the terminal, knocking passengers out of its way. Its weird rabbit ears swiveled back and forth. Foam dripped from its curved, toothy snout, and its forked tail lashed around, looking for something to sting.

"Moose!" a lady screamed. "Rabid moose!"

Everyone started screaming, running in different directions and blocking the Set animal's path.

"Moose?" I wondered.

Bast shrugged. "No telling what mortals will perceive. Now the idea will spread by power of suggestion."

Sure enough, more passengers started yelling "Moose!" and running around as the Set animal plowed through the lines and got tangled up in the stanchions. TSA officers surged forward, but the Set animal tossed them aside like rag dolls.

"Come on!" Bast told me.

"I can't just let it hurt these people."

"We can't stop it!"

But I didn't move. I wanted to believe Horus was giving me courage, or that maybe the past few days had finally woken up some dormant bravery gene I'd inherited from my parents. But the truth was scarier. This time, nobody was making me take a stand. I *wanted* to do it.

People were in trouble because of us. I *had* to fix it. I felt the same kind of instinct I felt when Sadie needed my help, like it was time for me to step up. And yes, it terrified me. But it also felt *right*.

"Go to the gate," I told Bast. "Take Sadie. I'll meet you there."

"What? Carter—"

"Go!" I imagined opening my invisible locker: 13/32/33. I reached out my hand, but not for my dad's magic box. I concentrated on something I'd lost in Luxor. It *had* to be there. For a moment, I felt nothing. Then my hand closed around a hard leather grip, and I pulled my sword out of nowhere.

Bast's eyes widened. "Impressive."

"Get moving," I said. "It's my turn to run interference."

"You realize it'll kill you."

"Thanks for the vote of confidence. Now, scat!"

Bast took off at top speed, Sadie flapping to stay balanced on her arm.

A shot rang out. I turned and saw the Set animal plow into a cop who'd just fired at its head to no effect. The poor cop flew backward and toppled over the metal detector gate.

"Hey, moose!" I screamed.

The Set animal locked its glowing eyes on me.

Well done! Horus said. *We will die with honor!*

Shut up, I thought.

I glanced behind me to make sure Bast and Sadie were out of sight. Then I approached the creature.

"So you've got no name?" I asked. "They couldn't think of one ugly enough?"

The creature snarled, stepping over the unconscious policeman.

"*Set animal* is too hard to say," I decided. "I'll call you Leroy."

Apparently, Leroy didn't like his name. He lunged.

I dodged his claws and managed to smack him in the snout with the flat of my blade, but that barely fazed him. Leroy backed up and charged again, slavering, baring his fangs. I slashed at his neck, but Leroy was too smart. He darted to the left and sank his teeth into my free arm. If it hadn't been for my makeshift leather armguard, I would've been minus one arm. As it was, Leroy's fangs still bit clear through the leather. Red-hot pain shot up my arm.

I yelled, and a primal surge of power coursed through my body. I felt myself rising off the ground and the golden aura of the hawk warrior forming around me. The Set animal's jaws were pried open so fast that it yelped and let go of my arm. I stood, now encased in a magical barrier twice my normal size, and kicked Leroy into the wall.

Good! said Horus. *Now dispatch the beast to the netherworld!*

Quiet, man. I'm doing all the work.

I was vaguely aware of security guards trying to regroup, yelling into their walkie-talkies and calling for help. Travelers were still screaming and running around. I heard a little girl shout: "Chicken man, get the moose!"

You know how hard it is to feel like an extreme falcon-headed combat machine when somebody calls you "chicken man"?

I raised my sword, which was now at the center of a ten-foot-long energy blade.

Leroy shook the dust off his cone-shaped ears, and came at me again. My armored form might've been powerful, but it was also clumsy and slow; moving it around felt like moving through Jell-O. Leroy dodged my sword strike and landed on my chest, knocking me down. He was a lot heavier than he looked. His tail and claws raked against my armor. I caught his neck in my glowing fists and tried to keep his fangs away from my face, but everywhere he drooled, my magical shield hissed and steamed. I could feel my wounded arm going numb.

Alarms blared. More passengers crowded toward the

checkpoint to see what was happening. I had to end this soon—before I passed out from pain or more mortals got hurt.

I felt my strength fading, my shield flickering. Leroy's fangs were an inch from my face, and Horus was offering no words of encouragement.

Then I thought about my invisible locker in the Duat. I wondered if other things could be put in there too...large, evil things.

I closed my hands around Leroy's throat and wedged my knee against his rib cage. Then I imagined an opening in the Duat—in the air right above me: 13/32/33. I imagined my locker opening as wide as it could go.

With my last bit of strength, I pushed Leroy straight up. He flew toward the ceiling, his eyes widening with surprise as he passed through an unseen rift and disappeared.

"Where'd it go?" someone yelled.

"Hey, kid!" another guy called. "You okay?"

My energy shield was gone. I wanted to pass out, but I had to leave before the security guys came out of their shock and arrested me for moose fighting. I got to my feet and threw my sword at the ceiling. It disappeared into the Duat. Then I wrapped the torn leather around my bleeding arm as best I could and ran for the gates.

I reached our flight just as they were closing the door.

Apparently, word of the chicken man incident hadn't spread quite yet. The gate agent gestured back toward the checkpoint as she took my ticket. "What's all the noise up there?"

"A moose got through security," I said. "It's under control now." Before she could ask questions, I raced down the jetway.

I collapsed into my seat across the aisle from Bast. Sadie, still in kite form, was pacing in the window seat next to me.

Bast let out a huge sigh of relief. "Carter, you made it! But you're hurt. What happened?"

I told her.

Bast's eyes widened. "You put the Set animal in your locker? Do you know how much strength that requires?"

"Yeah," I said. "I was there."

The flight attendant started making her announcements. Apparently, the security incident hadn't affected our flight. The plane pushed back from the gate on time.

I doubled forward in pain, and only then did Bast notice how bad my arm was. Her expression turned grim.

"Hold still." She whispered something in Egyptian, and my eyes began to feel heavy.

"You'll need sleep to heal that wound," she said.

"But if Leroy comes back—"

"Who?"

"Nothing."

Bast studied me as if seeing me for the first time. "That was extraordinarily brave, Carter. Facing the Set monster—you have more tomcat in you than I realized."

"*Um*—thanks?"

She smiled and touched my forehead. "We'll be in the air soon, my tomcat. Sleep."

I couldn't really object. Exhaustion washed over me, and I closed my eyes.

Naturally my soul decided to take a trip.

I was in *ba* form, circling above Phoenix. It was a brilliant winter morning. The cool desert air felt good under my wings. The city looked different in the daylight—a vast grid of beige and green squares dotted with palm trees and swimming pools. Stark mountains rose up here and there like chunks of the moon. The most prominent mountain was right below me—a long ridge with two distinct peaks. What had Set's minion called it on my first soul visit? Camelback Mountain.

Its foothills were crowded with luxury homes, but the top was barren. Something caught my attention: a crevice between two large boulders, and a shimmer of heat coming from deep within the mountain—something that no human eye would've noticed.

I folded my wings and dove toward the crevice.

Hot air vented out with such force that I had to push my way through. About fifty feet down, the crevice opened up, and I found myself in a place that simply couldn't exist.

The entire inside of the mountain had been hollowed out. In the middle of the cavern, a giant pyramid was under construction. The air rang with the sound of pickaxes. Hordes of demons cut blood-red limestone into blocks and hauled it to the middle of the cave, where more swarms of demons used ropes and ramps to hoist the blocks into place, the way my dad said the Giza pyramids were built. But the Giza pyramids had taken, like, twenty years each to complete. This pyramid was already halfway done.

There was something odd about it, too—and not just the

blood-red color. When I looked at it I felt a familiar tingle, as if the whole structure were humming with a tone ... no, a *voice* I almost recognized.

I spotted a smaller shape floating in the air above the pyramid—a reed barge like Uncle Amos's riverboat. On it stood two figures. One was a tall demon in leather armor. The other was a burly man in red combat fatigues.

I circled closer, trying to stay in the shadows because I wasn't sure I was really invisible. I landed on the top of the mast. It was a tricky maneuver, but neither of the boat's occupants looked up.

"How much longer?" asked the man in red.

He had Set's voice, but he looked completely different than he had in my last vision. He wasn't a slimy black thing, and he wasn't on fire—except for the scary mixture of hatred and amusement burning in his eyes. He had a big thick body like a linebacker's, with meaty hands and a brutish face. His short bristly hair and trimmed goatee were as red as his combat fatigues. I'd never seen camouflage that color before. Maybe he was planning on hiding out in a volcano.

Next to him, the demon bowed and scraped. It was the weird rooster-footed guy I'd seen before. He was at least seven feet tall and scarecrow thin, with bird talons for feet. And unfortunately, this time I could see his face. It was almost too hideous to describe. You know those anatomy exhibits where they show dead bodies without skin? Imagine one of those faces alive, only with solid black eyes and fangs.

"We're making excellent progress, master!" the demon

promised. "We conjured a hundred more demons today. With luck, we will be done at sunset on your birthday!"

"That is unacceptable, Face of Horror," Set said calmly.

The servant flinched. I guessed his name was Face of Horror. I wondered how long it had taken his mom to think of that. *Bob? No. Sam? No. How about Face of Horror?*

"B-but, master," Face stammered. "I thought—"

"Do not think, demon. Our enemies are more resourceful than I imagined. They have temporarily disabled my favorite pet and are now speeding toward us. We must finish before they arrive. *Sunrise* on my birthday, Face of Horror. No later. It will be the dawn of my new kingdom. I will scour all life from this continent, and this pyramid shall stand as a monument to my power—the final and eternal tomb of Osiris!"

My heart almost stopped. I looked down at the pyramid again, and I realized why it felt so familiar. It had an energy to it—*my father's* energy. I can't explain how, but I knew his sarcophagus lay hidden somewhere inside that pyramid.

Set smiled cruelly, as if he would be just as happy to have Face obey him or to rip Face to pieces. "You understand my order?"

"Yes, lord!" Face of Horror shifted his bird feet, as if building up his courage. "But may I ask, lord . . . why stop there?"

Set's nostrils flared. "You are one sentence away from destruction, Face of Horror. Choose your next words carefully."

The demon ran his black tongue across his teeth. "Well, my lord, is the annihilation of only one god worthy of your glorious self? What if we could create even more chaos energy—to feed your pyramid for all time and make you the eternal lord of all worlds?"

A hungry light danced in Set's eyes. "'Lord of all worlds' ...that has a nice ring to it. And how would you accomplish this, puny demon?"

"Oh, not I, my lord. I am an insignificant worm. But if we were to capture the others: Nephthys—"

Set kicked Face in the chest, and the demon collapsed, wheezing. "I told you never to speak her name."

"Yes, master," Face panted. "Sorry, master. But if we were to capture her, and the others...think on the power you could consume. With the right plan..."

Set began nodding, warming to the idea. "I think it's time we put Amos Kane to use."

I tensed. Was Amos here?

"Brilliant, master. A brilliant plan."

"Yes, I'm glad I thought of it. Soon, Face of Horror, *very* soon, Horus, Isis, and my treacherous wife will bow at my feet—and Amos will help. We'll have a nice little family reunion."

Set looked up—straight at me, as if he'd known I was there all along, and gave me that rip-you-to-pieces smile. "Isn't that right, boy?"

I wanted to spread my wings and fly. I had to get out of the cavern and warn Sadie. But my wings wouldn't work. I sat there paralyzed as Set reached out to grab me.

23. Professor Thoth's Final Exam

SADIE HERE. SORRY FOR THE DELAY, though I don't suppose you'd notice on a recording. My nimble-fingered brother dropped the microphone into a pit full of...oh, never mind. Back to the story.

Carter woke with such a start, he banged his knees against the drinks tray, which was quite funny.

"Sleep well?" I asked.

He blinked at me in confusion. "You're human."

"How kind of you to notice."

I took another bite of my pizza. I'd never eaten pizza from a china plate or had a Coke in a glass (with ice no less—Americans are so odd) but I was enjoying first class.

"I changed back an hour ago." I cleared my throat. "It—ah—was helpful, what you said, about focusing on what's important."

Awkward saying even that much, as I remembered everything he'd told me while I was in kite form about his travels

277

with Dad—how he'd gotten lost in the Underground, gotten sick in Venice, squealed like a baby when he'd found a scorpion in his sock. So much ammunition to tease him with, but oddly I wasn't tempted. The way he'd poured out his soul . . . Perhaps he thought I didn't understand him in kite form—but he'd been so honest, so unguarded, and he'd done it all to calm me down. If he hadn't given me something to focus on, I'd probably still be hunting field mice over the Potomac.

Carter had spoken about Dad as if their travels together had been a great thing, yes, but also quite a chore, with Carter always struggling to please and be on his best behavior, with no one to relax with, or talk to. Dad *was*, I had to admit, quite a presence. You'd be hard-pressed *not* to want his approval. (No doubt that's where I get my own stunningly charismatic personality.) I saw him only twice a year, and even so I had to prepare myself mentally for the experience. For the first time, I began to wonder if Carter really had the better end of the bargain. Would I trade my life for his?

I also decided not to tell him what had finally changed me back to human. I hadn't focused on Dad at all. I'd imagined Mum alive, imagined us walking down Oxford Street together, gazing in the shop windows and talking and laughing—the kind of ordinary day we'd never gotten to share. An impossible wish, I know. But it had been powerful enough to remind me of who I was.

Didn't say any of that, but Carter studied my face, and I sensed that he picked up my thoughts a little too well.

I took a sip of Coke. "You missed lunch, by the way."

"You didn't try to wake me?"

On the other side of the aisle, Bast burped. She'd just finished off her plate of salmon and was looking quite satisfied. "I could summon more Friskies," she offered. "Or cheese sandwiches."

"No thanks," Carter muttered. He looked devastated.

"God, Carter," I said. "If it's that important to you, I've got some pizza left—"

"It's not that," he said. And he told us how his *ba* had almost been captured by Set.

The news gave me trouble breathing. I felt as if I were stuck in kite form again, unable to think clearly. Dad trapped in a red pyramid? Poor Amos used as some sort of pawn? I looked at Bast for some kind of reassurance. "Isn't there anything we can do?"

Her expression was grim. "Sadie, I don't know. Set will be most powerful on his birthday, and sunrise is the most auspicious moment for magic. If he's able to generate one great explosion of storm energy at sunrise on that day—using not only his own magic, but augmenting it with the power of other gods he's managed to enslave . . . the amount of chaos he could unleash is almost unimaginable." She shuddered. "Carter, you say a simple demon gave him this idea?"

"Sounded like it," Carter said. "Or he tweaked the original plan, anyway."

She shook her head. "This is not like Set."

I coughed. "What do you mean? It's *exactly* like him."

"No," Bast insisted. "This is horrendous, even for him. Set wishes to be king, but such an explosion might leave him nothing to rule. It's almost as if . . ." She stopped herself, the thought seemingly too disturbing. "I don't understand it, but we'll be landing soon. You'll have to ask Thoth."

"You make it sound like you're not coming," I said.

"Thoth and I don't get along very well. Your chances of surviving might be better—"

The seat belt light came on. The captain announced we'd started our descent into Memphis. I peered out the window and saw a vast brown river cutting across the landscape—a river larger than any I'd ever seen. It reminded me uncomfortably of a giant snake.

The flight attendant came by and pointed to my lunch plate. "Finished, dear?"

"It seems so," I told her gloomily.

Memphis hadn't gotten word that it was winter. The trees were green and the sky was a brilliant blue.

We'd insisted Bast not "borrow" a car this time, so she agreed to rent one as long as she got a convertible. I didn't ask where she got the money, but soon we were cruising through the mostly deserted streets of Memphis with our BMW's top down.

I remember only snapshots of the city. We passed through one neighborhood that might've been a set from *Gone with the Wind*—big white mansions on enormous lawns shaded by cypress trees, although the plastic Santa Claus displays on the rooftops rather ruined the effect. On the next block, we almost got killed by an old woman driving a Cadillac out of a church parking lot. Bast swerved and honked her horn, and the woman just smiled and waved. Southern hospitality, I suppose.

After a few more blocks, the houses turned to rundown shacks. I spotted two African American boys wearing jeans and muscle shirts, sitting on their front porch, strumming acoustic guitars and singing. They sounded so good, I was tempted to stop.

On the next corner stood a cinder block restaurant with a hand-painted sign that read CHICKEN & WAFFLES. There was a queue of twenty people outside.

"You Americans have the strangest taste. What planet is this?" I asked.

Carter shook his head. "And where would Thoth be?"

Bast sniffed the air and turned left onto a street called Poplar. "We're getting close. If I know Thoth, he'll find a center of learning. A library, perhaps, or a cache of books in a magician's tomb."

"Don't have a lot of those in Tennessee," Carter guessed.

Then I spotted a sign and grinned broadly. "The University of Memphis, perhaps?"

"Well done, Sadie!" Bast purred.

Carter scowled at me. The poor boy gets jealous, you know.

A few minutes later, we were strolling through the campus of a small college: red brick buildings and wide courtyards. It was eerily quiet, except for the sound of a ball echoing on concrete.

As soon as Carter heard it, he perked up. "Basketball."

"Oh, please," I said. "We need to find Thoth."

But Carter followed the sound of the ball, and we followed him. He rounded the corner of a building and froze. "Let's ask them."

I didn't understand what he was on about. Then I turned the corner and yelped. On the basketball court, five players were in the middle of an intense game. They wore an assortment of jerseys from different American teams, and they all seemed keen to win—grunting and snarling at each other, stealing the ball and pushing.

Oh...and the players were all baboons.

"The sacred animal of Thoth," Bast said. "We must be in the right place."

One of the baboons had lustrous golden hair much lighter than the others, and a more, er, colorful bottom. He wore a purple jersey that seemed oddly familiar.

"Is that...a Lakers jersey?" I asked, hesitant to even name Carter's silly obsession.

He nodded, and we both grinned.

"Khufu!" we yelled.

True, we hardly knew the baboon. We'd spent less than a day with him, and our time at Amos's mansion seemed like ages ago, but still I felt like we'd recovered a long-lost friend.

Khufu jumped into my arms and barked at me. *"Agh! Agh!"* He picked through my hair, looking for bugs, I suppose [No comments from you, Carter!], and dropped to the ground, slapping the pavement to show how pleased he was.

Bast laughed. "He says you smell like flamingos."

"You speak Baboon?" Carter asked.

The goddess shrugged. "He also wants to know where you've been."

"Where *we've* been?" I said. "Well, first off, tell him I've spent the better part of the day as a kite, which is *not* a fla-mingo and does not end in *-o*, so it shouldn't be on his diet. Secondly—"

"Hold on." Bast turned to Khufu and said, *"Agh!"* Then she looked back at me. "All right, go ahead."

I blinked. "Okay . . . *um,* and secondly, where has *he* been?"

She relayed this in a single grunt.

Khufu snorted and grabbed the basketball, which sent his baboon friends into a frenzy of barking and scratching and snarling.

"He dove into the river and swam back," Bast translated, "but when he returned, the house was destroyed and we were gone. He waited a day for Amos to return, but he never did. So Khufu made his way to Thoth. Baboons are under his protection, after all."

"Why is that?" Carter asked. "I mean, no offense, but Thoth is the god of knowledge, right?"

"Baboons are very wise animals," Bast said.

"Agh!" Khufu picked his nose, then turned his Technicolor bum our direction. He threw his friends the ball. They began to fight over it, showing one another their fangs and slapping their heads.

"Wise?" I asked.

"Well, they're not *cats,* mind you," Bast added. "But, yes, wise. Khufu says that as soon as Carter keeps his promise, he'll take you to the professor."

I blinked. "The prof— Oh, you mean . . . right."

"What promise?" Carter asked.

The corner of Bast's mouth twitched. "Apparently, you promised to show him your basketball skills."

Carter's eyes widened in alarm. "We don't have time!"

"Oh, it's fine," Bast promised. "It's best that I go now."

"But where, Bast?" I asked, as I wasn't anxious to be separated from her again. "How will we find you?"

The look in her eyes changed to something like guilt, as if she'd just caused a horrible accident. "I'll find you when you get out, if you get out...."

"What do you mean *if*?" Carter asked, but Bast had already turned into Muffin and raced off.

Khufu barked at Carter most insistently. He tugged his hand, pulling him onto the court. The baboons immediately broke into two teams. Half took off their jerseys. Half left them on. Carter, sadly, was on the no-jersey team, and Khufu helped him pull his shirt off, exposing his bony chest. The teams began to play.

Now, I know nothing about basketball. But I'm fairly sure one isn't supposed to trip over one's shoes, or catch a pass with one's forehead, or dribble (is that the word?) with both hands as if petting a possibly rabid dog. But that is exactly the way Carter played. The baboons simply ran him over, quite literally. They scored basket after basket as Carter staggered back and forth, getting hit with the ball whenever it came close to him, tripping over monkey limbs until he was so dizzy he turned in a circle and fell over. The baboons stopped playing and watched him in disbelief. Carter lay in the middle of the court, covered in sweat and panting. The other baboons looked at Khufu. It was quite obvious what they were thinking: *Who invited this human?* Khufu covered his eyes in shame.

"Carter," I said with glee, "all that talk about basketball and the Lakers, and you're absolute *rubbish*! Beaten by monkeys!"

He groaned miserably. "It was ... it was Dad's favorite game."

I stared at him. Dad's favorite game. God, why hadn't that occurred to me?

Apparently he took my gobsmacked expression as further criticism.

"I ... I can tell you any NBA stat you want," he said a bit desperately. "Rebounds, assists, free throw percentages."

The other baboons went back to their game, ignoring Carter and Khufu both. Khufu let out a disgusted noise, half gag and half bark.

I understood the sentiment, but I came forward and offered Carter my hand. "Come on, then. It doesn't matter."

"If I had better shoes," he suggested. "Or if I wasn't so tired—"

"Carter," I said with a smirk. "It *doesn't* matter. And I'll not breathe a word to Dad when we save him."

He looked at me with obvious gratitude. (Well, I am rather wonderful, after all.) Then he took my hand, and I hoisted him up.

"Now for god's sake, put on your shirt," I said. "And Khufu, it's time you took us to the professor."

Khufu led us into a deserted science building. The air in the hallways smelled of vinegar, and the empty classroom labs looked like something from an American high school, not the sort of place a god would hang out. We climbed the stairs and found a row of professors' offices. Most of the doors were closed. One had been left open, revealing a space no bigger than a broom closet stuffed with books, a tiny desk, and one chair. I wondered if that professor had done something bad to get such a small office.

"*Agh!*" Khufu stopped in front of a polished mahogany door, much nicer than the others. A newly stenciled name glistened on the glass: DR. THOTH.

Without knocking, Khufu opened the door and waddled inside.

"After you, chicken man," I said to Carter. (And yes, I'm sure he was regretting telling me about that particular incident. After all, I couldn't *completely* stop teasing him. I have a reputation to maintain.)

I expected another broom closet. Instead, the office was impossibly big.

The ceiling rose at least ten meters, with one side of the office all windows, looking out over the Memphis skyline. Metal stairs led up to a loft dominated by an enormous telescope, and from somewhere up there came the sound of an electric guitar being strummed quite badly. The other walls of the office were crammed with bookshelves. Worktables overflowed with weird bits and bobs—chemistry sets, half-assembled computers, stuffed animals with electrical wires sticking out of their heads. The room smelled strongly of cooked beef, but with a smokier, tangier scent than I'd ever smelled.

Strangest of all, right in front of us, half a dozen longnecked birds—ibises—sat behind desks like receptionists, typing on laptop computers with their beaks.

Carter and I looked at each other. For once I was at a loss for words.

"Agh!" Khufu called out.

Up in the loft, the strumming stopped. A lanky man in his twenties stood up, electric guitar in hand. He had an unruly mane of blond hair like Khufu's, and he wore a stained white lab coat over faded jeans and a black T-shirt. At first I thought blood was trickling from the corner of his mouth. Then I realized it was some sort of meat sauce.

"Fascinating." He broke into a wide grin. "I've discovered something, Khufu. This is not Memphis, Egypt."

Khufu gave me a sideways look, and I could swear his expression meant, Duh.

"I've also discovered a new form of magic called blues music," the man continued. "And barbecue. Yes, you must try barbecue."

Khufu looked unimpressed. He climbed to the top of a bookshelf, grabbed a box of Cheerios, and began to munch.

The guitar man slid down the banister with perfect balance and landed in front of us. "Isis and Horus," he said. "I see you've found new bodies."

His eyes were a dozen colors, shifting like a kaleidoscope, with hypnotic effect.

I managed to stutter, "Um, we're not—"

"Oh, I see," he said. "Trying to share the body, eh? Don't think I'm fooled for a minute, Isis. I know you're in charge."

"But she's not!" I protested. "My name is Sadie Kane. I assume you're Thoth?"

He raised an eyebrow. "You claim not to know me? Of course I'm Thoth. Also called Djehuti. Also called—"

I stifled a laugh. "Ja-hooty?"

Thoth looked offended. "In Ancient Egyptian, it's a perfectly fine name. The Greeks called me Thoth. Then later they confused me with their god Hermes. Even had the nerve to rename my sacred city Hermopolis, though we're nothing alike. Believe me, if you've ever met Hermes—"

"*Agh!*" Khufu yelled through a mouthful of Cheerios.

"You're right," Thoth agreed. "I'm getting off track. So you claim to be Sadie Kane. And..." He swung a finger toward Carter, who was watching the ibises type on their laptops. "I suppose you're not Horus."

"Carter Kane," said Carter, still distracted by the ibises' screens. "What *is* that?"

Thoth brightened. "Yes, they're called computers. Marvelous, aren't they? Apparently—"

"No, I mean what are the birds typing?" Carter squinted and read from the screen. "'A Short Treatise on the Evolution of Yaks'?"

"My scholarly essays," Thoth explained. "I try to keep several projects going at once. For instance, did you know this university does not offer majors in astrology or leechcraft? Shocking! I intend to change that. I'm renovating new headquarters right now down by the river. Soon Memphis will be a true center of learning!"

"That's brilliant," I said halfheartedly. "We need help defeating Set."

The ibises stopped typing and stared at me.

Thoth wiped the barbecue sauce off his mouth. "You have the nerve to ask this after last time?"

"Last time?" I repeated.

"I have the account here somewhere...." Thoth patted the pockets of his lab coat. He pulled out a rumpled piece of paper and read it. "No, grocery list."

He tossed it over his shoulder. As soon as the paper hit the floor, it became a loaf of wheat bread, a jug of milk, and a six-pack of Mountain Dew.

Thoth checked his sleeves. I realized the stains on his coat were smeared words, printed in every language. The stains moved and changed, forming hieroglyphs, English letters, Demotic symbols. He brushed a stain off his lapel and seven letters fluttered to the floor, forming a word: *crawdad*. The word morphed into a slimy crustacean, like a shrimp, which wiggled its legs for only a moment before an ibis snapped it up.

"Ah, never mind," Thoth said at last. "I'll just tell you the short version: To avenge his father, Osiris, Horus challenged Set to a duel. The winner would become king of the gods."

"Horus won," Carter said.

"You do remember!"

"No, I read about it."

"And do you remember that without my help, Isis and you both would've died? Oh, I tried to mediate a solution to prevent the battle. That is one of my jobs, you know: to keep balance between order and chaos. But no-o-o, Isis convinced me to help your side because Set was getting too powerful. And the battle almost destroyed the world."

He complains too much, Isis said inside my head. *It wasn't so bad.*

"No?" Thoth demanded, and I got the feeling he could hear her voice as well as I could. "Set stabbed out Horus's eye."

"Ouch." Carter blinked.

"Yes, and I replaced it with a new eye made of moonlight. The Eye of Horus—your famous symbol. That was *me,* thank you very much. And when you cut off Isis's head—"

"Hold up." Carter glanced at me. "I cut off her *head?*"

I got better, Isis assured me.

"Only because I healed you, Isis!" Thoth said. "And yes, Carter, Horus, whatever you call yourself, you were so mad, you cut off her head. You were reckless, you see—about to charge Set while you were still weak, and Isis tried to stop you. That made you so angry you took your sword— Well, the point is, you almost destroyed each other before you could defeat Set. If you start another fight with the Red Lord, beware. He will use chaos to turn you against each other."

We'll defeat him again, Isis promised. *Thoth is just jealous.*

"Shut up," Thoth and I said at the same time.

He looked at me with surprise. "So, Sadie...you *are* trying to stay in control. It won't last. You may be blood of the pharaohs, but Isis is a deceptive, power-hungry—"

"I can contain her," I said, and I had to use all my will to keep Isis from blurting out a string of insults.

Thoth fingered the frets of his guitar. "Don't be so sure. Isis probably told you she helped defeat Set. Did she also tell you she was the reason Set got out of control in the first place? She exiled our first king."

"You mean Ra?" Carter said. "Didn't he get old and decide to leave the earth?"

Thoth snorted. "He was old, yes, but he was *forced* to leave. Isis got tired of waiting for him to retire. She wanted her husband, Osiris, to become king. She also wanted more power. So one day, while Ra was napping, Isis secretly collected a bit of the sun god's drool."

"*Eww,*" I said. "Since when does drool make you powerful?"

Thoth scowled at me accusingly. "You mixed the spit with clay to create a poisonous snake. That night, the serpent slipped into Ra's bedroom and bit him on the ankle. No amount of magic, even mine, could heal him. He would've died—"

"Gods can die?" Carter asked.

"Oh, yes," Thoth said. "Of course most of the time we rise again from the Duat—eventually. But this poison ate away at Ra's very being. Isis, of course, acted innocent. She cried to see Ra in pain. She tried to help with her magic. Finally she told Ra there was only one way to save him: Ra must tell her his secret name."

"Secret name?" I asked. "Like Bruce Wayne?"

"Everything in Creation has a secret name," Thoth said. "Even gods. To know a being's secret name is to have power over that creature. Isis promised that with Ra's secret name, she could heal him. Ra was in so much pain, he agreed. And Isis healed him."

"But it gave her power over him," Carter guessed.

"Extreme power," Thoth agreed. "She forced Ra to retreat into the heavens, opening the way for her beloved, Osiris, to become the new king of the gods. Set had been an important lieutenant to Ra, but he could not bear to see his brother Osiris become king. This made Set and Osiris enemies, and here we are five millennia later, still fighting that war, all because of Isis."

"But that's not my fault!" I said. "I would never do something like that."

"Wouldn't you?" Thoth asked. "Wouldn't you do anything to save your family, even if it upset the balance of the cosmos?"

His kaleidoscope eyes locked on mine, and I felt a surge of defiance. Well, why shouldn't I help my family? Who was this nutter in a lab coat telling me what I could and couldn't do?

Then I realized I didn't know who was thinking that: Isis or me. Panic started building in my chest. If I couldn't tell my own thoughts from those of Isis, how long before I went completely mad?

"No, Thoth," I croaked. "You have to believe me. I'm in control—me, Sadie—and I need your help. Set has our father."

I let it spill out, then—everything from the British Museum to Carter's vision of the red pyramid. Thoth listened without comment, but I could swear new stains developed on his lab coat as I talked, as if some of my words were being added to the mix.

"Just look at something for us," I finished. "Carter, hand him the book."

Carter rummaged through his bag and brought out the

book we'd stolen in Paris. "You wrote this, right?" he said. "It tells how to defeat Set."

Thoth unfolded the papyrus pages. "Oh, dear. I hate reading my old work. Look at this sentence. I'd never write it that way now." He patted his lab coat pockets. "Red pen—does anyone have one?"

Isis chafed against my willpower, insisting that we blast some sense into Thoth. *One fireball,* she pleaded. *Just one enormous magical fireball, please?*

I can't say I wasn't tempted, but I kept her under control.

"Look, Thoth," I said. "Ja-hooty, whatever. Set is about to destroy North America at the very least, possibly the world. Millions of people will die. You said you care about balance. Will you help us or not?"

For a moment, the only sounds were ibis beaks tapping on keyboards.

"You *are* in trouble," Thoth agreed. "So let me ask, why do you think your father put you in this position? Why did he release the gods?"

I almost said, *To bring back Mum.* But I didn't believe that anymore.

"My mum saw the future," I guessed. "Something bad was coming. I think she and Dad were trying to stop it. They thought the only way was to release the gods."

"Even though using the power of the gods is incredibly dangerous for mortals," Thoth pressed, "and against the law of the House of Life—a law that I convinced Iskandar to make, by the way."

I remembered something the old Chief Lector had told me

in the Hall of Ages. "Gods have great power, but only humans have creativity." "I think my mum convinced Iskandar that the rule was wrong. Maybe he couldn't admit it publicly, but she made him change his mind. Whatever is coming—it's so bad, gods and mortals are going to need each other."

"And what is coming?" Thoth asked. "The rise of Set?" His tone was coy, like a teacher trying a trick question.

"Maybe," I said carefully, "but I don't know."

Up on the bookshelf, Khufu belched. He bared his fangs in a messy grin.

"You have a point, Khufu," Thoth mused. "She does not sound like Isis. Isis would never admit she doesn't know something."

I had to clamp a mental hand over Isis's mouth.

Thoth tossed the book back to Carter. "Let's see if you act as well as you talk. I will explain the spell book, provided you prove to me that you truly have control of your gods, that you're not simply repeating the same old patterns."

"A test?" Carter said. "We accept."

"Now, hang on," I protested. Maybe being homeschooled, Carter didn't realize that "test" is normally a bad thing.

"Wonderful," Thoth said. "There is an item of power I require from a magician's tomb. Bring it to me."

"Which magician's tomb?" I asked.

But Thoth took a piece of chalk from his lab coat and scribbled something in the air. A doorway opened in front of him.

"How did you do that?" I asked. "Bast said we can't summon portals during the Demon Days."

"Mortals can't," Thoth agreed. "But a god of magic can. If you succeed, we'll have barbecue."

The doorway pulled us into a black void, and Thoth's office disappeared.

24. I Blow Up Some Blue Suede Shoes

"WHERE ARE WE?" I ASKED.

We stood on a deserted avenue outside the gates of a large estate. We still seemed to be in Memphis—at least the trees, the weather, the afternoon light were all the same.

The estate must've been several acres at least. The white metal gates were done in fancy designs of silhouetted guitar players and musical notes. Beyond them, the driveway curved through the trees up to a two-story house with a white-columned portico.

"Oh, no," Carter said. "I recognize those gates."

"What? Why?"

"Dad brought me here once. A great magician's tomb... Thoth has got to be kidding."

"Carter, what are you talking about? Is someone buried here?"

He nodded. "This is Graceland. Home to the most famous musician in the world."

"Michael Jackson lived here?"

"No, dummy," Carter said. "Elvis Presley."

I wasn't sure whether to laugh or curse. "Elvis Presley. You mean white suits with rhinestones, big slick hair, Gran's record collection—*that* Elvis?"

Carter looked around nervously. He drew his sword, even though we seemed to be totally alone. "This is where he lived and died. He's buried in back of the mansion."

I stared up at the house. "You're telling me Elvis was a magician?"

"Don't know." Carter gripped his sword. "Thoth did say something about music being a kind of magic. But something's not right. Why are we the only ones here? There's usually a mob of tourists."

"Christmas holidays?"

"But no security?"

I shrugged. "Maybe it's like what Zia did at Luxor. Maybe Thoth cleared everyone out."

"Maybe." But I could tell Carter was still uneasy. He pushed the gates, and they opened easily. "Not right," he muttered.

"No," I agreed. "But let's go pay our respects."

As we walked up the drive, I couldn't help thinking that the home of "the King" wasn't very impressive. Compared to some of the rich and famous homes I'd seen on TV, Elvis's place looked awfully small. It was just two stories high, with that white-columned portico and brick walls. Ridiculous plaster lions flanked the steps. Perhaps things were simpler back in Elvis's day, or maybe he spent all his money on rhinestone suits.

We stopped at the foot of the steps.

"So Dad brought you here?" I asked.

"Yeah." Carter eyed the lions as if expecting them to attack. "Dad loves blues and jazz, mostly, but he said Elvis was important because he took African American music and made it popular for white people. He helped invent rock and roll. Anyway, Dad and I were in town for a symposium or something. I don't remember. Dad insisted I come here."

"Lucky you." And yes, perhaps I was beginning to understand that Carter's life with Dad hadn't been all glamour and holiday, but still I couldn't help being a bit jealous. Not that I'd ever wanted to see Graceland, of course, but Dad had never insisted on taking me anywhere—at least until the British Museum trip when he disappeared. I hadn't even known Dad was an Elvis fan, which was rather horrifying.

We walked up the steps. The front door swung open all by itself.

"I don't like that," Carter said.

I turned to look behind us, and my blood went ice cold. I grabbed my brother's arm. "*Um*, Carter, speaking of things we don't like..."

Coming up the driveway were two magicians brandishing staffs and wands.

"Inside," Carter said. "Quick!"

I didn't have much time to admire the house. There was a dining room to our left and a living room–music room to our right, with a piano and a stained glass archway decorated with peacocks. All the furniture was roped off. The house smelled like old people.

"Item of power," I said. "Where?"

"I don't know," Carter snapped. "They didn't have 'items of power' listed on the tour!"

I glanced out the window. Our enemies were getting close. The bloke in front wore jeans, a black sleeveless shirt, boots, and a battered cowboy hat. He looked more like an outlaw than a magician. His friend was similarly dressed but much heftier, with tattooed arms, a bald head, and a scraggly beard. When they were ten meters away, the man with the cowboy hat lowered his staff, which morphed into a shotgun.

"Oh, please!" I yelled, and pushed Carter into the living room.

The blast shattered Elvis's front door and set my ears ringing. We scrambled to our feet and ran deeper into the house. We passed through an old-fashioned kitchen, then into the strangest den I'd ever seen. The back wall was made of vine-covered bricks, with a waterfall trickling down the side. The carpet was green shag (floor *and* ceiling, mind you) and the furniture was carved with creepy animal shapes. Just in case all that wasn't dreadful enough, plaster monkeys and stuffed lions had been strategically placed around the room. Despite the danger we were in, the place was so horrid, I just had to stop and marvel.

"God," I said. "Did Elvis have *no* taste?"

"The Jungle Room," Carter said. "He decorated it like this to annoy his dad."

"I can respect that."

Another shotgun blast roared through the house.

"Split up," Carter said.

"Bad idea!" I could hear the magicians tromping through the rooms, smashing things as they came closer.

"I'll distract them," Carter said. "You search. The trophy room is through there."

"Carter!"

But the fool ran off to protect me. I *hate* it when he does that. I should have followed him, or run the other way, but I stood frozen in shock as he turned the corner with his sword raised, his body beginning to glow with a golden light...and everything went wrong.

Blam! An emerald flash brought Carter to his knees. For a heartbeat, I thought he'd been hit with the shotgun, and I had to stifle a scream. But immediately, Carter collapsed and began to shrink, clothes, sword and all—melting into a tiny sliver of green.

The lizard that used to be my brother raced toward me, climbed up my leg and into my palm, where it looked at me desperately.

From around the corner, a gruff voice said, "Split up and find the sister. She'll be somewhere close."

"Oh, Carter," I whispered fondly to the lizard. "I will *so* kill you for this."

I stuffed him in my pocket and ran.

The two magicians continued to smash and crash their way through Graceland, knocking over furniture and blasting things to bits. Apparently they were not Elvis fans.

I ducked under some ropes, crept through a hallway, and found the trophy room. Amazingly, it was full of trophies. Gold records crowded the walls. Rhinestone Elvis jumpsuits glittered in four glass cases. The room was dimly lit, probably to keep the jumpsuits from blinding visitors, and music played softly from overhead speakers: Elvis warning everyone not to step on his blue suede shoes.

I scanned the room but found nothing that looked magical. The suits? I hoped Thoth did not expect me to wear one. The gold records? Lovely Frisbees, but no.

"Jerrod!" a voice called to my right. A magician was coming down the hallway. I darted toward the other exit, but a voice just outside it called back, "Yeah, I'm over here."

I was surrounded.

"Carter," I whispered. "Curse your lizard brain."

He fluttered nervously in my pocket but was no help.

I fumbled through my magician's bag and grasped my wand. Should I try drawing a magic circle? No time, and I didn't want to duel toe-to-toe with two older magicians. I had to stay mobile. I took out my rod and willed it into a full-length staff. I could set it on fire, or turn it into a lion, but what good would that do? My hands started to tremble. I wanted to crawl into a ball and hide beneath Elvis's gold record collection.

Let me take over, Isis said. *I can turn our enemies to dust.*

No, I told her.

You will get us both killed.

I could feel her pressing against my will, trying to bust out. I could taste her anger with these magicians. How dare they challenge us? With a word, we could destroy them.

No, I thought again. Then I remembered something Zia had said: *Use whatever you have available.* The room was dimly lit...perhaps if I could make it darker.

"Darkness," I whispered. I felt a tugging sensation in my stomach, and the lights flickered off. The music stopped. The light continued to dim—even the sunlight faded from the windows until the entire room went black.

Somewhere to my left, the first magician sighed in exasperation. "Jerrod!"

"Wasn't me, Wayne!" Jerrod insisted. "You always blame me!"

Wayne muttered something in Egyptian, still moving towards me. I needed a distraction.

I closed my eyes and imagined my surroundings. Although it was pitch-black, I could still sense Jerrod in the hallway to my left, stumbling through the darkness. I sensed Wayne on the other side of the wall to the right, only a few steps from the doorway. And I could visualize the four glass display cases with Elvis's suits.

They're tossing your house, I thought. *Defend it!*

A stronger pull in my gut, as if I were lifting a heavy weight—then the display cases blew open. I heard the shuffling of stiff cloth, like sails in the wind, and was dimly aware of four pale white shapes in motion—two heading to either door.

Wayne yelled first as the empty Elvis suits tackled him. His shotgun lit up the dark. Then to my left, Jerrod shouted in surprise. A heavy *clump!* told me he'd been knocked over. I decided to go in Jerrod's direction—better an off-balance bloke than one with a shotgun. I slipped through the doorway and down a hall, leaving Jerrod scuffling behind me and yelling, "Get off! Get off!"

Take him while he's down, Isis urged. *Burn him to ashes!*

Part of me knew she had a point: if I left Jerrod in one piece, he would be up in no time and after me again; but it didn't seem right to hurt him, especially while he was being tackled by Elvis suits. I found a door and burst outside into the afternoon sunlight.

I was in the backyard of Graceland. A large fountain gurgled nearby, ringed by grave markers. One had a glass-encased flame at the top and was heaped with flowers. I took a wild guess: it must be Elvis's.

A magician's tomb.

Of course. We'd been searching the house, but the item of power would be at his gravesite. But what exactly *was* the item?

Before I could approach the grave, the door burst open. The big bald man with the straggly beard stumbled out. A tattered Elvis suit had its sleeves wrapped around his neck like it was getting a piggyback ride.

"Well, well." The magician threw off the jumpsuit. His voice confirmed for me that he was the one called Jerrod. "You're just a little girl. You've caused us a lot of trouble, missy."

He lowered his staff and fired a shot of green light. I raised my wand and deflected the bolt of energy straight up. I heard a surprised coo—the cry of a pigeon—and a newly made lizard fell out of the sky at my feet.

"Sorry," I told it.

Jerrod snarled and threw down his staff. Apparently, he specialized in lizards, because the staff morphed into a komodo dragon the size of a London taxicab.

The monster charged me with unnatural speed. It opened

its jaws and would've bitten me in half, but I just had time to wedge my staff in its mouth.

Jerrod laughed. "Nice try, girl!"

I felt the dragon's jaws pressing on the staff. It was only a matter of seconds before the wood snapped, and then I'd be a komodo dragon's snack. *A little help*, I told Isis. Carefully, very carefully, I tapped in to her strength. Doing so without letting her take over was like riding a surfboard over a tidal wave, trying desperately to stay on my feet. I felt five thousand years of experience, knowledge, and power course through me. She offered me options, and I selected the simplest. I channeled power through my staff and felt it grow hot in my hands, glowing white. The dragon hissed and gurgled as my staff elongated, forcing the creature's jaws open wider, wider, and then: *boom!*

The dragon shattered into kindling and sent the splintered remains of Jerrod's staff raining down around me.

Jerrod had only a moment to look stunned before I threw my wand and whapped him solidly on the forehead. His eyes crossed, and he collapsed on the pavement. My wand returned to my hand.

That would've been a lovely happy ending...except I'd forgotten about Wayne. The cowboy-hatted magician stumbled out the door, almost tripping over his friend, but he recovered with lightning speed.

He shouted, "Wind!" and my staff flew out of my hands and into his.

He smiled cruelly. "Well fought, darlin'. But elemental magic is always quickest."

He struck the ends of both staffs, his and mine, against the pavement. A wave rippled over the dirt and pavement as if the ground had become liquid, knocking me off my feet and sending my wand flying. I scrambled backwards on hands and knees, but I could hear Wayne chanting, summoning fire from the staffs.

Rope, Isis said. *Every magician carries rope.*

Panic had made my mind go blank, but my hand instinctively went for my magic bag. I pulled out a small bit of twine. Hardly a rope, but it triggered a memory—something Zia had done in the New York museum. I threw the twine at Wayne and yelled a word Isis suggested: *"Tas!"*

A golden hieroglyph burned in the air over Wayne's head:

The twine whipped toward him like an angry snake, growing longer and thicker as it flew. Wayne's eyes widened. He stumbled back and sent jets of flame shooting from both staffs, but the rope was too quick. It lashed round his ankles and toppled him sideways, wrapping round his whole body until he was encased in a twine cocoon from chin to toes. He struggled and screamed and called me quite a few unflattering names.

I got up unsteadily. Jerrod was still out cold. I retrieved my staff, which had fallen next to Wayne. He continued straining against the twine and cursing in Egyptian, which sounded strange with an American Southern accent.

Finish him, Isis warned. *He can still speak. He will not rest until he destroys you.*

"Fire!" Wayne screamed. "Water! Cheese!"

Even the cheese command did not work. I reckoned his rage was throwing his magic off balance, making it impossible to focus, but I knew he would recover soon.

"Silence," I said.

Wayne's voice abruptly stopped working. He kept screaming, but no sound came out.

"I'm not your enemy," I told him. "But I can't have you killing me, either."

Something wriggled in my pocket, and I remembered Carter. I took him out. He looked okay, except of course for the fact he was still a lizard.

"I'll try to change you back," I told him. "Hopefully I don't make things worse."

He made a little croak that didn't convey much confidence.

I closed my eyes and imagined Carter as he should be: a tall boy of fourteen, badly dressed, very human, very annoying. Carter began to feel heavy in my hands. I put him down and watched as the lizard grew into a vaguely human blob. By the count of three, my brother was lying on his stomach, his sword and pack next to him on the lawn.

He spit grass out of his mouth. "How'd you do that?"

"I don't know," I admitted. "You just seemed . . . wrong."

"Thanks a lot." He got up and checked to make sure he had all his fingers. Then he saw the two magicians and his mouth fell open. "What did you do to them?"

"Just tied one up. Knocked one out. Magic."

"No, I mean . . ." He faltered, searching for words, then gave up and pointed.

I looked at the magicians and yelped. Wayne wasn't moving. His eyes and mouth were open, but he wasn't blinking or breathing. Next to him, Jerrod looked just as frozen. As we watched, their mouths began to glow as if they'd swallowed matches. Two tiny yellow orbs of fire popped out from between their lips and shot into the air, disappearing in the sunlight.

"What—what was that?" I asked. "Are they dead?"

Carter approached them cautiously and put his hand on Wayne's neck. "It doesn't even feel like skin. More like rock."

"No, they were human! I didn't turn them to rock!"

Carter felt Jerrod's forehead where I'd whacked him with my wand. "It's cracked."

"What?"

Carter picked up his sword. Before I could even scream, he brought the hilt down on Jerrod's face and the magician's head cracked into shards like a flowerpot.

"They're made of clay," Carter said. "They're both *shabti*."

He kicked Wayne's arm and I heard it crunch under the twine.

"But they were casting spells," I said. "And talking. They were *real*."

As we watched, the *shabti* crumbled to dust, leaving nothing behind but my bit of twine, two staffs, and some grungy clothes.

"Thoth was testing us," Carter said. "Those balls of fire, though . . ." He frowned as if trying to recall something important.

"Probably the magic that animated them," I guessed. "Flying back to their master—like a recording of what they did?"

It sounded like a solid theory to me, but Carter seemed awfully troubled. He pointed to the blasted back door of Graceland. "Is the whole house like that?"

"Worse." I looked at the ruined Elvis jumpsuit under Jerrod's clothes and scattered rhinestones. Maybe Elvis had no taste, but I still felt bad about trashing the King's palace. If the place had been important to Dad...Suddenly an idea perked me up. "What was it Amos said, when he repaired that saucer?"

Carter frowned. "This is a whole house, Sadie. Not a saucer."

"Got it," I said. "*Hi-nehm!*"

A gold hieroglyphic symbol flickered to life in my palm.

I held it up and blew it towards the house. The entire outline of Graceland began to glow. The pieces of the door flew back into place and mended themselves. The tattered bits of Elvis clothing disappeared.

"Wow," Carter said. "Do you think the inside is fixed too?"

"I—" My vision blurred, and my knees buckled. I would've knocked my head on the pavement if Carter hadn't caught me.

"It's okay," he said. "You did a lot of magic, Sadie. That was amazing."

"But we haven't even found the item Thoth sent us for."

"Yeah," Carter said. "Maybe we have."

He pointed to Elvis's grave, and I saw it clearly: a memento left behind by some adoring fan—a necklace with a silver loop-topped cross, just like the one on Mum's T-shirt in my old photograph.

"An ankh," I said. "The Egyptian symbol for eternal life."

Carter picked it up. There was a small papyrus scroll attached to the chain.

"What's this?" he murmured, and unrolled the sheet. He stared at it so hard I thought he'd burn a hole in it.

"What?" I looked over his shoulder.

The painting looked quite ancient. It showed a golden, spotted cat holding a knife in one paw and chopping the head off a snake.

Beneath it, in black marker, someone had written: *Keep up the fight!*

"That's vandalism, isn't it?" I asked. "Marking up an ancient drawing like that? Rather an odd thing to leave for Elvis."

Carter didn't seem to hear. "I've seen this picture before. It's in a lot of tombs. Don't know why it never occurred to me..."

I studied the picture more closely. Something about it did seem rather familiar.

"You know what it means?" I asked.

"It's the Cat of Ra, fighting the sun god's main enemy, Apophis."

"The snake," I said.

"Yeah, Apophis was—"

"The embodiment of chaos," I said, remembering what Nut had said.

Carter looked impressed, as well he should have. "Exactly. Apophis was even worse than Set. The Egyptians thought Doomsday would come when Apophis ate the sun and destroyed all of Creation."

"But... the cat killed it," I said hopefully.

"The cat had to kill it over and over again," Carter said. "Like what Thoth said about repeating patterns. The thing is ... I asked Dad one time if the cat had a name. And he said nobody knows for sure, but most people assume it's Sekhmet, this fierce lion goddess. She was called the Eye of Ra because she did his dirty work. He saw an enemy; she killed it."

"Fine. So?"

"So the cat doesn't look like Sekhmet. It just occurred to me..."

I finally saw it, and a shiver went down my back. "The Cat of Ra looks exactly like Muffin. It's Bast."

Just then the ground rumbled. The memorial fountain began to glow, and a dark doorway opened.

"Come on," I said. "I've got some questions for Thoth. And then I'm going to punch him in the beak."

25. We Win an All-Expenses-Paid Trip to Death

BEING TURNED INTO A LIZARD can really mess up your day. As we stepped through the doorway, I tried to hide it, but I was feeling pretty bad.

You're probably thinking: *Hey, you already turned into a falcon. What's the big deal?* But someone else *forcing* you into another form—that's totally different. Imagine yourself in a trash compactor, your entire body smashed into a shape smaller than your hand. It's painful and it's humiliating. Your enemy pictures you as a stupid harmless lizard, then imposes their will on you, overpowering your thoughts until you have to be what *they* want you to be. I guess it could've been worse. He could've pictured me as a fruit bat, but still...

Of course I felt grateful to Sadie for saving me, but I also felt like a complete loser. It was bad enough that I'd embarrassed myself on the basketball court with a troop of baboons. But I'd also totally failed in battle. Maybe I'd done okay with

Leroy, the airport monster, but faced with a couple of magicians (even clay ones), I got turned into a reptile in the first two seconds. How would I stand a chance against Set?

I was shaken out of those thoughts when we emerged from the portal, because we were definitely not in Thoth's office.

In front of us loomed a life-size glass-and-metal pyramid, almost as big as the ones at Giza. The skyline of downtown Memphis rose up in the distance. At our backs were the banks of the Mississippi River.

The sun was setting, turning the river and the pyramid to gold. On the pyramid's front steps, next to a twenty-foot-tall pharaoh statue labeled RAMESSES THE GREAT, Thoth had set out a picnic with barbecued ribs and brisket, bread and pickles, the works. He was playing his guitar with a portable amp. Khufu stood nearby, covering his ears.

"Oh, good." Thoth strummed a chord that sounded like the death cry of a sick donkey. "You lived."

I stared up at the pyramid in amazement. "Where did this come from? You didn't just . . . build it, did you?" I remembered my *ba* trip to Set's red pyramid, and suddenly pictured gods building monuments all over the U.S.

Thoth chuckled. "I didn't have to build it. The people of Memphis did that. Humans never really forget Egypt, you know. Every time they build a city on the banks of a river, they remember their heritage, buried deep in their subconscious. This is the Pyramid Arena—sixth largest pyramid in the world. It used to be a sports arena for . . . what is that game you like, Khufu?"

"*Agh!*" Khufu said indignantly. And I swear he gave me a dirty look.

"Yes, basketball," Thoth said. "But the arena fell on hard times. It's been abandoned for years. Well, no longer. I'm moving in. You do have the ankh?"

For a moment, I wondered if it had been such a good idea helping Thoth, but we needed him. I tossed him the necklace.

"Excellent," he said. "An ankh from the tomb of Elvis. Powerful magic!"

Sadie clenched her fists. "We almost died getting that. You tricked us."

"Not a trick," he insisted. "A test."

"Those *things*," Sadie said, "the *shabti*—"

"Yes, my best work in centuries. A shame to break them, but I couldn't have you beating up on *real* magicians, could I? *Shabti* make excellent stunt doubles."

"So you saw the whole thing," I muttered.

"Oh, yes." Thoth held out his hand. Two little fires danced across his palm—the magic essences we'd seen escape from the *shabti*'s mouths. "These are . . . recording devices, I suppose you'd say. I got a full report. You defeated the *shabti* without killing. I must admit I'm impressed, Sadie. You controlled your magic and controlled Isis. And you, Carter, did well turning into a lizard."

I thought he was teasing me. Then I realized there was genuine sympathy in his eyes, as if my failure had also been some kind of test.

"You will find worse enemies ahead, Carter," he warned.

"Even now, the House of Life sends its best against you. But you will also find friends where you least expect them."

I didn't know why, but I got the feeling he was talking about Zia...or maybe that was just wishful thinking.

Thoth stood and handed Khufu his guitar. He tossed the ankh at the statue of Ramesses, and the necklace fastened itself around the pharaoh's neck.

"There you are, Ramesses," Thoth said to the statue. "Here's to our new life."

The statue glowed faintly, as if the sunset had just gotten ten times brighter. Then the glow spread to the entire pyramid before slowly fading.

"Oh, yes," Thoth mused. "I think I'll be happy here. Next time you children visit me, I'll have a much bigger laboratory."

Scary thought, but I tried to stay focused.

"That's not all we found," I said. "You need to explain *this*."

I held out the painting of the cat and the snake.

"It's a cat and a snake," Thoth said.

"Thank you, god of wisdom. You placed it for us to find, didn't you? You're trying to give us some kind of clue."

"Who, me?"

Just kill him, Horus said.

Shut up, I said.

At least kill the guitar.

"The cat is Bast," I said, trying to ignore my inner psycho falcon. "Does this have something to do with why our parents released the gods?"

Thoth gestured toward the picnic plates. "Did I mention we have barbecue?"

Sadie stomped her foot. "We had a deal, Ja-hooty!"

"You know...I like that name," Thoth mused, "but not so much when *you* say it. I believe our deal was that I would explain how to use the spell book. May I?"

He held out his hand. Reluctantly I dug the magic book out of my bag and handed it over.

Thoth unfolded the pages. "Ah, this takes me back. So many formulae. In the old days, we believed in ritual. A good spell might take weeks to prepare, with exotic ingredients from all over the world."

"We don't have weeks," I said.

"Rush, rush, rush." Thoth sighed.

"*Agh,*" Khufu agreed, sniffing the guitar.

Thoth closed the book and handed it back to me. "Well, it's an incantation for destroying Set."

"We *know* that," Sadie said. "Will it destroy him forever?"

"No, no. But it will destroy his form in this world, banishing him deep into the Duat and reducing his power so he will not be able to appear again for a long, long time. Centuries, most likely."

"Sounds good," I said. "How do we read it?"

Thoth stared at me like the answer should be obvious. "You cannot read it now because the words can only be spoken in Set's presence. Once before him, Sadie should open the book and recite the incantation. She'll know what to do when the time comes."

"Right," Sadie said. "And Set will just stand there calmly while I read him to death."

Thoth shrugged. "I did not say it would be easy. You'll also require two ingredients for the spell to work—a verbal ingredient, Set's secret name—"

"*What?*" I protested. "How are we supposed to get that?"

"With difficulty, I'd imagine. You can't simply read a secret name from a book. The name must come from the owner's own lips, in his own pronunciation, to give you power over him."

"Great," I said. "So we just force Set to tell us."

"Or trick him," Thoth said. "Or convince him."

"Isn't there any other way?" Sadie asked.

Thoth brushed an ink splotch off his lab coat. A hieroglyph turned into a moth and fluttered away. "I suppose . . . yes. You could ask the person closest to Set's heart—the person who loves him most. She would also have the ability to speak the name."

"But nobody loves Set!" Sadie said.

"His wife," I guessed. "That other goddess, Nephthys."

Thoth nodded. "She's a river goddess. Perhaps you could find her in a river."

"This just gets better and better," I muttered.

Sadie frowned at Thoth. "You said there was another ingredient?"

"A physical ingredient," Thoth agreed, "a feather of truth."

"A what?" Sadie asked.

But I knew what he was talking about, and my heart sank. "You mean from the Land of the Dead."

Thoth beamed. "Exactly."

"Wait," Sadie said. "What is he talking about?"

I tried to conceal my fear. "When you died in Ancient

Egypt, you had to take a journey to the Land of the Dead," I explained. "A really *dangerous* journey. Finally, you made it to the Hall of Judgment, where your life was weighed on the Scales of Anubis: your heart on one side, the feather of truth on the other. If you passed the test, you were blessed with eternal happiness. If you failed, a monster ate your heart and you ceased to exist."

"Ammit the Devourer," Thoth said wistfully. "Cute little thing."

Sadie blinked. "So we're supposed to get a feather from this Hall of Judgment *how*, exactly?"

"Perhaps Anubis will be in a good mood," Thoth suggested. "It happens every thousand years or so."

"But how do we even get to the Land of the Dead?" I asked. "I mean...without dying."

Thoth gazed at the western horizon, where the sunset was turning blood-red. "Down the river at night, I should think. That's how most people pass into the Land of the Dead. I would take a boat. You'll find Anubis at the end of the river—" He pointed north, then changed his mind and pointed south. "Forgot, rivers flow south here. Everything is backward."

"*Agh!*" Khufu ran his fingers down the frets of the guitar and ripped out a massive rock 'n' roll riff. Then he belched as if nothing had happened and set down the guitar. Sadie and I just stared at him, but Thoth nodded as if the baboon had said something profound.

"Are you sure, Khufu?" Thoth asked.

Khufu grunted.

"Very well." Thoth sighed. "Khufu says he would like to go

with you. I told him he could stay here and type my doctoral thesis on quantum physics, but he's not interested."

"Can't imagine why," Sadie said. "Glad to have Khufu along, but where do we find a boat?"

"You are the blood of pharaohs," Thoth said. "Pharaohs always have access to a boat. Just make sure you use it wisely."

He nodded toward the river. Churning toward the shore was an old-fashioned paddlewheel steamboat with smoke billowing from its stacks.

"I wish you a good journey," Thoth said. "Until we meet again."

"We're supposed to take *that*?" I asked. But when I turned to look at Thoth, he was gone, and he'd taken the barbecue with him.

"Wonderful," Sadie muttered.

"*Agh!*" Khufu agreed. He took our hands and led us down to the shore.

26. Aboard the *Egyptian Queen*

As far as rides to the Land of Death go, the boat was pretty cool. It had multiple decks with ornate railings painted black and green. The side paddlewheels churned the river into froth, and along the paddlewheel housings the name of the boat glittered in gold letters: EGYPTIAN QUEEN.

At first glance, you'd think the boat was just a tourist attraction: one of those floating casinos or cruise boats for old people. But if you looked closer you started noticing strange little details. The boat's name was written in Demotic and in hieroglyphics underneath the English. Sparkly smoke billowed from the stacks as if the engines were burning gold. Orbs of multicolored fire flitted around the decks. And on the prow of the ship, two painted eyes moved and blinked, scanning the river for trouble.

"That's odd," Sadie remarked.

I nodded. "I've seen eyes painted on boats before. They still do that all over the Mediterranean. But usually they don't move."

"What? No, not the stupid eyes. That lady on the highest deck. Isn't that..." Sadie broke into a grin. "Bast!"

Sure enough, our favorite feline was leaning out the window of the pilot's house. I was about to wave to her, when I noticed the creature standing next to Bast, gripping the wheel. He had a human body and was dressed in the white uniform of a boat captain. But instead of a head, a double-bladed axe sprouted from his collar. And I'm not talking about a *small* axe for chopping wood. I'm talking *battle*-axe: twin crescent-shaped iron blades, one in front where his face should be, one in the back, the edges splattered with suspicious-looking dried red splotches.

The ship pulled up to the dock. Balls of fire began zipping around—lowering the gangplank, tying off ropes, and basically doing crew-type stuff. How they did it without hands, and without setting everything on fire, I don't know, but it wasn't the strangest thing I'd seen that week.

Bast climbed down from the wheelhouse. She hugged us as we came aboard—even Khufu, who tried to return the favor by grooming her for lice.

"I'm glad you survived!" Bast told us. "What happened?"

We gave her the basics and her hair poofed out again. "Elvis? *Gah!* Thoth is getting cruel in his old age. Well, I can't say I'm glad to be on this boat again. I *hate* the water, but I suppose—"

"You've been on this boat before?" I asked.

Bast's smile wavered. "A million questions as usual, but let's eat first. The captain is waiting."

I wasn't anxious to meet a giant axe, and I wasn't

enthusiastic about another one of Bast's grilled-cheese-and-Friskies dinners, but we followed her inside the boat.

The dining parlor was lavishly decorated in Egyptian style. Colorful murals depicting the gods covered the walls. Gilded columns supported the ceiling. A long dining table was laden with every kind of food you could want—sandwiches, pizzas, hamburgers, Mexican food, you name it. It *way* made up for missing Thoth's barbecue. On a side table stood an ice chest, a line of golden goblets, and a soda dispenser with about twenty different choices. The mahogany chairs were carved to look like baboons, which reminded me a little too much of Graceland's Jungle Room, but Khufu thought they were okay. He barked at his chair just to show it who was top monkey, then sat on its lap. He picked an avocado from a basket of fruit and started peeling it.

Across the room, a door opened, and the axe dude came in. He had to duck to avoid cleaving the doorframe.

"Lord and Lady Kane," the captain said, bowing. His voice was a quivery hum that resonated along his front blade. I saw a video one time of a guy playing music by hitting a saw with a hammer, and that's sort of the way the captain sounded. "It is an honor to have you aboard."

"'Lady Kane,'" Sadie mused. "I like that."

"I am Bloodstained Blade," the captain said. "What are your orders?"

Sadie raised an eyebrow at Bast. "He takes orders from us?"

"Within reason," Bast said. "He is bound to your family. Your father…" She cleared her throat. "Well, he and your mother summoned this boat."

The axe demon made a disapproving hum. "You haven't told them, goddess?"

"I'm getting to it," Bast grumbled.

"Told us what?" I asked.

"Just details." She rushed on. "The boat can be summoned once a year, and only in times of great need. You'll need to give the captain your orders now. He must have clear directions if we're to proceed, ah, *safely*."

I wondered what was bothering Bast, but the axe dude was waiting for orders, and the flecks of dried blood on his blades told me I'd better not keep him in suspense.

"We need to visit the Hall of Judgment," I told him. "Take us to the Land of the Dead."

Bloodstained Blade hummed thoughtfully. "I will make the arrangements, Lord Kane, but it will take time."

"We don't have a lot of that." I turned to Sadie. "It's... what, the evening of the twenty-seventh?"

She nodded in agreement. "Day after tomorrow, at sunrise, Set completes his pyramid and destroys the world unless we stop him. So, yes, Captain Very Large Blade, or whatever it is, I'd say we're in a bit of a rush."

"We will, of course, do our best," said Bloodstained Blade, though his voice sounded a little, well, sharp. "The crew will prepare your staterooms. Will you dine while you wait?"

I looked at the table laden with food and realized how hungry I was. I hadn't eaten since we were in the Washington Monument. "Yeah. *Um*, thanks, BSB."

The captain bowed again, which made him look a little too much like a guillotine. Then he left us to our dinner.

At first, I was too busy eating to talk. I inhaled a roast beef sandwich, a couple of pieces of cherry pie with ice cream, and three glasses of ginger ale before I finally came up for air.

Sadie didn't eat as much. Then again she'd had lunch on the plane. She settled for a cheese-and-cucumber sandwich and one of those weird British drinks she likes—a Ribena. Khufu carefully picked out everything that ended with -o— Doritos, Oreos, and some chunks of meat. Buffalo? Armadillo? I was scared to even guess.

The balls of fire floated attentively around the room, refilling our goblets and clearing away our plates as we finished.

After so many days spent running for our lives, it felt good to just sit at a dinner table and relax. The captain's informing us that he couldn't transport us instantly to the Land of the Dead was the best news I'd had in a long time.

"*Agh!*" Khufu wiped his mouth and grabbed one of the balls of fire. He fashioned it into a glowing basketball and snorted at me.

For once I was pretty sure what he'd said in Baboon. It wasn't an invitation. It meant something like: "I'm going to play basketball by myself now. I will not invite you because your lack of skill would make me throw up."

"No problem, man," I said, though my face felt hot with embarrassment. "Have fun."

Khufu snorted again, then loped off with the ball under his arm. I wondered if he'd find a court somewhere on board.

At the far end of the table, Bast pushed her plate away. She'd hardly touched her tuna Friskies.

"Not hungry?" I asked.

"*Hmm?* Oh...I suppose not." She turned her goblet listlessly. She was wearing an expression I didn't associate with cats: guilt.

Sadie and I locked eyes. We had a brief, silent exchange, something like:

You ask her.

No, you.

Of course Sadie's better at giving dirty looks, so I lost the contest.

"Bast?" I said. "What did the captain want you to tell us?"

She hesitated. "Oh, that? You shouldn't listen to demons. Bloodstained Blade is bound by magic to serve, but if he ever got loose, he'd use that axe on all of us, believe me."

"You're changing the subject," I said.

Bast traced her finger across the table, drawing hieroglyphs in the condensation ring from her goblet. "The truth? I haven't been on board since the night your mother died. Your parents had docked this boat on the Thames. After the...accident, your father brought me here. This is where we made our deal."

I realized she meant *right* here, at this table. My father had sat here in despair after Mom's death—with no one to console him except the cat goddess, an axe demon, and a bunch of floating lights.

I studied Bast's face in the dim light. I thought about the painting we'd found at Graceland. Even in human form, Bast looked so much like that cat—a cat drawn by some artist thousands of years ago.

"It wasn't just a chaos monster, was it?" I asked.

Bast eyed me. "What do you mean?"

"The thing you were fighting when our parents released you from the obelisk. It wasn't just a chaos monster. You were fighting Apophis."

All around the parlor, the servant fires dimmed. One dropped a plate and fluttered nervously.

"Don't say the Serpent's name," Bast warned. "Especially as we head into the night. Night is his realm."

"It's true, then." Sadie shook her head in dismay. "Why didn't you say anything? Why did you lie to us?"

Bast dropped her gaze. Sitting in the shadows, she looked weary and frail. Her face was etched with the traces of old battle scars.

"I was the Eye of Ra." She spoke quietly. "The sun god's champion, the instrument of his will. Do you have any idea what an honor it was?"

She extended her claws and studied them. "When people see pictures of Ra's warrior cat, they assume it's Sekhmet, the lioness. And she *was* his first champion, it's true. But she was too violent, too out of control. Eventually Sekhmet was forced to step down, and Ra chose *me* as his fighter: little Bast."

"Why do you sound ashamed?" Sadie asked. "You said it's an honor."

"At first I was proud, Sadie. I fought the Serpent for ages. Cats and snakes are mortal enemies. I did my job well. But then Ra withdrew to the heavens. He bound me to the Serpent with his last spell. He cast us both into that abyss, where I was charged to fight the Serpent and keep it down forever."

A realization crept over me. "So you *weren't* a minor prisoner. You were imprisoned longer than any of the other gods."

She closed her eyes. "I still remember Ra's words: 'My loyal cat. This is your greatest duty.' And I was proud to do it...for centuries. Then millennia. Can you imagine what it was like? Knives against fangs, slashing and thrashing, a never-ending war in the darkness. Our life forces grew weaker, my enemy's and mine, and I began to realize that was Ra's plan. The Serpent and I would rip each other to nothingness, and the world would be safe. Only in this way could Ra withdraw in peace of mind, knowing chaos would not overcome Ma'at. I would have done my duty, too. I had no choice. Until your parents—"

"Gave you an escape route," I said. "And you took it."

Bast looked up miserably. "I am the queen of cats. I have many strengths. But to be honest, Carter...cats are not very brave."

"And Ap—your enemy?"

"He stayed trapped in the abyss. Your father and I were sure of it. The Serpent was already greatly weakened from eons of fighting with me, and when your mother used her own life force to close the abyss, well...she worked a powerful feat of magic. There should've been no way for the Serpent to break through that kind of seal. But as the years have gone by...we became less and less sure the prison would hold him. If somehow he managed to escape and regain his strength, I cannot imagine what would happen. And it would be my fault."

I tried to imagine the serpent, Apophis—a creature of chaos even worse than Set. I pictured Bast with her knives, locked in combat with that monster for eons. Maybe I should've been angry at Bast for not telling us the truth earlier. Instead, I felt sorry for her. She'd been put in the same position we were now in—forced to do a job that was way too big for her.

"So why did my parents release you?" I asked. "Did they say?"

She nodded slowly. "I was losing my fight. Your father told me that your mother had foreseen…horrible things if the Serpent overcame me. They had to free me, give me time to heal. They said it was the first step in restoring the gods. I don't pretend to understand their whole plan. I was relieved to take your father's offer. I convinced myself I was doing the right thing for the gods. But it does not change the fact that I was a coward. I failed in my duty."

"It isn't your fault," I told her. "It wasn't fair of Ra to ask of you."

"Carter's right," Sadie said. "That's too much sacrifice for one person—one cat goddess, whatever."

"It was my king's will," Bast said. "The pharaoh can command his subjects for the good of the kingdom—even to lay down their lives—and they must obey. Horus knows this. He was the pharaoh many times."

She speaks truly, Horus said.

"Then you had a stupid king," I said.

The boat shuddered as if we'd ground the keel over a sandbar.

"Be careful, Carter," Bast warned. "Ma'at, the order of creation, hinges on loyalty to the rightful king. If you question it, you'll fall under the influence of chaos."

I felt so frustrated, I wanted to break something. I wanted to yell that order didn't seem much better than chaos if you had to get yourself killed for it.

You are being childish, Horus scolded. *You are a servant of Ma'at. These thoughts are unworthy.*

My eyes stung. "Then maybe *I'm* unworthy."

"Carter?" Sadie asked.

"Nothing," I said. "I'm going to bed."

I stormed off. One of the flickering lights joined me, guiding me upstairs to my quarters. The stateroom was probably very nice. I didn't pay attention. I just fell on the bed and passed out.

I seriously needed an extra-strength magic pillow, because my *ba* refused to stay put. [And no, Sadie, I don't think wrapping my head in duct tape would've worked either.]

My spirit floated up to the steamboat's wheelhouse, but it wasn't Bloodstained Blade at the wheel. Instead, a young man in leather armor navigated the boat. His eyes were outlined with kohl, and his head was bald except for a braided ponytail. The guy definitely worked out, because his arms were ripped. A sword like mine was strapped to his belt.

"The river is treacherous," he told me in a familiar voice. "A pilot cannot get distracted. He must always be alert for sandbars and hidden snags. That's why boats are painted with my eyes, you know—to see the dangers."

"The Eyes of Horus," I said. "You."

The falcon god glanced at me, and I saw that his eyes were two different colors—one blazing yellow like the sun, the other reflective silver like the moon. The effect was so disorienting, I had to look away. And when I did, I noticed that Horus's shadow didn't match his form. Stretched across the wheelhouse was the silhouette of a giant falcon.

"You wonder if order is better than chaos," he said. "You become distracted from our real enemy: Set. You should be taught a lesson."

I was about to say, *No really, that's okay*.

But immediately my *ba* was whisked away. Suddenly, I was on board an airplane—a big international aircraft like planes my dad and I had taken a million times. Zia Rashid, Desjardins, and two other magicians were scrunched up in a middle row, surrounded by families with screaming children. Zia didn't seem to mind. She meditated calmly with her eyes closed, while Desjardins and the other two men looked so uncomfortable, I almost wanted to laugh.

The plane rocked back and forth. Desjardins spilled wine all over his lap. The seat belt light blinked on, and a voice crackled over the intercom: "This is the captain. It looks like we'll be experiencing some minor turbulence as we make our descent into Dallas, so I'm going to ask the flight attendants—"

Boom! A blast rattled the windows—lightning followed immediately by thunder.

Zia's eyes snapped open. "The Red Lord."

The passengers screamed as the plane plummeted several hundred feet.

"*Il commence!*" Desjardins shouted over the noise. "Quickly!"

As the plane shook, passengers shrieked and grabbed

their seats. Desjardins got up and opened the overhead compartment.

"Sir!" a flight attendant yelled. "Sir, sit down!"

Desjardins ignored the attendant. He grabbed four familiar bags—magical tool kits—and threw them to his colleagues.

Then things really went wrong. A horrible shudder passed through the cabin and the plane lurched sideways. Outside the right-hand windows, I saw the plane's wing get sheared off by a five-hundred-mile-an-hour wind.

The cabin devolved into chaos—drinks, books, and shoes flying everywhere, oxygen masks dropping and tangling, people screaming for their lives.

"Protect the innocents!" Desjardins ordered.

The plane began to shake and cracks appeared in the windows and walls. The passengers went silent, slumping into unconsciousness as the air pressure dropped. The four magicians raised their wands as the airplane broke to pieces.

For a moment, the magicians floated in a maelstrom of storm clouds, chunks of fuselage, luggage, and spinning passengers still strapped to their seats. Then a white glow expanded around them, a bubble of power that slowed the breakup of the plane and kept the pieces swirling in a tight orbit. Desjardins reached out his hand and the edge of a cloud stretched toward him—a tendril of cottony white mist, like a safety line. The other magicians did likewise, and the storm bent to their will. White vapor wrapped around them and began to send out more tendrils, like funnel clouds, which snatched pieces of the plane and pulled them back together.

A child fell past Zia, but she pointed her staff and murmured a spell. A cloud enveloped the little girl and brought her back. Soon the four magicians were reassembling the plane around them, sealing the breaches with cloudy cobwebs until the entire cabin was encased in a glowing cocoon of vapor. Outside, the storm raged and thunder boomed, but the passengers slept soundly in their seats.

"Zia!" Desjardins shouted. "We can't hold this for long."

Zia ran past him up the aisle to the flight deck. Somehow the front of the plane had survived the breakup intact. The door was armored and locked, but Zia's staff flared, and the door melted like wax. She stepped through and found three unconscious pilots. The view through the window was enough to make me sick. Through the spiraling clouds, the ground was coming up fast—*very* fast.

Zia slammed her wand against the controls. Red energy surged through the displays. Dials spun, meters blinked, and the altimeter leveled out. The plane's nose came up, its speed dropping. As I watched, Zia glided the plane toward a cow pasture and landed it without even a bump. Then her eyes rolled back in her head, and she collapsed.

Desjardins found her and gathered her in his arms. "Quickly," he told his colleagues, "the mortals will wake soon."

They dragged Zia out of the cockpit, and my *ba* was swept away through a blur of images.

I saw Phoenix again—or at least *some* of the city. A massive red sandstorm churned across the valley, swallowing buildings and mountains. In the harsh, hot wind, I heard Set laughing, reveling in his power.

Then I saw Brooklyn: Amos's ruined house on the East

River and a winter storm raging overhead, howling winds slamming the city with sleet and hail.

And then I saw a place I didn't recognize: a river winding through a desert canyon. The sky was a blanket of pitch-black clouds, and the river's surface seemed to boil. Something was moving under the water, something huge, evil, and powerful—and I knew it was waiting for me.

This is only the beginning, Horus warned me. *Set will destroy everyone you care about. Believe me, I know.*

The river became a marsh of tall reeds. The sun blazed overhead. Snakes and crocodiles slid through the water. At the water's edge sat a thatched hut. Outside it, a woman and a child of about ten stood examining a battered sarcophagus. I could tell the coffin had once been a work of art—gold encrusted with gems—but now it was dented and black with grime.

The woman ran her hands over the coffin's lid.

"Finally." She had my mother's face—blue eyes and caramel-colored hair—but she glowed with magical radiance, and I knew I was looking at the goddess Isis.

She turned to the boy. "We have searched so long, my son. Finally we have retrieved him. I will use my magic and give him life again!"

"Papa?" The boy gazed wide-eyed at the box. "He's really inside?"

"Yes, Horus. And now—"

Suddenly their hut erupted into flames. The god Set stepped from the inferno—a mighty red-skinned warrior with smoldering black eyes. He wore the double crown of Egypt and the robes of a pharaoh. In his hands, an iron staff smoldered.

"Found the coffin, did you?" he said. "Good for you!"

Isis reached toward the sky. She summoned lightning against the god of chaos, but Set's rod absorbed the attack and reflected it back at her. Arcs of electricity blasted the goddess and sent her sprawling.

"Mother!" The boy drew a knife and charged Set. "I'll kill you!"

Set bellowed with laughter. He easily sidestepped the boy and kicked him into the dirt.

"You have spirit, nephew," Set admitted. "But you won't live long enough to challenge me. As for your father, I'll just have to dispose of him more permanently."

Set slammed his iron staff against the coffin's lid.

Isis screamed as the coffin shattered like ice.

"Make a wish." Set blew with all his might, and the shards of coffin flew into the sky, scattering in all directions. "Poor Osiris—he's gone to pieces, scattered all over Egypt now. And as for you, sister Isis—run! That's what you do best!"

Set lunged forward. Isis grabbed her son's hand and they both turned into birds, flying for their lives.

The scene faded, and I was back in the steamboat's wheelhouse. The sun rose in fast-forward as towns and barges sped past and the banks of the Mississippi blurred into a play of light and shadow.

"He destroyed my father," Horus told me. "He will do the same to yours."

"No," I said.

Horus fixed me with those strange eyes—one blazing gold, one full-moon silver. "My mother and Aunt Nephthys spent years searching for the pieces of the coffin and Father's body. When they collected all fourteen, my cousin Anubis helped bind my father back together with mummy wrappings, but still Mother's magic could not bring him back to life fully. Osiris became an undead god, a half-living shadow of my father, fit to rule only in the Duat. But his loss gave me anger. Anger gave me the strength to defeat Set and take the throne for myself. You must do the same."

"I don't want a throne," I said. "I want my dad."

"Don't deceive yourself. Set is merely toying with you. He will bring you to despair, and your sorrow will make you weak."

"I have to save my dad!"

"That is not your mission," Horus chided. "The world is at stake. Now, wake!"

Sadie was shaking my arm. She and Bast stood over me, looking concerned.

"What?" I asked.

"We're here," Sadie said nervously. She'd changed into a fresh linen outfit, black this time, which matched her combat boots. She'd even managed to redye her hair so the streaks were blue.

I sat up and realized I felt rested for the first time in a week. My soul may have been traveling, but at least my body had gotten some sleep. I glanced out the stateroom window. It was pitch-black outside.

"How long was I out?" I demanded.

"We've sailed down most of the Mississippi and into the Duat," Bast said. "Now we approach the First Cataract."

"The First Cataract?" I asked.

"The entrance," Bast said grimly, "to the Land of the Dead."

27. A Demon with Free Samples

ME? I SLEPT LIKE THE DEAD, which I hoped wasn't a sign of things to come.

I could tell Carter's soul had been wandering through some frightening places, but he wouldn't talk about them.

"Did you see Zia?" I asked. He looked so rattled I thought his face would fall off. "Knew it," I said.

We followed Bast up to the wheelhouse, where Bloodstained Blade was studying a map while Khufu manned—*er*, babooned—the wheel.

"The baboon is driving," I noted. "Should I be worried?"

"Quiet, please, Lady Kane." Bloodstained Blade ran his fingers over a long stretch of papyrus map. "This is delicate work. Two degrees to starboard, Khufu."

"*Agh!*" Khufu said.

The sky was already dark, but as we chugged along, the stars disappeared. The river turned the color of blood. Darkness swallowed the horizon, and along the riverbanks, the lights of towns changed to flickering fires, then winked out completely.

Now our only lights were the multicolored servant fires and the glittering smoke that bloomed from the smokestacks, washing us all in a weird metallic glow.

"Should be just ahead," the captain announced. In the dim light, his red-flecked axe blade looked scarier than ever.

"What's that map?" I asked.

"*Spells of Coming Forth by Day*," he said. "Don't worry. It's a good copy."

I looked at Carter for a translation.

"Most people call it *The Book of the Dead*," he told me. "Rich Egyptians were always buried with a copy, so they could have directions through the Duat to the Land of the Dead. It's like an *Idiot's Guide to the Afterlife*."

The captain hummed indignantly. "I am no idiot, Lord Kane."

"No, no, I just meant..." Carter's voice faltered. "*Uh, what is that?*"

Ahead of us, crags of rock jutted from the river like fangs, turning the water into a boiling mass of rapids.

"The First Cataract," Bloodstained Blade announced. "Hold on."

Khufu pushed the wheel to the left, and the steamboat skidded sideways, shooting between two rocky spires with only centimeters to spare. I'm not much of a screamer, but I'll readily admit that I screamed my head off. [And don't look at me like that, Carter. You weren't much better.]

We dropped over a stretch of white water—or red

water—and swerved to avoid a rock the size of Paddington Station. The steamboat made two more suicidal turns between boulders, did a three-sixty spin round a swirling vortex, launched over a ten-meter waterfall, and came crashing down so hard, my ears popped like a gunshot.

We continued downstream as if nothing had happened, the roar of the rapids fading behind us.

"I don't like cataracts," I decided. "Are there more?"

"Not as large, thankfully," said Bast, who was also looking seasick. "We've crossed over into—"

"The Land of the Dead," Carter finished.

He pointed to the shore, which was shrouded in mist. Strange things lurked in the darkness: flickering ghost lights, giant faces made of fog, hulking shadows that seemed unconnected to anything physical. Along the riverbanks, old bones dragged themselves through the mud, linking with other bones in random patterns.

"I'm guessing this isn't the Mississippi," I said.

"The River of Night," Bloodstained Blade hummed. "It is every river and no river—the shadow of the Mississippi, the Nile, the Thames. It flows throughout the Duat, with many branches and tributaries."

"Clears that right up," I muttered.

The scenes got stranger. We saw ghost villages from ancient times—little clusters of reed huts made of flickering smoke. We saw vast temples crumbling and reconstructing themselves over and over again like a looped video. And everywhere, ghosts turned their faces towards our boat as we passed. Smoky hands reached out. Shades silently called to us, then turned away in despair as we passed.

"The lost and confused," Bast said. "Spirits who never found their way to the Hall of Judgment."

"Why are they so sad?" I asked.

"Well, they're dead," Carter speculated.

"No, it's more than that," I said. "It's like they're … expecting someone."

"Ra," Bast said. "For eons, Ra's glorious sun boat would travel this route each night, fighting off the forces of Apophis." She looked round nervously as if remembering old ambushes. "It was dangerous: every night, a fight for existence. But as he passed, Ra would bring sunlight and warmth to the Duat, and these lost spirits would rejoice, remembering the world of the living."

"But that's a legend," Carter said. "The earth revolves around the sun. The sun never actually descends under the earth."

"Have you learned nothing of Egypt?" Bast asked. "Conflicting stories can be equally true. The sun is a ball of fire in space, yes. But its image you see as it crosses the sky, the life-giving warmth and light it brings to the earth—that was embodied by Ra. The sun was his throne, his source of power, his very spirit. But now Ra has retreated into the heavens. He sleeps, and the sun is just the sun. Ra's boat no longer travels on its cycle through the Duat. He no longer lights the dark, and the dead feel his absence most keenly."

"Indeed," Bloodstained Blade said, though he didn't sound

very upset about it. "Legend says the world will end when Ra gets too tired to continue living in his weakened state. Apophis will swallow the sun. Darkness will reign. Chaos will overcome Ma'at, and the Serpent will reign forever."

Part of me thought this was absurd. The planets would not simply stop spinning. The sun would not cease to rise.

On the other hand, here I was riding a boat through the Land of the Dead with a demon and a god. If Apophis was real too, I didn't fancy meeting him.

And to be honest, I felt guilty. If the story Thoth told me was true, Isis had *caused* Ra to retreat into the heavens with that secret name business. Which meant, in a ridiculous, maddening way, the end of the world would be my fault. Bloody typical. I wanted to punch myself to get even with Isis, but I suspected it would hurt.

"Ra should wake up and smell the *sahlab*," I said. "He should come back."

Bast laughed without humor. "And the world should be young again, Sadie. I wish it could be so...."

Khufu grunted and gestured ahead. He gave the captain back the wheel and ran out of the wheelhouse and down the stairs.

"The baboon is right," said Bloodstained Blade. "You should get to the prow. A challenge will be coming soon."

"What sort of challenge?" I asked.

"It's hard to tell," Bloodstained Blade said, and I thought I detected smug satisfaction in his voice. "I wish you luck, Lady Kane."

"Why me?" I grumbled.

Bast, Carter, and I stood at the prow of the boat, watching the river appear out of the darkness. Below us, the boat's painted eyes glowed faintly in the dark, sweeping beams of light across the red water. Khufu had climbed to the top of the gangplank, which stood straight up when retracted, and cupped his hand over his eyes like a sailor in a crow's-nest.

But all that vigilance didn't do much good. With the dark and the mist, our visibility was nil. Massive rocks, broken pillars, and crumbling statues of pharaohs loomed out of nowhere, and Bloodstained Blade yanked the wheel to avoid them, forcing us to grab hold of the rails. Occasionally we'd see long slimy lines cutting through the surface of the water, like tentacles, or the backs of submerged creatures—I really didn't want to know.

"Mortal souls are always challenged," Bast told me. "You must prove your worth to enter the Land of the Dead."

"Like it's such a big treat?"

I'm not sure how long I stared into the darkness, but after a good while a reddish smudge appeared in the distance, as if the sky were becoming lighter.

"Is that my imagination, or—"

"Our destination," Bast said. "Strange, we really should've been challenged by now—"

The boat shuddered, and the water began to boil. A giant figure erupted from the river. I could see him only from the waist up, but he towered several meters over the boat. His body was humanoid—bare-chested and hairy with purplish skin. A rope belt was tied around his waist, festooned with leather pouches, severed demon heads, and other charming bits and bobs. His head was a strange combination of lion and human, with gold eyes and a black mane done in dreadlocks. His blood-splattered mouth was feline, with bristly whiskers and razor-sharp fangs. He roared, scaring Khufu right off the gangplank. The poor baboon did a flying leap into Carter's arms, which knocked them both to the deck.

"You *had* to say something," I told Bast weakly. "This a relative of yours, I hope?"

Bast shook her head. "I cannot help you with this, Sadie. *You* are the mortals. You must deal with the challenge."

"Oh, thanks for that."

"I am Shezmu!" the bloody lion man said.

I wanted to say, "Yes, you certainly are." But I decided to keep my mouth shut.

He turned his golden eyes on Carter and tilted his head. His nostrils quivered. "I smell the blood of pharaohs. A tasty treat...or do you dare to name me?"

"N-name you?" Carter sputtered. "Do you mean your secret name?"

The demon laughed. He grabbed a nearby spire of rock, which crumpled like old plaster in his fist.

I looked desperately at Carter. "You don't happen to have his secret name lying around somewhere?"

"It may be in *The Book of the Dead*," Carter said. "I forgot to check."

"Well?" I said.

"Keep him busy," Carter replied, and scrambled off to the wheelhouse.

Keep a demon busy, I thought. *Right. Maybe he fancies a game of tiddlywinks.*

"Do you give up?" Shezmu bellowed.

"No!" I yelled. "No, we don't give up. We will name you. Just...Gosh, you're quite well muscled, aren't you? Do you work out?"

I glanced at Bast, who nodded approval.

Shezmu rumbled with pride and flexed his mighty arms. Never fails with men, does it? Even if they're twenty meters tall and lion-headed.

"I am Shezmu!" he bellowed.

"Yes, you might've mentioned that already," I said. "I'm wondering, *um,* what sort of titles you've earned over the years, eh? Lord of this and that?"

"I am Osiris's royal executioner!" he yelled, smashing a fist into the water and rocking our boat. "I am the Lord of Blood and Wine!"

"Brilliant," I said, trying not to get sick. "Er, how are blood and wine connected, exactly?"

"*Garrr!*" He leaned forward and bared his fangs, which were not any prettier up close. His mane was matted with nasty bits of dead fish and river moss. "Lord Osiris lets me behead the wicked! I crush them in my wine press, and make wine for the dead!"

I made a mental note never to drink the wine of the dead.

You're doing well. Isis's voice gave me a start. She'd been quiet so long, I'd almost forgotten her. *Ask him about his other duties.*

"And what are your other duties...O powerful wine demon guy?"

"I am Lord of..." He flexed his muscles for maximum effect. "Perfume!"

He grinned at me, apparently waiting for terror to set it.

"Oh, my!" I said. "That must make your enemies tremble."

"Ha, ha, ha! Yes! Would you like to try a free sample?" He ripped a slimy leather pouch off his belt, and brought out a clay pot filled with sweet-smelling yellow powder. "I call this ...Eternity!"

"Lovely," I gagged. I glanced behind me, wondering where Carter had gone to, but there was no sign of him.

Keep him talking, Isis urged.

"And, *um*...perfume is part of your job because...wait, I've got it, you squeeze it out of plants, like you squeeze wine..."

"Or blood!" Shezmu added.

"Well, naturally," I said. "The blood goes without saying."

"Blood!" he said.

Khufu yelped and covered his eyes.

"So you serve Osiris?" I asked the demon.

"Yes! At least..." He hesitated, snarling in doubt. "I did. Osiris's throne is empty. But he will return. He will!"

"Of course," I said. "And so your friends call you what... Shezzy? Bloodsiekins?"

"I have no friends! But if I did, they would call me Slaughterer of Souls, Fierce of Face! But I don't have any friends, so my name is not in danger. Ha, ha, ha!"

I looked at Bast, wondering if I'd just gotten as lucky as I thought. Bast beamed at me.

Carter came stumbling down the stairs, holding *The Book*

of the Dead. "I've got it! Somewhere here. Can't read this part, but—"

"Name me or be eaten!" Shezmu bellowed.

"I name you!" I shouted back. "Shezmu, Slaughterer of Souls, Fierce of Face!"

"GAAAAHHHHH!" He writhed in pain. "How do they always know?"

"Let us pass!" I commanded. "Oh, and one more thing… my brother wants a free sample."

I just had time to step away, and Carter just had time to look confused before the demon blew yellow dust all over him. Then Shezmu sank under the waves.

"What a nice fellow," I said.

"*Pah!*" Carter spit perfume. He looked like a piece of breaded fish. "What was *that* for?"

"You smell lovely," I assured him. "What's next, then?"

I was feeling very pleased with myself until our boat rounded a bend in the river. Suddenly the reddish glow on the horizon became a blaze of light. Up in the wheelhouse, the captain rang the alarm bell.

Ahead of us, the river was on fire, rushing through a steaming stretch of rapids towards what looked like a bubbling volcanic crater.

"The Lake of Fire," Bast said. "This is where it gets interesting."

28. I Have a Date with the God of Toilet Paper

BAST HAD AN INTERESTING DEFINITION of *interesting*: a boiling lake several miles wide that smelled like burning petrol and rotten meat. Our steamboat stopped short where the river met the lake, because a giant metal gate blocked our path. It was a bronze disk like a shield, easily as wide as our boat, half submerged in the river. I wasn't sure how it avoided melting in the heat, but it made going forward impossible. On either bank of the river, facing the disk, was a giant bronze baboon with its arms raised.

"What is this?" I asked.

"The Gates of the West," Bast said. "Ra's sunboat would pass through and be renewed in the fires of the lake, then pass through to the other side and rise through the Gates of the East for a new day."

Looking up at the huge baboons, I wondered if Khufu had some sort of secret baboon code that would get us in. But instead he barked at the statues and cowered heroically behind my legs.

"How do we get past?" I wondered.

"Perhaps," a new voice said, "you should ask me."

The air shimmered. Carter backed up quickly, and Bast hissed.

In front of me appeared a glowing bird spirit: a *ba*. It had the usual combination of human head and killer turkey body, with its wings tucked back and its entire form glowing, but something about this *ba* was different. I realized I knew the spirit's face—an old bald man with brown, papery skin, milky eyes, and a kindly smile.

"Iskandar?" I managed.

"Hello, my dear." The old magician's voice echoed as if from the bottom of a well.

"But..." I found myself tearing up. "You're really dead, then?"

He chuckled. "Last I checked."

"But *why*? I didn't make you—"

"No, my dear. It wasn't your fault. It was simply the right time."

"It was horrible timing!" My surprise and sadness abruptly turned to anger. "You *left* us before we got trained or anything, and now Desjardins is after us and—"

"My dear, look how far you've come. Look how well you have done. You didn't need me, nor would more training have helped. My brethren would have found out the truth about you soon enough. They are excellent at sniffing out godlings, I fear, and they would not have understood."

"You knew, didn't you? You knew we were possessed by gods."

"*Hosts* of the gods."

"Whatever! You knew."

"After our second meeting, yes. My only regret is that I did not realize it sooner. I could not protect you and your brother as much as—"

"As much as who?"

Iskandar's eyes became sad and distant. "I made choices, Sadie. Some seemed wise at the time. Some, in retrospect..."

"Your decision to forbid the gods. My mum convinced you it was a bad idea, didn't she?"

His spectral wings fluttered. "You must understand, Sadie. When Egypt fell to the Romans, my spirit was crushed. Thousands of years of Egyptian power and tradition toppled by that foolish Queen Cleopatra, who thought she could host a goddess. The blood of the pharaohs seemed weak and diluted—lost forever. At the time I blamed everyone—the gods who used men to act out their petty quarrels, the Ptolemaic rulers who had driven Egypt into the ground, my own brethren in the House for becoming weak and greedy and corrupt. I communed with Thoth, and we agreed: the gods must be put away, banished. The magicians must find their way without them. The new rules kept the House of Life intact for another two thousand years. At the time, it was the right choice."

"And now?" I asked.

Iskandar's glow dimmed. "Your mother foresaw a great imbalance. She foresaw the day—very soon—when Ma'at would be destroyed, and chaos would reclaim all of Creation. She insisted that only the gods and the House together could prevail. The old way—the path of the gods—would have to be reestablished. I was a foolish old man. I knew in my heart she was right, but I refused to believe...and your parents took it upon themselves to act. They sacrificed themselves trying to put things right, because I was too stubborn to change. For that, I am truly sorry."

As much as I tried, I found it hard to stay angry at the old turkey. It's a rare thing when an adult admits they are wrong to a child—especially a wise, two-thousand-year-old adult. You rather have to cherish those moments.

"I forgive you, Iskandar," I said. "Honestly. But Set is about to destroy North America with a giant red pyramid. What do I *do* about it?"

"That, my dear, I can't answer. Your choice..." He tilted his head back toward the lake, as if hearing a voice. "Our time is at an end. I must do my job as gatekeeper, and decide whether or not to grant you access to the Lake of Fire."

"But I've got more questions!"

"And I wish we had more time," Iskandar said. "You have a strong spirit, Sadie Kane. Someday, you will make an excellent guardian *ba*."

"Thanks," I muttered. "Can't wait to be poultry forever."

"I can only tell you this: your choice approaches. Don't let your feelings blind you to what is best, as I did."

"What choice? Best for whom?"

"That's the key, isn't it? Your father—your family—the gods—the world. Ma'at and Isfet, order and chaos, are about to collide more violently than they have in eons. You and your brother will be instrumental in balancing those forces, or destroying everything. That, also, your mother foresaw."

"Hang on. What do you—"

"Until we meet again, Sadie. Perhaps some day, we will have a chance to talk further. But for now, pass through! My job is to assess your courage—and you have that in abundance."

I wanted to argue that no, in fact, I didn't. I wanted Iskandar to stay and tell me exactly what my mother had foreseen in my future. But his spirit faded, leaving the deck quiet and still. Only then did I realize that no one else on board had said a thing.

I turned to face Carter. "Leave everything to me, eh?"

He was staring into space, not even blinking. Khufu still clung to my legs, absolutely petrified. Bast's face was frozen in mid-hiss.

"*Um*, guys?" I snapped my fingers, and they all unfroze.

"*Ba!*" Bast hissed. Then she looked around and scowled. "Wait, I thought I saw...what just happened?"

I wondered how powerful a magician had to be to stop time, to freeze even a goddess. Some day, Iskandar was going to teach me that trick, dead or no.

"Yeah," I said. "I reckon there was a *ba*. Gone now."

The baboon statues began to rumble and grind as their arms lowered. The bronze sun disk in the middle of the river sank below the surface, clearing the way into the lake. The boat shot forward, straight into the flames and the boiling red waves. Through the shimmering heat, I could just make out an island in the middle of the lake. On it rose a glittering black temple that looked not at all friendly.

"The Hall of Judgment," I guessed.

Bast nodded. "Times like this, I'm glad I don't have a mortal soul."

As we docked at the island, Bloodstained Blade came down to say good-bye.

"I hope to see you again, Lord and Lady Kane," he hummed. "Your rooms will be waiting aboard the *Egyptian Queen*. Unless, of course, you see fit to release me from service."

Behind his back, Bast shook her head adamantly.

"*Um*, we'll keep you around," I told the captain. "Thanks for everything."

"As you wish," the captain said. If axes could frown, I'm sure he would have.

"Stay sharp," Carter told him, and with Bast and Khufu, we walked down the gangplank. Instead of pulling away, the ship simply sank into the boiling lava and disappeared.

I scowled at Carter. "'Stay sharp?'"

"I thought it was funny."

"You're hopeless."

We walked up the steps of the black temple. A forest of stone pillars held up the ceiling. Every surface was carved with hieroglyphs and images, but there was no color—just black on black. Haze from the lake drifted through the temple, and despite reed torches that burned on each pillar, it was impossible to see very far through the gloom.

"Stay alert," Bast warned, sniffing the air. "He's close."

"Who?" I asked.

"The Dog," Bast said with disdain.

There was a snarling noise, and a huge black shape leaped out of the mist. It tackled Bast, who rolled over and wailed in feline outrage, then raced off, leaving us alone with the beast. I suppose she had warned us that she wasn't brave.

The new animal was sleek and black, like the Set animal we'd seen in Washington, D.C., but more obviously canine, graceful and rather cute, actually. A jackal, I realized, with a golden collar around its neck.

Then it morphed into a young man, and my heart almost stopped. He was the boy from my dreams, quite literally—the guy in black I'd seen twice before in my *ba* visions.

In person, if possible, Anubis was even more drop-dead gorgeous. [Oh . . . ha, ha. I didn't catch the pun, but thank you, Carter. God of the dead, drop-dead gorgeous. Yes, hilarious. Now, may I continue?]

He had a pale complexion, tousled black hair, and rich brown eyes like melted chocolate. He was dressed in black jeans, combat boots (like mine!), a ripped T-shirt, and a black leather jacket that suited him quite nicely. He was long and lean like a jackal. His ears, like a jackal's, stuck out a bit (which I found cute), and he wore a gold chain around his neck.

Now, please understand, I am *not* boy crazy. I'm not! I'd spent most of the school term making fun of Liz and Emma, who were, and I was very glad they weren't with me just then, because they would've teased me to no end.

The boy in black stood and brushed off his jacket. "I'm *not* a dog," he grumbled.

"No," I agreed. "You're . . ."

No doubt I would've said *delicious* or something equally embarrassing, but Carter saved me.

"You're Anubis?" he asked. "We've come for the feather of truth."

Anubis frowned. He locked his very nice eyes with mine. "You're not dead."

"No," I said. "Though we're trying awfully hard."

"I don't deal with the living," he said firmly. Then he looked at Khufu and Carter. "However, you travel with a baboon. That shows good taste. I won't kill you until you've had a chance to explain. Why did Bast bring you here?"

"Actually," Carter said, "Thoth sent us."

Carter started to tell him the story, but Khufu broke in impatiently. *"Agh! Agh!"*

Baboon-speak must have been quite efficient, because Anubis nodded as if he'd just gotten the whole tale. "I see."

He scowled at Carter. "So you're Horus. And you're..." His finger drifted towards me.

"I'm—I'm, *um*—" I stammered. Quite unlike me to be tongue-tied, I'll admit, but looking at Anubis, I felt as if I'd just gotten a large shot of Novocain from the dentist. Carter looked at me as if I'd gone daft.

"I'm not Isis," I managed. "I mean, Isis is milling about inside, but I'm not her. She's just... visiting."

Anubis tilted his head. "And the two of you intend to challenge Set?"

"That's the general idea," Carter agreed. "Will you help?"

Anubis glowered. I remembered Thoth saying Anubis was

only in a good mood once an eon or so. I had the feeling this was not one of those days.

"No," he said flatly. "I'll show you why."

He turned into a jackal and sped back the way he'd come. Carter and I exchanged looks. Not knowing what else to do, we ran after Anubis, deeper into the gloom.

In the center of the temple was a large circular chamber that seemed to be two places at once. On the one hand, it was a great hall with blazing braziers and an empty throne at the far end. The center of the room was dominated by a set of scales—a black iron T with ropes linked to two golden dishes, each big enough to hold a person—but the scales were broken. One of the golden dishes was bent into a V, as if something very heavy had jumped up and down on it. The other dish was hanging by a single rope.

Curled at the base of the scales, fast asleep, was the oddest monster I'd seen yet. It had the head of crocodile with a lion's mane. The front half of its body was lion, but the back end was sleek, brown, and fat—a hippo, I decided. The odd bit was, the animal was tiny—I mean, no larger than an average poodle, which I suppose made him a hippodoodle.

So that was the hall, at least *one* layer of it. But at the same time, I seemed to be standing in a ghostly graveyard—like a three-dimensional projection superimposed on the room. In some places, the marble floor gave way to patches of mud and moss-covered paving stones. Lines of aboveground tombs like miniature row houses radiated from the center of the chamber in a wheel-spokes pattern. Many of the tombs had cracked open. Some were bricked up, others ringed with iron fences. Around the edges of the chamber, the black pillars shifted form, sometimes changing into ancient cypress trees. I felt as if I were stepping between two different worlds, and I couldn't tell which one was real.

Khufu loped straight over to the broken scales and climbed to the top, making himself right at home. He paid no attention to the hippodoodle.

The jackal trotted to the steps of the throne and changed back into Anubis.

"Welcome," he said, "to the last room you will ever see."

Carter looked around in awe. "The Hall of Judgment." He focused on the hippodoodle and frowned. "Is that..."

"Ammit the Devourer," Anubis said. "Look upon him and tremble."

Ammit apparently heard his name in his sleep. He made a yipping sound and turned on his back. His lion and hippo legs twitched. I wondered if netherworld monsters dreamed of chasing rabbits.

"I always pictured him...bigger," Carter admitted.

Anubis gave Carter a harsh look. "Ammit only has to be big enough to eat the hearts of the wicked. Trust me, he does his job well. Or...he *did* it well, anyway."

Up on the scales, Khufu grunted. He almost lost his balance on the central beam, and the dented saucer clanged against the floor.

"Why are the scales broken?" I asked.

Anubis frowned. "Ma'at is weakening. I've tried to fix them, but..." He spread his hands helplessly.

I pointed to the ghostly rows of tombs. "Is that why the, ah, graveyard is butting in?"

Carter looked at me strangely. "What graveyard?"

"The tombs," I said. "The trees."

"What are you talking about?"

"He can't see them," Anubis said. "But you, Sadie—you're perceptive. What do you hear?"

At first I didn't know what he meant. All I heard was the blood rushing through my ears, and the distant rumble and crackle of the Lake of Fire. (And Khufu scratching himself and grunting, but that was nothing new.)

Then I closed my eyes, and I heard another distant sound—music that triggered my earliest memories, my father smiling as he danced me round our house in Los Angeles.

"Jazz," I said.

I opened my eyes, and the Hall of Judgment was gone. Or not *gone*, but faded. I could still see the broken scales and the empty throne. But no black columns, no roar of fire. Even Carter, Khufu, and Ammit had disappeared.

The cemetery was *very* real. Cracked paving stones wobbled under my feet. The humid night air smelled of spices and fish stew and old mildewed places. I might've been back in England—a churchyard in some corner of London, perhaps—but the writing on the graves was in French, and the air was much too mild for an English winter. The trees hung low and lush, covered with Spanish moss.

And there was music. Just outside the cemetery's fence, a jazz band paraded down the street in somber black suits and brightly colored party hats. Saxophonists bobbed up and down. Cornets and clarinets wailed. Drummers grinned and swayed, their sticks flashing. And behind them, carrying flowers and torches, a crowd of revelers in funeral clothes danced round an old-fashioned black hearse as it drove along.

"Where *are* we?" I said, marveling.

Anubis jumped from the top of a tomb and landed next to me. He breathed in the graveyard air, and his features relaxed. I found myself studying his mouth, the curve of his lower lip.

"New Orleans," he said.

"Sorry?"

"The Drowned City," he said. "In the French Quarter, on the west side of the river—the shore of the dead. I love it here. That's why the Hall of Judgment often connects to this part of the mortal world."

The jazz procession made its way down the street, drawing more onlookers into the party.

"What are they celebrating?"

"A funeral," Anubis said. "They've just put the deceased in his tomb. Now they're 'cutting the body loose.' The mourners celebrate the dead one's life with song and dance as they escort the empty hearse away from the cemetery. Very Egyptian, this ritual."

"How do you know so much?"

"I'm the god of funerals. I know every death custom in the world—how to die properly, how to prepare the body and soul for the afterlife. I live for death."

"You must be fun at parties," I said. "Why have you brought me here?"

"To talk." He spread his hands, and the nearest tomb

rumbled. A long white ribbon shot out of a crack in the wall. The ribbon just kept coming, weaving itself into some kind of shape next to Anubis, and my first thought was, *My god, he's got a magic roll of toilet paper.*

Then I realized it was cloth, a length of white linen wrappings—*mummy* wrappings. The cloth twisted itself into the form of a bench, and Anubis sat down.

"I don't like Horus." He gestured for me to join him. "He's loud and arrogant and thinks he's better than me. But Isis always treated me like a son."

I crossed my arms. "You're *not* my son. And I told you I'm *not* Isis."

Anubis tilted his head. "No. You don't act like a godling. You remind me of your mother."

That hit me like a bucket of cold water (and sadly, I knew exactly what *that* felt like, thanks to Zia). "You've met my mother?"

Anubis blinked, as if realizing he'd done something wrong. "I—I know all the dead, but each spirit's path is secret. I should not have spoken."

"You can't just say something like that and then clam up! Is she in the Egyptian afterlife? Did she pass your little Hall of Judgment?"

Anubis glanced uneasily at the golden scales, which shimmered like a mirage in the graveyard. "It is not *my* hall. I merely oversee it until Lord Osiris returns. I'm sorry if I upset you, but I can't say anything more. I don't know why I said anything at all. It's just... your soul has a similar glow. A strong glow."

"How flattering," I grumbled. "My soul glows."

"I'm sorry," he said again. "Please, sit."

I had no interest in letting the matter drop, or sitting with him on a bunch of mummy wrappings, but my direct approach to information gathering didn't seem to be working. I plopped down on the bench and tried to look as annoyed as possible.

"So." I gave him a sulky glare. "What's *that* form, then? Are you a godling?"

He frowned and put his hand to his chest. "You mean, am I inhabiting a human body? No, I can inhabit any graveyard, any place of death or mourning. This is my natural appearance."

"Oh." Part of me had hoped there was an actual boy sitting next to me—someone who just happened to be hosting a god. But I should've known that was too good to be true. I felt disappointed. Then I felt angry with myself for feeling disappointed.

It's not like there was any potential, Sadie, I chided myself. *He's the bloody god of funerals. He's like five thousand years old.*

"So," I said, "if you can't tell me anything useful, at least help me. We need a feather of truth."

He shook his head. "You don't know what you're asking. The feather of truth is too dangerous. Giving it to a mortal would be against the rules of Osiris."

"But Osiris isn't here." I pointed at the empty throne. "That's his seat, isn't it? Do you see Osiris?"

Anubis eyed the throne. He ran his fingers along his gold chain as if it were getting tighter. "It's true that I've waited here for ages, keeping my station. I was not imprisoned like the rest. I don't know why ... but I did the best I could. When

I heard the five had been released, I hoped Lord Osiris would return, but..." He shook his head dejectedly. "Why would he neglect his duties?"

"Probably because he's trapped inside my dad."

Anubis stared at me. "The baboon did not explain this."

"Well, I can't explain as well as a baboon. But basically my dad wanted to release some gods for reasons I don't quite... Maybe he thought, *I'll just pop down to the British Museum and blow up the Rosetta Stone!* And he released Osiris, but he also got Set and the rest of that lot."

"So Set imprisoned your father while he was hosting Osiris," Anubis said, "which means Osiris has also been trapped by my—" He stopped himself. "By Set."

Interesting, I thought.

"You understand, then," I said. "You've got to help us."

Anubis hesitated, then shook his head. "I can't. I'll get in trouble."

I just stared at him and laughed. I couldn't help it, he sounded so ridiculous. "You'll get in *trouble*? How old are you, sixteen? You're a god!"

It was hard to tell in the dark, but I could swear he blushed. "You don't understand. The feather cannot abide the smallest lie. If I gave it to you, and you spoke a single untruth while you carried it, or acted in a way that was not truthful, you would burn to ashes."

"You're assuming I'm a liar."

He blinked. "No, I simply—"

"You've never told a lie? What were you about to say just now—about Set? He's your father, I'm guessing. Is that it?"

Anubis closed his mouth, then opened it again. He looked as if he wanted to get angry but couldn't quite remember how. "Are you always this infuriating?"

"Usually more," I admitted.

"Why hasn't your family married you off to someone far, far away?"

He asked as if it were an honest question, and now it was my turn to be flabbergasted. "Excuse me, death boy! But I'm twelve! Well...almost thirteen, and a very mature almost thirteen, but that's *not* the point. We don't 'marry off' girls in my family, and you may know everything about funerals, but apparently you aren't very up to speed on courtship rituals!"

Anubis looked mystified. "Apparently not."

"Right! Wait—what were we talking about? Oh, thought you could distract me, eh? I remember. Set's your father, yes? Tell the truth."

Anubis gazed across the graveyard. The sound of the jazz funeral was fading into the streets of the French Quarter.

"Yes," he said. "At least, that's what the legends say. I've never met him. My mother, Nephthys, gave me to Osiris when I was a child."

"She...gave you away?"

"She said she didn't want me to know my father. But in truth, I'm not sure she knew what to do with me. I wasn't like my cousin Horus. I wasn't a warrior. I was a...*different* child."

He sounded so bitter, I didn't know what to say. I mean, I'd asked for the truth, but usually you don't actually *get* it, especially from guys. I also knew something about being the different child—and feeling like my parents had given me away.

"Maybe your mum was trying to protect you," I said. "Your dad being Lord of Evil, and all."

"Maybe," he said halfheartedly. "Osiris took me under his wing. He made me the Lord of Funerals, the Keeper of the Ways of Death. It's a good job, but... you asked how old I am. The truth is I don't know. Years don't pass in the Land of the Dead. I still feel quite young, but the world has gotten old around me. And Osiris has been gone so long... He's the only family I had."

Looking at Anubis in the dim light of the graveyard, I saw a lonely teenage guy. I tried to remind myself that he was a god, thousands of years old, probably able to control vast powers *well* beyond magic toilet paper, but I still felt sorry for him.

"Help us rescue my dad," I said. "We'll send Set back to the Duat, and Osiris will be free. We'll all be happy."

Anubis shook his head again. "I told you—"

"Your scales are broken," I noticed. "That's because Osiris isn't here, I'm guessing. What happens to all the souls that come for judgment?"

I knew I'd hit a nerve. Anubis shifted uncomfortably on the bench. "It increases chaos. The souls become confused. Some cannot go to the afterlife. Some manage, but they must find other ways. I try to help, but... the Hall of Judgment is also called the Hall of Ma'at. It is meant to be the center of order, a stable foundation. Without Osiris, it is falling into disrepair, crumbling."

"Then what are you waiting for? Give us the feather. Unless you're afraid your dad will ground you."

His eyes flashed with irritation. For a moment I thought

he was planning *my* funeral, but he simply sighed in exasperation. "I do a ceremony called the opening of the mouth. It lets the soul of the dead person come forth. For you, Sadie Kane, I would invent a new ceremony: the closing of the mouth."

"Ha, ha. Are you going to give me the feather or not?"

He opened his hand. There was a burst of light, and a glowing feather floated above his palm—a snowy plume like a writing quill. "For Osiris's sake—but I will insist on several conditions. First, only you may handle it."

"Well, of course. You don't think I'd let Carter—"

"Also, you must listen to my mother, Nephthys. Khufu told me you were looking for her. If you manage to find her, listen to her."

"Easy," I said, though the request did leave me strangely uncomfortable. Why would Anubis ask something like that?

"And before you go," Anubis continued, "you must answer three questions for me as you hold the feather of truth, to prove that you are honest."

My mouth suddenly felt dry. "Um . . . what sort of questions?"

"Any that I want. And remember, the slightest lie will destroy you."

"Give me the bloody feather."

As he handed it to me, the feather stopped glowing, but it felt warmer and heavier than a feather should.

"It's the tail feather from a *bennu*," Anubis explained, "what you'd call a phoenix. It weighs exactly the same as a human soul. Are you ready?"

"No," I said, which must've been truthful, as I didn't burn up. "Does that count as one question?"

Anubis actually smiled, which was quite dazzling. "I suppose it does. You bargain like a Phoenician sea trader, Sadie Kane. Second question, then: Would you give your life for your brother?"

"Yes," I said immediately.

(I know. It surprised me too. But holding the feather forced me to be truthful. Obviously it didn't make me any wiser.)

Anubis nodded, apparently not surprised. "Final question: If it means saving the world, are you prepared to lose your father?"

"That's not a fair question!"

"Answer it honestly."

How could I answer something like that? It wasn't a simple yes/no.

Of course I knew the "right" answer. The heroine is supposed to refuse to sacrifice her father. Then she boldly goes off and saves her dad *and* the world, right? But what if it really *was* one or the other? The whole world was an awfully large place: Gran and Gramps, Carter, Uncle Amos, Bast, Khufu, Liz and Emma, everyone I'd ever known. What would my dad say if I chose him instead?

"If . . . if there really was no other way," I said, "no other way *at all*— Oh, come off. It's a ridiculous question."

The feather began to glow.

"All right," I relented. "If I had to, then I suppose . . . I suppose I would save the world."

Horrible guilt crushed down on me. What kind of daughter was I? I clutched the *tyet* amulet on my necklace—my one remembrance of Dad. I know some of you lot will be thinking:

You hardly ever saw your dad. You barely knew him. Why would you care so much?

But that didn't make him any less my dad, did it? Or the thought of losing him forever any less horrible. And the thought of failing him, of *willingly* choosing to let him die even to save the world—what sort of awful person was I?

I could barely meet Anubis's eyes, but when I did, his expression softened.

"I believe you, Sadie."

"Oh, really. I'm holding the bloody feather of truth, and you believe me. Well, thanks."

"The truth is harsh," Anubis said. "Spirits come to the Hall of Judgment all the time, and they *cannot* let go of their lies. They deny their faults, their true feelings, their mistakes... right up until Ammit devours their souls for eternity. It takes strength and courage to admit the truth."

"Yeah. I feel so strong and courageous. Thanks."

Anubis stood. "I should leave you now. You're running out of time. In just over twenty-four hours, the sun will rise on Set's birthday, and he will complete his pyramid—unless you stop him. Perhaps when next we meet—"

"You'll be just as annoying?" I guessed.

He fixed me with those warm brown eyes. "Or perhaps you could bring me up to speed on modern courtship rituals."

I sat there stunned until he gave me a glimpse of a smile—just enough to let me know he was teasing. Then he disappeared.

"Oh, very funny!" I yelled. The scales and the throne vanished. The linen bench unraveled and dumped me in the middle of the graveyard. Carter and Khufu appeared next to me, but I just kept yelling at the spot where Anubis had stood, calling him some choice names.

"What's going on?" Carter demanded. "Where are we?"

"He's horrible!" I growled. "Self-important, sarcastic, incredibly hot, insufferable—"

"*Agh!*" Khufu complained.

"Yeah," Carter agreed. "Did you get the feather or not?"

I held out my hand, and there it was—a glowing white plume floating above my fingers. I closed my fist and it disappeared again.

"Whoa," Carter said. "But what about Anubis? How did you—"

"Let's find Bast and get out of here," I interrupted. "We've got work to do."

And I marched out of the graveyard before he could ask me more questions, because I was in *no* mood to tell the truth.

29. Zia Sets a Rendezvous

[Yeah, thanks a lot, Sadie. You get to tell the part about the Land of the Dead. I get to describe Interstate 10 through Texas.]

Long story short: It took forever and was totally boring, unless your idea of fun is watching cows graze.

We left New Orleans about 1 A.M. on December twenty-eighth, the day before Set planned to destroy the world. Bast had "borrowed" an RV—a FEMA leftover from Hurricane Katrina. At first Bast suggested taking a plane, but after I told her about my dream of the magicians on the exploding flight, we agreed planes might not be a good idea. The sky goddess Nut had promised us safe air travel as far as Memphis, but I didn't want to press our luck the closer we got to Set.

"Set is not our only problem," Bast said. "If your vision is correct, the magicians are closing in on us. And not just *any* magicians—Desjardins himself."

"And Zia," Sadie put in, just to annoy me.

In the end, we decided it was safer to drive, even though it was slower. With luck, we'd make Phoenix just in time to challenge Set. As for the House of Life, all we could do was hope to avoid them while we did our job. Maybe once we dealt with Set, the magicians would decide we were cool. Maybe...

I kept thinking about Desjardins, wondering if he really could be a host for Set. A day ago, it had made perfect sense. Desjardins wanted to crush the Kane family. He'd hated our dad, and he hated us. He'd probably been waiting for decades, even centuries, for Iskandar to die, so he could become Chief Lector. Power, anger, arrogance, ambition: Desjardins had it all. If Set was looking for a soulmate, literally, he couldn't do much better. And if Set could start a war between the gods and magicians by controlling the Chief Lector, the only winner would be the forces of chaos. Besides, Desjardins was an easy guy to hate. *Somebody* had sabotaged Amos's house and alerted Set that Amos was coming.

But the way Desjardins saved all those people on the plane—that just didn't seem like something the Lord of Evil would do.

Bast and Khufu took turns driving while Sadie and I dozed off and on. I didn't know baboons could drive recreational vehicles, but Khufu did okay. When I woke up around dawn, he was navigating through early morning rush hour in Houston, baring his fangs and barking a lot, and none of the other drivers seemed to notice anything out of the ordinary.

For breakfast, Sadie, Bast, and I sat in the RV's kitchen while the cabinets banged open and the dishes clinked and miles and miles of nothing went by outside. Bast had snagged us some snacks and drinks (and Friskies, of course) from a New Orleans all-night convenience store before we left, but nobody seemed very hungry. I could tell Bast was anxious. She'd already shredded most of the RV's upholstery, and was now using the kitchen table as a scratching post.

As for Sadie, she kept opening and closing her hand, staring at the feather of truth as if it were a phone she wished would ring. Ever since her disappearance in the Hall of Judgment, she'd been acting all distant and quiet. Not that I'm complaining, but it wasn't like her.

"What happened with Anubis?" I asked her for the millionth time.

She glared at me, ready to bite my head off. Then she apparently decided I wasn't worth the effort. She fixed her eyes on the glowing feather that hovered over her palm.

"We talked," she said carefully. "He asked me some questions."

"What kind of questions?"

"Carter, don't ask. Please."

Please? Okay, that really wasn't like Sadie.

I looked at Bast, but she wasn't any help. She was slowly gouging the Formica to bits with her claws.

"What's wrong?" I asked her.

She kept her eyes on the table. "In the Land of the Dead, I abandoned you. *Again.*"

"Anubis startled you," I said. "It's no big deal."

Bast gave me the big yellow eyes, and I got the feeling I'd only made things worse.

"I made a promise to your father, Carter. In exchange for

my freedom, he gave me a job even more important than fighting the Serpent: protecting Sadie—and if it ever became necessary, protecting *both* of you."

Sadie flushed. "Bast, that's...I mean, thank you and all, but we're hardly more important than fighting...you know, *him*."

"You don't understand," Bast said. "The two of you are not just blood of the pharaohs. You're the most powerful royal children to be born in centuries. You're the only chance we have of reconciling the gods and the House of Life, of relearning the old ways before it's too late. If you could learn the path of the gods, you could find others with royal blood and teach *them*. You could revitalize the House of Life. What your parents did—*everything* they did, was to prepare the way for you."

Sadie and I were silent. I mean, what do you say to something like that? I guessed I'd always felt like my parents loved me, but willing to *die* for me? Believing it was necessary so Sadie and I could do some amazing world-saving stuff? I didn't ask for that.

"They didn't want to leave you alone," Bast said, reading my expression. "They didn't plan on it, but they knew releasing the gods would be dangerous. Believe me, they understood how special you are. At first I was protecting you two because I promised. Now even if I hadn't promised, I would. You two are like kittens to me. I won't fail you again."

I'll admit I got a lump in my throat. I'd never been called someone's kitten before.

Sadie sniffled. She brushed something from under her eye. "You're not going to wash us, are you?"

It was good to see Bast smile again. "I'll try to resist. And by the way, Sadie, I'm proud of you. Dealing with Anubis on your own—those death gods can be nasty customers."

Sadie shrugged. She seemed strangely uncomfortable. "Well, I wouldn't call him *nasty*. I mean, he looked hardly more than a teenager."

"What are you talking about?" I said. "He had the head of a jackal."

"No, when he turned human."

"Sadie..." I was starting to get worried about her now. "When Anubis turned human he *still* had the head of a jackal. He was huge and terrifying and, yeah, pretty nasty. Why, what did he look like to you?"

Her cheeks reddened. "He looked...like a mortal guy."

"Probably a glamour," Bast said.

"No," Sadie insisted. "It couldn't have been."

"Well, it's not important," I said. "We got the feather."

Sadie fidgeted, as if it was *very* important. But then she closed her fist, and the feather of truth disappeared. "It won't do us any good without the secret name of Set."

"I'm working on that." Bast's gaze shifted around the room—she seemed afraid of being overheard. "I've got a plan. But it's dangerous."

I sat forward. "What is it?"

"We'll have to make a stop. I'd rather not jinx us until we get closer, but it's on our way. Shouldn't cause much of a delay."

I tried to calculate. "This is the morning of the second Demon Day?"

Bast nodded. "The day Horus was born."

"And Set's birthday is tomorrow, the third Demon Day. That means we have about twenty-four hours until he destroys North America."

"And if he gets his hands on us," Sadie added, "he'll ramp up his power even more."

"It'll be enough time," Bast said. "It's roughly twenty-four hours driving from New Orleans to Phoenix, and we've already been on the road over five hours. If we don't have any more nasty surprises—"

"Like the kind we have every day?"

"Yes," Bast admitted. "Like those."

I took a shaky breath. Twenty-four hours and it would be over, one way or the other. We'd save Dad and stop Set, or everything would've been for nothing—not just what Sadie and I had done, but all our parents' sacrifices too. Suddenly I felt like I was underground again, in one of those tunnels in the First Nome, with a million tons of rock over my head. One little shift in the ground, and everything would come crashing down.

"Well," I said. "If you need me, I'll be outside, playing with sharp objects."

I grabbed my sword and headed for the back of the RV.

I'd never seen a mobile home with a porch before. The sign on the back door warned me not to use it while the vehicle was in motion, but I did anyway.

It wasn't the best place to practice swordplay. It was too small, and two chairs took up most of the space. The cold wind whipped around me, and every bump in the road threw me off balance. But it was the only place I could go to be alone. I needed to clear my thoughts.

I practiced summoning my sword from the Duat and putting it back. Soon I could do it almost every time, as long as I kept my focus. Then I practiced some moves—blocks, jabs, and strikes—until Horus couldn't resist offering his advice.

Lift the blade higher, he coached. *More of an arc, Carter. The blade is designed to hook an enemy's weapon.*

Shut up, I grumbled. *Where were you when I needed help on the basketball court?* But I tried holding the sword his way and found he was right.

The highway wound through long stretches of empty scrubland. Once in a while we'd pass a rancher's truck or a family SUV, and the driver would get wide-eyed when he saw me: a black kid swinging a sword on the back of an RV. I'd just smile and wave, and Khufu's driving soon left them in the dust.

After an hour of practice, my shirt was stuck to my chest with cold sweat. My breathing was heavy. I decided to sit and take a break.

"It approaches," Horus told me. His voice sounded more substantial, no longer in my head. I looked next to me and saw him shimmering in a golden aura, sitting back in the other deck chair in his leather armor with his sandaled feet up on the railing. His sword, a ghostly copy of *my* sword, was propped next to him.

"What's approaching?" I asked. "The fight with Set?"

"That, of course," Horus said. "But there is another challenge before that, Carter. Be prepared."

"Great. As if I didn't have enough challenges already."

Horus's silver and gold eyes glittered. "When I was growing up, Set tried to kill me many times. My mother and I fled from place to place, hiding from him until I was old enough to face him. The Red Lord will send the same forces against you. The next will come—"

"At a river," I guessed, remembering my last soul trip. "Something bad is going is happen at a river. But what's the challenge?"

"You must beware—" Horus's image began to fade, and the god frowned. "What's this? Someone is trying to—a different force—"

He was replaced by the glowing image of Zia Rashid.

"Zia!" I stood up, suddenly conscious of the fact that I was sweaty and gross and looked like I'd just been dragged through the Land of the Dead.

"Carter?" Her image flickered. She was clutching her staff, and wore a gray coat wrapped over her robes as if she were standing somewhere cold. Her short black hair danced around her face. "Thank Thoth I found you."

"How did you get here?"

"No time! Listen: we're coming after you. Desjardins, me, and two others. We don't know exactly where you are. Desjardins' tracking spells are having trouble finding you, but he knows we're getting close. And he knows where you're going—Phoenix."

My mind started racing. "So he finally believes Set is free? You're coming to help us?"

Zia shook her head. "He's coming to stop you."

"*Stop* us? Zia, Set's about to blow up the continent! My

dad—" My voice cracked. I hated how scared and powerless I sounded. "My dad's in trouble."

Zia reached out a shimmering hand, but it was just an image. Our fingers couldn't touch. "Carter, I'm sorry. You have to see Desjardins' point of view. The House of Life has been trying to keep the gods locked up for centuries to prevent something like *this* from happening. Now that you've unleashed them—"

"It wasn't *my* idea!"

"I know, but you're trying to fight Set with divine magic. Gods can't be controlled. You could end up doing even more damage. If you let the House of Life handle this—"

"Set is too strong," I said. "And I *can* control Horus. I can do this."

Zia shook her head. "It will get harder as you get closer to Set. You have no idea."

"And you do?"

Zia glanced nervously to her left. Her image turned fuzzy, like a bad television signal. "We don't have much time. Mel will be out of the restroom soon."

"You've got a magician named Mel?"

"Just listen. Desjardins is splitting us into two teams. The plan is for us to cut you off on either side and intercept you. If *my* team reaches you first, I think I can keep Mel from attacking long enough for us all to talk. Then maybe we can figure out how to approach Desjardins, to convince him we have to cooperate."

"Don't take this the wrong way, but why should I trust you?"

She pursed her lips, looking genuinely hurt. Part of me felt guilty, while part of me worried this was some kind of trick.

"Carter...I have something to tell you. Something that might help, but it has to be said in person."

"Tell me now."

"Thoth's beak! You are impossibly stubborn."

"Yeah, it's a gift."

We locked eyes. Her image was fading, but I didn't want her to go. I wanted to talk longer.

"If you won't trust me, I'll have to trust you," Zia said. "I will arrange to be in Las Cruces, New Mexico, tonight. If you choose to meet me, perhaps we can convince Mel. Then together, we'll convince Desjardins. Will you come?"

I wanted to promise, just to see her, but I imagined myself trying to convince Sadie or Bast that this was a good idea. "I don't know, Zia."

"Just think about it," she pleaded. "And Carter, don't trust Amos. If you see him—" Her eyes widened. "Mel's here!" she whispered.

Zia slashed her staff in front of her, and her image vanished.

30. Bast Keeps a Promise

HOURS LATER, I WOKE UP ON THE RV's couch with Bast shaking my arm.

"We're here," she announced.

I had no idea how long I'd been asleep. At some point, the flat landscape and complete boredom had zonked me out, and I'd started having bad dreams about tiny magicians flying around in my hair, trying to shave me bald. Somewhere in there, I'd had a nightmare about Amos too, but it was fuzzy. I still didn't understand why Zia would mention him.

I blinked the sleep out of my eyes and realized my head was in Khufu's lap. The baboon was foraging my scalp for munchies.

"Dude." I sat up groggily. "Not cool."

"But he gave you a lovely hairdo," Sadie said.

"*Agh-agh!*" Khufu agreed.

Bast opened the door of the trailer. "Come on," she said. "We'll have to walk from here."

When I got to the door I almost had a heart attack. We

were parked on a mountain road so narrow, the RV would've toppled over if I'd sneezed wrong.

For a second, I was afraid we were already in Phoenix, because the landscape looked similar. The sun was just setting on the horizon. Rugged mountain ranges stretched out on either side, and the desert floor between them seemed to go on forever. In a valley to our left lay a colorless city—hardly any trees or grass, just sand, gravel, and buildings. The city was much smaller than Phoenix, though, and a large river traced its southern edge, glinting red in the fading light. The river curved around the base of the mountains below us before snaking off to the north.

"We're on the moon," Sadie murmured.

"El Paso, Texas," Bast corrected. "And that's the Rio Grande." She took a big breath of the cool dry air. "A river civilization in the desert. Very much like Egypt, actually! *Er*, except for the fact that Mexico is next door. I think this is the best spot to summon Nephthys."

"You really think she'll tell us Set's secret name?" Sadie asked.

Bast considered. "Nephthys is unpredictable, but she has sided against her husband before. We can hope."

That didn't sound very promising. I stared at the river far below. "Why did you park us on the mountain? Why not closer?"

Bast shrugged, as if this hadn't occurred to her. "Cats like to get as high up as possible. In case we have to pounce on something."

"Great," I said. "So if we have to pounce, we're all set."

"It's not so bad," Bast said. "We just climb our way down to the river through a few miles of sand, cacti, and rattlesnakes, looking out for the Border Patrol, human traffickers, magicians, and demons—and summon Nephthys."

Sadie whistled. "Well, I'm excited!"

"*Agh*," Khufu agreed miserably. He sniffed the air and snarled.

"He smells trouble," Bast translated. "Something bad is about to happen."

"Even *I* could smell that," I grumbled, and we followed Bast down the mountain.

Yes, Horus said. *I remember this place.*

It's El Paso, I told him. *Unless you went out for Mexican food, you've never been here.*

I remember it well, he insisted. *The marsh, the desert.*

I stopped and looked around. Suddenly I remembered this place, too. About fifty yards in front of us, the river spread out into a swampy area—a web of slow-moving tributaries cutting a shallow depression through the desert. Marsh grass grew tall along the banks. There must've been some kind of surveillance, its being an international border and all, but I couldn't spot any.

I'd been here in *ba* form. I could picture a hut right there in the marsh, Isis and young Horus hiding from Set. And just downriver—that's where I'd sensed something dark moving under the water, waiting for me.

I caught Bast's arm when she was a few steps from the bank. "Stay away from the water."

She frowned. "Carter, I'm a *cat*. I'm not going for a swim. But if you want to summon a river goddess, you really need to do it at the riverbank."

She made it sound so logical that I felt stupid, but I couldn't help it. Something bad was about to happen.

What is it? I asked Horus. *What's the challenge?*

But my ride-along god was unnervingly silent, as if waiting.

Sadie tossed a rock into the murky brown water. It sank with a loud *ker-plunk!*

"Seems quite safe to me," she said, and trudged down to the banks.

Khufu followed hesitantly. When he reached the water, he sniffed at it and snarled.

"See?" I said. "Even Khufu doesn't like it."

"It's probably ancestral memory," Bast said. "The river was a dangerous place in Egypt. Snakes, hippos, all kinds of problems."

"Hippos?"

"Don't take it lightly," Bast warned. "Hippos can be *deadly*."

"Was that what attacked Horus?" I asked. "I mean in the old days, when Set was looking for him?"

"Haven't heard that story," Bast said. "Usually you hear that Set used scorpions first. Then later, crocodiles."

"Crocodiles," I said, and a chill went down my back.

Is that it? I asked Horus. But again he didn't answer. "Bast, does the Rio Grande have crocodiles?"

"I very much doubt it." She knelt by the water. "Now, Sadie, if you'd do the honors?"

"How?"

"Just ask for Nephthys to appear. She was Isis's sister. If she's anywhere on this side of the Duat, she should hear your voice."

Sadie looked doubtful, but she knelt next to Bast and touched the water. Her fingertips caused ripples that seemed much too large, rings of force emanating all the way across the river.

"Hullo, Nephthys?" she said. "Anyone home?"

I heard a splash downriver, and turned to see a family of immigrants crossing midstream. I'd heard stories about how thousands of people cross the border from Mexico illegally each year, looking for work and a better life, but it was startling to actually see them in front of me—a man and a woman hurrying along, carrying a little girl between them. They were dressed in ragged clothes and looked poorer than the poorest Egyptian peasants I'd ever seen. I stared at them for a few seconds, but they didn't appear to be any kind of supernatural threat. The man gave me a wary look and we seemed to come to a silent understanding: we both had enough problems without bothering each other.

Meanwhile Bast and Sadie stayed focused on the water, watching the ripples spread out from Sadie's fingers.

Bast tilted her head, listening intently. "What's she saying?"

"I can't make it out," Sadie whispered. "Very faint."

"You can actually hear something?" I asked.

"*Shhh,*" they both said at once.

"'*Caged*'..." Sadie said. "No, what is that word in English?"

"Sheltered," Bast suggested. "She is sheltered far away. A *sleeping host*. What is *that* supposed to mean?"

I didn't know what they were talking about. I couldn't hear a thing.

Khufu tugged at my hand and pointed downriver. "*Agh.*"

The immigrant family had disappeared. It seemed impossible they could cross the river so quickly. I scanned both banks—no sign of them—but the water was more turbulent where they'd been standing, as if someone had stirred it with a giant spoon. My throat tightened.

"*Um*, Bast—"

"Carter, we can barely hear Nephthys," she said. "Please."

I gritted my teeth. "Fine. Khufu and I are going to check something—"

"*Shh!*" Sadie said again.

I nodded to Khufu, and we started down the riverbank. Khufu hid behind my legs and growled at the river.

I looked back, but Bast and Sadie seemed fine. They were still staring at the water as if it were some amazing Internet video.

Finally we got to the place where I'd seen the family, but the water had calmed. Khufu slapped the ground and did a handstand, which meant he was either break dancing or really nervous.

"What is it?" I asked, my heart pounding.

"*Agh, agh, agh!*" he complained. That was probably an entire lecture in Baboon, but I had no idea what he was saying.

"Well, I don't see any other way," I said. "If that family got pulled into the water or something...I have to find them. I'm going in."

"*Agh!*" He backed away from the water.

"Khufu, those people had a little girl. If they need help, I can't just walk away. Stay here and watch my back."

Khufu grunted and slapped his own face in protest as I stepped into the water. It was colder and swifter than I'd imagined. I concentrated, and summoned my sword and wand out of the Duat. Maybe it was my imagination, but that seemed to make the river run even faster.

I was midstream when Khufu barked urgently. He was jumping around on the riverbank, pointing frantically at a nearby clump of reeds.

The family was huddled inside, trembling with fear, their eyes wide. My first thought: *Why are they hiding from me?*

"I won't hurt you," I promised. They stared at me blankly, and I wished I could speak Spanish.

Then the water churned around me, and I realized they weren't scared of me. My next thought: *Man, I'm stupid.*

Horus's voice yelled: *Jump!*

I sprang out of the water as if shot from a cannon—twenty, thirty feet into the air. No way I should've been able to do that, but it was a good thing, because a monster erupted from the river beneath me.

At first all I saw were hundreds of teeth—a pink maw three times as big as me. Somehow I managed to flip and land on my feet in the shallows. I was facing a crocodile as long as our

RV—and that was just the half sticking out of the water. Its gray-green skin was ridged with thick plates like a camouflage suit of armor, and its eyes were the color of moldy milk.

The family screamed and started scrambling up the banks. That caught the crocodile's attention. He instinctively turned toward the louder, more interesting prey. I'd always thought of crocodiles as slow animals, but when it charged the immigrants, I'd never seen anything move so fast.

Use the distraction, Horus urged. *Get behind it and strike.*

Instead I yelled, "Sadie, Bast, help!" and I threw my wand.

Bad throw. The wand hit the river right in front of the croc, then skipped off the water like a stone, smacked the croc between the eyes, and shot back into my hand.

I doubt I did any damage, but the croc glanced over at me, annoyed.

Or you can smack it with a stick, Horus muttered.

I charged forward, yelling to keep the croc's attention. Out of the corner of my eye, I could see the family scrambling to safety. Khufu ran along behind them, waving his arms and barking to herd them out of harm's way. I wasn't sure if they were running from the croc or the crazy monkey, but as long as they kept running, I didn't care.

I couldn't see what was happening with Bast and Sadie. I heard shouting and splashing behind me, but before I could look, the crocodile lunged.

I ducked to the left, slashing with my sword. The blade just bounced off the croc's hide. The monster thrashed sideways, and its snout would've bashed my head in; but I instinctively raised my wand and the croc slammed into a wall of force, bouncing off as if I were protected by a giant invisible energy bubble.

I tried to summon the falcon warrior, but it was too hard to concentrate with a six-ton reptile trying to bite me in half.

Then I heard Bast scream, "NO!" and I knew immediately, without even looking, that something was wrong with Sadie.

Desperation and rage turned my nerves to steel. I thrust out my wand and the wall of energy surged outward, slamming into the crocodile so hard, it went flying through the air, tumbling out of the river and onto the Mexican shore. While it was on its back, flailing and off balance, I leaped, raising my sword, which was now glowing in my hands, and drove the blade into the monster's belly. I held on while the crocodile thrashed, slowly disintegrating from its snout to the tip of its tail, until I stood in the middle of a giant pile of wet sand.

I turned and saw Bast battling a crocodile just as big as mine. The crocodile lunged, and Bast dropped beneath it, raking her knives across its throat. The croc melted into the river until it was only a smoky cloud of sand, but the damage had been done: Sadie lay in a crumpled heap on the riverbank.

By the time I got there, Khufu and Bast were already at her side. Blood trickled from Sadie's scalp. Her face was a nasty shade of yellow.

"What happened?" I asked.

"It came out of nowhere," Bast said miserably. "Its tail hit Sadie and sent her flying. She never had a chance. Is she ...?"

Khufu put his hand on Sadie's forehead and made popping noises with his mouth.

Bast sighed with relief. "Khufu says she'll live, but we have to get her out of here. Those crocodiles could mean..."

Her voice trailed off. In the middle of the river, the water was boiling. Rising from it was a figure so horrible, I knew we were doomed.

"Could mean *that*," Bast said grimly.

To start with, the guy was twenty feet tall—and I don't mean with a glowing avatar. He was all flesh and blood. His chest and arms were human, but he had light green skin, and his waist was wrapped in a green armored kilt like reptile hide. He had the head of a crocodile, a massive mouth filled with white crooked teeth, and eyes that glistened with green mucus (yeah, I know—real attractive). His black hair hung in plaits down to his shoulders, and bull's horns curved from his head. If that wasn't weird enough, he appeared to be sweating at an unbelievable rate—oily water poured off him in torrents and pooled in the river.

He raised his staff—a length of green wood as big as a telephone pole.

Bast yelled, "Move!" and pulled me back as the crocodile man smashed a five-foot-deep trench in the riverbank where I'd been standing.

He bellowed: "Horus!"

The last thing I wanted to do was say, *Here!* But Horus spoke urgently in my mind: *Face him down. Sobek only understands strength. Do not let him grasp you, or he will pull you down and drown you.*

I swallowed my fear and yelled, "Sobek! You, uh, weakling! How the heck are ya?"

Sobek bared his teeth. Maybe it was his version of a friendly smile. Probably not.

"That form does not serve you, falcon god," he said. "I will snap you in half."

Next to me, Bast slipped her knives from her sleeves. "Don't let him grasp you," she warned.

"Already got the memo," I told her. I was conscious of Khufu off to my right, slowly lugging Sadie uphill. I had to keep this green guy distracted, at least until they were safe. "Sobek, god of...I'm guessing crocodiles! Leave us in peace or we'll destroy you!"

Good, Horus said. *"Destroy" is good.*

Sobek roared with laughter. "Your sense of humor has improved, Horus. You and your kitty will destroy me?" He turned his mucus-filmed eyes on Bast. "What brings you to my realm, cat goddess? I thought you didn't like the *water!*"

On the last word, he aimed his staff and shot forth a torrent of green water. Bast was too quick. She jumped and came down behind Sobek with her avatar fully formed—a massive, glowing cat-headed warrior. "Traitor!" Bast yelled. "Why do you side with chaos? Your duty is to the king!"

"What king?" Sobek roared. "Ra? Ra is gone. Osiris is dead *again,* the weakling! And this boy child cannot restore the empire. There was a time I supported Horus, yes. But he has no strength in this form. He has no followers. Set offers power. Set offers fresh meat. I think I will start with godling flesh!"

He turned on me and swung his staff. I rolled away from his strike, but his free hand shot out and grabbed me around the waist. I just wasn't quick enough. Bast tensed, preparing to launch herself at the enemy, but before she could, Sobek dropped his staff, grasped me with both massive hands, and dragged me into the water. The next thing I knew I was drowning in the cold green murk. I couldn't see or breathe. I sank into the depths as Sobek's hands crushed the air out of my lungs.

Now or never! Horus said. *Let me take control.*

No, I replied. *I'll die first.*

I found the thought strangely calming. If I was already dead, there was no point in being afraid. I might as well go down fighting.

I focused my power and felt strength coursing through my body. I flexed my arms and felt Sobek's grip weaken. I summoned the avatar of the hawk warrior and was instantly encased in a glowing golden form as large as Sobek. I could just see him in the dark water, his slimy eyes wide with surprise.

I broke his grip and head-butted him, breaking off a few of his teeth. Then I shot out of the water and landed on the riverbank next to Bast, who was so startled, she almost slashed me.

"Thank Ra!" she exclaimed.

"Yeah, I'm alive."

"No, I almost jumped in after you. I hate the water!"

Then Sobek exploded out of the river, roaring in rage. Green blood oozed from one of his nostrils.

"You cannot defeat me!" He held out his arms, which were raining perspiration. "I am lord of the water! My sweat creates the rivers of the world!"

Eww. I decided not to swim in rivers anymore. I glanced

back, looking for Khufu and Sadie, but they were nowhere in sight. Hopefully Khufu had gotten Sadie to safety, or at least found a good place to hide.

Sobek charged, and he brought the river with him. A massive wave smashed into me, toppling me to the ground, but Bast jumped and came down on Sobek's back in full avatar form. The weight hardly seemed to bother him. He tried to grab her without any luck. She slashed repeatedly at his arms, back and neck, but his green skin seemed to heal as quickly as she could cut him.

I struggled to my feet, which in avatar form is like trying to get up with a mattress strapped to your chest. Sobek finally managed to grab Bast and throw her off. She tumbled to a stop without getting hurt, but her blue aura was flickering. She was losing power.

We played tag team with the crocodile god—stabbing and slashing—but the more we wounded him, the more enraged and powerful he seemed to get.

"More minions!" he shouted. "Come to me!"

That couldn't be good. Another round of giant crocs and we'd be dead.

Why don't we get minions? I complained to Horus, but he didn't answer. I could feel him struggling to channel his power through me, trying to keep up our combat magic.

Sobek's fist smashed into Bast, and she went flying again. This time when she hit the ground, her avatar flickered off completely.

I charged, trying to draw Sobek's attention. Unfortunately,

it worked. Sobek turned and blasted me with water. While I was blind, he slapped me so hard I flew across the riverbank, tumbling through the reeds.

My avatar collapsed. I sat up groggily and found Khufu and Sadie right next to me, Sadie still passed out and bleeding, Khufu desperately murmuring in Baboon and stroking her forehead.

Sobek stepped out of the water and grinned at me. Far downstream in the dim evening light, about a quarter of a mile away, I could see two wake lines in the river, coming toward us fast—Sobek's reinforcements.

From the river, Bast yelled, "Carter, hurry! Get Sadie out of here!"

Her face went pale with strain, and her cat warrior avatar appeared around her one more time. It was weak, though—barely substantial.

"Don't!" I called. "You'll die!"

I tried to summon the falcon warrior, but the effort made my insides burn with pain. I was out of power, and Horus's spirit was slumbering, completely spent.

"Go!" Bast yelled. "And tell your father I kept my promise."

"NO!"

She leaped at Sobek. The two grappled—Bast slashing furiously across his face while Sobek howled in pain. The two gods toppled into the water, and down they went.

I ran to the riverbank. The river bubbled and frothed. Then a green explosion lit the entire length of the Rio Grande, and a small black-and-gold creature shot out of the river as if it had been tossed. It landed on the grass at my feet—a wet, unconscious, half-dead cat.

"Bast?" I picked up the cat gingerly. It wore Bast's collar, but as I watched, the talisman of the goddess crumbled to dust. It wasn't Bast anymore. Only Muffin.

Tears stung my eyes. Sobek had been defeated, forced back to the Duat or something, but there were still two wake lines coming toward us in the river, close enough now that I could see the monsters' green backs and beady eyes.

I cradled the cat against my chest and turned toward Khufu. "Come on, we have to—"

I froze, because standing right behind Khufu and my sister, glaring at me, was a different crocodile—one that was pure white.

We're dead, I thought. And then, *Wait . . . a white crocodile?*

It opened its mouth and lunged—straight over me. I turned and saw it slam into the two other crocodiles—the giant green ones that had been about to kill me.

"Philip?" I said in amazement, as the crocodiles thrashed and fought.

"Yes," said a man's voice.

I turned again and saw the impossible. Uncle Amos was kneeling next to Sadie, frowning as he examined her head wound. He looked up at me urgently. "Philip will keep Sobek's minions busy, but not for long. Follow me now, and we have a slim chance of surviving!"

31. I Deliver a Love Note

I'M GLAD CARTER TOLD THAT LAST BIT—partly because I was unconscious when it happened, partly because I can't talk about what Bast did without going to pieces.

Ah, but more on that later.

I woke feeling as if someone had overinflated my head. My eyes weren't seeing the same things. Out my left, I saw a baboon bum, out my right, my long-lost uncle Amos. Naturally, I decided to focus on the right.

"Amos?"

He laid a cool cloth on my forehead. "Rest, child. You had quite a concussion."

That at least I could believe.

As my eyes began to focus, I saw we were outside under a starry night sky. I was lying on a blanket on what felt like soft sand. Khufu stood next to me, his colorful side a bit too close to my face. He was stirring a pot over a small fire, and whatever he was cooking smelled like burning tar. Carter sat nearby at the top of a sand dune, looking despondent and holding... was that Muffin in his lap?

Amos appeared much as he had when we last saw him, ages ago. He wore his blue suit with matching coat and fedora. His long hair was neatly braided, and his round glasses glinted in the sun. He appeared fresh and rested—not like someone who'd been the prisoner of Set.

"How did you—"

"Get away from Set?" His expression darkened. "I was a fool to go looking for him, Sadie. I had no idea how powerful he'd become. His spirit is tied to the red pyramid."

"So...he doesn't *have* a human host?"

Amos shook his head. "He doesn't need one as long as he has the pyramid. As it gets closer to completion, he gets stronger and stronger. I sneaked into his lair under the mountain and walked right into a trap. I'm ashamed to say he took me without a fight."

He gestured at his suit, showing off how perfectly fine he was. "Not a scratch. Just—*bam*. I was frozen like a statue. Set stood me outside his pyramid like a trophy and let his demons laugh and mock me as they passed by."

"Did you see Dad?" I asked.

His shoulders slumped. "I heard the demons talking. The coffin is inside the pyramid. They're planning to use Osiris's power to augment the storm. When Set unleashes it at sunrise—and it will be *quite* an explosion—Osiris and your father will be obliterated. Osiris will be exiled so deep into the Duat he may never rise again."

My head began to throb. I couldn't believe we had so

little time, and if Amos couldn't save Dad, how could Carter and I?

"But you got away," I said, grasping for any good news. "So there must be weaknesses in his defenses or—"

"The magic that froze me eventually began to weaken. I concentrated my energy and worked my way out of the binding. It took many hours, but finally I broke free. I sneaked out at midday, when the demons were sleeping. It was much too easy."

"It doesn't sound easy," I said.

Amos shook his head, obviously troubled. "Set allowed me to escape. I don't know why, but I shouldn't be alive. It's a trick of some sort. I'm afraid..." Whatever he was going to say, he changed his mind. "At any rate, my first thought was to find you, so I summoned my boat."

He gestured behind him. I managed to lift my head and saw we were in a strange desert of white dunes that stretched as far as I could see in the starlight. The sand under my fingers was so fine and white, it might've been sugar. Amos's boat, the same one that had carried us from the Thames to Brooklyn, was beached at the top of a nearby dune, canted at a precarious angle as if it had been thrown there.

"There's a supply locker aboard," Amos offered, "if you'd like fresh clothes."

"But where are we?"

"White Sands," Carter told me. "In New Mexico. It's a government range for testing missiles. Amos said no one would look for us here, so we gave you some time to heal. It's about seven in the evening, still the twenty-eighth. Twelve hours or so until Set...you know."

"But..." Too many questions swam round in my mind. The last thing I remembered, I'd been at the river talking to Nephthys. Her voice had seemed to come from the other side of the world. She'd spoken faintly through the current—so hard to understand, yet quite insistent. She'd told me she was sheltered far away in a sleeping host, which I couldn't make sense of. She'd said she could not appear in person, but that she would send a message. Then the water had started to boil.

"We were attacked." Carter stroked Muffin's head, and I finally noticed that the amulet—*Bast's* amulet—was missing. "Sadie, I've got some bad news."

He told me what had happened, and I closed my eyes. I started to weep. Embarrassing, yes, but I couldn't help it. Over the last few days, I'd lost everything—my home, my ordinary life, my father. I'd been almost killed half a dozen times. My mother's death, which I'd never gotten over to begin with, hurt like a reopened wound. And now Bast was gone too?

When Anubis had questioned me in the Underworld, he'd wanted to know what I would sacrifice to save the world.

What haven't I sacrificed already? I wanted to scream. *What have I got left?*

Carter came over and gave me Muffin, who purred in my arms, but it wasn't the same. It wasn't Bast.

"She'll come back, won't she?" I looked at Amos imploringly. "I mean she's immortal, isn't she?"

Amos tugged at the rim of his hat. "Sadie...I just don't know. It seems she sacrificed herself to defeat Sobek. Bast forced him back to the Duat at the expense of her own life force. She even spared Muffin, her host, probably with the last shred of her power. If that's true, it would be very difficult for Bast to come back. Perhaps some day, in a few hundred years—"

"No, not a few hundred years! I can't—" My voice broke.

Carter put his hand on my shoulder, and I knew he understood. We *couldn't* lose anyone else. We just couldn't.

"Rest now," Amos said. "We can spare another hour, but then we'll have to get moving."

Khufu offered me a bowl of his concoction. The chunky liquid looked like soup that had died long ago. I glanced at Amos, hoping he'd give me a pass, but he nodded encouragingly.

Just my luck, on top of everything else I had to take baboon medicine.

I sipped the brew, which tasted almost as bad as it smelled, and immediately my eyelids felt heavy. I closed my eyes and slept.

And just when I thought I had this soul-leaving-the-body business sorted, my soul decided to break the rules. Well, it is *my* soul after all, so I suppose that makes sense.

As my *ba* left my body, it kept its human form, which was better than the winged poultry look, but it kept growing and growing until I towered above White Sands. I'd been told many times that I have a lot of spirit (usually not as a compliment), but this was absurd. My *ba* was as tall as the Washington Monument.

To the south, past miles and miles of desert, steam rose from the Rio Grande—the battle site where Bast and Sobek had perished. Even as tall as I was, I shouldn't have been able to see all the way to Texas, especially at night, but somehow I could. To the north, even farther away, I saw a distant red glow and I knew it was the aura of Set. His power was growing as his pyramid neared completion.

I looked down. Next to my foot was a tiny cluster of specks—our camp. Miniature Carter, Amos, and Khufu sat talking round the cooking fire. Amos's boat was no larger than my little toe. My own sleeping form lay curled in a blanket, so small I could've crushed myself with one misstep.

I was enormous, and the world was small.

"That's how gods see things," a voice told me.

I looked around but saw nothing, just the vast expanse of rolling white dunes. Then, in front of me, the dunes shifted. I thought it was the wind, until an entire dune rolled sideways like a wave. Another moved, and another. I realized I was looking at a human form—an enormous man lying in the fetal position. He got up, shaking white sand everywhere. I knelt down and cupped my hands over my companions to keep them from getting buried. Oddly, they didn't seem to notice, as if the disruption were no more than a sprinkle of rain.

The man rose to his full height—at least a head taller than my own giant form. His body was made of sand that curtained off his arms and chest like waterfalls of sugar. The sand shifted across his face until he formed a vague smile.

"Sadie Kane," he said. "I have been waiting for you."

"Geb." Don't ask me how, but I knew instantly that this was the god of the earth. Maybe the sand body was a giveaway. "I have something for you."

It didn't make sense that my *ba* would have the envelope,

but I reached into my shimmering ghostly pocket and pulled out the note from Nut.

"Your wife misses you," I said.

Geb took the note gingerly. He held it to his face and seemed to sniff it. Then he opened the envelope. Instead of a letter, fireworks burst out. A new constellation blazed in the night sky above us—the face of Nut, formed by a thousand stars. The wind rose quickly and ripped the image apart, but Geb sighed contentedly. He closed the envelope and tucked it inside his sandy chest as if there were a pocket right where his heart should be.

"I owe you thanks, Sadie Kane," Geb said. "It has been many millennia since I saw the face of my beloved. Ask me a favor that the earth can grant, and it shall be yours."

"Save my father," I said immediately.

Geb's face rippled with surprise. "*Hmm*, what a loyal daughter! Isis could learn a thing from you. Alas, I cannot. Your father's path is twined with that of Osiris, and matters between the gods cannot be solved by the earth."

"Then I don't suppose you could collapse Set's mountain and destroy his pyramid?" I asked.

Geb's laughter was like the world's largest sand shaker. "I cannot intervene so directly between my children. Set is my son too."

I almost stamped my foot in frustration. Then I remembered I was giant and might smash the whole camp. Could a *ba* do that? Better not to find out. "Well, your favors aren't very useful, then."

Geb shrugged, sloughing off a few tons of sand from his

shoulders. "Perhaps some advice to help you achieve what you desire. Go to the place of the crosses."

"And where is that?"

"Close," he promised. "And, Sadie Kane, you are right. You have lost too much. Your family has suffered. I know what that is like. Just remember, a parent would do anything to save his children. I gave up my happiness, my wife—I took on the curse of Ra so that my children could be born." He looked up at the sky wistfully. "And while I miss my beloved more each millennium, I know neither of us would change our choice. I have five children whom I love."

"Even Set?" I asked incredulously. "He's about to destroy millions of people."

"Set is more than he appears," Geb said. "He is our flesh and blood."

"Not mine."

"No?" Geb shifted, lowering himself. I thought he was crouching, until I realized he was melting into the dunes. "Think on it, Sadie Kane, and proceed with care. Danger awaits you at the place of crosses, but you will also find what you need most."

"Could you be a little more vague?" I grumbled.

But Geb was gone, leaving only a taller than normal dune in the sands; and my *ba* sank back into my body.

32. The Place of Crosses

I WOKE WITH MUFFIN SNUGGLED on my head, purring and chewing my hair. For a moment, I thought I was home. I used to wake with Muffin on my head all the time. Then I remembered I *had* no home, and Bast was gone. My eyes started tearing up again.

No, Isis's voice chided. *We must stay focused.*

For once, the goddess was right. I sat up and brushed the white sand off my face. Muffin meowed in protest, then waddled two steps and decided she could settle for my warm place on the blanket.

"Good, you're up," Amos said. "We were about to wake you."

It was still dark. Carter stood on the deck of the boat, pulling on a new linen coat from Amos's supply locker. Khufu loped over to me and made a purring sound at the cat. To my surprise, Muffin leaped into his arms.

"I've asked Khufu to take the cat back to Brooklyn," Amos said. "This is no place for her."

Khufu grunted, clearly unhappy with his assignment.

"I know, my old friend," Amos said. His voice had a hard edge; he seemed to be asserting himself as the alpha baboon. "It is for the best."

"*Agh*," Khufu said, not meeting Amos's eyes.

Unease crept over me. I remembered what Amos said: that his release might have been a trick of Set's. And Carter's vision: Set was *hoping* that Amos would lead us to the mountain so we could be captured. What if Set was influencing Amos somehow? I didn't like the idea of sending Khufu away.

On the other hand, I didn't see much choice but to accept Amos's help. And seeing Khufu there, holding Muffin, I couldn't bear the idea of putting either of them in danger. Maybe Amos had a point.

"Can he travel safely?" I asked. "Out here all by himself?"

"Oh, yes," Amos promised. "Khufu—and all baboons—have their own brand of magic. He'll be fine. And just in case..."

He brought out a wax figurine of a crocodile. "This will help if the need arises."

I coughed. "A crocodile? After what we just—"

"It's Philip of Macedonia," Amos explained.

"Philip is wax?"

"Of course," Amos said. "Real crocodiles are much too difficult to keep. And I *did* tell you he's magic."

Amos tossed the figurine to Khufu, who sniffed it, then

stuffed it into a pouch with his cooking supplies. Khufu gave me one last nervous look, glanced fearfully at Amos, then ambled over the dune with his bag in one arm and Muffin in the other.

I didn't see how they would survive out here, magic or no. I waited for Khufu to appear on the crest of the next dune, but he never did. He simply vanished.

"Now, then," Amos said. "From what Carter has told me, Set means to unleash his destruction tomorrow at sunrise. That gives us very little time. What Carter would *not* explain is how you plan to destroy Set."

I glanced at Carter and saw warning in his eyes. I understood immediately, and felt a flush of gratitude. Perhaps the boy wasn't completely thick. He shared my concerns about Amos.

"It's best we keep that to ourselves," I told Amos flatly. "You said so yourself. What if Set attached a magic listening device to you or something?"

Amos's jaw tightened. "You're right," he said grudgingly. "I can't trust myself. It's just…so frustrating."

He sounded truly anguished, which made me feel guilty. I was tempted to change my mind and tell him our plan, but one look at Carter and I kept my resolve.

"We should head to Phoenix," I said. "Perhaps along the way…"

I slipped my hand into my pocket. Nut's letter was gone. I wanted to tell Carter about my talk with the earth god, Geb, but I didn't know if it was safe in front of Amos. Carter and I had been a team for so many days now, I realized that I resented Amos's presence a little. I didn't want to confide in anyone else. God, I can't believe I just said that.

Carter spoke up. "We should stop in Las Cruces."

I'm not sure who was more surprised: Amos or me.

"That's near here," Amos said slowly. "But..." He picked up a handful of sand, murmured a spell, and threw the sand into the air. Instead of scattering, the grains floated and formed a wavering arrow, pointing southwest toward a line of rugged mountains that made a dark silhouette against the horizon.

"As I thought," Amos said, and the sand fell to the earth. "Las Cruces is out of our way by forty miles—over those mountains. Phoenix is northwest."

"Forty miles isn't so bad," I said. "Las Cruces..." The name seemed strangely familiar to me, but I couldn't decide why. "Carter, why there?"

"I just..." He looked so uncomfortable I knew it must have something to do with Zia. "I had a vision."

"A vision of loveliness?" I ventured.

He looked like he was trying to swallow a golf ball, which confirmed my suspicions. "I just think we should go there," he said. "We might find something important."

"Too risky," Amos said. "I can't allow it with the House of Life on your trail. We should stay in the wilderness, away from cities."

Then suddenly: *click*. My brain had one of those amazing moments when it actually works correctly.

"No, Carter's right," I said. "We have to go there."

It was my brother's turn to look surprised. "I am? We do?"

"Yes." I took the plunge and told them about my talk with Geb.

Amos brushed some sand off his jacket. "That's interesting, Sadie. But I don't see how Las Cruces comes into play."

"Because it's Spanish, isn't it?" I said. "Las Cruces. *The crosses.* Just as Geb told me."

Amos hesitated, then nodded reluctantly. "Get in the boat."

"A bit short on water for a boat ride, aren't we?" I asked.

But I followed him on board. Amos took off his coat and uttered a magic word. Instantly, the coat came to life, drifted to the stern and grasped the tiller.

Amos smiled at me, and some of that old twinkle came back into his eyes. "Who needs water?"

The boat shuddered and lifted into the sky.

If Amos ever got tired of being a magician, he could've gotten a job as a sky boat tour operator. The vista coming over the mountains was quite stunning.

At first, the desert had seemed barren and ugly to me compared to the lush greens of England, but I was starting to appreciate that the desert had its own stark beauty, especially at night. The mountains rose like dark islands in a sea of lights. I'd never seen so many stars above us, and the dry wind smelled of sage and pine. Las Cruces spread out in the valley below—a glowing patchwork of streets and neighborhoods.

As we got closer, I saw that most of the town was nothing very remarkable. It might've been Manchester or Swindon or any place, really, but Amos aimed our ship toward the south of the city, to an area that was obviously much older—with adobe buildings and tree-lined streets.

As we descended, I began to get nervous.

"Won't they notice us in a flying boat?" I asked. "I mean, I know magic is hard to see, but—"

"This is New Mexico," Amos said. "They see UFOs here all the time."

And with that, we landed on the roof of a small church.

It was like dropping back in time, or onto a Wild West film set. The town square was lined with stucco buildings like an Indian pueblo. The streets were brightly lit and crowded—it looked like a festival—with stall vendors selling strings of red peppers, Indian blankets, and other curios. An old stagecoach was parked next to a clump of cacti. In the plaza's bandstand, men with large guitars and loud voices played mariachi music.

"This is the historic area," Amos said. "I believe they call it Mesilla."

"Have a lot of Egyptian stuff here, do they?" I asked dubiously.

"Oh, the ancient cultures of Mexico have a lot in common with Egypt," Amos said, retrieving his coat from the tiller. "But that's a talk for another day."

"Thank god," I muttered. Then I sniffed the air and smelled something strange but wonderful—like baking bread and melting butter, only spicer, yummier. "I—am—*starving*."

It didn't take long, walking the plaza, to discover handmade tortillas. God, they were good. I suppose London has Mexican restaurants. We've got everything else. But I'd never been to one, and I doubt the tortillas would've tasted this heavenly.

A large woman in a white dress rolled out balls of dough in her flour-caked hands, flattened and baked the tortillas on a hot skillet, and handed them to us on paper napkins. They didn't need butter or jam or anything. They were so delicate, they just melted in my mouth. I made Amos pay for about a dozen, just for me.

Carter was enjoying himself too until he tried the red-chili tamales at another booth. I thought his face would explode. "Hot!" he announced. "Drink!"

"Eat more tortilla," Amos advised, trying not to laugh. "Bread cuts the heat better than water."

I tried the tamales myself and found they were excellent, not nearly as hot as a good curry, so Carter was just being a wimp, as usual.

Soon we'd eaten our fill and began wandering the streets, looking for... well, I wasn't sure, exactly. Time was a-wasting. The sun was going down, and I knew this would be the last night for all of us unless we stopped Set, but I had no idea why Geb had sent me here. *You will also find what you need most.* What did that mean?

I scanned the crowds and caught a glimpse of a tall young guy with dark hair. A thrill went up my spine—*Anubis?* What if he was following me, making sure I was safe? What if *he* was what I needed most?

Wonderful thought, except it wasn't Anubis. I scolded myself for thinking I could have luck that good. Besides, Carter had seen Anubis as a jackal-headed monster. Perhaps Anubis's appearance with me was just a trick to befuddle my brain—a trick that worked *quite* well.

I was daydreaming about that, and about whether or not they had tortillas in the Land of the Dead, when I locked eyes with a girl across the plaza.

"Carter." I grabbed his arm and nodded in the direction of Zia Rashid. "Someone's here to see you."

Zia was ready for battle in her loose black linen clothes, staff and wand in hand. Her dark choppy hair was blown to one side like she'd flown here on a strong wind. Her amber eyes looked about as friendly as a jaguar's.

Behind her was a vendor's table full of tourist souvenirs, and a poster that read: NEW MEXICO: LAND OF ENCHANTMENT. I doubted the vendor knew just how much enchantment was standing right in front of his merchandise.

"You came," Zia said, which seemed a bit on the obvious side. Was it my imagination, or was she looking at Amos with apprehension—even fear?

"Yeah," Carter said nervously. "You, uh, remember Sadie. And this is—"

"Amos," Zia said uneasily.

Amos bowed. "Zia Rashid, it's been several years. I see Iskandar sent his best."

Zia looked as if he'd smacked her in the face, and I realized Amos hadn't heard the news.

"*Um*, Amos," I said. "Iskandar is dead."

He stared at us in disbelief as we told him the story.

"I see," he said at last. "Then the new Chief Lector is—"

"Desjardins," I said.

"Ah. Bad news."

Zia frowned. Instead of addressing Amos, she turned to me.

"Do not dismiss Desjardins. He's very powerful. You'll need his help—*our* help—to challenge Set."

"Has it ever occurred to you," I said, "that Desjardins might be *helping* Set?"

Zia glared at me. "Never. *Others* might. But not Desjardins."

Clearly she meant Amos. I suppose that should've made me even more suspicious of him, but instead I got angry.

"You're blind," I told Zia. "Desjardins' first order as Chief Lector was to have us killed. He's trying to stop us, even though he *knows* Set is about to destroy the continent. And Desjardins was there that night at the British Museum. If Set needed a body—"

The top of Zia's staff burst into flame.

Carter quickly moved between us. "Whoa, both of you just calm down. We're here to talk."

"I *am* talking," Zia said. "You need the House of Life on your side. You have to convince Desjardins you're not a threat."

"By surrendering?" I asked. "No, thank you. I'd rather not be turned into a bug and squashed."

Amos cleared his throat. "I'm afraid Sadie is right. Unless Desjardins has changed since I last saw him, he is not a man who will listen to reason."

Zia fumed. "Carter, could we speak in *private?*"

He shifted from foot to foot. "Look, Zia, I—I agree we need to work together. But if you're going to try to convince me to surrender to the House—"

"There's something I must tell you," she insisted. "Something you *need* to know."

The way she said that made the hairs stand up on the back of my neck. Could this be what Geb meant? Was it possible that Zia held the key to defeating Set?

Suddenly Amos tensed. He pulled his staff out of thin air and said, "It's a trap."

Zia looked stunned. "What? No!"

Then we all saw what Amos had sensed. Marching towards us from the east end of the plaza was Desjardins himself. He wore cream-colored robes with the Chief Lector's leopard-skin cape tied across his shoulders. His staff glowed purple. Tourists and pedestrians veered out of his way, confused and nervous, as if they weren't sure what was going on but they knew enough to clear off.

"Other way," I urged.

I turned and saw two more magicians in black robes marching in from the west.

I pulled my wand and pointed it at Zia. "You set us up!"

"No! I swear—" Her face fell. "Mel. Mel must've told him."

"Right," I grumbled. "Blame Mel."

"No time for explanations," Amos said, and he blasted Zia with a bolt of lightning. She crashed into the souvenir table.

"Hey!" Carter protested.

"She's the enemy," Amos said. "And we have enough enemies."

Carter rushed to Zia's side (naturally) while more pedestrians panicked and scattered for the edges of the square.

"Sadie, Carter," Amos said, "if things go bad, get to the boat and flee."

"Amos, we're not leaving you," I said.

"You're more important," he insisted. "I can hold off Desjardins for— Look out!"

Amos spun his staff towards the two magicians in black. They'd been muttering spells, but Amos's gust of wind swept them off their feet, sending them swirling out of control at the center of a dust devil. They churned along the street, picking up trash, leaves, and tamales, until the miniature tornado tossed the screaming magicians over the top of a building and out of sight.

On the other side of the plaza, Desjardins roared in anger: "Kane!"

The Chief Lector slammed his staff into the ground. A crack opened in the pavement and began snaking towards us. As the crevice grew wider, the buildings trembled. Stucco flaked off the walls. The fissure would've swallowed us, but Isis's voice spoke in my mind, telling me the word I needed.

I raised my wand. "Quiet. *Hah-ri.*"

Hieroglyphs blazed to life in front of us:

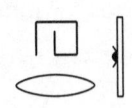

The fissure stopped just short of my feet. The earthquake died.

Amos sucked in a breath. "Sadie, how did you—"

"Divine Words, Kane!" Desjardins stepped forward, his face livid. "The child dares speak the Divine Words. She is corrupted by Isis, and you are guilty of assisting the gods."

"Step off, Michel," Amos warned.

Part of me found it amusing that Desjardins' first name was Michel, but I was too scared to enjoy the moment.

Amos held out his wand, ready to defend us. "We must stop Set. If you're wise—"

"I would what?" Desjardins said. "Join you? Collaborate? The gods bring nothing but destruction."

"No!" Zia's voice. With Carter's help, she'd somehow managed to struggle to her feet. "Master, we can't fight each other. That's not what Iskandar wanted."

"Iskandar is dead!" Desjardins bellowed. "Now, step away from them, Zia, or be destroyed with them."

Zia looked at Carter. Then she set her jaw and faced Desjardins. "No. We must work together."

I regarded Zia with a new respect. "You really didn't lead him here?"

"I do not lie," she said.

Desjardins raised his staff, and huge cracks appeared in the buildings all around him. Chunks of cement and adobe brick flew at us, but Amos summoned the wind and deflected them.

"Children, get out of here!" Amos yelled. "The other magicians won't stay gone forever."

"For once, he's right," Zia warned. "But we can't make a portal—"

"We've got a flying boat," Carter offered.

Zia nodded appreciatively. "Where?"

We pointed towards the church, but unfortunately Desjardins was between it and us.

Desjardins hurled another volley of stones. Amos deflected them with wind and lightning.

"Storm magic!" Desjardins sneered. "Since when is Amos Kane an expert in the powers of chaos? Do you see this, children? How can he be your protector?"

"Shut up," Amos growled, and with a sweep of his staff he raised a sandstorm so huge that it blanketed the entire square.

"Now," Zia said. We made a wide arc around Desjardins, then ran blindly towards the church. The sandstorm bit my skin and stung my eyes, but we found the stairs and climbed to the roof. The wind subsided, and across the plaza I could see Desjardins and Amos still facing each other, encased in shields of force. Amos was staggering; the effort was clearly taking too much out of him.

"I have to help," Zia said reluctantly, "or Desjardins will kill Amos."

"I thought you didn't trust Amos," Carter said.

"I don't," she agreed. "But if Desjardins wins this duel, we're all dead. We'll never escape." She clenched her teeth as if she were preparing for something really painful.

She held out her staff and murmured an incantation. The air became warm. The staffed glowed. She released it and it burst into flame, growing into a column of fire a full meter thick and four meters tall.

"Hunt Desjardins," she intoned.

Immediately, the fiery column floated off the roof and began moving slowly but deliberately towards the Chief Lector.

Zia crumpled. Carter and I had to grab her arms to keep her from falling on her face.

Desjardins looked up. When he saw the fire, his eyes widened with fear. "Zia!" he cursed. "You *dare* attack me?"

The column descended, passing through the branches of a tree and burning a hole straight through them. It landed in the street, hovering just a few centimeters above the pavement. The heat was so intense that it scorched the concrete curb and melted the tarmac. The fire came to a parked car, and instead of going round, it burned its way straight through the metal chassis, sawing the car in two.

"Good!" Amos yelled from the street. "Well done, Zia!"

In desperation, Desjardins staggered to his left. The column adjusted course. He blasted it with water, but the liquid evaporated into steam. He summoned boulders, but they just passed through the fire and dropped into melted, smoking lumps on the opposite side.

"What *is* that thing?" I asked.

Zia was unconscious, and Carter shook his head in wonder. But Isis spoke in my mind. *A pillar of fire,* she said with admiration. *It is the most powerful spell a master of fire can summon. It is impossible to defeat, impossible to escape. It can be used to lead the summoner toward a goal. Or it can be used to pursue any enemy, forcing him to run. If Desjardins tries to focus on anything else, it will overtake him and consume him. It will not leave him alone until it dissipates.*

How long? I asked.

Depends on the strength of the caster. Between six and twelve hours.

I laughed aloud. Brilliant! Of course Zia had passed out creating it, but it was still brilliant.

Such a spell has depleted her energy, Isis said. *She will not be able to work any magic until the pillar is gone. In order to help you, she has left herself completely powerless.*

"She'll be all right," I told Carter. Then I shouted down to the plaza: "Amos, come on! We've got to go!"

Desjardins kept backing up. I could tell he was scared of the fire, but he wasn't quite done with us. "You will be sorry for this! You wish to play gods? Then you leave me no choice." Out of the Duat, he pulled a cluster of sticks. No, they were arrows—about seven of them.

Amos looked at the arrows in horror. "You wouldn't! No Chief Lector would ever—"

"I summon Sekhmet!" Desjardins bellowed. He threw the arrows into the air and they began to twirl, orbiting Amos.

Desjardins allowed himself a satisfied smile. He looked straight at me. "You choose to place your faith in the gods?" he called. "Then die by the hands of a god."

He turned and ran. The pillar of fire picked up speed and followed.

"Children, get out of here!" Amos yelled, encircled by the arrows. "I'll try to distract her!"

"Who?" I demanded. I knew I'd heard the name Sekhmet before, but I'd heard *a lot* of Egyptian names. "Which one is Sekhmet?"

Carter turned to me, and even with all we'd been through over the last week, I had never seen him look so scared. "We need to leave," he said. *"Now."*

33. We Go Into the Salsa Business

YOU'RE FORGETTING SOMETHING, Horus told me.

A little busy here! I thought back.

You might think it's easy steering a magic boat through the sky. You'd be wrong. I didn't have Amos's animated coat, so I stood in the back trying to shift the tiller myself, which was like stirring cement. I couldn't see where we were going. We kept tilting back and forth while Sadie tried her best to keep an unconscious Zia from flopping over the side.

It's my birthday, Horus insisted. *Wish me happy birthday!*

"Happy birthday!" I yelled. "Now, shut up!"

"Carter, what are you on about?" Sadie screamed, grabbing the railing with one hand and Zia with the other as the boat tipped sideways. "Have you lost your mind?"

"No, I was talking to—Oh, forget it."

I glanced behind us. *Something* was approaching—a blazing figure that lit up the night. Vaguely humanoid, definitely bad news. I urged the boat to go faster.

Did you get me anything? Horus urged.

Will you please do something helpful? I demanded. *That thing following us—is that what I think it is?*

Oh. Horus sounded bored. *That's Sekhmet. The Eye of Ra, destroyer of the wicked, the great huntress, lady of flame, et cetera.*

Great, I thought. *And she's following us because . . .*

The Chief Lector has the power to summon her once during his lifetime, Horus explained. *It's an old, old gift—goes back to the days when Ra first blessed man with magic.*

Once during his lifetime, I thought. *And Desjardins chooses now?*

He never was very good at being patient.

I thought that the magicians don't like gods!

They don't, Horus agreed. *Just shows you what a hypocrite he is. But I suppose killing you was more important than standing on principle. I can appreciate that.*

I looked back again. The figure was definitely getting closer—a giant golden woman in glowing red armor, with a bow in one hand and a quiver of arrows slung across her back—and she was hurtling toward us like a rocket.

How do we beat her? I asked.

You pretty much don't, Horus said. *She is the incarnation of the sun's wrath. Back in the days when Ra was active, she would've been much more impressive, but still. . . . She's unstoppable. A born killer. A slaying machine—*

"Okay, I get it!" I yelled.

"What?" Sadie demanded, so loud that Zia stirred.

"Wha—what?" Her eyes fluttered open.

"Nothing," I shouted. "We're being followed by a slaying machine. Go back to sleep."

Zia sat up woozily. "A slaying machine? You don't mean—"

"Carter, veer right!" Sadie yelled.

I did, and a flaming arrow the size of a predator drone grazed our port side. It exploded above us, setting the roof of our boathouse on fire.

I steered the boat into a dive, and Sekhmet shot past but then pirouetted in the air with irritating agility and dove after us.

"We're burning," Sadie pointed out helpfully.

"Noticed!" I yelled back.

I scanned the landscape below us, but there was nowhere safe to land—just subdivisions and office parks.

"Die, enemies of Ra!" Sekhmet yelled. "Perish in agony!"

She's almost as annoying as you, I told Horus.

Impossible, Horus said. *No one bests Horus.*

I took another evasive turn, and Zia yelled, "There!"

She pointed toward a well-lit factory complex with trucks, warehouses, and silos. A giant chili pepper was painted on the side of the biggest warehouse, and a floodlit sign read: MAGIC SALSA, INC.

"Oh, please," Sadie said. "It's not really magic! That's just a name."

"No," Zia insisted. "I've got an idea."

"Those Seven Ribbons?" I guessed. "The ones you used on Serqet?"

Zia shook her head. "They can only be summoned once a year. But my plan—"

Another arrow blazed past us, only inches from our starboard side.

"Hang on!" I yanked at the tiller and spun the boat upside down just before the arrow exploded. The hull shielded us from the brunt of the blast, but the entire bottom of the ship was now on fire, and we were going down.

With my last bit of control, I aimed the boat toward the roof of the warehouse, and we crashed through, slamming into a huge mound of . . . something crunchy.

I clawed my way clear of the boat and sat up in a daze. Fortunately, the stuff we'd crashed into was soft. Unfortunately, it was a twenty-foot pile of dried chili peppers, and the boat had set them on fire. My eyes began to sting, but I knew better than to rub them, because my hands were now covered in chili oil.

"Sadie?" I called. "Zia?"

"Help!" Sadie yelled. She was on the other side of the boat, dragging Zia out from under the flaming hull. We managed to pull her free and slide down the pile onto the floor.

The warehouse seemed to be a massive facility for drying peppers, with thirty or forty mountains of chilis and rows of wooden drying racks. The wreckage of our boat filled the air with spicy smoke, and through the hole we'd made in the roof, I could see the blazing figure of Sekhmet descending.

We ran, plowing through another pile of peppers. [No, I didn't pick a peck of them, Sadie—just shut up.] We hid behind a drying rack, where shelves of peppers made the air burn like hydrochloric acid.

Sekhmet landed, and the warehouse floor shuddered. Up close, she was even more terrifying. Her skin glowed like liquid gold, and her chest armor and skirt seemed to be woven of tiles made from molten lava. Her hair was like a thick lion's mane. Her eyes were feline, but they didn't sparkle like Bast's or betray any kindness or humor. Sekhmet's eyes blazed like her arrows, designed only to seek and destroy. She was beautiful the way an atomic explosion is beautiful.

"I smell blood!" she roared. "I will feast on enemies of Ra until my belly is full!"

"Charming," Sadie whispered. "So Zia...this plan?"

Zia didn't look so well. She was shivering and pale, and seemed to have trouble focusing on us. "When Ra...when he first called Sekhmet to punish humans because they were rebelling against him...she got out of hand."

"Hard to imagine," I whispered, as Sekhmet ripped through the burning wreckage of our boat.

"She started killing *everyone*," Zia said, "not just the wicked. None of the other gods could stop her. She would just kill all day until she was gorged on blood. Then she'd leave until the next day. So the people begged the magicians to come up with a plan, and—"

"You dare hide?" Flames roared as Sekhmet's arrows destroyed pile after pile of dried peppers. "I will roast you alive!"

"Run now," I decided. "Talk later."

Sadie and I dragged Zia between us. We managed to get out of the warehouse just before the whole place imploded from the heat, billowing a spicy-hot mushroom cloud into the sky. We ran through a parking lot filled with semitrailers and hid behind a sixteen-wheeler.

I peeked out, expecting to see Sekhmet walk through the

flames of the warehouse. Instead, she leaped out in the form of a giant lion. Her eyes blazed, and floating over her head was a disk of fire like a miniature sun.

"The symbol of Ra," Zia whispered.

Sekhmet roared: "Where are you, my tasty morsels?" She opened her maw and breathed a blast of hot air across the parking lot. Wherever her breath touched, the asphalt melted, cars disintegrated into sand, and the parking lot turned into barren desert.

"How did she do that?" Sadie hissed.

"Her breath creates the deserts," Zia said. "That is the legend."

"Better and better." Fear was closing up my throat, but I knew we couldn't hide much longer. I summoned my sword. "I'll distract her. You two run—"

"No," Zia insisted. "There is another way." She pointed at a row of silos on the other side of the lot. Each one was three stories tall and maybe twenty feet in diameter, with a giant chili pepper painted on the side.

"Petrol tanks?" Sadie asked.

"No," I said. "Must be salsa, right?"

Sadie stared at me blankly. "Isn't that a type of music?"

"It's a hot sauce," I said. "That's what they make here."

Sekhmet breathed in our direction, and the three trailers next to us melted into sand. We scuttled sideways and jumped behind a cinder block wall.

"Listen," Zia gasped, her face beading with sweat. "When the people needed to stop Sekhmet, they got huge vats of beer and colored them bright red with pomegranate juice."

"Yeah, I remember now," I interrupted. "They told Sekhmet it was blood, and she drank until she passed out. Then Ra was able to recall her into the heavens. They transformed her into something gentler. A cow goddess or something."

"Hathor," Zia said. "That is Sekhmet's other form. The flip side of her personality."

Sadie shook her head in disbelief. "So you're saying we offer to buy Sekhmet a few pints, and she'll turn into a cow."

"Not exactly," Zia said. "But salsa is red, is it not?"

We skirted the factory grounds as Sekhmet chewed up trucks and blasted huge swathes of the parking lot to sand.

"I hate this plan," Sadie grumbled.

"Just keep her occupied for a few seconds," I said. "And don't die."

"Yeah, that's the hard bit, isn't it?"

"One..." I counted. "Two...three!"

Sadie burst into the open and used her favorite spell: "*Ha-di!*"

The glyphs blazed over Sekhmet's head:

And everything around her exploded. Trucks burst to pieces. The air shimmered with energy. The ground heaved upward, creating a crater fifty feet deep into which the lioness tumbled.

It was pretty impressive, but I didn't have time to admire Sadie's work. I turned into a falcon and launched myself toward the salsa tanks.

"*RRAAAARR!*" Sekhmet leaped out of the crater and breathed desert wind in Sadie's direction, but Sadie was long gone. She ran sideways, ducking behind trailers and releasing a few lengths of magical rope as she fled. The ropes whipped through the air and tried to tie themselves around the lioness's mouth. They failed, of course, but they did annoy the Destroyer.

"Show yourself!" Sekhmet bellowed. "I will feast on your flesh!"

Perched on a silo, I concentrated all my power and turned straight from falcon to avatar. My glowing form was so heavy, its feet sank into the top of the tank.

"Sekhmet!" I yelled.

The lioness whirled and snarled, trying to locate my voice.

"Up here, kitty!" I called.

She spotted me and her ears went back. "Horus?"

"Unless you know another guy with a falcon head."

She padded back and forth uncertainly, then roared in challenge. "Why do you speak to me when I am in my raging form? You know I must destroy everything in my path, even you!"

"If you must," I said. "But first, you might like to feast on the blood of your enemies!"

I drove my sword into the tank and salsa gushed out in a chunky red waterfall. I leaped to the next tank and sliced it open. And again, and again, until six silofuls of Magic Salsa were spewing into the parking lot.

"Ha, ha!" Sekhmet loved it. She leaped into the red sauce torrent, rolling in it, lapping it up. "Blood. Lovely blood!"

Yeah, apparently lions aren't too bright, or their taste buds aren't very developed, because Sekhmet didn't stop until her belly was bulging and her mouth literally began to smoke.

"Tangy," she said, stumbling and blinking. "But my eyes hurt. What kind of blood is this? Nubian? Persian?"

"Jalapeño," I said. "Try some more. It gets better."

Her ears were smoking too now as she tried to drink more. Her eyes watered, and she began to stagger.

"I . . ." Steam curled from her mouth. "Hot . . . hot mouth . . ."

"Milk is good for that," I suggested. "Maybe if you were a cow."

"Trick," Sekhmet groaned. "You . . . you tricked . . ."

But her eyes were too heavy. She turned in a circle and collapsed, curling into a ball. Her form twitched and shimmered as her red armor melted into spots on her golden skin, until I was looking down at an enormous sleeping cow.

I dropped off the silo and stepped carefully around the sleeping goddess. She was making cow snoring sounds, like "*Moo-zzz, moo-zzz.*" I waved my hand in front of her face, and when I was convinced she was out cold, I dispelled my avatar. Sadie and Zia emerged from behind a trailer.

"Well," said Sadie, "that was different."

"I will never eat salsa again," I decided.

"You both did wonderfully," Zia said. "But your boat is burned. How do we get to Phoenix?"

"*We?*" Sadie said. "I don't recall inviting you."

Zia's face turned salsa red. "Surely you don't *still* think I led you into a trap?"

"I don't know," Sadie said. "Did you?"

423

I couldn't believe I was hearing this.

"Sadie." My voice sounded dangerously angry, even to myself. "*Lay off.* Zia summoned that pillar-of-fire thing. She sacrificed her magic to save us. *And* she told us how to beat the lioness. We need her."

Sadie stared at me. She glanced back and forth between Zia and me, probably trying to judge how far she could push things.

"Fine." She crossed her arms and pouted. "But we need to find Amos first."

"No!" Zia said. "That would be a very bad idea."

"Oh, so we can trust you, but not Amos?"

Zia hesitated. I got the feeling that was *exactly* what she meant, but she decided to try a different approach. "Amos would not want you to wait. He said to keep going, didn't he? If he survived Sekhmet, he will find us on the road. If not..."

Sadie huffed. "So how do we get to Phoenix? Walk?"

I gazed across the parking lot, where one sixteen-wheeler was still intact. "Maybe we don't have to." I took off the linen coat I'd borrowed from Amos's supply locker. "Zia, Amos had a way of animating his coat so it could steer his boat. Do you know the spell?"

She nodded. "It's fairly simple with the right ingredients. I could do it if I had my magic."

"Can you teach me?"

She pursed her lips. "The hardest part is the figurine. The first time you enchant the piece of clothing, you'd need to smash a *shabti* into the fabric and speak a binding charm to meld them together. It would require a clay or wax figure that has already been imbued with a spirit."

Sadie and I looked at each other, and simultaneously said, "Doughboy!"

34. Doughboy Gives Us a Ride

I SUMMONED DAD'S MAGIC TOOLKIT out of the Duat and grabbed our little legless friend. "Doughboy, we need to talk."

Doughboy opened his wax eyes. "Finally! You realize how stuffy it is in there? At last you've remembered that you need my brilliant guidance."

"Actually we need you to become a coat. Just for a while."

His tiny mouth fell open. "Do I look like an article of clothing? I am the lord of all knowledge! The mighty—"

I smashed him into my jacket, wadded it up, threw it on the pavement and stepped on it. "Zia, what's that spell?"

She told me the words, and I repeated the chant. The coat inflated and hovered in front of me. It brushed itself off and ruffled its collar. If coats can look indignant, this one did.

Sadie eyed it suspiciously. "Can it drive a lorry with no feet for the pedals?"

"Shouldn't be a problem," Zia said. "It's a nice long coat."

I sighed with relief. For a moment, I'd imagined myself having to animate my pants, too. That could get awkward.

"Drive us to Phoenix," I told the coat.

The coat made a rude gesture at me—or at least, it would've been rude if the coat had hands. Then it floated into the driver's seat.

The cab was bigger than I'd thought. Behind the seat was a curtained area with a full-size bed, which Sadie claimed immediately.

"I'll let you and Zia have some quality time," she told me. "Just the two of you and your coat."

She ducked behind the curtains before I could smack her.

The coat drove us west on I-10 as a bank of dark clouds swallowed the stars. The air smelled like rain.

After a long time, Zia cleared her throat. "Carter, I'm sorry about . . . I mean, I wish the circumstances were better."

"Yeah," I said. "I guess you'll get in a lot of trouble with the House."

"I will be shunned," she said. "My staff broken. My name blotted from the books. I'll be cast into exile, assuming they don't kill me."

I thought about Zia's little shrine in the First Nome—all those pictures of her village and her family that she didn't remember. As she talked about getting exiled, she had the same expression on her face that she had worn then: not regret or sadness, more like confusion, as if she herself couldn't figure out why she was rebelling, or what the First Nome had meant to her. She'd said Iskandar was like her only family. Now she had no one.

"You could come with us," I said.

She glanced over. We were sitting close together, and I was very aware of her shoulder pressing against mine. Even with the reek of burned peppers on both of us, I could smell her Egyptian perfume. She had a dried chili stuck in her hair, and somehow that made her look even cuter.

Sadie says my brain was just addled. [Seriously, Sadie, I don't interrupt this much when *you're* telling the story.]

Anyway, Zia looked at me sadly. "Where would we go, Carter? Even if you defeat Set and save this continent, what will you do? The House will hunt you down. The gods will make your life miserable."

"We'll figure it out," I promised. "I'm used to traveling. I'm good at improvising, and Sadie's not *all* bad."

"I heard that!" Sadie's muffled voice came through the curtain.

"And with you," I continued, "I mean, you know, with your magic, things would be easier."

Zia squeezed my hand, which sent a tingle up my arm. "You're kind, Carter. But you don't know me. Not really. I suppose Iskandar saw this coming."

"What do you mean?"

Zia took her hand away, which kind of bummed me out. "When Desjardins and I came back from the British Museum, Iskandar spoke to me privately. He said I was in danger. He said he would take me somewhere safe and..." Her eyebrows knit together. "That's odd. I don't remember."

A cold feeling started gnawing at me. "Wait, *did* he take you somewhere safe?"

428

"I...I think so." She shook her head. "No, he couldn't have, obviously. I'm still here. Perhaps he didn't have time. He sent me to find you in New York almost immediately."

Outside, a light rain began to fall. The coat turned on our windshield wipers.

I didn't understand what Zia had told me. Perhaps Iskandar had sensed a change in Desjardins, and he was trying to protect his favorite student. But something else about the story bothered me—something I couldn't quite put my finger on.

Zia stared into the rain as if she saw bad things out there in the night.

"We're running out of time," she said. "He's coming back."

"Who's coming back?"

She looked at me urgently. "The thing I needed to tell you—the thing you need. It's Set's secret name."

The storm surged. Thunder crackled and the truck shuddered in the wind.

"H-hold on," I stammered. "How could you know Set's name? How did you even know we needed it?"

"You stole Desjardins' book. Desjardins told us about it. He said it didn't matter. He said you could not use the spell without Set's secret name, which is impossible to get."

"So how do *you* know it? Thoth said it could only come from Set himself, or from the person..." My voice trailed off as a horrible thought occurred to me. "Or from the person closest to him."

Zia shut her eyes as if in pain. "I—I can't explain it, Carter. I just have this voice telling me the name—"

"The fifth goddess," I said, "Nephthys. You were there too at the British Museum."

Zia looked completely stunned. "No. That's impossible."

"Iskandar said you were in danger. He wanted to take you somewhere safe. That's what he meant. You're a godling."

She shook her head stubbornly. "But he *didn't* take me away. I'm right here. If I were hosting a god, the other magicians of the House would've figured it out days ago. They know me too well. They would've noticed the changes in my magic. Desjardins would've destroyed me."

She had a point—but then another terrible thought occurred to me. "Unless Set is controlling him," I said.

"Carter, are you really so blind? Desjardins is not Set."

"Because you think it's Amos," I said. "Amos who risked his life to save us, who told us to keep going without him. Besides, Set doesn't need a human form. He's using the pyramid."

"Which you know because . . . ?"

I hesitated. "Amos told us."

"This is getting us nowhere," Zia said. "I know Set's secret name, and I can tell you. But you must promise you will not tell Amos."

"Oh, come on. Besides, if you know the name, why can't you just use it yourself?"

She shook her head, looking almost as frustrated as I felt. "I don't know why. . . . I just know it's not my role to play. It must be you or Sadie—blood of the pharaohs. If you don't—"

The truck slowed abruptly. Out the front windshield, about twenty yards ahead, a man in a blue coat was standing in our headlights. It was Amos. His clothes were tattered like he'd been sprayed with a shotgun, but otherwise he looked okay. Before the truck had even stopped completely, I jumped out of the cab and ran to meet him.

"Amos!" I cried. "What happened?"

"I distracted Sekhmet," he said, putting a finger through one of the holes in his coat. "For about eleven seconds. I'm glad to see you survived."

"There was a salsa factory," I started to explain, but Amos held up his hand.

"Time for explanations later," he said. "Right now we have to get going."

He pointed northwest, and I saw what he meant. The storm was worse up ahead. A *lot* worse. A wall of black blotted out the night sky, the mountains, the highway, as if it would swallow the whole world.

"Set's storm is gathering," Amos said with a twinkle in his eyes. "Shall we drive into it?"

S
A
D
I
E

35. Men Ask for Directions (and Other Signs of the Apocalypse)

I DON'T KNOW HOW I MANAGED IT with Carter and Zia yammering, but I got some sleep in the back of the truck. Even after the excitement of seeing Amos alive, as soon as we got going again I was back in the bunk and drifting off. I suppose a good *ha-di* spell can really take it out of you.

Naturally, my *ba* took this as an opportunity to travel. Heaven forbid I get some *peaceful* rest.

I found myself back in London, on the banks of the Thames. Cleopatra's Needle rose up in front of me. It was a gray day, cool and calm, and even the smell of the low-tide muck made me feel homesick.

Isis stood next to me in a cloud-white dress, her dark hair braided with diamonds. Her multicolored wings faded in and out behind her like the Northern Lights.

"Your parents had the right idea," she said. "Bast was failing."

"She was my friend," I said.

432

"Yes. A good and loyal servant. But chaos cannot be kept down forever. It grows. It seeps into the cracks of civilization, breaks down the edges. It cannot be kept in balance. That is simply its nature."

The obelisk rumbled, glowing faintly.

"Today it is the American continent," Isis mused. "But unless the gods are rallied, unless we achieve our full strength, chaos will soon destroy the entire human world."

"We're doing our best," I insisted. "We'll beat Set."

Isis looked at me sadly. "You know that's not what I mean. Set is only the beginning."

The image changed, and I saw London in ruins. I'd seen some horrific photos of the Blitz in World War II, but that was nothing compared to this. The city was leveled: rubble and dust for miles, the Thames choked with flotsam. The only thing standing was the obelisk, and as I watched, it began to crack open, all four sides peeling away like some ghastly flower unfolding.

"Don't show me this," I pleaded.

"It will happen soon enough," Isis said, "as your mother foresaw. But if you cannot face it..."

The scene changed again. We stood in the throne room of a palace—the same one I'd seen before, where Set had entombed Osiris. The gods were gathering, materializing as streams of light that shot through the throne room, curled round the pillars, and took on human form. One became Thoth with his stained lab coat, his wire-rimmed glasses, and his hair standing out all over his head. Another became Horus, the proud young warrior with silver and gold eyes. Sobek, the crocodile god, gripped his watery staff and snarled at me. A mass of scorpions scuttled behind a column and emerged on the other side as Serqet, the brown-robed arachnid goddess. Then my heart leaped, because I noticed a boy in black standing in the shadows behind the throne: Anubis, his dark eyes studying me with regret.

He pointed at the throne, and I saw it was empty. The palace was missing its heart. The room was cold and dark, and it was impossible to believe this had once been a place of celebrations.

Isis turned to me. "We need a ruler. Horus must become pharaoh. He must unite the gods and the House of Life. It is the only way."

"You can't mean Carter," I said. "My mess of a brother—pharaoh? Are you joking?"

"We have to help him. You and I."

The idea was so ridiculous I would have laughed had the gods not been staring at me so gravely.

"Help him?" I said. "Why doesn't he help *me* become pharaoh?"

"There have been strong women pharaohs," Isis admitted. "Hatshepsut ruled well for many years. Nefertiti's power was equal to her husband's. But you have a different path, Sadie. Your power will not come from sitting on a throne. I think you know this."

I looked at the throne, and I realized Isis had a point. The idea of sitting there with a crown on my head, trying to rule this lot of bad-tempered gods, did not appeal to me in the slightest. Still . . . Carter?

"You've grown strong, Sadie," Isis said. "I don't think you realize *how* strong. Soon, we will face the test together. We will prevail, if you maintain your courage and faith."

"Courage and faith," I said. "Not my two strong suits."

"Your moment comes," Isis said. "We depend on you."

The gods gathered round, staring at me expectantly. They began to crowd in, pressing so close I couldn't breathe, grabbing my arms, shaking me....

I woke to find Zia poking my shoulder. "Sadie, we've stopped."

I instinctively reached for my wand. "What? Where?"

Zia pushed aside the curtains of the sleeping berth and leaned over me from the front seat, unnervingly like a vulture. "Amos and Carter are in the gas station. You need to be prepared to move."

"Why?" I sat up and looked out the windshield, straight into a raging sandstorm. "Oh..."

The sky was black, so it was impossible to tell if it was day or night. Through the gale of wind and sand, I could see we were parked in front of a lighted petrol station.

"We're in Phoenix," Zia said, "but most of the city is shut down. People are evacuating."

"Time?"

"Half past four in the morning," Zia said. "Magic isn't working very well. The closer we get to the mountain, the worse it is. And the truck's GPS system is down. Amos and Carter went inside to ask directions."

That didn't sound promising. If two male magicians were desperate enough to stop for directions, we were in dire straits.

The truck's cab shook in the howling wind. After all we'd been through, I felt silly being scared of a storm, but I climbed over the seat so I could sit next to Zia and have some company.

"How long have they been in there?" I asked.

"Not long," Zia said. "I wanted to talk to you before they come back."

I raised an eyebrow. "About Carter? Well, if you're wondering whether he likes you, the way he stammers might be an indication."

Zia frowned. "No, I'm—"

"Asking if I mind? Very considerate. I must say at first I had my doubts, what with you threatening to kill us and all, but I've decided you're not a bad sort, and Carter's mad about you, so—"

"It's not about Carter."

I wrinkled my nose. "Oops. Could you just forget what I said, then?"

"It's about Set."

"God," I sighed. "Not this again. Still suspicious of Amos?"

"You're blind not to see it," Zia said. "Set loves deception and traps. It is his favorite way to kill."

Part of me knew she had a point. No doubt you'll think I was foolish not to listen. But have you ever sat by while someone talks badly about a member of your family? Even if it's not your favorite relative, the natural reaction is to defend them—at least it was for me, possibly because I didn't have that much family to begin with. "Look, Zia, I can't believe Amos would—"

"*Amos* wouldn't," Zia agreed. "But Set can bend the mind

and control the body. I'm not a specialist on possession, but it was a very common problem in ancient times. Minor demons are difficult enough to dislodge. A major god—"

"He's *not* possessed. He *can't* be." I winced. A sharp pain was burning in my palm, in the spot where I'd last held the feather of truth. But I wasn't telling a lie! I *did* believe Amos was innocent...didn't I?

Zia studied my expression. "You need Amos to be all right. He is your uncle. You've lost too many members of your family. I understand that."

I wanted to snap back that she didn't understand anything, but her tone made me suspect she had known grief—possibly even more than I.

"We've got no choice," I said. "There's what, three hours till sunrise? Amos knows the best way into the mountain. Trap or no, we have to go there and try to stop Set."

I could almost see the gears spinning in her head as she searched for some way, *any* way to convince me.

"All right," she said at last. "I wanted to tell Carter something but I never got the opportunity. I'll tell you instead. The last thing you need to stop Set—"

"You couldn't possibly know his secret name."

Zia held my gaze. Maybe it was the feather of truth, but I was certain she wasn't bluffing. She *did* have the name of Set. Or at least, she *believed* she did.

And honestly, I'd overheard bits of her conversation with Carter while I was in the back of the cab. I hadn't meant to eavesdrop, but it was hard not to. I looked at Zia, and tried to believe she was hosting Nephthys, but it didn't make any sense. I'd spoken with Nephthys. She'd told me she was far away in some sort of sleeping host. And Zia was right here in front of me.

"It will work," Zia insisted. "But I can't do it. It must be *you*."

"Why not use it yourself?" I demanded. "Because you spent all your magic?"

She waved away the question. "Just promise me you will use it *now*, on Amos, before we reach the mountain. It may be your only chance."

"And if you're wrong, we waste the only chance we have. The book disappears once it's used, right?"

Grudgingly, Zia nodded. "Once read, the book will dissolve and appear somewhere else in the world. But if you wait any longer, we're doomed. If Set lures you into his base of power, you'll never have the strength to confront him. Sadie, please—"

"Tell me the name," I said. "I promise I'll use it at the right time."

"*Now* is the right time."

I hesitated, hoping Isis would drop some words of wisdom, but the goddess was silent. I don't know if I would've relented. Perhaps things would've turned out differently if I'd agreed to Zia's plan. But before I could make that choice, the truck's doors opened, and Amos and Carter climbed in with a gust of sand.

"We're close." Amos smiled as if this were good news. "Very, very close."

36. Our Family Is Vaporized

LESS THAN A MILE FROM Camelback Mountain, we broke through into a circle of perfect calm.

"Eye of the storm," Carter guessed.

It was eerie. All around the mountain swirled a cylinder of black clouds. Traces of smoke drifted back and forth from Camelback's peak to the edges of the maelstrom like the spokes of a wheel, but directly above us, the sky was clear and starry, beginning to turn gray. Sunrise wasn't far off.

The streets were empty. Mansions and hotels clustered round the mountain's base, completely dark; but the mountain itself glowed. Ever hold your hand over a torch (sorry, a *flashlight* for you Americans) and watch the way your skin glows red? That's the way the mountain looked: something very bright and hot was trying to burn through the rock.

"Nothing's moving on the streets," Zia said. "If we try to drive up to the mountain—"

"We'll be seen," I said.

"What about that spell?" Carter looked at Zia. "You know ...the one you used in the First Nome."

"What spell?" I asked.

Zia shook her head. "Carter is referring to an invisibility spell. But I have no magic. And unless you have the proper components, it can't be done on a whim."

"Amos?" I asked.

He pondered the question. "No invisibility, I'm afraid. But I have another idea."

I thought turning into a bird was bad, until Amos turned us into storm clouds.

He explained what he was going to do in advance, but it didn't make me any less nervous.

"No one will notice a few wisps of black cloud in the midst of a storm," he reasoned.

"But this is impossible," Zia said. "This is storm magic, *chaos* magic. We should not—"

Amos raised his wand, and Zia disintegrated.

"No!" Carter yelled, but then he too was gone, replaced by a swirl of black dust.

Amos turned to me.

"Oh, no," I said. "Thanks, but—"

Poof. I was a storm cloud. Now, that may sound amazing to you, but imagine your hands and feet disappearing, turning into wisps of wind. Imagine your body replaced by dust and vapor, and having a tingly feeling in your stomach without even *having* a stomach. Imagine having to concentrate just to keep yourself from dispersing to nothing.

I got so angry, a flash of lightning crackled inside me.

"Don't be that way," Amos chided. "It's only for a few minutes. Follow me."

He melted into a heavier, darker bit of storm and raced towards the mountain. Following wasn't easy. At first I could only float. Every wind threatened to take some part of me away. I tried swirling and found it helped keep my particles together. Then I imagined myself filling with helium, and suddenly I was off.

I couldn't be sure if Carter and Zia were following or not. When you're a storm, your vision isn't human. I could vaguely sense what was around me, but what I "saw" was scattered and fuzzy, as if through heavy static.

I headed towards the mountain, which was an almost irresistible beacon to my storm self. It glowed with heat, pressure, and turbulence—everything a little dust devil like me could want.

I followed Amos to a ridge on the side of the mountain, but I returned to human form a little too soon. I tumbled out of the sky and knocked Carter to the ground.

"Ouch," he groaned.

"Sorry," I offered, though mostly I was concentrating on not getting sick. My stomach still felt like it was mostly storm.

Zia and Amos stood next to us, peeping into a crevice between two large sandstone boulders. Red light seeped from within and made their faces look devilish.

Zia turned to us. Judging from her expression, what she'd seen wasn't good. "Only the pyramidion left."

"The what?" I looked through the crevice, and the view

was almost as disorienting as being a storm cloud. The entire mountain was hollowed out, just as Carter had described. The cavern floor was about six hundred meters below us. Fires blazed everywhere, bathing the rock walls in blood-colored light. A giant crimson pyramid dominated the cave, and at its base, masses of demons milled about like a rock concert crowd waiting for the show to begin. High above them, eye-level to us, two magic barges manned by crews of demons floated slowly, ceremoniously towards the pyramid. Suspended in a mesh of ropes between the boats was the only piece of the pyramid not yet installed—a golden capstone to top off the structure.

"They know they've won," Carter guessed. "They're making a show of it."

"Yes," Amos said.

"Well, let's blow up the boats or something!" I said.

Amos looked at me. "Is *that* your strategy, honestly?"

His tone made me feel completely stupid. Looking down on the demon army, the enormous pyramid...what had I been thinking? I couldn't battle this. I was a bloody twelve-year-old.

"We have to try," Carter said. "Dad's in there."

That shook me out of my self-pity. If we were going to die, at least we would do it trying to rescue my father (oh, and North America, too, I suppose).

"Right," I said. "We fly to those boats. We stop them from placing the capstone—"

"Pyramidion," Zia corrected.

"Whatever. Then we fly into the pyramid and find Dad."

"And when Set tries to stop you?" Amos asked.

I glanced at Zia, who was silently warning me not to say more.

"First things first," I said. "How do we fly to the boats?"

"As a storm," Amos suggested.

"No!" the rest of us said.

"I will not be part of more chaos magic," Zia insisted. "It is *not* natural."

Amos waved at the spectacle below us. "Tell me *this* is natural. You have another plan?"

"Birds," I said, hating myself for even considering it. "I'll become a kite. Carter can do a falcon."

"Sadie," Carter warned, "what if—"

"I have to try." I looked away before I could lose my resolve. "Zia, it's been almost ten hours since your pillar of fire, hasn't it? Still no magic?"

Zia held out her hand and concentrated. At first, nothing happened. Then red light flickered along her fingers, and her staff appeared in her grip, still smoking.

"Good timing," Carter said.

"Also bad timing," Amos observed. "It means Desjardins is no longer pursued by the pillar of fire. He'll be here soon, and I'm sure he'll bring backup. More enemies for us."

"My magic will still be weak," Zia warned. "I won't be much help in a fight, but I can perhaps manage to summon a ride." She brought out the vulture pendant she'd used at Luxor.

"Which leaves me," Amos said. "No worries there. Let's meet on the left boat. We'll take that one out, then deal with the right. And let's hope for surprise."

I wasn't in the mood to let Amos set our plans, but I

couldn't find any fault with his logic. "Right. We'll have to finish the boats off quickly, then head into the pyramid itself. Perhaps we can seal off the entrance or something."

Carter nodded. "Ready."

At first, the plan seemed to go well. Turning into a kite was no problem, and to my surprise, once I reached the prow of the ship, I managed to turn back into a human on the first try, with my staff and wand ready. The only person more surprised was the demon right in front of me, whose switchblade head popped straight up in alarm.

Before he could slice me or even cry out, I summoned wind from my staff and blew him off the side of the boat. Two of his brethren charged forward, but Carter appeared behind them, sword drawn, and sliced them into piles of sand.

Unfortunately, Zia was a bit less stealthy. A giant vulture with a girl hanging from its feet tends to attract attention. As she flew towards the boat, demons below pointed and yelled. Some threw spears that fell short of their mark.

Zia's grand entrance did manage to distract the remaining two demons on our boat, however, which allowed Amos to appear behind them. He'd taken the form of a fruit bat, which brought back bad memories; but he quickly returned to human form and body-slammed the demons, sending them tumbling into the air.

"Hold on!" he told us. Zia landed just in time to grab the tiller. Carter and I grabbed the sides of the boat. I had no idea what Amos was planning, but after my last flying boat ride, I wasn't taking chances. Amos began to chant, pointing his staff towards the other boat, where the demons were just beginning to shout and point at us.

One of them was tall and very thin, with black eyes and a disgusting face, like muscle with the skin peeled away.

"That's Set's lieutenant," Carter warned. "Face of Horror."

"You!" the demon screamed. "Get them!"

Amos finished his spell. "Smoke," he intoned.

Instantly, the second boat evaporated into gray mist. The demons fell screaming. The golden capstone plummeted until the lines attached to it from our side yanked taut, and our boat nearly flipped over. Canted sideways, we began to sink towards the cavern floor.

"Carter, cut the lines!" I screamed.

He sliced them with his sword, and the boat leveled out, rising several meters in an instant and leaving my stomach behind.

The pyramidion crashed to the cavern floor with much crunching and squishing. I had the feeling we'd just made a nice stack of demon griddlecakes.

"So far so good," Carter noted, but as usual, he'd spoken too soon.

Zia pointed below us. "Look."

All those demons who had wings—a small percentage, but still a good forty or fifty—had launched themselves towards us, filling the air like a swarm of angry wasps.

"Fly to the pyramid," Amos said. "I'll distract the demons."

The pyramid's entrance, a simple doorway between two columns at the base of the structure, was not far from us. It was guarded by a few demons, but most of Set's forces were running towards our boat, screaming and throwing rocks (which tended to fall back down and hit them, but no one says demons are bright).

"They're too many," I argued. "Amos, they'll kill you."

"Don't worry about me," he said grimly. "Seal the entrance behind you."

He pushed me over the side, giving me no choice but to turn into a kite. Carter in falcon form was already spiraling towards the entrance, and I could hear Zia's vulture flapping its great wings behind us.

I heard Amos yell, "For Brooklyn!"

It was an odd battle cry. I glanced back, and the boat burst into flames. It began drifting away from the pyramid and down towards the army of monsters. Fireballs shot from the boat in all directions as pieces of the hull crumbled away. I didn't have time to marvel at Amos's magic, or worry what had happened to him. He distracted many of the demons with his pyrotechnics, but some noticed us.

Carter and I landed just inside the pyramid's entrance and returned to human form. Zia tumbled in next to us and turned her vulture back into an amulet. The demons were only a few steps behind—a dozen massive blokes with the heads of insects, dragons, and assorted Swiss Army knife attachments.

Carter thrust out his hand. A giant shimmering fist appeared and mimicked his move—pushing right between Zia and me and slamming the doors shut. Carter closed his eyes in concentration, and a burning golden symbol etched itself across the doors like a seal: the Eye of Horus. The lines glowed faintly as demons hammered against the barrier, trying to get in.

"It won't hold them long," Carter said.

I was duly impressed, though of course I didn't say that. Looking at the sealed doors, all I could think about was Amos, out there on a burning boat, surrounded by an evil army.

"Amos knew what he was doing," Carter said, though he didn't sound very convinced. "He's probably fine."

"Come on," Zia prodded us. "No time for second guessing."

The tunnel was narrow, red, and humid, so I felt like I was crawling through an artery of some enormous beast. We made our way down single file, as the tunnel sloped at about forty degrees—which would've made a lovely waterslide but wasn't so good for stepping carefully. The walls were decorated with intricate carvings, like most Egyptian walls we'd seen, but Carter obviously didn't like them. He kept stopping, scowling at the pictures.

"What?" I demanded, after the fifth or sixth time.

"These aren't normal tomb drawings," he said. "No afterlife pictures, no pictures of the gods."

Zia nodded. "This pyramid is not a tomb. It is a platform, a body to contain the power of Set. All these pictures are to increase chaos, and make it reign forever."

As we kept walking, I paid more attention to the carvings, and I saw what Zia meant. The pictures showed horrible monsters, scenes of war, cities such as Paris and London in flames, full-color portraits of Set and the Set animal tearing into modern armies—scenes so gruesome, no Egyptian would ever commit them to stone. The farther we went, the weirder and more vivid the pictures became, and the queasier I felt.

Finally we reached the heart of the pyramid.

Where the burial chamber should've been in a regular pyramid, Set had designed a throne room for himself. It was about the size of a tennis court, but around the edges, the floor dropped off into a deep trench like a moat. Far, far below, red liquid bubbled. Blood? Lava? Evil ketchup? None of the possibilities were good.

The trench looked easy enough to jump, but I wasn't anxious to do so because inside the room, the entire floor was carved with red hieroglyphs—all spells invoking the power of Isfet, chaos. Far above in the center of the ceiling, a single square hole let in blood-red light. Otherwise, there seemed to be no exits. Along either wall crouched four obsidian statues of the Set animal, their faces turned towards us with pearl teeth bared and emerald eyes glittering.

But the worst part was the throne itself. It was a horrid misshapen thing, like a red stalagmite that had grown haphazardly from centuries of dripping sediment. And it had formed itself around a gold coffin—*Dad's* coffin—which was buried in the throne's base, with just enough of it sticking out to form a kind of footrest.

"How do we get him out?" I said, my voice trembling.

Next to me, Carter caught his breath. "Amos?"

I followed his gaze up to the glowing red vent in the middle of the ceiling. A pair of legs dangled from the opening. Then Amos dropped down, opening his cloak like a parachute so that he floated to the floor. His clothes were still smoking, his hair dusted with ash. He pointed his staff towards the ceiling and spoke a command. The shaft he'd come through rumbled, spilling dust and rubble, and the light was abruptly cut off.

Amos dusted off his clothes and smiled at us. "That should hold them for a while."

"How did you do that?" I asked.

He gestured for us to join him in the room.

Carter jumped the trench without hesitation. I didn't like it, but I wasn't going to let him go without me, so I hopped the trench too. Immediately I felt even queasier than before, as if the room were tilting, throwing my senses off balance.

Zia came over last, eyeing Amos carefully.

"You should not be alive," she said.

Amos chuckled. "Oh, I've heard that before. Now, let's get to business."

"Yes." I stared at the throne. "How do we get the coffin out?"

"Cut it?" Carter drew his sword, but Amos held up his hand.

"No, children. That's not the business I mean. I've made sure no one will interrupt us. Now it's time we talked."

A cold tingle started up my spine. "Talked?"

Suddenly Amos fell to his knees and began to convulse. I ran towards him, but he looked up at me, his face racked with pain. His eyes were molten red.

"*Run!*" he groaned.

He collapsed, and red steam issued from his body.

"We have to go!" Zia grabbed my arm. "*Now!*"

But I watched, frozen in horror, as the steam rose from

Amos's unconscious form and drifted towards the throne, slowly taking the shape of a seated man—a red warrior in fiery armor, with an iron staff in his hand and the head of a canine monster.

"Oh, dear," Set laughed. "I suppose Zia gets to say 'I told you so.'"

37. Leroy Gets His Revenge

MAYBE I'M A SLOW LEARNER, OKAY?

Because it wasn't until that moment, facing the god Set in the middle of his throne room, in the heart of an evil pyramid, with an army of demons outside and the world about to explode, that I thought, *Coming here was a really* bad *idea.*

Set rose from his throne. He was red skinned and muscular, with fiery armor and a black iron staff. His head shifted from bestial to human. One moment he had the hungry stare and slavering jaws of my old friend Leroy, the monster from the D.C. airport. The next he had sandy hair and a handsome but harsh face, with intelligent eyes that sparkled with humor and a cruel, crooked smile. He kicked our uncle out of the way and Amos groaned, which at least meant he was alive.

I was clenching my sword so tight, the blade trembled.

"Zia was right," I said. "You possessed Amos."

Set spread his hands, trying to look modest. "Well, you know... It wasn't a *full* possession. Gods can exist in many places at once, Carter. Horus could tell you that if he was being honest. I'm sure Horus has been looking for a nice war monument to occupy, or a military academy somewhere—anything but that scrawny little form of yours. Most of my being has now transferred to this magnificent structure."

He swept his arm proudly around the throne room. "But a sliver of my soul was quite enough to control Amos Kane."

He held out his pinky, and a wisp of red smoke snaked toward Amos, sinking into his clothes. Amos arched his back like he'd been hit by lightning.

"Stop it!" I yelled.

I ran toward Amos, but the red mist had already dissipated. Our uncle's body went slack.

Set dropped his hand as if bored with the attack. "Not much left, I'm afraid. Amos fought well. He was very entertaining, demanding much more of my energy than I had anticipated. That chaos magic—that was *his* idea. He tried his best to warn you, to make it obvious I was controlling him. The funny thing is, I forced him to use his own magic reserves to pull off those spells. He almost burned out his soul trying to send you those warning flares. Turn you into a storm? Please. Who does that anymore?"

"You're a beast!" Sadie shouted.

Set gasped in mock surprise. "Really? Me?"

Then he roared with laughter as Sadie tried to drag Amos out of harm's way.

"Amos was in London that night," I said, hoping to keep his attention on me. "He must've followed us to the

British Museum, and you've been controlling him ever since. Desjardins was never your host."

"Oh, that commoner? Please," Set sneered. "We always prefer blood of the pharaohs, as I'm sure you've heard. But I did love fooling you. I thought the *bon soir* was an especially nice touch."

"You knew my *ba* was there, watching. You forced Amos to sabotage his own house so your monsters could get in. You made him walk into an ambush. Why didn't you just have him kidnap us?"

Set spread his hands. "As I said, Amos put up a good fight. There were certain things I could not make him do without destroying him completely, and I didn't want to ruin my new plaything quite so soon."

Anger burned inside me. Amos's odd behavior finally made sense. Yes, he had been controlled by Set, but he'd been fighting it all the way. The conflict I'd felt in him had been his attempts to warn us. He'd almost destroyed himself trying to save us, and Set had thrown him aside like a broken toy.

Give me control, Horus urged. *We will avenge him.*

I've got this, I said.

No! Horus said. *You must let me. You are not ready.*

Set laughed as if he could sense our struggle. "Oh, poor Horus. Your host needs training wheels. You seriously expect to challenge me with *that*?"

For the first time, Horus and I had the same feeling at exactly the same moment: *rage.*

Without thinking, we raised our hand, extending our

energy toward Set. A glowing fist slammed into him, and the Red God flew backward with such force, he cracked a column, which tumbled down on top of him.

For a heartbeat, the only sound was the trickle of dust and debris. Then out of the rubble came a deep howl of laughter. Set rose from the ruins, tossing aside a huge chunk of stone.

"Nice!" he roared. "Completely ineffective, but nice! It will be a pleasure chopping you to bits, Horus, as I did your father before you. I will entomb you all in this chamber to increase my storm—all four of my precious siblings, and the storm will be large enough to envelop the world!"

I blinked, momentarily losing my focus. "Four?"

"Oh, yes." Set's eyes drifted to Zia, who had quietly retreated to one side of the room. "I haven't forgotten you, my dear."

Zia glanced at me in desperation. "Carter, don't worry about me. He's trying to distract you."

"Lovely goddess," Set purred. "The form does not do you justice, but your choices were limited, weren't they?"

Set moved toward her, his staff beginning to glow.

"No!" I shouted. I advanced, but Set was just as good at magical shoving as I was. He pointed at me, and I slammed against the wall, pinned as if an entire football team were holding me down.

"Carter!" Sadie cried. "She's Nephthys. She can take care of herself!"

"No." All my instincts told me Zia couldn't be Nephthys. At first I'd thought so, but the more I considered, the more it seemed wrong. I felt no divine magic from her, and something told me I would have if she were really hosting a goddess.

Set would crush her unless I helped. But if Set was trying to distract me, it was working. As he stalked toward Zia, I struggled against his magic, but I couldn't free myself. The more I tried to combine my power with Horus's, the way I'd done before, the more my fear and panic got in the way.

You must yield to me! Horus insisted, and the two of us wrestled for control of my mind, which gave me a splitting headache.

Set took another step toward Zia.

"Ah, Nephthys," he crooned. "At the beginning of time, you were my treacherous sister. In another incarnation, in another age, you were my treacherous wife. Now, I think you'll make a nice appetizer. True, you're the weakest of us all, but you're still one of the five, and there *is* power in collecting the complete set."

He paused, then grinned. "The complete Set! That's funny! Now let's consume your energy and entomb your soul, shall we?"

Zia thrust out her wand. A red sphere of defensive energy glowed around her, but even I could tell it was weak. Set shot a blast of sand from his staff and the sphere collapsed. Zia stumbled backward, the sand ripping at her hair and clothes. I struggled to move, but Zia yelled, "Carter, I'm not important! Stay focused! Don't resist!"

She raised her staff and shouted, "The House of Life!"

She launched a bolt of fire at Set—an attack that must have cost all of her remaining energy. Set batted the flames aside, straight at Sadie, who had to raise her wand quickly to protect herself and Amos from getting fried. Set tugged at the air as if pulling an invisible rope, and Zia flew toward him like a rag doll, straight into his hand.

Don't resist. How could Zia say that? I resisted like crazy, but it didn't do me any good. All I could do was stare helplessly as Set lowered his face to Zia's and examined her.

At first Set seemed triumphant, gleeful, but his expression quickly turned to confusion. He scowled, his eyes flaring.

"What trick is this?" he growled. "Where have you hidden her?"

"You will not possess her," Zia managed, her breath choked off by his grip.

"Where *is* she?" He threw Zia aside.

She slammed against the wall and would've slid into the moat, but Sadie yelled "Wind!" and a gust of air lifted Zia's body just enough for her to tumble onto the floor.

Sadie ran over and dragged her away from the glowing trench.

Set roared, "Is this your trickery, Isis?" He sent another blast of sandstorm against them, but Sadie held up her wand. The storm met a shield of force that deflected the wind around it—the sand pitted the walls behind Sadie, making a halo-shaped scar in the rock.

I didn't understand what Set was so angry about, but I couldn't allow him to hurt Sadie.

Seeing her alone, protecting Zia from the wrath of a god, something inside me clicked, like an engine shifting into higher gear. My thinking suddenly became faster and clearer. The anger and fear didn't go away, but I realized they weren't important. They weren't going to help me save my sister.

Don't resist, Zia had told me.

She didn't mean resisting Set. She meant Horus. The falcon god and I had been wrestling with each other for days as he tried to take control of my body.

But *neither* of us could be in control. That was the answer. We had to act in unison, trust each other completely, or we were both dead.

Yes, Horus thought, and he stopped pushing. I stopped resisting, letting our thoughts flow together. I understood his power, his memories, and his fears. I saw every host he had ever been over a thousand lifetimes. And he saw my mind—everything, even the stuff I wasn't proud of.

It's hard to describe the feeling. And I knew from Horus's memory that this kind of union was *very* rare—like the one time when the coin doesn't land heads *or* tails, but stands on its edge, perfectly balanced. He did not control me. I did not use him for power. We acted as one.

Our voices spoke in harmony: "Now."

And the magic bonds that held us shattered.

My combat avatar formed around me, lifting me off the floor and encasing me with golden energy. I stepped forward and raised my sword. The falcon warrior mimicked the movement, perfectly attuned to my wishes.

Set turned and regarded me with cold eyes.

"So, Horus," he said. "You managed to find the pedals of your little bike, eh? That does not mean you can ride."

"I am Carter Kane," I said. "Blood of the Pharaohs, Eye of Horus. And now, Set—brother, uncle, traitor—I'm going to crush you like a gnat."

38. The House Is in the House

IT WAS A FIGHT TO THE DEATH, and I felt great.

Every move was perfect. Every strike was so much fun I wanted to laugh out loud. Set grew in size until he was larger than me, and his iron staff the size of a boat's mast. His face would flicker, sometimes human, sometimes the feral maw of the Set animal.

We clashed sword against staff and sparks flew. He pushed me off balance, and I smashed into one of his animal statues, which toppled to the floor and broke. I regained my balance and charged, my blade biting into a chink of Set's shoulder guard. He howled as black blood seeped from the wound.

He swung his staff, and I rolled before the strike could split my head. His staff cracked the floor instead. We fought back and forth, smashing pillars and walls, with chunks of the ceiling falling around us, until I realized Sadie was yelling to get my attention.

Out of the corner of my eye, I saw her trying to shield Zia

and Amos from the destruction. She'd drawn a hasty protective circle on the floor, and her shields were deflecting the falling debris, but I understood why she was worried: much more of this, and the entire throne room would collapse, crushing all of us. I doubted it would hurt Set much. He was probably counting on that. He *wanted* to entomb us here.

I had to get him into the open. Maybe if I gave Sadie time, she could free Dad's coffin from that throne.

Then I remembered how Bast had described her fight with Apophis: grappling with the enemy for eternity.

Yes, Horus agreed.

I raised my fist and channeled a burst of energy toward the air vent above us, blasting it open until red light once again poured through. Then I dropped my sword and launched myself at Set. I grabbed his shoulders with my bare hands, trying to get him in a wrestler's hold. He attempted to pummel me, but his staff was useless at close range. He growled and dropped the weapon, then grabbed my arms. He was much stronger than I was, but Horus knew some good moves. I twisted and got behind Set, my forearm slipping under his arm and grabbing his neck in a vise. We stumbled forward, almost stepping on Sadie's protective shields.

Now we've got him, I thought. *What do we do with him?*

Ironically, it was Amos who gave me the answer. I remembered how he'd turned me into a storm, overcoming my sense of self by sheer mental force. Our minds had had a brief battle, but he had imposed his will with absolute confidence, imagining me as a storm cloud, and that's what I'd become.

You're a fruit bat, I told Set.

No! his mind yelled, but I had surprised him. I could feel his confusion, and I used it against him. It was easy to imagine him as a bat, since I'd seen Amos become one when he was possessed by Set. I pictured my enemy shrinking, growing leathery wings and an even uglier face. I shrank too, until I was a falcon with a fruit bat in my claws. No time to waste; I shot toward the air vent, wrestling with the bat as we spun in circles up the shaft, slashing and biting. Finally we burst into the open, reverting to our warrior forms on the side of the red pyramid.

I stood uneasily on the slope. My avatar shimmered with damage along the right arm, and my own arm was cut and bleeding in the same spot. Set rose, wiping black blood from his mouth.

He grinned at me, and his face flickered with the snarl of a predator. "You can die knowing you made a good effort, Horus. But it's much too late. Look."

I gazed out over the cavern, and my heart crawled into my throat. The army of demons had engaged a new enemy in battle. Magicians—dozens of them—had appeared in a loose circle around the pyramid and were fighting their way forward. The House of Life must have gathered all its available forces, but they were pathetically few against Set's legions. Each magician stood inside a moving protective circle, like a spotlight beam, wading through the enemy with staff and wand glowing. Flames, lightning, and tornadoes ripped through the demon host. I spotted all kinds of summoned beasts—lions, serpents, sphinxes, and even some hippos charging through the enemy like tanks. Here and there, hieroglyphs glowed in the air, causing explosions and earthquakes that destroyed Set's forces. But more demons just kept coming, surrounding the magicians in deeper and deeper ranks. I watched as one magician was completely overwhelmed, his circle broken in a flash of green light, and he went down under the enemy wave.

"This is the end of the House," Set said with satisfaction. "They cannot prevail as long as my pyramid stands."

The magicians seemed to know this. As they got closer, they sent fiery comets and bolts of lightning toward the pyramid; but each blast dissipated harmlessly against its stone slopes, consumed in the red haze of Set's power.

Then I spotted the golden capstone. Four snake-headed giants had retrieved it and were carrying it slowly but steadily through the melee. Set's lieutenant Face of Horror shouted orders to them, lashing them with a whip to keep them moving. They pressed forward until they reached the pyramid's base and began to climb.

I charged toward them, but Set intervened in an instant, placing himself in my path.

"I don't think so, Horus," he laughed. "You won't ruin this party."

We both summoned our weapons to our hands and fought with renewed ferocity, slicing and dodging. I brought my sword down in a deadly arc, but Set ducked aside and my blade hit stone, sending a shock wave through my whole body. Before I could recover, Set spoke a word: *"Ha-wi!"*

Strike.

The hieroglyphs exploded in my face and sent me tumbling down the side of the pyramid.

When my vision cleared, I saw Face of Horror and the snake-headed giants far above me, lugging their golden load up the side of the monument, only a few steps from the top.

"No," I muttered. I tried to rise, but my avatar form was sluggish.

Then out of nowhere a magician catapulted into the midst of the demons and unleashed a gale of wind. Demons went flying, dropping the capstone, and the magician struck it with his staff, stopping it from sliding. The magician was Desjardins. His forked beard and robes and leopard-skin cape were singed with fire, and his eyes were full of rage. He pressed his staff against the capstone, and its golden shape began to glow; but before Desjardins could destroy it, Set rose up behind him and swung his iron rod like a baseball bat.

Desjardins tumbled, broken and unconscious, all the way down the pyramid, disappearing into the mob of demons. My heart twisted. I'd never liked Desjardins, but no one deserved a fate like that.

"Annoying," Set said. "But not effective. This is what the House of Life has reduced itself to, eh, Horus?"

I charged up the slope, and again our weapons clanged together. We fought back and forth as gray light began to seep through the cracks in the mountain above us.

Horus's keen senses told me we had about two minutes until sunrise, maybe less.

Horus's energy kept surging through me. My avatar was only mildly damaged, my attacks still swift and strong. But it wasn't enough to defeat Set, and Set knew it. He was in no hurry. With every minute, another magician went down on the battlefield, and chaos got closer to winning.

Patience, Horus urged. *We fought him for seven years the first time.*

But I knew we didn't have seven minutes, much less seven years. I wished Sadie were here, but I could only hope she'd managed to free Dad and keep Zia and Amos safe.

That thought distracted me. Set swept his staff at my feet, and instead of jumping, I tried to back up. The blow cracked against my right ankle, knocking me off balance and sending me somersaulting down the pyramid's side.

Set laughed. "Have a nice trip!" Then he picked up the capstone.

I rose, groaning, but my feet were like lead. I staggered up the slope, but before I'd closed even half the distance, Set placed the capstone and completed the structure. Red light flowed down the sides of the pyramid with a sound like the world's largest bass guitar, shaking the entire mountain and making my whole body go numb.

"Thirty seconds to sunrise!" Set yelled with glee. "And this land will be mine forever. You can't stop me alone, Horus—especially not in the desert, the source of my strength!"

"You're right," said a nearby voice.

I glanced over and saw Sadie rising from the air vent—radiant with multicolored light, her staff and wand glowing.

"Except Horus is *not* alone," she said. "And we're *not* going to fight you in the desert."

She struck her staff against the pyramid and shouted a name: the last words I'd ever expect her to utter as a battle cry.

39. Zia Tells Me a Secret

CHEERS, CARTER, FOR MAKING ME LOOK dramatic and all that.

The truth was a bit less glamorous.

Back up, shall we? When my brother, the crazy chicken warrior, turned into a falcon and went up the pyramid's chimney with his new friend, the fruit bat, he left me playing nurse to two very wounded people—which I didn't appreciate, and which I wasn't particularly good at.

Poor Amos's wounds seemed more magical than physical. He didn't have a mark on him, but his eyes were rolled up in his head, and he was barely breathing. Steam curled from his skin when I touched his forehead, so I decided I'd best leave him for the moment.

Zia was another story. Her face was deathly pale, and she was bleeding from several nasty cuts on her leg. One of her arms was twisted at a bad angle. Her breath rattled with a sound like wet sand.

"Hold still." I ripped some cloth from the hem of my pants

and tried to bind her leg. "Maybe there's some healing magic or—"

"Sadie." She gripped my wrist feebly. "No time. Listen."

"If we can stop the bleeding—"

"His name. You need his name."

"But you're not Nephthys! Set said so."

She shook her head. "A message . . . I speak with her voice. The name—Evil Day. Set was born, and it was an *Evil Day*."

True enough, I thought, but could that really be Set's secret name? What Zia was talking about, not being Nephthys but speaking with her voice—it made no sense. Then I remembered the voice at the river. Nephthys had said she would send a message. And Anubis had made me promise I would listen to Nephthys.

I shifted uncomfortably. "Look, Zia—"

Then the truth hit me in face. Some things Iskandar had said, some things Thoth had said—they all clicked together. Iskandar had wanted to protect Zia. He'd told me if he'd realized Carter and I were godlings sooner, he could've protected us as well as . . . someone. As well as *Zia*. Now I understood how he'd tried to protect her.

"Oh, god." I stared at her. "That's it, isn't it?"

She seemed to understand, and she nodded. Her face contorted with pain, but her eyes remained as fierce and insistent as ever. "Use the name. Bend Set to your will. Make him help."

"*Help?* He just tried to kill you, Zia. He's not the *helping* type."

"Go." She tried to push me away. Flames sputtered weakly from her fingers. "Carter needs you."

That was the one thing she might've said to spur me on. Carter was in trouble.

"I'll be back, then," I promised. "Don't...um, go anywhere."

I stood and stared at the hole in the ceiling, dreading the idea of turning into a kite again. Then my eyes fixed on Dad's coffin, buried in the red throne. The sarcophagus was glowing like something radioactive, heading for meltdown. If I could only break the throne...

Set must be dealt with first, Isis warned.

But if I can free Dad... I stepped towards the throne.

No, Isis warned. *What you might see is too dangerous.*

What are you talking about? I thought irritably. I put my hand on the golden coffin. Instantly I was ripped from the throne room and into a vision.

I was back in the Land of the Dead, in the Hall of Judgment. The crumbling monuments of a New Orleans graveyard shimmered around me. Spirits of the dead stirred restlessly in the mist. At the base of the broken scales, a tiny monster slept—Ammit the Devourer. He opened one glowing yellow eye to study me, then went back to sleep.

Anubis stepped out of the shadows. He was dressed in a black silk suit with his tie unknotted, like he'd just come back from a funeral or possibly a convention for really gorgeous undertakers. "Sadie, you shouldn't be here."

"Tell me about it," I said, but I was so glad to see him, I wanted to sob with relief.

He took my hand and led me towards the empty black throne. "We have lost all balance. The throne cannot be empty. The restoration of Ma'at must begin here, in this hall."

He sounded sad, as if he were asking me to accept something terrible. I didn't understand, but a profound sense of loss crept over me.

"It's not fair," I said.

"No, it's not." He squeezed my hand. "I'll be here, waiting. I'm sorry, Sadie. I truly am..."

He started to fade.

"Wait!" I tried to hold on to his hand, but he melted into mist along with the graveyard.

I found myself back in the throne room of the gods, except it looked like it had been abandoned for centuries. The roof had fallen in, along with half of the columns. The braziers were cold and rusty. The beautiful marble floor was as cracked as a dry lakebed.

Bast stood alone next to the empty throne of Osiris. She gave me a mischievous smile, but seeing her again was almost too painful to bear.

"Oh, don't be sad," she chided. "Cats don't do regret."

"But aren't you—aren't you dead?"

"That all depends." She gestured around her. "The Duat is in turmoil. The gods have gone too long without a king. If Set doesn't take over, someone else must. The enemy is coming. Don't let me die in vain."

"But will you come back?" I asked, my voice breaking. "Please, I never even got to say good-bye to you. I can't—"

"Good luck, Sadie. Keep your claws sharp." Bast vanished, and the scenery changed again.

I stood in the Hall of Ages, in the First Nome—another

empty throne—and Iskandar sat at its feet, waiting for a pharaoh who hadn't existed for two thousand years.

"A leader, my dear," he said. "Ma'at demands a leader."

"It's too much," I said. "Too many thrones. You can't expect Carter—"

"Not alone," Iskandar agreed. "But this is your family's burden. You started the process. The Kanes alone will heal us or destroy us."

"I don't know what you mean!"

Iskandar opened his hand, and in a flash of light, the scene changed one more time.

I was back at the Thames. It must've been the dead of the night, three o'clock in the morning, because the Embankment was empty. Mist obscured the lights of the city, and the air was wintry.

Two people, a man and a woman, stood bundled against the cold, holding hands in front of Cleopatra's Needle. At first I thought they were a random couple on a date. Then, with a shock, I realized I was looking at my parents.

My dad lifted his face and scowled at the obelisk. In the dim glow of the streetlamps, his features looked like chiseled marble—like the pharaoh statues he loved to study. He *did* have the face of a king, I thought—proud and handsome.

"You're sure?" he asked my mother. "Absolutely sure?"

Mum brushed her blond hair out of her face. She was even more beautiful than her pictures, but she looked worried— eyebrows furrowed, lips pressed together. Like *me* when I was upset, when I looked in the mirror and tried to convince myself things weren't so bad. I wanted to call to her, to let her know I was there, but my voice wouldn't work.

"She told me this is where it begins," my mother said. She pulled her black coat around her, and I caught a glimpse of her necklace—the amulet of Isis, *my* amulet. I stared at it, stunned, but then she pulled her collar closed, and the amulet disappeared. "If we want to defeat the enemy, we must start with the obelisk. We must find out the truth."

My father frowned uneasily. He'd drawn a protective circle around them—blue chalk lines on the pavement. When he touched the base of the obelisk, the circle began to glow.

"I don't like it," he said. "Won't you call on her help?"

"No," my mother insisted. "I know my limits, Julius. If I tried it again..."

My heart skipped a beat. Iskandar's words came back to me: *She saw things that made her seek advice from unconventional places.* I recognized the look in my mother' eyes, and I knew: my mother had communed with Isis.

Why didn't you tell me? I wanted to scream.

My father summoned his staff and wand. "Ruby, if we fail—"

"We can't fail," she insisted. "The world depends on it."

They kissed one last time, as if they sensed they were saying good-bye. Then they raised their staffs and wands and began to chant. Cleopatra's Needle glowed with power.

I yanked my hand away from the sarcophagus. My eyes stung with tears.

You knew my mother, I shouted at Isis. *You encouraged her to open that obelisk. You got her killed!*

I waited for her to answer. Instead, a ghostly image appeared in front of me—a projection of my father, shimmering in the light of the golden coffin.

"Sadie." He smiled. His voice sounded tinny and hollow, the way it used to on the phone when he'd call me from far away—from Egypt or Australia or god knows where. "Don't blame Isis for your mother's fate. None of us understood exactly what would happen. Even your mother could only see bits and pieces of the future. But when the time came, your mother accepted her role. It was her decision."

"To *die?*" I demanded. "Isis should've helped her. *You* should've helped her. I *hate* you!"

As soon as I said it, something broke inside me. I started to cry. I realized I'd wanted to say that to my dad for years. I blamed him for Mum's death, blamed him for leaving me. But now that I'd said it, all the anger drained out me, leaving me nothing but guilt.

"I'm sorry," I sputtered. "I didn't—"

"Don't apologize, my brave girl. You have every right to feel that way. You had to get it out. What you're about to do—you have to believe it's for the right reasons, not because you resent me."

"I don't know what you mean."

He reached out to brush a tear from my cheek, but his hand was just a shimmer of light. "Your mother was the first in many centuries to commune with Isis. It was dangerous, against the teachings of the House, but your mother was a diviner. She had a premonition that chaos was rising. The House was failing. We *needed* the gods. Isis could not cross the Duat. She could barely manage a whisper, but she told us what she could about their imprisonment. She counseled Ruby on what must be done. The gods could rise again, she said, but it would take many *hard* sacrifices. We thought the obelisk would release all the gods, but that was only the beginning."

"Isis could've given Mum more power. Or at least Bast! Bast *offered*—"

"No, Sadie. Your mother knew her limits. If she had tried to host a god, *fully* use divine power, she would have been consumed or worse. She freed Bast, and used her own power to seal the breach. With her life, she bought you some time."

"Me? But..."

"You and your brother have the strongest blood of any Kane in three thousand years. Your mother studied the lineage of the pharaohs—she knew this to be true. You have the best chance at relearning the old ways, and healing the breach between magicians and gods. Your mother began the stirring. I unleashed the gods from the Rosetta Stone. But it will be your job to restore Ma'at."

"You can help," I insisted. "Once we free you."

"Sadie," he said forlornly, "when you become a parent, you may understand this. One of my hardest jobs as a father, one of my greatest duties, was to realize that my own dreams, my own goals and wishes, are secondary to my children's. Your mother and I have set the stage. But it is *your* stage. This pyramid is designed to feed chaos. It consumes the power of other gods and makes Set stronger."

"I know. If I break the throne, maybe open the coffin..."

"You might save me," Dad conceded. "But the power of Osiris, the power inside me, would be consumed by the pyramid. It would only hasten the destruction and make Set stronger. The pyramid must be destroyed, *all* of it. And you know how that must be done."

I was about to protest that I *didn't* know, but the feather of truth kept me honest. The way was inside me—I'd seen it in Isis's thoughts. I'd known what was coming ever since Anubis asked me that impossible question: "To save the world, would you sacrifice your father?"

"I don't want to," I said. "Please."

"Osiris must take his throne," my father said. "Through death, life. It is the only way. May Ma'at guide you, Sadie. I love you."

And with that, his image dissipated.

Someone was calling my name.

I looked back and saw Zia trying to sit up, clutching weakly at her wand. "Sadie, what are you doing?"

All around us, the room was shaking. Cracks split the walls, as if a giant were using the pyramid as a punching bag.

How long had I been in a trance? I wasn't sure, but I was out of time.

I closed my eyes and concentrated. The voice of Isis spoke almost immediately: *Do you see now? Do you understand why I could not say more?*

Anger built inside me, but I forced it down. *We'll talk about that later. Right now, we have a god to defeat.*

I pictured myself stepping forward, merging with the soul of the goddess.

I'd shared power with Isis before, but this was different. My resolve, my anger, even my grief gave me confidence. I looked Isis straight in the eye (spiritually speaking), and we understood one another.

I saw her entire history—her early days grasping for power, using tricks and schemes to find the name of Ra. I saw her wedding with Osiris, her hopes and dreams for a new empire. Then I saw those dreams shattered by Set. I felt her anger and bitterness, her fierce pride and protectiveness for her young son, Horus. And I saw the pattern of her life repeating itself over and over again through the ages, through a thousand different hosts.

Gods have great power, Iskandar had said. *But only humans have creativity, the power to change history.*

I also felt my mother's thoughts, like an imprint on the goddess's memory: Ruby's final moments and the choice she'd made. She'd given her life to start a chain of events. And the next move was mine.

"Sadie!" Zia called again, her voice weakening.

"I'm fine," I said. "I'm going now."

Zia studied my face, and obviously didn't like what she saw. "You're not fine. You've been badly shaken. Fighting Set in your condition would be suicide."

"Don't worry," I said. "We have a plan."

With that, I turned into a kite and flew up the airshaft towards the top of the pyramid.

40. I Ruin a Rather Important Spell

I FOUND THAT THINGS WEREN'T GOING WELL UPSTAIRS.

Carter was a crumpled heap of chicken warrior on the slope of the pyramid. Set had just placed the capstone and was shouting, "Thirty seconds to sunrise!" In the cavern below, magicians from the House of Life waded through an army of demons, fighting a hopeless fight.

The scene would've been frightening enough, but now I saw it as Isis did. Like a crocodile with eyes at water level—seeing both below and above the surface—I saw the Duat entwined with the regular world. The demons had fiery souls in the Duat that made them look like an army of birthday candles. Where Carter stood in the mortal world, a falcon warrior stood in the Duat—not an avatar, but the real thing, with feathered head, sharp bloodstained beak, and gleaming black eyes. His sword rippled with golden light. As for Set—imagine a mountain of sand, doused with petrol, set on fire, spinning in the world's largest blender. That's what he looked like in the Duat—a column of destructive force so powerful that the stones at his feet bubbled and blistered.

I'm not sure what I looked like, but I felt powerful. The force of Ma'at coursed through me; the Divine Words were at my command. I was Sadie Kane, blood of the pharaohs. And I was Isis, goddess of magic, holder of the secret names.

As Carter struggled his way up the pyramid, Set gloated: "You can't stop me by yourself, Horus—especially not in the desert, the source of my strength!"

"You're right!" I called.

Set turned, and the look on his face was priceless. I raised my staff and wand, gathering my magic.

"Except that Horus is *not* alone," I said. "And we're *not* going to fight you in the desert."

I slammed my staff against the stones and shouted, "Washington, D.C.!"

The pyramid shook. For a moment, nothing else happened.

Set seemed to realize what I was doing. He let out a nervous laugh. "Magic one-oh-one, Sadie Kane. You can't open a portal during the Demon Days!"

"A mortal can't," I agreed. "But a goddess of magic can."

Above us, the air crackled with lightning. The top of the cavern dissolved into a churning vortex of sand as large as the pyramid.

Demons stopped fighting and looked up in horror. Magicians stammered midspell, their faces slack with awe.

The vortex was so powerful that it ripped blocks off the

pyramid and sucked them into the sand. And then, like a giant lid, the portal began to descend.

"No!" Set roared. He blasted the portal with flames, then turned on me and hurled stones and lightning, but it was too late. The portal swallowed us all.

The world seemed to flip upside down. For a heartbeat, I wondered if I'd made a terrible miscalculation—if Set's pyramid would explode in the portal, and I'd spend eternity floating through the Duat as a billion little particles of Sadie sand. Then, with a sonic boom, we appeared in the cold morning air with a brilliant blue sky above us. Spread out below us were the snow-covered fields of the National Mall in Washington, D.C.

The red pyramid was still intact, but cracks had appeared on its surface. The gold capstone glowed, trying to maintain its magic, but we weren't in Phoenix anymore. The pyramid had been ripped from its source of power, the desert, and in front us loomed the default gateway for North America, the tall white obelisk that was the most powerful focal point of Ma'at on the continent: the Washington Monument.

Set screamed something at me in Ancient Egyptian. I was fairly sure it wasn't a compliment.

"I will rend your limbs from their sockets!" he shouted. "I will—"

"Die?" Carter suggested. He rose behind Set and swung his sword. The blade cut into Set's armor at the ribs—not a killing blow, but enough to knock the Red God off balance and send him tumbling down the side of his pyramid. Carter bounded after him, and in the Duat I could see arcs of white energy pulsing from the Washington Monument to the Horus avatar, charging it with new power.

"The book, Sadie!" Carter shouted as he ran. "Do it now!"

I must've been dazed from summoning the portal, because Set understood what Carter was saying a lot faster than I did.

"No!" the Red God shouted. He charged towards me, but Carter intercepted him halfway up the slope.

He grappled with Set, holding him back. The stones of the pyramid cracked and crumbled under the weight of their godly forms. All around the base of the pyramid, demons and magicians who'd been pulled through the portal and knocked momentarily unconscious were starting to stir.

The book, Sadie . . . Sometimes it's helpful to have someone other than yourself inside your head, because one can slap the other. *Duh, the book!*

I held out my hand and summoned the little blue tome we'd stolen from Paris: *The Book of Overcoming Set.* I unfolded the papyrus; the hieroglyphs were as clear as a nursery school primer. I called for the feather of truth, and instantly it appeared, glowing above the pages.

I began the spell, speaking the Divine Words, and my body rose into the air, hovering a few centimeters above the pyramid. I chanted the story of creation: the first mountain rising above the waters of chaos, the birth of the gods Ra, Geb, and Nut, the rise of Ma'at, and the first great empire of men, Egypt.

The Washington Monument began to glow as hieroglyphs appeared along its sides. The capstone gleamed silver.

Set tried to lash out at me, but Carter intercepted him. And the red pyramid began to break apart.

I thought about Amos and Zia, trapped inside under tons of stone, and I almost faltered, but my mother's voice spoke in my mind: *Stay focused, dearest. Watch for your enemy.*

Yes, Isis said. *Destroy him!*

But somehow I knew that wasn't what my mother meant. She was telling me to watch. Something important was about to happen.

Through the Duat, I saw magic forming around me, weaving a white sheen over the world, reinforcing Ma'at and expelling chaos. Carter and Set wrestled back and forth as huge chunks of the pyramid collapsed.

The feather of truth glowed, shining like a spotlight on the Red God. As I neared the end of the spell, my words began tearing Set's form to shreds.

In the Duat, his fiery whirlwind was being stripped away, revealing a black-skinned, slimy thing like an emaciated Set animal—the evil essence of the god. But in the mortal world, occupying the same space, there stood a proud warrior in red armor, blazing with power and determined to fight to the death.

"I name you Set," I chanted. "I name you Evil Day."

With a thunderous roar, the pyramid imploded. Set fell crashing into the ruins. He tried to rise, but Carter swung his sword. Set barely had time to raise his staff. Their weapons crossed, and Horus slowly forced Set to one knee.

"Now, Sadie!" Carter yelled.

"You have been my enemy," I chanted, "and a curse on the land."

A line of white light shot down the length of the

Washington Monument. It widened into a rift—a doorway between this world and the brilliant white abyss that would lock Set away, trapping his life force. Maybe not forever, but for a long, long time.

To complete the spell, I only had to speak one more line: "Deserving no mercy, an enemy of Ma'at, you are exiled beyond the earth."

The line had to be spoken with absolute conviction. The feather of truth required it. And why shouldn't I believe it? It was the truth. Set deserved no mercy. He *was* an enemy of Ma'at.

But I hesitated.

"Watch for your enemy," my mother had said.

I looked towards the top of the monument, and in the Duat I saw chunks of pyramid flying skyward and the souls of demons lifting off like fireworks. As Set's chaos magic dispersed, all the force that had been charging up, ready to destroy a continent, was being sucked into the clouds. And as I watched, the chaos tried to form a shape. It was like a red reflection of the Potomac—an enormous crimson river at least a mile long and a hundred meters wide. It writhed in the air, trying to become solid, and I felt its rage and bitterness. This was not what it had wanted. There was not enough power or chaos for its purpose. To form properly, it needed the death of millions, the wasting of an entire continent.

It was not a river. It was a snake.

"Sadie!" Carter yelled. "What are you waiting for?"

He couldn't see it, I realized. No one could but me.

Set was on his knees, writhing and cursing as white energy

encircled him, pulling him towards the rift. "Lost your stomach, witch?" he bellowed. Then he glared at Carter. "You see, Horus? Isis was always a coward. She could never complete the deed!"

Carter looked at me, and for a moment I saw the doubt on his face. Horus would be urging him towards bloody vengeance. I was hesitating. This is what had turned Isis and Horus against each other before. I couldn't let it happen now.

But more than that, in Carter's wary expression I saw the way he used to look at me on our visiting days—when we were practically strangers, forced to spend time together, pretending we were a happy family because Dad expected it of us. I didn't want to go back to that. I wasn't pretending anymore. We *were* a family, and we had to work together.

"Carter, look." I threw the feather of truth into the sky, breaking the spell.

"No!" Carter screamed.

But the feather exploded into silver dust that clung to the form of the serpent, forcing it to become visible, just for an instant.

Carter's mouth fell open as the serpent writhed in the air above Washington, slowly losing power.

Next to me, a voice screamed: "Wretched gods!"

I turned to see Set's minion, Face of Horror, with his fangs bared and his grotesque face only inches from mine, a jagged knife raised above my head. I only had time to think: *I'm dead,* before a flash of metal registered in the corner of my eye. There was a sickening thud, and the demon froze.

Carter had thrown his sword with deadly accuracy. The

demon dropped his knife, fell to his knees, and stared down at the blade that was now sheathed in his side.

He crumpled to his back, exhaling with an angry hiss. His black eyes fixed on me, and he spoke in a completely different voice—a rasping, dry sound, like a reptile's belly scraping over sand. "This is not over, godling. All this I have wrought with a wisp of my voice, the merest bit of my essence wriggling from my weakened cage. Imagine what I shall do when fully formed."

He gave me a ghastly smile, and then his face went slack. A tiny line of red mist curled from his mouth—like a worm or a fresh-hatched snake—and writhed upward into the sky to join its source. The demon's body disintegrated into sand.

I looked up once more at the giant red serpent slowly dissolving in the sky. Then I summoned a good strong wind and dispersed it completely.

The Washington Monument stopped glowing. The rift closed, and the little spellbook disappeared from my hand.

I moved towards Set, who was still ensnared in ropes of white energy. I'd spoken his true name. He wasn't going anywhere just yet.

"You both saw the serpent in the clouds," I said. "Apophis."

Carter nodded, stunned. "He was trying to break into the mortal world, using the Red Pyramid as a gateway. If its power had been unleashed..." He looked down in revulsion at the pile of sand that had once been a demon. "Set's lieutenant—Face of Horror—he was possessed by Apophis all along, using Set to get what he wanted."

"Ridiculous!" Set glared at me and struggled against his

bonds. "The snake in the clouds was one of your tricks, Isis. An illusion."

"You know it wasn't," I said. "I could've sent you into the abyss, Set, but you saw the real enemy. Apophis was trying to break out of his prison in the Duat. His voice possessed Face of Horror. He was using you."

"No one uses me!"

Carter let his warrior form disperse. He floated to the ground and summoned his sword back to his hand. "Apophis wanted your explosion to feed *his* power, Set. As soon as he came through the Duat and found us dead, I'm betting *you* would've been his first meal. Chaos would've won."

"I *am* chaos!" Set insisted.

"Partially," I said. "But you're still one of the gods. True, you're evil, faithless, ruthless, vile—"

"You make me blush, sister."

"But you're also the strongest god. In the ancient times, you were Ra's faithful lieutenant, defending his boat against Apophis. Ra couldn't have defeated the Serpent without you."

"I am pretty great," Set admitted. "But Ra is gone forever, thanks to you."

"Maybe not forever," I said. "We'll have to find him. Apophis is rising, which means we'll need all the gods to battle him. Even you."

Set tested his bonds of white energy. When he found he couldn't break them, he gave me a crooked smile. "You suggest an alliance? You'd trust me?"

Carter laughed. "You've got to be kidding. But we've got your number, now. Your secret name. Right, Sadie?"

I closed my fingers, and the bonds tightened around Set. He cried out in pain. It took a great deal of energy, and I knew I couldn't hold him like this for long, but there was no point telling that to Set.

"The House of Life tried banishing the gods," I said. "It didn't work. If we lock you away, we're no better than they are. It doesn't solve anything."

"I couldn't agree more," Set groaned. "So if you'll just loosen these bonds—"

"You're still a villainous piece of scum," I said. "But you have a role to play, and you'll need controlling. I'll agree to release you—*if* you swear to behave, to return to the Duat, and not cause trouble until we call you. And then you'll make trouble only for us, fighting against Apophis."

"Or I could chop off your head," Carter suggested. "That would probably exile you for a good long while."

Set glanced back and forth between us. "Make trouble for you, eh? That *is* my specialty."

"Swear by your own name and the throne of Ra," I said. "You will leave now and not reappear until you are called."

"Oh, I swear," he said, much too quickly. "By my name and Ra's throne and our mother's starry elbows."

"If you betray us," I warned, "I have your name. I won't show you mercy a second time."

"You always were my favorite sister."

I gave him one last shock, just to remind him of my power, and then let the bindings dissolve.

Set stood up and flexed his arms. He appeared as a warrior with red armor and red skin, a black, forked beard, and twinkling, cruel eyes; but in the Duat, I saw his other side, a raging inferno just barely contained, waiting to be unleashed and burn everything in its path. He winked at Horus, then pretended to shoot me with a finger gun. "Oh, this will be *good*. We're going to have so much fun."

"Begone, Evil Day," I said.

He turned into a pillar of salt and dissolved.

The snow in the National Mall had melted in a perfect square, the exact size of Set's pyramid. Around the edges, a dozen magicians still lay passed out. The poor dears had started to stir when our portal closed, but the explosion of the pyramid had knocked them all out again. Other mortals in the area had also been affected. An early-morning jogger was slumped on the sidewalk. On nearby streets, cars idled while the drivers took naps over the steering wheels.

Not everyone was asleep, though. Police sirens wailed in the distance, and seeing as how we'd teleported practically into the president's backyard, I knew it wouldn't be long before we had a great deal of heavily armed company.

Carter and I ran to the center of the melted square, where Amos and Zia lay crumpled in the grass. There was no sign of Set's throne or the golden coffin, but I tried to push those thoughts out of my mind.

Amos groaned. "What…" His eyes clouded over with terror. "Set…he…he…"

"Rest." I put my hand on his forehead. He was burning with fever. The pain in his mind was so sharp, it cut me like a razor. I remembered a spell Isis had taught me in New Mexico.

"Quiet," I whispered. *"Hah-ri."*

Faint hieroglyphs glowed over his face:

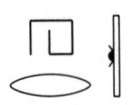

Amos drifted back to sleep, but I knew it was only a temporary fix.

Zia was even worse off. Carter cradled her head and spoke reassuringly about how she would be fine, but she looked bad. Her skin was a strange reddish color, dry and brittle, as if she'd suffered a horrible sunburn. In the grass around her, hieroglyphs were fading—the remains of a protective circle—and I thought I understood what had happened. She'd used her last bit of energy to shield herself and Amos when the pyramid imploded.

"Set?" she asked weakly. "Is he gone?"

"Yes." Carter glanced at me, and I knew we'd be keeping the details to ourselves. "Everything's fine, thanks to you. The secret name worked."

She nodded, satisfied, and her eyes began to close.

"Hey." Carter's voice quavered. "Stay awake. You're not going to leave me alone with Sadie, are you? She's bad company."

Zia tried to smile, but the effort made her wince. "I was . . . never here, Carter. Just a message—a placeholder."

"Come on. No. That's no way to talk."

"Find her, will you?" Zia said. A tear traced its way down her nose. "She'd . . . like that . . . a date at the mall." Her eyes drifted away from him and stared blankly into the sky.

"Zia!" Carter clutched her hand. "Stop that. You can't . . . You can't just . . ."

I knelt next to him and touched Zia's face. It was cold as stone. And even though I understood what had happened, I couldn't think of anything to say, or any way to console my brother. He shut his eyes tight and lowered his head.

Then it happened. Along the path of Zia's tear, from the corner of her eye to the base of her nose, Zia's face cracked. Smaller fractures appeared, webbing her skin. Her flesh dried out, hardening . . . turning to clay.

"Carter," I said.

"What?" he said miserably.

He looked up just as a small blue light drifted out of Zia's mouth and flew into the sky. Carter backed away in shock. "What—what did you do?"

"Nothing," I said. "She's a *shabti*. She said she wasn't really here. She was just a placeholder."

Carter looked bewildered. But then a small light started to burn in his eyes—a tiny bit of hope. "Then . . . the real Zia is alive?"

"Iskandar was protecting her," I said. "When the spirit of Nephthys joined with the real Zia in London, Iskandar knew she was in danger. Iskandar hid her away and replaced her with a *shabti*. Remember what Thoth said: 'Shabti make excellent stunt doubles?' That's what she was. And Nephthys told me she was sheltered somewhere, inside a sleeping host."

"But where—"

"I don't know," I said. And in Carter's present state, I was too afraid to raise the *real* question: If Zia had been a *shabti* all this time, had we ever known her at all? The real Zia had never gotten close to us. She'd never discovered what an incredibly amazing person I was. God forbid, she might not even like Carter.

Carter touched her face and it crumbled to dust. He picked up her wand, which remained solid ivory, but he held it gingerly as if he were afraid it too would dissolve. "That blue light," he began to ramble, "I saw Zia release one in the First Nome, too. Just like the *shabti* in Memphis—they sent their thoughts back to Thoth. So Zia must've been in contact with her *shabti*. That's what the light was. They must've been, like, sharing memories, right? She must *know* what the *shabti*'s been through. If the real Zia is alive somewhere, she might be locked up or in some kind of magic sleep or— We have to find her!"

I wasn't sure it would be so simple, but I didn't want to argue. I could see the desperation on his face.

Then a familiar voice sent a cold shiver down my back: "What have you done?"

Desjardins was literally fuming. His tattered robes still smoked from battle. (Carter says I shouldn't mention that his pink boxer shorts were showing, but they were!) His staff was aglow, and the whiskers in his beard smoldered. Behind him stood three equally battered magicians, who all looked as if they'd just regained consciousness.

"Oh, good," I muttered. "You're alive."

"You bargained with Set?" Desjardins demanded. "You let him *go*?"

"We don't answer to you," Carter growled. He stepped

forward, hand on his sword, but I put out my arm to hold him back.

"Desjardins," I said as calmly as I could, "Apophis is rising, in case you missed that part. We need the gods. The House of Life has to relearn the old ways."

"The old ways destroyed us!" he yelled.

A week ago, the look in his eyes would've made me tremble. He fairly glowed with rage, and hieroglyphs blazed in the air around him. He was the Chief Lector, and I'd just undone everything the House had worked for since the fall of Egypt. Desjardins was a heartbeat away from turning me into an insect, and the thought should've terrified me.

Instead, I looked him in the eye. Right now, I was more powerful than he was. *Much* more powerful. And I let him know it.

"Pride destroyed you," I said. "Greed and selfishness and all of that. It's hard to follow the path of the gods. But it is part of magic. You can't just shut it down."

"You are drunk with power," he snarled. "The gods have possessed you, as they always do. Soon you will forget you are even human. We will fight you and destroy you." Then he glared at Carter. "And *you*—I know what Horus would demand. You will never reclaim the throne. With my last breath—"

"Save it," I said. Then I faced my brother. "You know what we have to do?"

Understanding passed between us. I was surprised how easily I could read him. I thought it might be the influence of the gods, but then I realized it was because we were both

Kanes, brother and sister. And Carter, god help me, was also my friend.

"Are you sure?" he asked. "We're leaving ourselves open." He glared at Desjardins. "Just one more good smack with the sword?"

"I'm sure, Carter."

I closed my eyes and focused.

Consider carefully, Isis said. *What we've done so far is only the beginning of the power we could wield together.*

That's the problem, I said. *I'm not ready for that. I've got to get there on my own, the hard way.*

You are wise for a mortal, Isis said. *Very well.*

Imagine giving up a fortune in cash. Imagine throwing away the most beautiful diamond necklace in the world. Separating myself from Isis was harder than that, *much* harder.

But it wasn't impossible. *I know my limits,* my mother had said, and now I understood how wise she'd been.

I felt the spirit of the goddess leave me. Part of her flowed into my necklace, but most of her streamed into the Washington Monument, back into the Duat, where Isis would go . . . somewhere else. Another host? I wasn't sure.

When I opened my eyes, Carter stood next to me looking grief-stricken, holding his Eye of Horus amulet.

Desjardins was so stunned, he momentarily forgot how to speak English. *"Ce n'est pas possible. On ne pourrait pas—"*

"Yes, we could," I said. "We've given up the gods of our own free will. And you've got a lot to learn about what's possible."

Carter threw down his sword. "Desjardins, I'm not after the throne. Not unless I earn it by myself, and that's going to take time. We're going to learn the path of the gods. We're going to teach others. You can waste time trying to destroy us, or you can help."

The sirens were much closer now. I could see the lights of emergency vehicles coming from several directions, slowly cordoning off the National Mall. We had only minutes before we were surrounded.

Desjardins looked at the magicians behind him, probably gauging how much support he could rally. His brethren looked in awe. One even started to bow to me, then caught himself.

Alone, Desjardins might've been able to destroy us. We were just magicians now—very tired magicians, with hardly any formal training.

Desjardins' nostrils flared. Then he surprised me by lowering his staff. "There has been too much destruction today. But the path of the gods shall remain closed. If you cross the House of Life again..."

He let the threat hang in the air. He slammed his staff down, and with a final burst of energy, the four magicians dissolved into wind and gusted away.

Suddenly I felt exhausted. The terror of what I'd been through began to sink in. We'd survived, but that was little consolation. I missed my parents. I missed them terribly. I wasn't a goddess anymore. I was just a regular girl, alone with only my brother.

Then Amos groaned and started sitting up. Police cars and sinister-looking black vans blocked the curbs all around us. Sirens blared. A helicopter sliced through the air over the Potomac, closing fast. God only knew what the mortals thought had happened at the Washington Monument, but I didn't want my face on the nightly news.

"Carter, we have to get out of here," I said. "Can you summon enough magic to change Amos into something small—a mouse maybe? We can fly him out."

He nodded, still in a daze. "But Dad . . . we didn't . . ."

He looked around helplessly. I knew how he felt. The pyramid, the throne, the golden coffin—all of it was gone. We'd come so far to rescue our father, only to lose him. And Carter's first girlfriend lay at his feet in a pile of pottery shards. That probably didn't help either. (Carter protests that she wasn't really his girlfriend. Oh, please!)

I couldn't dwell on it, though. I had to be strong for both of us or we'd end up in prison.

"First things first," I said. "We have to get Amos to safety."

"Where?" Carter asked.

There was only one place I could think of.

41. We Stop the Recording, for Now

I CAN'T BELIEVE SADIE'S GOING TO let me have the last word. Our experience together must've really taught her something. Ow, she just hit me. Never mind.

Anyway, I'm glad she told that last part. I think she understood it better than I did. And the whole thing about Zia not being Zia and Dad not getting rescued...that was pretty hard to deal with.

If anybody felt worse than I did, it was Amos. I had just enough magic to turn myself into a falcon and him into a hamster (hey, I was rushed!), but a few miles from the National Mall, he started struggling to change back. Sadie and I were forced to land outside a train station, where Amos turned back into a human and curled into a shivering ball. We tried to talk to him, but he could barely complete a sentence.

Finally we got him into the station. We let him sleep on a bench while Sadie and I warmed up and watched the news.

According to Channel 5, the whole city of Washington

was under lockdown. There'd been reports of explosions and weird lights at the Washington Monument, but all the cameras could show us was a big square of melted snow on the mall, which kind of made for boring video. Experts came on and talked about terrorism, but eventually it became clear that there'd been no permanent damage—just a bunch of scary lights. After a while, the media started speculating about freak storm activity or a rare southern appearance of the Northern Lights. Within an hour, the authorities opened up the city.

I wished we had Bast with us, because Amos was in no shape to be our chaperone; but we managed to buy tickets for our "sick" uncle and ourselves as far as New York.

I slept on the way, the amulet of Horus clutched in my hand.

We got back to Brooklyn at sunset.

We found the mansion burned out, which we'd expected, but we had nowhere else to go. I knew we'd made the right choice when we guided Amos through the doorway and heard a familiar, *"Agh! Agh!"*

"Khufu!" Sadie cried.

The baboon tackled her in a hug and climbed onto her shoulders. He picked at her hair, seeing if she'd brought him any good bugs to eat. Then he jumped off and grabbed a half-melted basketball. He grunted at me insistently, pointing to a makeshift basket he'd made out of some burned beams and a laundry basket. It was a gesture of forgiveness, I realized. He had forgiven me for sucking at his favorite game, and he was offering lessons. Looking around, I realized that he'd tried to clean up in his own baboon way, too. He'd dusted off the one surviving sofa, stacked Cheerios boxes in the fireplace, and even put a dish of water and fresh food out for Muffin, who was curled up asleep on a little pillow. In the clearest part of the living room, under an intact section of roof, Khufu had made three separate mounds of pillows and sheets—sleeping places for us.

I got a lump in my throat. Seeing the care that he'd taken getting ready for us, I couldn't imagine a better welcome home present.

"Khufu," I said, "you are one freaking awesome baboon."

"*Agh!*" he said, pointing to the basketball.

"You want to school me?" I said. "Yeah, I deserve it. Just give us a second to..."

My smile melted when I saw Amos.

He'd drifted over to the ruined statue of Thoth. The god's cracked ibis head lay at his feet. His hands had broken off, and his tablet and stylus lay shattered on the ground. Amos stared at the headless god—the patron of magicians—and I could guess what he was thinking. *A bad omen for a homecoming.*

"It's okay," I told him. "We're going to make it right."

If Amos heard me, he gave no sign. He drifted over to the couch and plopped down, putting his head in his hands.

Sadie glanced at me uneasily. Then she looked around at the blackened walls, the crumbling ceilings, the charred remains of the furniture.

"Well," she said, trying to sound upbeat. "How about *I* play basketball with Khufu, and you can clean the house?"

Even with magic, it took us several weeks to put the house back in order. That was just to make it livable. It was hard without Isis and Horus helping, but we could still do magic. It just took a lot more concentration and a lot more time. Every day, I went to sleep feeling as if I'd done twelve hours of hard labor; but eventually we got the walls and ceilings repaired, and cleaned up the debris until the house no longer smelled of smoke. We even managed to fix the terrace and the pool. We brought Amos out to watch as we released the wax crocodile figurine into the water, and Philip of Macedonia sprang to life.

Amos almost smiled when he saw that. Then he sank into a chair on the terrace and stared desolately at the Manhattan skyline.

I began to wonder if he would ever be the same. He'd lost too much weight. His face looked haggard. Most days he wore his bathrobe and didn't even bother to comb his hair.

"He was taken over by Set," Sadie told me one morning, when I mentioned how worried I was. "Do you have any idea how *violating* that is? His will was broken. He doubts himself and... Well, it may be a long time...."

We tried to lose ourselves in work. We repaired the statue of Thoth, and fixed the broken *shabti* in the library. I was better at grunt work—moving blocks of stone or heaving ceiling beams into place. Sadie was better at fine details, like repairing the hieroglyphic seals on the doors. Once, she really impressed me by imagining her bedroom just as it had been and speaking the joining spell, *hi-nehm*. Pieces of furniture flew together out of the debris, and *boom!*: instant repair job. Of course, Sadie passed out for twelve hours afterward, but still…pretty cool. Slowly but surely, the mansion began to feel like home.

At night I would sleep with my head on a charmed headrest, which mostly kept my *ba* from drifting off; but sometimes I still had strange visions—the red pyramid, the serpent in the sky, or the face of my father as he was trapped in Set's coffin. Once I thought I heard Zia's voice trying to tell me something from far away, but I couldn't make out the words.

Sadie and I kept our amulets locked in a box in the library. Every morning I would sneak down to make sure they were still there. I would find them glowing, warm to the touch, and I would be tempted—*very* tempted—to put on the Eye of Horus. But I knew I couldn't. The power was too addictive, too dangerous. I'd achieved a balance with Horus once, under extreme circumstances, but I knew it would be too easy to get overwhelmed if I tried it again. I had to train first, become a more powerful magician, before I would be ready to tap that much power.

One night at dinner, we had a visitor.

Amos had gone to bed early, as he usually did. Khufu was inside watching ESPN with Muffin on his lap. Sadie and I sat exhausted on the deck overlooking the river. Philip of Macedonia floated silently in his pool. Except for the hum of the city, the night was quiet.

I'm not sure how it happened, but one minute we were alone, and the next there was a guy standing at the railing. He was lean and tall, with messed-up hair and pale skin, and his clothes were all black, as if he'd mugged a priest or something. He was probably around sixteen, and even though I'd never seen his face before, I had the weirdest feeling that I knew him.

Sadie stood up so quickly she knocked over her split-pea soup—which is gross enough in the bowl, but running all over the table? Yuck.

"Anubis!" she blurted.

Anubis? I thought she was kidding, because this guy did not look anything like the slavering jackal-headed god I'd seen in the Land of the Dead. He stepped forward, and my hand crept for my wand.

"Sadie," he said. "Carter. Would you come with me, please?"

"Sure," Sadie said, her voice a little strangled.

"Hold on," I said. "Where are we going?"

Anubis gestured behind him, and a door opened in the air—a pure black rectangle. "Someone wants to see you."

Sadie took his hand and stepped through into the darkness, which left me no choice but to follow.

The Hall of Judgment had gotten a makeover. The golden scales still dominated the room, but they had been fixed. The black pillars still marched off into the gloom on all four sides. But now I could see the overlay—the strange holographic image of the real world—and it was no longer a graveyard, as Sadie had described. It was a white living room with tall ceilings and huge picture windows. Double doors led to a terrace that looked out over the ocean.

I was struck speechless. I looked at Sadie, and judging from the shock on her face, I guessed she recognized the place too: our house in Los Angeles, in the hills overlooking the Pacific—the last place we'd lived as a family.

"The Hall of Judgment is intuitive," a familiar voice said. "It responds to strong memories."

Only then did I notice the throne wasn't empty anymore. Sitting there, with Ammit the Devourer curled at his feet, was our father.

I almost ran to him, but something held me back. He looked the same in many ways—the long brown coat, the rumpled suit and dusty boots, his head freshly shaven and his beard trimmed. His eyes gleamed the way they did whenever I made him proud.

But his form shimmered with a strange light. Like the room itself, I realized, he existed in two worlds. I concentrated hard, and my eyes opened to a deeper level of the Duat.

Dad was still there, but taller and stronger, dressed in the robes and jewels of an Egyptian pharaoh. His skin was a dark shade of blue like the deep ocean.

Anubis walked over and stood at his side, but Sadie and I were a little more cautious.

"Well, come on," Dad said. "I won't bite."

Ammit the Devourer growled as we came close, but Dad stroked his crocodile head and shushed him. "These are my children, Ammit. Behave."

"D-Dad?" I stammered.

Now I want to be clear: even though weeks had passed since the battle with Set, and even though I'd been busy rebuilding the mansion the whole time, I hadn't stopped thinking about my dad for a minute. Every time I saw a picture in the library, I thought of the stories he used to tell me. I kept my clothes in a suitcase in my bedroom closet, because I couldn't bear the idea that our life traveling together was over. I missed him so much I would sometimes turn to tell him something before I forgot that he was gone. In spite of all that, and all the emotion boiling around inside me, all I could think of to say was: "You're blue."

My dad's laugh was so normal, so *him*, that it broke the tension. The sound echoed through the hall, and even Anubis cracked a smile.

"Goes with the territory," Dad said. "I'm sorry I didn't bring you here sooner, but things have been..." He looked at Anubis for the right word.

"Complicated," Anubis suggested.

"Complicated. I have meant to tell you both how proud I am of you, how much the gods are in your debt—"

"Hang on," Sadie said. She stomped right up to the throne. Ammit growled at her, but Sadie growled back, which confused the monster into silence.

"What *are* you?" she demanded. "My dad? Osiris? Are you even alive?"

Dad looked at Anubis. "What did I tell you about her? Fiercer than Ammit, I said."

"You didn't need to tell me." Anubis's face was grave. "I've learned to fear that sharp tongue."

Sadie looked outraged. "Excuse me?"

"To answer your question," Dad said, "I am both Osiris and Julius Kane. I am alive *and* dead, though the term *recycled* might be closer to the truth. Osiris is the god of the dead, and the god of new life. To return him to his throne—"

"You had to die," I said. "You knew this going into it. You *intentionally* hosted Osiris, knowing you would die."

I was shaking with anger. I didn't realize how strongly I'd felt about it, but I couldn't believe what my dad had done. "This is what you meant by 'making things right'?"

My dad's expression didn't change. He was still looking at me with pride and downright *joy*, as if everything I did delighted him—even my shouting. It was infuriating.

"I missed you, Carter," he said. "I can't tell you how much. But we made the right choice. We *all* did. If you had saved me in the world above, we would have lost everything. For the first time in millennia, we have a chance at rebirth, and a chance to stop chaos because of you."

"There had to be another way," I said. "You could've fought as a mortal, without . . . without—"

"Carter, when Osiris was alive, he was a great king. But when he died—"

"He became a thousand times more powerful," I said, remembering the story Dad used to tell me.

My father nodded. "The Duat is the foundation for the real world. If there is chaos here, it reverberates in the upper world. Helping Osiris to his throne was a first step, a thousand times more important than anything I could've done in the world above—except being your father. And I am still your father."

My eyes stung. I guess I understood what he was saying, but I didn't like it. Sadie looked even angrier than me, but she was glaring at Anubis.

"Sharp tongue?" she demanded.

Dad cleared his throat. "Children, there is another reason I made my choice, as you can probably guess." He held out his hand, and a woman in a black dress appeared next to him. She had golden hair, intelligent blue eyes, and a face that looked familiar. She looked like Sadie.

"Mom," I said.

She gazed back and forth from Sadie to me in amazement, as if *we* were the ghosts. "Julius told me how much you'd grown, but I couldn't believe it. Carter, I bet you're shaving—"

"Mom."

"—and dating girls—"

"Mom!" Have you ever noticed how parents can go from the most wonderful people in the world to totally embarrassing in three seconds?

She smiled at me, and I had to fight with about twenty different feelings at once. I'd spent years dreaming of being back with my parents, together in our house in L.A. But not like this: not with the house just an afterimage, and my mom a spirit, and my dad . . . recycled. I felt like the world was shifting under my feet, turning into sand.

"We can't go back, Carter," Mom said, as if reading my mind. "But nothing is lost, even in death. Do you remember the law of conservation?"

It had been six years since we'd sat together in the living room—*this* living room, and she'd read me the laws of physics the way most parents read bedtime stories. But I still remembered. "Energy and matter can't be created or destroyed."

"Only changed," my mother agreed. "And sometimes changed for the better."

She took Dad's hand, and I had to admit—blue and ghostly or not—they kind of looked happy.

"Mum." Sadie swallowed. For once, her attention wasn't on Anubis. "Did you really . . . was that—"

"Yes, my brave girl. My thoughts mixed with yours. I'm so proud of you. And thanks to Isis, I feel like I know you as well." She leaned forward and smiled conspiratorially. "I like chocolate caramels, too, though your grandmum never approved of keeping sweets in the flat."

Sadie broke into a relieved grin. "I know! She's impossible!"

I got the feeling they were going to start chatting for hours, but just then the Hall of Judgment rumbled. Dad checked his watch, which made me wonder what time zone the Land of the Dead was in.

"We should wrap things up," he said. "The others are expecting you."

"Others?" I asked.

"A gift before you go." Dad nodded to Mom.

She stepped forward and handed me a palm-size package of folded black linen. Sadie helped me unwrap it, and inside was a new amulet—one that looked like a column or a tree trunk or . . .

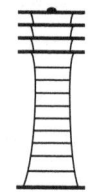

"Is that a spine?" Sadie demanded.

"It is called a *djed*," Dad said. "My symbol—the spine of Osiris."

"Yuck," Sadie muttered.

Mom laughed. "It is a bit yuck, but honestly, it's a powerful symbol. Stands for stability, strength—"

"Backbone?" I asked.

"Literally." Mom gave me an approving look, and again I had that surreal shifting feeling. I couldn't believe I was standing here, having a chat with my somewhat dead parents.

Mom closed the amulet into my hands. Her touch was warm, like a living person's. "*Djed* also stands for the power of Osiris—renewed life from the ashes of death. This is exactly what you will need if you are to stir the blood of the pharaohs in others and rebuild the House of Life."

"The House won't like that," Sadie put in.

"No," Mom said cheerfully. "They certainly won't."

The Hall of Judgment rumbled again.

"It is time," Dad said. "We'll meet again, children. But until then, take care."

"Be mindful of your enemies," Mom added.

"And tell Amos..." Dad's voice trailed off thoughtfully. "Remind my brother that Egyptians believe in the power of the sunrise. They believe each morning begins not just a new day, but a new world."

Before I could figure out what that meant, the Hall of Judgment faded, and we stood with Anubis in a field of darkness.

"I'll show you the way," Anubis said. "It is my job."

He ushered us to a space in the darkness that looked no

different from any other. But when he pushed with his hand, a door swung open. The entrance blazed with daylight.

Anubis bowed formally to me. Then he looked at Sadie with a glint of mischief in his eyes. "It's been...stimulating."

Sadie flushed and pointed at him accusingly. "We're not done, mister. I expect you to look after my parents. And next time I'm in the Land of the Dead, you and I will have words."

A smile tugged at the corner of his mouth. "I'll look forward to that."

We stepped through the doorway and into the palace of the gods.

It looked just like Sadie had described from her visions: soaring stone columns, fiery braziers, a polished marble floor, and in the middle of the room, a gold-and-red throne. All around us, gods had gathered. Many were just flashes of light and fire. Some were shadowy images that shifted from animal to human. I recognized a few: Thoth flickered into view as a wild-haired guy in a lab coat before turning into a cloud of green gas; Hathor, the cow-headed goddess, gave me a puzzled look, as if she vaguely recognized me from the Magic Salsa incident. I looked for Bast, but my heart fell. She didn't seem to be in the crowd. In fact, most of the gods I didn't recognize.

"What have we started?" Sadie murmured.

I understood what she meant. The throne room was full of hundreds of gods, major and minor, all darting through the palace, forming new shapes, glowing with power. An entire supernatural army...and they all seemed to be staring at us.

Thankfully, two old friends stood next to the throne. Horus wore full battle armor and a *khopesh* sword at his side.

His kohl-lined eyes—one gold, one silver—were as piercing as ever. At his side stood Isis in a shimmering white gown, with wings of light.

"Welcome," Horus said.

"*Um*, hi," I said.

"He has a way with words," Isis muttered, which made Sadie snort.

Horus gestured to the throne. "I know your thoughts, Carter, so I think I know what you will say. But I have to ask you one more time. Will you join me? We could rule the earth and the heavens. Ma'at demands a leader."

"Yeah, so I've heard."

"I would be stronger with you as my host. You've only touched the surface of what combat magic can do. We could accomplish great things, and it *is* your destiny to lead the House of Life. You could be the king of two thrones."

I glanced at Sadie, but she just shrugged. "Don't look at me. I find the idea horrifying."

Horus scowled at her, but the truth was, I agreed with Sadie. All those gods waiting for direction, all those magicians who hated us—the idea of trying to lead them made my knees turn to water.

"Maybe some day," I said. "Much later."

Horus sighed. "Five thousand years, and I still do not understand mortals. But—very well."

He stepped up to the throne and looked around at the assembled gods.

"I, Horus, son of Osiris, claim the throne of the heavens

as my birthright!" he shouted. "What was once mine shall be mine again. Is there any who would challenge me?"

The gods flickered and glowed. A few scowled. One muttered something that sounded like "Cheese," although that could've been my imagination. I caught a glimpse of Sobek, or possibly another crocodile god, snarling in the shadows. But no one raised a challenge.

Horus took his seat on the throne. Isis brought him a crook and flail—the twin scepters of the pharaohs. He crossed them over his chest and all the gods bowed before him.

When they'd risen again, Isis stepped toward us. "Carter and Sadie Kane, you have done much to restore Ma'at. The gods must gather their strength, and you have bought us time, though we do not know how much. Apophis will not stay locked away forever."

"I'd settle for a few hundred years," Sadie said.

Isis smiled. "However that may be, today you are heroes. The gods owe you a debt, and we take our debts seriously."

Horus rose from the throne. With a wink at me, he knelt before us. The other gods shifted uncomfortably, but then followed his example. Even the gods in fire form dimmed their flames.

I probably looked pretty stunned, because when Horus got up again he laughed. "You look like that time when Zia told you—"

"Yeah, could we skip that?" I said quickly. Letting a god into your head has serious disadvantages.

"Go in peace, Carter and Sadie," Horus said. "You will find our gift in the morning."

"Gift?" I asked nervously, because if I got one more magic amulet, I was going to break out in a cold sweat.

"You'll see," Isis promised. "We will be watching you, and waiting."

"That's what scares me," Sadie said.

Isis waved her hand, and suddenly we were back on the mansion's terrace as if nothing had happened.

Sadie turned toward me wistfully. "'Stimulating.'"

I held out my hand. The *djed* amulet was glowing and warm in its linen wrapping. "Any idea what this thing does?"

She blinked. "*Hmm?* Oh, don't care. What did Anubis look like to you?"

"What did...he looked like a guy. So?"

"A good-looking guy, or a slobbering dog-headed guy?"

"I guess...not the dog-headed guy."

"I knew it!" Sadie pointed at me as if she'd won an argument. "Good-looking. I knew it!"

And with a ridiculous grin, she spun around and skipped into the house.

My sister, as I may have mentioned, is a little strange.

The next day, we got the gods' gift.

We woke to find that the mansion had been completely repaired down to the smallest detail. Everything we hadn't finished yet—probably another month's worth of work—was done.

The first thing I found were new clothes in my closet, and after a moment's hesitation, I put them on. I went downstairs and found Khufu and Sadie dancing around the restored Great

Room. Khufu had a new Lakers jersey and a brand-new basketball. The magical brooms and mops were busy doing their cleaning routine. Sadie looked up at me and grinned—and then her expression changed to shock.

"Carter, what—what are you *wearing?*"

I came down the stairs, feeling even more self-conscious. The closet had offered me several choices this morning, not just my linen robes. My old clothes had been there, freshly cleaned—a button-down shirt, starched khaki slacks, loafers. But there had also been a third choice, and I'd taken it: some Reeboks, blue jeans, a T-shirt, and a hoodie.

"It's, *um*, all cotton," I said. "Okay for magic. Dad would probably think I look like a gangster...."

I thought for sure Sadie would tease me about that, and I was trying to beat her to the punch. She scrutinized every detail of my outfit.

Then she laughed with absolute delight. "It's brilliant, Carter. You look almost like a regular teenager! And *Dad* would think..." She pulled my hoodie over my head. "Dad would think you look like an impeccable magician, because that's what you are. Now, come on. Breakfast is waiting on the patio."

We were just digging in when Amos came outside, and his change of clothes was even more surprising than mine. He wore a crisp new chocolate-colored suit with matching coat and fedora. His shoes were shined, his round glasses polished, his hair freshly braided with amber beads. Sadie and I both stared at him.

"What?" he demanded.

"Nothing," we said in unison. Sadie looked at me and mouthed O-M-G, then went back to her bangers and eggs. I attacked my pancakes. Philip thrashed around happily in his swimming pool.

Amos joined us at the table. He flicked his fingers and coffee magically filled his cup. I raised my eyebrows. He hadn't used magic since the Demon Days.

"I thought I'd go away for a while," he announced. "To the First Nome."

Sadie and I exchanged glances.

"Are you sure that's a good idea?" I asked.

Amos sipped his coffee. He stared across the East River as if he could see all the way to Washington, D.C. "They have the best magic healers there. They will not turn away a petitioner seeking aid—even me. I think...I think I should try."

His voice was fragile, like it would crack apart any moment. But still, it was the most he'd said in weeks.

"I think that's brilliant," Sadie offered. "We'll watch after the place, won't we, Carter?"

"Yeah," I said. "Absolutely."

"I may be gone for a while," Amos said. "Treat this as your home. It *is* your home." He hesitated, as if choosing his next words carefully. "And I think, perhaps, you should start recruiting. There are many children around the world with the blood of the pharaohs. Most do not know what they are. What you two said in Washington—about rediscovering the path of the gods—it may be our only chance."

Sadie got up and kissed Amos on the forehead. "Leave it to us, Uncle. I've got a plan."

"That," I said, "sounds like very bad news."

Amos managed a smile. He squeezed Sadie's hand, then got up and ruffled my hair as he headed inside.

I took another bite of my pancakes and wondered why—on such a great morning—I still felt sad, and a little incomplete. I suppose with so many things suddenly getting better, the things that were still missing hurt even worse.

Sadie picked at her scrambled eggs. "I suppose it would be selfish to ask for more."

I stared at her, and I realized we were thinking the same thing. When the gods had said a gift...Well, you can hope for things, but as Sadie said, I guess you can't get greedy.

"It's going to be hard to travel if we need to go recruiting," I said cautiously. "Two unaccompanied minors."

Sadie nodded. "No Amos. No responsible adult. I don't think Khufu counts."

And that's when the gods completed their gift.

A voice from the doorway said, "Sounds like you have a job opening."

I turned and felt a thousand pounds of grief drop from my shoulders. Leaning against the door in a leopard-spotted jumpsuit was a dark-haired lady with golden eyes and two very large knives.

"Bast!" Sadie cried.

The cat goddess gave us a playful smile, as if she had all kinds of trouble in mind. "Someone call for a chaperone?"

A few days later, Sadie had a long phone conversation with Gran and Grandpa Faust in London. They didn't ask to talk to me, and I didn't listen in. When Sadie came back down to the Great Room, she had a faraway look in her eyes. I was afraid—*very* afraid—that she was missing London.

"Well?" I asked reluctantly.

"I told them we were all right," she said. "They told me the police have stopped bothering them about the explosion at the British Museum. Apparently the Rosetta Stone turned up unharmed."

"Like magic," I said.

Sadie smirked. "The police decided it might've been a gas explosion, some sort of accident. Dad's off the hook, as are we. I could go home to London, they said. Spring term starts in a few weeks. My mates Liz and Emma have been asking about me."

The only sound was the crackle of fire in the hearth. The Great Room suddenly seemed bigger to me, emptier.

At last I said, "What did you tell them?"

Sadie raised an eyebrow. "God, you're thick sometimes. What do you think?"

"Oh." My mouth felt like sandpaper. "I guess it'll be good to see your friends and get back your old room, and—"

Sadie punched my arm. "Carter! I told them I couldn't very well go home, because I already *was* home. This is where I belong. Thanks to the Duat, I can see my friends whenever I want. And besides, you'd be lost without me."

I must've grinned like a fool, because Sadie told me to wipe the silly look off my face—but she sounded pleased about it. I suppose she knew she was right, for once. I would've been lost without her. [And no, Sadie, I can't believe I just said that either.]

Just when things were settling down to a nice safe routine, Sadie and I embarked on our new mission. Our destination was a school that Sadie had seen in a dream. I won't tell you which school, but Bast drove us a long way to get there. We recorded this tape along the way. Several times the forces of chaos tried to stop us. Several times we heard rumors that our enemies were starting to hunt down other descendants of the pharaohs, trying to thwart our plans.

We got to the school the day before the spring term started. The hallways were empty, and it was easy to slip inside. Sadie and I picked a locker at random, and she told me to set the combination. I summoned some magic and mixed around the numbers: 13/32/33. Hey, why mess with a good formula?

Sadie said a spell and the locker began to glow. Then she put the package inside and closed the door.

"Are you sure about this?" I asked.

She nodded. "The locker is partially in the Duat. It'll store the amulet until the right person opens it."

"But if the *djed* falls into the wrong hands—"

"It won't," she promised. "The blood of the pharaohs is strong. The right kids will find the amulet. If they figure out how to use it, their powers should awaken. We have to trust that the gods will guide them to Brooklyn."

"We won't know how to train them," I argued. "No one has studied the path of the gods for two thousand years."

"We'll figure it out," Sadie said. "We have to."

"Unless Apophis gets us first," I said. "Or Desjardins and the House of Life. Or unless Set breaks his word. Or a thousand other things go wrong."

"Yes," Sadie said with a smile. "Be fun, eh?"

We locked the locker and walked away.

Now we're back at the Twenty-first Nome in Brooklyn.

We're going to send out this tape to a few carefully chosen people and see if it gets published. Sadie believes in fate. If the story falls into your hands, there's probably a reason. Look for the *djed*. It won't take much to awaken your power. Then the trick is learning to use that power without dying.

As I said at the beginning: the whole story hasn't happened yet. Our parents promised to see us again, so I know we'll have to go back to the Land of the Dead eventually, which I think is fine with Sadie, as long as Anubis is there.

Zia is out there somewhere—the real Zia. I intend to find her.

Most of all, chaos is rising. Apophis is gaining strength. Which means we have to gain strength too—gods and men, united like in olden times. It's the only way the world won't be destroyed.

So the Kane family has a lot of work to do. And so do you.

Maybe you'll want to follow the path of Horus or Isis, Thoth or Anubis, or even Bast. I don't know. But whatever you decide, the House of Life needs new blood if we're going to survive.

So this is Carter and Sadie Kane signing off.

Come to Brooklyn. We'll be waiting.

AUTHOR'S NOTE

Much of this story is based on fact, which makes me think that either the two narrators, Sadie and Carter, did a great deal of research . . . or they are telling the truth.

The House of Life did exist, and was an important part of Egyptian society for several millennia. Whether or not it still exists today—that is something I cannot answer. But it is undeniable that Egyptian magicians were famed throughout the ancient world, and many of the spells they could supposedly cast are exactly as described in this story.

The way the narrators portray Egyptian magic is also supported by archaeological evidence. Shabti, curved wands, and magicians' boxes have survived, and can be viewed in many museums. All of the artifacts and monuments Sadie and Carter mention actually exist—with the possible exception of the red pyramid. There is a "Red Pyramid" at Giza, but it is only called that because the original white casing stones were stripped away, revealing the pink granite blocks underneath. In fact the pyramid's owner, Senefru, would be horrified to learn his pyramid is now red, the color of Set.

As for the magical red pyramid mentioned in the story, we can only hope that it has been destroyed.

Should further recordings fall into my hands, I will relay the information. Until then, we can only hope that Carter and Sadie are wrong in their predictions about the rise of chaos. . . .